Demon *Rising*

Book One in the *Gravity* Series

by **Karma** *Rose*

Demon Rising,
1st Edition

by Karma Rose

<u>Skyborn</u>

He walks with the stars,
Where there can be no scars,
Grown in a womb of flame.

With wings of the skies,
He sings where he flies,
And the hunter who shoots will know shame.

The arrow can kill him,
But the angel with a whim
Will cure him with kindness and care.

A wound through his mind,
Without one of his kind,
He wakes to a world of warfare.

Demon *Rising*

July 17th, 1956

Dear Diary,

I met the strangest boy today, the boy that Grandma used to tell me about. He's very shy and quiet and polite. Oh, and he does look...different. I don't want to say anything that might be mean or impolite, but he's very different.

To be honest, I don't think he's human. Mother says that people are born differently sometimes, that they're very special people who need special care. But that's not often that people are born that way, and not like this. Normally, only one or two things are not wrong but different about someone, not everything.

It's no small wonder all of the other kids say that the Lawrence house is cursed, though. That boy...I'm not surprised he frightens people without meaning to, since he does look rather frightening. He doesn't scare me much, though. I think he's harmless, all scared and alone the way he is.

I find it funny, though. Grandma said he was a demon, but he was a good one. Does that mean that there are bad ones, too? Or is it like angels falling because they're bad, only because he's good the Devil won't let him stay in Hell anymore? I wonder if that means he can go to Heaven with the rest of us. Or does he have to stay here if no one wants him?

Sincerely,
Katelyn

1

<u>Prologue</u>

Robert Smith possessed a more than generic name, had lived an average life as a therapist—working with average patients—and adored his wife and two children. He had come to discover that the level of life he had achieved was unsatisfying and unbearably dull. He went to work six days a week to pay for his suburban home and ensure his children a place in decent colleges.

The repetitive schedule had begun to drill a numbing hole in his skull where he could feel all of his life's potential leaking from.

When the elite researchers, studying a sentient, as-of-yet-unnamed specie tapped his shoulder then, he was thrilled to accept the job. They wanted him to evaluate their specimen to see if it was stable enough to be released into society. A wonderful change in pace to Mr. Smith; a break away from the ordinary. How hard could it have been to speak to it? After all, even the press called it an animal.

Arriving at the institute—trimmed brown hair combed back neatly and brown eyes sparkling with anticipation—he was unnerved by the number of halls they took him down. First one, then to the left, then the right and back again. It was enough to drive him mad before, at last, his guide stopped at a plain silver door. Robert smiled tentatively.

"Is this it?" he asked, nervous now that he was genuinely there.

The guide nodded, "Yeah. He's in there. And don't worry, he's not half as terrifying as he looks."

Robert's eyes widened as the guide walked away. He stared at the door a moment longer before taking a deep breath to steady himself. He turned the knob and the door swung open noiselessly.

He was surprised to find the creature look up at him with a start when he entered the room. To be honest, Robert was shocked to see it. It was tall, to be sure, even when sitting and appeared as though it could have modeled for David were it not for the rich crimson skin. It had large, leathery wings and a snaking tail that ended in a broad arrow-head the size of Robert's hand. Two thick horns, of varying shades of brown, grew from its forehead and curved over its skull to the back of its head.

The beast watched Mr. Smith with bright green eyes set beneath heavy brows. "Good morning, sir. I would have dressed more appropriately had I known you were going to look so sharp."

Robert glanced down at his navy blue suit, frowning in confusion. "Ah, right. Erm, am I understanding correctly that you're the...patient?"

The demon chuckled and Robert's stunned mind was able to notice how deep the demon's voice was, causing him to shudder. "Such a polite term compared to what I have become accustomed to, but yes. Please, sit. I was told the appointment could last all day and no man I have met has stood that long before."

Robert nodded. Straightening his jacket nervously, he sat across from the demon with a sigh, setting his bag by his feet. His eyes widened when he realized that his suit matched the color of the demon's lips perfectly. "Are you alright?"

The demon nodded politely, "Yes, sir. Why do you ask?"

"Your lips! They're blue," cried Robert, outraged. It spoke like a person! How could these researchers mistreat it so horribly? Was there something they had not told him? He refrained from glancing at the door in his mild trepidation.

"Of course, sir, that is their natural color," replied the demon calmly, touching a curved claw to his pointed chin, appearing thoughtful, "Although, I do appreciate your concern."

Robert cleared his throat, sighing again. This was the strangest day he could recall ever having, "Right. So, let's get this started." He pulled a pen and pad of paper from his bag. "What's your name?"

"Cory Charles Lawrence," answered Cory, fidgeting and glancing at the door.

Robert frowned. "Is something wrong?"

"I apologize. I have nervous issues regarding an unending list of things that I am certain we will address at one point or another," sighed Cory, closing his eyes. Robert waited patiently for the demon to recover. Eyes snapping open, Cory waved a hand to Robert. "Please, continue."

"How old are you?"

"I will be 68 on the ninth of August."

Robert glanced at the demon's youthful appearance incredulously. "And how long have you been at this facility?"

Demon *Rising*

"Forty-one years, tomorrow," murmured Cory, eyes becoming distant. He sighed heavily, leaning back in his chair. He stared at his hands tearfully, "A very long time, sir. One's appearance, in every sense, can change drastically, their life even more so. You look like a young man. How old are you?"

Robert blinked in surprise. He had never had a patient ask him that before. "Forty-six."

"Mm, young indeed. Do you love your wife?" he asked, pointing to Robert's ring.

"Immensely," replied Robert reflexively.

Cory nodded. "Do you have any children?"

"Two girls. Why are you asking all of this?" inquired Robert, pen poised. Whatever the reason, it was sure to be useful in his diagnosis.

Cory smiled with a doleful look in his eyes, revealing a few sharply pointed teeth. "Forty years alone is…brutal. I find it comforting to know that others can still enjoy what I lost. When did you propose?"

"When I was twenty-four. Why do you find it comforting?"

A glistening droplet streaked down the demon's angular face. "It helps me imagine my life, had I not been brought here. From what I recall I was twenty-seven, bound to inherit a farm outside of a small town I called home. It was the most I could ever ask for being what I am and it was the curiosity of this facility that…Well, I would be impolite to finish that sentence, so I will not. Do you understand why it is I ask to know if a wife, children and home are enjoyable?"

Robert nodded numbly, pale skin paling further as an alien guilt shivered up his spine. "Yes. Yes, I do. Can you tell me what it was like for you growing up?"

Cory's eyes slid half-shut and became distant, but he nodded. "Yes. I remember all of it quite well and I miss it. Would you like me to make it a story for you, sir, since you seem so intrigued?"

"Please, do. I'll stop you if I have any questions that can't wait."

"Well, then. Let me see how best to begin..."

<u>Chapter One:</u>
<u>Darkest Hour</u>

I was found in the cornfields of my parents' farm the ninth of August, 1942. Mother had discovered me while checking for sick stalks. I remember hearing her tell the story to the other women in the town, every year near Christmas. I would always be sitting beside her, listening to the mothers' tales of their children while I watched others my age play.

The smell of the fire is the richest detail in my memory, but I still recall the slight hint of spiced pies, eggnog, and honeyed ham. Near the tree it smelled of peppermint and pine. Carols would be sung or played over the radio, as well as seasonal shows. That was the only time I could sit with all the other children and not be rejected silently.

I was different; I understood that. I did not understand why I should be shunned for the difference, though. They all had differences that they put aside every day to talk, play, work. So why should I be the outcast?

"It's not your fault, or the children's," my mother had explained when I was seven, after the older kids had chased me back to my house in a fury. It was the first time I can remember bleeding. The color of my blood horrified the kids and they fled to leave me staring at the black on my fingertips. "Their parents don't trust you, Cory, and that mistrust they can't escape. Once they can see for themselves, they'll be able to form their own opinions of you. Everything will work out."

She promised me that almost every night from then on. No matter how dark things got, I believed her. Things had to get better, because there was no way they could get any worse.

Since it was dangerous for me during the day—with the angry children and unknown people passing through the town—I could only leave the house at night. Coincidentally, I spent my time indoors reading whatever material we had. Fairy tales that Mother had read to my two older brothers and would read to my younger sister. They were not adopted, unlike myself. My eldest brother, Dustin, looked like Father; Ethan, the second eldest, looked like Mother's sister, Aunt Betty; my little sister, Lisa, looked like Mother. I looked like I was painted by a Renaissance artist for a church's demon portrait.

It took me until I was twelve to understand that I was something different, more than a look-alike to a widely disliked mythical image. I began to grasp at the reality that I was not human. Still, I saw no reason why others would fear or hate me. I was kind to them, yet...

When I turned thirteen, Father asked me to help him with the crops. It gave me something to do outside all night, where my eyes could see everything flawlessly by the light of the moon and stars. The sun will burn my eyes at times you see—quite randomly—with more pain than a knife through my skull.

That was the beginning of my favorite years: The

cool, rich night air filling my lungs, the moist earth between my toes and under my claws from planting seeds. Being able to at last feel a fuller range of movement with my powerful body. I had a freedom that some only dreamed of. I had no one to share that freedom with much to my dismay, but that somehow only heightens the magnificence of those times.

My favorite hour of every night was the hour just before dawn. The air was at its coldest, a rush of sensation against my skin. My work would be done and I would have an hour of my own time outdoors, one lonely hour trapped between hiding and fieldwork. It was around then that I had begun to teach myself to fly. I had seen birds out my window, bats overhead. I could feel my own wings and the potential they held. Every part of me yearned to leave the ground behind, to soar where there was no hatred or fear, with the truest freedom I could imagine.

When I first launched myself out of my window—the highest place I could find since I was clueless of how to get airborne otherwise—there was the sharpest second when I knew that things were on the upswing, that the darkest part of my early years was nearly over. At first I was falling, and then my wings caught the rush of air.

It hurt intensely, the membranes of my wings soft and weak from a lack of use. On the down stroke I felt a surge of emotion without words. It filled my chest, brought tears to my eyes and made the muscles of my unused wings burn. This was the first time I had ever felt like my body may tire out, or may not be strong enough for the task. I could run for miles, farm for hours or any other physical labor possible without rest and when any human would tire or fall ill I was barely out of breath.

But this...This was a daunting obstacle, something I had never encountered. As I made to pull up and away from the ground, a breeze by any standard rustled through the trees, knocking me off my balance to send me reeling into the ground. Tumbling over and over, I heard and felt my left horn snap off in the middle as something tore through the membrane of my right wing. I screamed, of course. Nothing had hurt so much before. Humans are weak after all, and any damage they could have caused me were minor bruises that healed within a day, with the exception of my one skinned knee. I had just been thrown out of the sky though, dragged down by my own weight.

To anyone who might have seen, I imagined it appeared as though I were one of the fallen angels I had read so much about, tumbling to the earth with the visage of a demon. Looking back on that thought, I realize that it was ignorant and amusing. Fallen angels are—yes—seen as demons, but they are described as handsome, too beautiful for mortals to lay eyes upon. As far from my own description as I am told it could ever get.

I was gasping when I could stop crying and screaming from the pain. Where my horn had snapped, I could feel the bitter air against it like acid, and the cut in my wing seared angrily. The blood that gushed from the wound on my wing and—I later discovered—from my horn was hot and felt like it should have burnt me.

When at last I found the ability to lift my bruised body from the patch of crushed plants I noticed the lights of the house were on and shadowy figures were rushing back and forth urgently. I could hear my name being shouted, see Father standing in the doorway. He was worried and even from such a distance the expression on his face was clearly etched and defined. Behind him I saw Ethan and Dustin. Then, I did not understand their slight smirks. Looking back now, I understand too perfectly.

When I stumbled onto the porch, right wing half dragged, Father exclaimed that my face looked "like it's been drenched in tar!" Both Ethan and Dustin glared from behind our parents, seething that their hopes were unfulfilled. Lisa had come to hug me, giving me some confidence that there was room for me in this family yet.

It was a rather messy and agonizing affair, patching me up. Blood was everywhere. It pooled and soaked so many towels that I thought I should have died already.

"You're lucky that the doctor taught those classes a few months ago," Mother had told me as she stitched my membrane. I only nodded and winced as I held the fourth towel to my broken horn. When they inquired as to how I had injured myself, I answered honestly.

Father laughed and was about to go into his explanation that people cannot fly when he paused, looking like he had been slapped. He stared at me as though he had never seen me before when I realized that I was shifting my uninjured wing anxiously. It had not dawned on him until then how different I was, how alien. "People" were limited by gravity, yet I was not. Where could I ever stand in this society built upon generalities and selfishness?

We both knew the answer: I never could. We silently agreed that we would try to make a place for me, however. All for Mother, of course. She would be heartbroken to think that one of her children was destined for such a lonely path, as I was, and it has been a lonely trek to be sure, but worth every moment. That was what she hoped for all of her children. A life that in spite of what came was worth while.

Once I had healed—it took two weeks for my wing, nearly two months for my horn—I was attempting to fly again. Both of my wings could be broken and it would never keep me from trying and failing to fly.

The oddest thing happened around then, as well. About a month after my first crash, a neighbor girl came over with a basket of goods and a note wishing me well. I heard the knock on the front door and immediately ran to my room on the second floor. It was a habit by then and I did not mind it. I rather appreciated having someplace to retreat to when potentially violent people came to my home.

There were the muted voices beneath me as I was accustomed to and then I heard the front door shut. I heard footsteps on the stairs, two people coming up to my room. I looked up in interest. No one ever needed to tell me when it was safe to come out again because I could hear everything that happened downstairs.

My door was opened by Mother and then she left. I frowned deeply, leaning forward from the suspense. What was going on? What was happening?

A girl stepped into my view and I rocketed backwards, off the floor and onto my bed in a sudden jolt of terror. It was a second before I realized that my teeth were bared, a growling hiss escaping me. She flinched at that too, nearly dropping the wicker basket she held tightly in her hands.

When I had control over myself again, I snapped my mouth shut and mumbled an apology. I kept my eyes low, ashamed of my behavior while I listened to her tentative steps into my room.

Demon *Rising*

I curled up with my eyes shut tight, tail smacking the bed with a muted thump. Behind my lids, I saw her terrified little face, framed by tight ringlets of dark brown hair. She was short, with skin that was a smooth, soft brown to complement her almost-black eyes. She was slight and so her yellow summer dress was baggy, but her face held gentle features that gave her an adorable appearance.

I shuddered, a new sensation seeping through me. I could not pinpoint it then, distracted as I was by her nearing steps and a swelling excitement inside me.

Oh, and what a sweet moment that was! If I pondered the world all over for anything better I would be lucky to count any higher than my one hand!

Her soft, trembling little fingers touched my hand and she whispered without fear, "I'm Katelyn."

I lifted my head slowly—more than aware of what my horns could do if I was rash—to blink at her in awe. Her eyes were wide with curiosity, no trace of fear in her scent or on her face.

Smiling tentatively I replied, "My name is Cory."

Katelyn smiled back and held out her basket, arm shaking from the effort of holding it. "I heard you got hurt. I couldn't come by any sooner, sorry. But all of the treats are fresh."

I reached out a hand, mindful of my claws as I took the basket from her easily. Her little body shuddered slightly in relief. To me, the basket was easy to hold, nearly mindless.

Sitting on the floor, she patted a spot beside her for me to sit with her. "I'm eleven. How old are you?"

"I will be fourteen next month." I brought the

basket to the floor with me, investigating its contents curiously. The smell of freshly baked cookies made my mouth water.

Her eyes widened in amazement. "Wow...You look...older."

I gasped quietly in surprise. A sentence that began with "You look" commonly ended in an insult directed at me. Unsure of what to say I shrugged at her statement and continued to dig through the basket.

Fresh apples, two berry jams, a warm loaf of cinnamon raisin bread, splendid varieties of cookies wrapped individually in tin foil and tied with ribbons. It made me laugh. I had read of such perfect creations but had yet to witness one. Now here in my hands, as a gift to me, there was one such wonder. I half dreaded indulging in the goods, since it meant that the gift would vanish.

"I don't mind if you eat anything in front of me," she told me after analyzing my expression. "I had plenty of cookie dough to last at least until Christmas."

I stared at her blankly, struggling to find something to say. "That would be in five months."

She nodded. "Yeah...Why do you sound so...?"

"Gruff? I cannot help it, that would be my voice." I kept my eyes down again, afraid that she would begin acting the only way I knew unfamiliar humans could act: violently.

"No," she laughed, "formal and quiet. Are you afraid of being loud and impolite?"

I laughed at that. "Maybe."

That was the beginning of what we could never have imagined. Every day she had a chance, Katelyn would come to the farm to visit me. Lisa was happy to play with another girl from time to time; more so that I had a friend. Mother was less concerned about me being alone. My brothers were envious, and as I grew older I began to understand why. Katelyn became more attractive as one season came and another went.

Some days she would stay until nightfall to watch me leap out of my window and practice landing or gliding. We would have been inseparable if I had been able to leave the house safely.

In the early summer of my fifteenth birthday, she stopped coming. Day after day, I waited for her to show up and explain that she had gone on some grand adventure to explore the world. I wanted to hear whatever stories she had to tell, or anything else she had to say.

It was September 2nd when the note appeared on our front porch; the words are ingrained into my memory from reading it endlessly. I cried every time I finished it. It read:

Dear Cory,

My parents don't think it's safe for me to spend time with you anymore. I can't come over, and this is the only letter they would let me give you. I hope you get to have a good life!

Sincerely, Katelyn

I had read the stories and felt each character's suffering, yet this far surpassed any grief I had ever felt before. My only friend was gone forever, leaving me alone in my home again staring out the windows longingly every day and working diligently throughout the night.

My brothers were snide and sharply enthusiastic about this turn of events; Lisa and my parents missed Katelyn. If you would have asked any of them—even my brothers—they would tell you that there is nothing as terrible as watching and hearing a demon cry. I imagine I appeared rather pathetic, curled into the darkest corner of my bed holding my wicker basket close, the long-worn letter folded as neatly as possible inside it.

Little did I realize my heart had broken. I was a timid dog, cast away by the only kind master it had ever known. The only thing I looked forward to was my steady progression toward flight. I would have wished to damn my life if not for that one thing to cling to. It became my lifeline.

By the time I was sixteen, I had at last begun to recover from Katelyn's abrupt disappearance. I was also "a monster" as Father put it. Six feet and three inches tall, with a nineteen foot wingspan I weighed 270 pounds, covered with layers of muscle. I understood Father's description and agreed wholly. Even Dustin—then 20— was barely six feet and had lost much of the mass he had achieved from working in the fields. He had moved out the winter I was fifteen and now worked in retail. He never defined his position to me and I assumed he was intimidated. I understood that he was justified in that intimidation, since most grown men would cower in front of me. Not a fact I have ever been proud of, merely one I have come to accept.

That August, at long last, I achieved flight. A full minute circling over the farm, the wind cascading around me as I pounded out a place for myself in the sky with my enormous crimson wings. It saddened me that the sun was rising to the east, but it also made me proud. The anger could not reach me here, high above the ground. I was unbound by them. I truly was free.

My feet touched the ground at the moment the sun shone over the horizon and I squinted about at the bright new world. Father was standing on the porch, smiling at me as he waved me back to the house, holding up a package for me.

I nodded, taking a moment to appreciate the morning as I strode to the house. I felt pleasantly tired, worn with exertion and flooded with emotion. I took the package with a thanks, mildly curious about what it could possibly contain.

Father's face was guilty. "She came by yesterday. You were sleeping and she didn't want to wake you up, so..."

I was frozen, the small package in my hand holding a new weight. It felt like I was choking, strangled by my own excitement and recurring grief.

"Did she...Did she look alright?" I asked. I was breathing heavily from the emotions, my mind reeling.

Father nodded. "She brought by a couple of photos, insisted you have them. They're inside."

It hurt to think that she had come to visit and did not wake me. Even now, after decades of time, I regret missing those few hours with her. Time is different for me than it is for humans. I can see and feel myself moving through it. Or rather, it moving around me and pulling me along. The best I can compare it to is being caught in a river and being unable to swim or drown. Every moment for me is sharp

17

and precise, but I can still be confused easily when I am spun about and beaten on the head by a few sharp rocks along the way. To imagine what I could have shared in that short time…It would be enough to make me build a time machine, if I were so irresponsible.

When I went inside, Mother wore a guilty expression as well. She welcomed me to breakfast as I sat in my usual chair beside Lisa and across from Ethan. My brother wore an evil grin while Lisa looked like she might cry.

"I'm sorry I didn't tell you," she gushed with a sniffle. "I wanted to wake you up, but that would've upset Katelyn and I thought that would upset you since you're upset when anyone's upset and that would've made for a bad visit. Can you ever forgive me?"

I nodded with a smile, reaching over to pat her on the head, careful not to injure her. She smiled, too, and then looked at Mother with a pointed nod in my direction. Mother picked up a small envelope and handed it to me. She and Father took their own seats, watching me carefully.

We ate in silence, the package from Katelyn clutched tightly in my stronger right hand, utensil in my left. When we were finished I took the photos and package up to my room. I remember all of this clearly: I shut the door behind me and took care when I sat on my old, dying bed. I stared at the objects in confusion for a minute.

I was indeed confounded. I believed that she would not be coming back. I thought all hope of having my friend was gone. This was a defiance of the reality I had come to face. This was one of those moments when—in that infinite river of time—I had been smacked on the head by rocks.

Demon *Rising*

I took out the pictures first. There were only three, yet still more than I had hoped for. The first image was of Katelyn standing in front of an orchard, grinning at the camera. She looked roughly an inch or so taller than my sister and, oh, that one year had been so generous to her. She was beautiful, her girlish appearance beginning to fade and hint at a more womanly figure. She had on a baggy shirt with a skirt; her hair had been pulled back into a ponytail, allowing her face a full expression of who she was.

In my mind, I imagined the color to her hair and skin. Vaguely, I wondered if her eyes were indeed their odd shade of black or acting kindly and remaining deep brown.

Before I knew it I was crying with joy! By now, I am sure this sounds like a classic tale of the fool and I have felt such many times in life. Trusting obviously dark persons or continuing along a certain path when every instinct told me it could only end in disaster. I would never call any of that a mistake, however. It all brought me to where I am and no matter the route it is a worthy destination.

Another photograph had her smiling tamely, an image of her shoulders and above. The final one was of her staring spitefully at the camera, arms crossed. She wore a formal dress, surrounded by other women in formal gowns. A wedding, perhaps?

Looking through the captured moments, it felt like I could remember her as if I were there. My eyes strayed to the floor where she had sat once and it seemed to brighten the room thinking that there had been someone else here with me.

Setting aside the photos, I picked up the package. It was wrapped in brown paper with my name scrawled haphazardly on one side. I tore off the paper with shaking hands; my heart was pounding with excitement. This was a genuine mystery to me—what could be inside the paper— as it was from my only friend. Excited was hardly a good enough word to describe how I felt.

Beneath the paper, there was a note attached to a small yellow journal. The note on the journal read:

Dear Cory,

Sorry it's been so long. My parents are away this weekend, so we can see each other if we keep it secret! Isn't that great? Also, I'm giving you my journal to let you know how I've been this last year. Hope to see you tomorrow (Saturday) night!

Sincerely, Katelyn

P.S. You drool and snore!

I laughed at the ending of the note and then paused as it occurred to me that she meant to see me tonight. I rechecked the note, flipping it over to look at the back as I searched for an address. On the back of the note it was scribbled somewhat hurriedly with the words "Meet at dusk" above it.

Life was too wonderful. It was magnificent! While I thought that everything possible had to go wrong now, I knew it would only go as right as it could. I wished the night could come that instant, even knowing that I had things to prepare for tonight.

I hid the pictures and journal before returning to the downstairs in search of Father. He was sitting in the living room, reading as he always did for an hour in the morning before he went to work. He looked up with a curious frown when I entered.

"Katelyn wants to see me tonight," I told him, finding myself nervous by this concept suddenly. I pushed that aside for the moment. "May I meet with her? I would rather not put off chores, and it feels wrong asking for permission to, however I—"

"Be back before dawn, for safety's sake," he interrupted. I stared at him silently, confounded by what he said. He sighed and motioned for me to take a seat beside him before he explained himself,

"Now, whatever it is you are or look like, we can't change and that's a shame. But I've watched you grow up and damn it, I wish there was something anyone could do so that you could enjoy the life every man dreams of living. I'm sorry you've got to spend all your time on this farm and it kills me that you have the same needs anyone else has," he told me honestly, keeping his eyes level with mine. He added as he set his book aside, "It's a lucky thing that your only friend's a girl, too."

I frowned deeply at his comment, "Why is that?"

He only raised one eyebrow at me, as though my past few months of mourning should have been explanation enough, "The point is that every man needs a woman to keep him sane, even if it's a woman in a man's body. Anyone who tells you otherwise is crazy or in denial. I'm not going to keep you deprived and tell you that you can't have friends if your chores aren't done."

"But Ethan and Dustin—"

"Can go out during normal and unreasonable hours of the day—you can't. And you've been doing your chores diligently for the past what, seven years? You've earned up more than a night's worth of a break, believe me." He smiled at me and patted my shoulder, "Go on and shower. I know you don't start stinking near as soon as any of us human men, but..."

I chuckled and shook my head in disbelief. Father was a strange individual, to be sure. As I got up to leave, he grabbed my hand and gave it a squeeze.

"I'm proud of you, Cory," he told me, then let me go. I stood in shock for a moment before continuing with my intended path. It was the first time Father had told me he was proud.

Some say there are people who can dream the future. I have come to believe this, not as anything supernatural, merely the slightest temporary overlap in time when the subconscious can completely comprehend the separate time and occurrences. The first time I experienced such an event was that day while I slept, anticipating the visit with Katelyn.

It was the most vivid dream I could recall ever having. I was flying—that sensation was too obvious—and it was black outside. There were no stars and no moon, a thick storm blocking out the sky. The wind was difficult to overcome, but I managed. My body felt larger than I knew it to be, and stronger. It was incomprehensible to me then, but I know how to control such mass and strength now.

Rain was spattering across my skin infrequently, but I knew that I had only minutes to reach my destination before it became too dangerous. I understood in the logic of dreams that I was off to meet with Katelyn and that she wanted to show me something. Or perhaps I wanted to show her something? It was a different place than our usual, but I was willing to go farther and explore. I had planned to...

There was a flash of lightning behind me, the force of it jostling me slightly. Then thunder rumbled and rolled through the air. I could feel it in my bones, and that frightened me.

A deep, dark sense weighed on my chest. It felt as though I should not have been able to breathe. Beneath me, I could see Katelyn's old truck parked next to a grove of trees. I circled and landed easily, grateful to be out of the sky.

Katelyn rushed over to me, tiny when wrapped in my arms as we hugged. She pulled back with an elated smile, face wet from looking up into the rain.

"Don't worry, I checked with the ranger about you coming out and he said it was sa—"

Her voice was drowned out by a loud bang that we thought was thunder at first. My back ached suddenly—sharply—and this time I genuinely could not breathe. My mouth worked silently while my body struggled, fought to bring in enough air to stand as another two thunder claps came and two more cores of pain shot through my back.

I fell to the ground as I was crushed by the agony while I listened to her panic, and then startled awake on my bed, gasping. My smaller body was mine again, mind free of the nightmare. I could then understand that the last three claps of thunder were gunshots in the dream, leaving me sick with leftover fear and pain.

The light of the setting sun brought me back to

myself as it seeped in through my open window, reminding me that I had someplace to be. I dressed nicely, which meant I wore a shirt with my worn jeans instead of going without one. Rubbing a muscle cramp from my neck after sleeping on my too-small bed, I went downstairs to eat before meeting with Katelyn. Her address was safely tucked into my pocket, a smile on my face.

Mother had already set the table and was serving the plates when she looked up at my entrance. "What, no shoes?"

"You remember what happened to the last pair I had, Mother. We agreed it was safer for the shoes if they stayed away from me," I reminded her, smile broadening. Nightmare forgotten, the world was glowing to me. I was ecstatic and nothing could ruin my night.

Dinner was wonderful. Mother had prepared her famous stew with pie for dessert. For the life of me, I cannot remember how they tasted exactly, only that then I had thought nothing could taste better. I was always in sharpest tune with the moment however, and anything could be the best if I had nothing to compare it to right then. Heh, a silly young man. I would learn just how silly, and what it means to truly treasure anything.

Dark fell faster than I would have expected. I yearned to fly to Katelyn's house, but I knew that would be foolish for only a half mile's walk. So I set off on foot.

The night was different now; the wind on my face felt softer. The evening was warm and smelled richly of the orchards and farms in the area. That strange emotion I had felt the first time I had seen Katelyn was taking me over again, refusing to allow me coherent thoughts. I felt very much alive as I listened to the crickets and frogs and

Demon *Rising*

watched fireflies blinking in and out, like stars on earth.

I took a deep breath to keep myself from shaking. This was my first venture beyond the farm alone in nearly a decade. There was no parent to protect me or kind human to hide behind for safety. I was wandering out into a world of angry, frightened people in search of kindness and hope. Anyone could have told me that it was a doomed mission.

I was happy, though. I felt safe. I felt invincible. I was not going to be foolish or arrogant because of it, however. It was nice to feel strong and like nobody could hurt me. After straying and being attacked too many times, the peaceful night was a welcomed relief.

It shocked me when I saw the small yellow house with its porch light on, little black numbers on the mailbox telling me that this was my desired location. Katelyn smiled and waved from where she sat on the porch swing. She patted the seat beside her eagerly and I hurried my stride, careful with my claws on the wooden porch.

I inspected the structure and condition of the swing. Still uncertain I asked, "Will I break it?"

She took a moment to think about what I had said before grinning suddenly. "Oh, my three cousins who play baseball can sit safely. I checked with my mom just in case, since you looked so *huge* yesterday! You look even bigger when you're standing! You've grown, like, twelve feet!"

"One," I corrected, taking my seat. "And a hundred pounds."

Her eyes bulged and she blinked, giving her an even more adorable face. "Wow…You really are *huge*. And…"

I tensed, ready to be turned away if I frightened her. "And?"

25

Demon *Rising*

She reached toward me slowly, touching her fingertips to my brow gently. "Your face..."

"It has gotten worse, hasn't it?" I sighed heavily, pulling my face out from under her fingers. My skin tingled slightly where she had touched me.

"No!" she gasped in horror. "It's fine, just different is all I meant. I've seen the face of ugly before and you're not it no matter how hard you try."

"How do I know you're not just trying to comfort me?" I asked skeptically, leaning forward to rest my arms on my knees. In spite of being beyond the farm's boundaries, I felt myself relaxing as I fell into the familiar rhythm of her company.

"I've seen newborn babies," she answered me grimly. "They're wrinkly, little and ugly. They're only cute after a few days to deprune."

I laughed. "So if I got pruny...?"

"The baby would still be ugly," she snickered. "And you would just look like a big red prune."

"Rather hard to imagine," I muttered with a grin. It was easier to be improper with her, knowing that I would not offend her no matter what I said.

We were quiet for awhile, swinging slowly and listening to the nighttime sounds. I watched moths gather around the porch light eagerly, fluttering about aimlessly. I was content where I was. Everything was perfect.

"It's so short," whispered Katelyn forlornly. I looked over to see tears in her eyes. She turned to me with a frown, brows creased. "Life. This last year feels so long, but I know it's not. And I know tonight's going to be over soon and it won't ever be like this again."

"Why does that make you so sad?" I asked quietly.

It made me sad, too, but why did it upset her? I loathed to see tears rolling down her cheeks and would bear whatever pain caused them for her. That new emotion spiked through me, intensified by her grief and fueling my determination.

"Because that means that eventually we won't be friends anymore," she sniffled, the lighting poor enough to make her eyes a depthless black. "Promise we can be friends forever?"

"I promise." Even when I had no inkling of how to fulfill my end of the bargain, I knew that I would. Any obstacles would be overcome and I would ensure the survival of our friendship.

She scooted closer to me on the swing to lean her head on my arm. I smiled and lifted my arm to hug her. She smiled back and readjusted to rest her head on my chest instead before jerking away in surprise.

She poked at where she had put her head. "I know you look like you have lots of muscle, but you feel it too? What on earth have you been doing, Cory, bench-lifting tanks?!"

I chuckled softly. "Farming. It would be a bit of a strain to push a tank, let alone bench-lift one. Maybe in another hundred pounds of muscle."

"Another?" she gasped, replacing her head. "No. Bad. No more growing for you, mister."

I rolled my eyes, not that she could see or discern the action. My eyes look similar to a cat's as you can well see, making many eye expressions difficult. It appears more like I am crossing my eyes than anything.

Katelyn groaned in irritation, shifting. "Have you ever wanted to not be tired?"

I thought of every time she came to visit during my regular sleeping hours. "Yes. Are you tired, then?"

She yawned pointedly. "Sorry. Maybe we should make coffee."

"Wonderful idea, give the energetic man with wings coffee. You can have some, I would rather stay sober." I was grinning enthusiastically, glad to be spending time with a friend off of the farm.

She looked up at me with a smile, grasping at my meaning. "You can fly now?"

"Last night, I was airborne for a full minute, the first time ever," I told her proudly. Boasting to her made me feel secure, tied with the undefined feeling. I was beginning to suspect its true nature by then, however.

"Can you show me, or would that not be safe?" she inquired. There was a hint of hope in her voice that was poorly concealed.

I sighed and shook my head. "No, it would be too dangerous. Come by the farm some night, though, and I would be happy to demonstrate."

"Thanks," she sighed, settling back down. A moment later she was snoring lightly, breathing more deeply and evenly in sleep. Moving slowly, I gently lowered her head to my lap for a more comfortable sleep.

I was saddened that she would be asleep for the rest of the night we had, yet I was content. The night was calm, lazily drifting by and granting me a wish of mine. Light inside the dark I felt on the fringes of my perception. A tempting, bribing darkness that I was afraid could consume me.

Was that the insanity Father had mentioned men possessed without a woman? An empty, greedily consuming shadow? It did not feel as if this were so, not then and not now that I know what that darkness is. Untamed...

I pondered Father's words further to pass the time with a smile, all the while I watched the moon move across the starlit sky. Katelyn would shift now and again with a moan or a sigh. Once, she grabbed my hand and would not let go. I imagine she had mistaken it for a favorite stuffed animal or pillow. It amused me greatly at the time.

As she had said, the time was over very soon. It felt like an hour's passing when the sky began to turn gray and weigh me down. I suppose I had lied to say that nothing could ruin my night, since the coming of morning would always shatter my peaceful dark.

Sighing heavily, I began to shake Katelyn awake gently, unthinking of the car driving down the lonely road until it turned into Katelyn's driveway. The windows were open, allowing me to hear the argument inside.

"...you we should have left sooner. We lost our reservation, and all the other hotels were full!" snapped a female voice.

"So it's my fault, not yours for talking so long with everyone? How generous of you! Maybe next time, I'll take a taxi to keep the reservation!" a male voice shouted back.

My heart raced and I trembled in fear. Katelyn groaned and stirred slowly at the sound of her parents' voices. I was frozen. Katelyn was still on my lap and if I moved too fast then I would hurt her with a claw or too much force. If I moved slowly, they would notice the disturbance on the porch faster than if I stayed still. Terror of many things locked me in place to wait for whatever wretched thing was to come.

"That's a good idea! Next time you can also—Oh, Jeff, what's on the porch?!" Her shouts of anger turned to screams of fright.

The gray sky lightened slightly.

"Holy—!" The driver's door opened and a man stumbled out. He wore glasses over near-black eyes. Clearly Katelyn's father.

"Is it a bear?!" demanded the woman in the car before exiting as well. She was small, with soft features that contrasted with her...forceful personality. Katelyn's mother.

"Whatever it is, we should scare it off," replied her husband.

The woman nodded and then froze with a gasp. "Jeff, it's Katelyn!"

"What? But Kate's not that—Oh, no! What did you do to Kate?!" shouted Jeff. He charged at me, face corrupt with rage.

I moved swiftly to cover my head in a moment of panic, begging, "Do not hurt me, please!"

Jeff's blows only stung but drove me further into my fear. If he could attack me so easily, what act of anger would he stop at, if he stopped at all?

"Daddy, stop it! You're hurting him!" I heard Katelyn scream. The attack halted and I dared to see what was happening, peering between a crack in my arms.

Katelyn's back took up much of my vision, though I could guess that she was keeping Jeff from continuing his assault. I saw a drop of scarlet fall onto her shoulder from her cheek, staining the soft pink dress she wore. I gasped in horror, guilt welling up in my chest. I had hurt her in my haste to protect myself.

"You *let* that thing onto our property?" demanded Katelyn's father.

"His name is Cory, Dad, and he's the Lawrences' third son." I heard the stubborn undertone in her voice. She would not back down now that her mind was set.

"Right, but that still doesn't change that it's an animal!" he barked back. "Now get out of my way so I can scare it off."

"Please!" I cried out, panicked. The sky was only getting brighter and more people were bound to join in to beat me. "I never meant to anger you and I will leave if you would let me!"

Katelyn did not move and her father fell silent. Her mother came up then, demanding what was going on and why on earth I had been allowed on the furniture.

"Please," I said again, voice shaking. "Let me go."

"Oh, it talks! Katelyn, get the talking thing off the porch swing," commanded her mother.

I stood immediately, lowering my arms cautiously. Katelyn's father straightened abruptly, horrified by my size. Her mother's glare dissolved into a smile and she thanked me for obeying. I nodded and stared around myself in confusion. The world was different in the minutes before the sun rose.

Accented with gold, pink and orange the sky was a gorgeous masterpiece. The houses, road, cars, trees, everything was cast into soft grays. I had never seen this previously, not from outside the farm. A chuckle escaped me before the sun's light exploded from the horizon to light the world and blind me.

I exclaimed at the sudden pain. My eyes felt burnt,

inside and out, my skull throbbing excruciatingly. Meanwhile, my entire mind panicked that this was the end of my time. I was away from home, facing hostile people, surrounded by houses filled with everyone who hated me for no reason.

I fell to the floor with an arm around my aching head, fighting to keep from hissing at the pain and the threats. I wanted to speak coherently to ask for a place to stay or hide for the day, but my body would not cooperate with me. It refused to do anything but stay curled on the floor and growl.

"Quick! Mom, open the door, Dad, move out of the way!" Katelyn cried out urgently. Hurried footsteps told me that they were following her lead. Katelyn's small hands guided me to my feet kindly and she put her hand in mine to lead me into her home.

I gasped and sighed in relief, blinking my eyes open. The pain lessened slowly as my sight came back to me. I heard the door close behind me and turned to find a disgruntled Jeff.

"I truly am sorry for disturbing you," I apologized sincerely. Jeff nodded curtly and stepped past me. I felt shunned, as always. It was more pronounced now, however. I was unwanted in their home, on their lawn or in this world. I was excruciatingly different and it had never been so painful as then, when I realized that without the approval of her parents I truly was doomed to loneliness for however long I lived.

"Kate, Cory, freshen up for church," called Katelyn's mother from another room.

Jeff went to find her, asking, "Jasmine? We're taking Cory?"

Demon *Rising*

"May I call my family to let them know where I am and that I will be safe?" I asked, a heavy feeling settling in my gut. A demon surrounded by hundreds of persons on hallowed ground was not my idea of entertaining. Far from. It was one of the scenes from some of my worst nightmares.

"Tell them to meet us there, too!" replied her mother. My shoulders slumped. This was not going to end well.

Katelyn showed me the phone before going to tidy up for church. My hands were shaking, heart pounding the fastest I could recall in years. All I could see was more evidence that a demon is in fact my specie. Demons are evil by make, and any good god worthy of worship could have planned this series of unfortunate events.

Father told me that I was in good hands with Katelyn's family before I told him where to meet. He then swore things and words I still am astounded he said. He was commonly such a mindful man, and here he was calling women names I never thought existed. He was in a foul mood, but he said that they would be there. I felt somewhat reassured, knowing my family would be waiting for me there.

Katelyn came back to where I was with a comb and blue ribbon, smiling apologetically. "Mother said tidy up, so I thought we should tie your hair back. This is all I have, sorry."

I nodded and found a place to sit on the floor out of the way, so that she could "tidy me up". It felt ridiculously humorous that I should be fancied up for what would likely turn into a beating. Putting a ribbon in my hair...Oh, that still amuses me. She was gentle with my hair, careful to not pull it or yank through knots. It felt...nice.

"Your hair's so fine," she commented, making me laugh. "It's thick, too, and such a pretty color..."

"Black is pretty?" I asked in curiosity. I had been told her favorite color was yellow. Was it still or had it changed?

"This black is," she told me. "It looks like it has blue in it."

"I think that would be the ribbon," I told her.

"Are you two ready yet?" asked Jasmine from behind us.

"Yes, Mother," answered Katelyn. I felt a slight tug on my hair. "There. Don't play with the bow or it'll come out."

"Yes, madam," I said quietly, standing.

Jasmine came close to straighten and smooth my shirt in a motherly fashion. "There. Now hurry on out to the car."

"May we eat?" asked Katelyn, face sincere as she followed her mother to the kitchen. I went to step out the door, praying the sun would not hurt my eyes now.

It did not, and I found that the homes and world were gorgeous. Green, lit brilliantly by the bright sun, covered the trees, the grass, the porches. Red roses bloomed in the yard across from Katelyn's, so rich in color I thought I might cry. I stepped off the porch, off the walk and into the grass. It tickled my feet and felt so spry and alive. The sun on my face was warm and filled me with a hope I had never known. It sprung from my chest to run through my veins, making me smile and tears fall from my eyes.

For a moment, I forgot my imminent doom.

Demon *Rising*

"You can cry?" asked Jeff, startling me.

I nodded. "Yes, as much as anyone. I feel everything the way anyone would. Sad, happy, sorrow and joy. The only thing I do not do is look like everyone."

Jeff nodded thoughtfully, empathy in his frown. "I know what that's like."

"Apple?" asked Katelyn with a smile, offering me two as she came up beside us.

"Kate, I don't think that's going to be enough," admitted Jeff, eyeing me with interest.

I accepted the offer with a grateful smile. "It will suffice until I may return home. Thank you very much."

Jasmine came out to examine our small congregation with a frown. "I don't think he's going to fit in the car."

"He can fly, though!" exclaimed Katelyn excitedly. "Right? You can fly?"

"Yes," I answered, unnerved by the idea.

"Or we could walk," suggested Jeff, noticing my slight terror. "It's only a couple miles. We'll be on time for the service, if not to help Paul set up."

"Will you be alright walking, Cory?" asked Jasmine politely.

I nodded. "Of course."

It was a pleasant walk. The road was strange to my bare feet. After a mile, it became somewhat painful to walk on it. My feet were accustomed to going without protection no matter the season, though it was commonly only across the fields and the occasional young briar plant. The road was sharp, even to my toughened skin. Small stones got caught beneath the claws on my toes, and with every step they scratched me and dug deeper into my flesh.

Demon *Rising*

It was only when we arrived at the porch of the church that Jeff noticed the black pooling from my toes like tar. I had noticed the pain and endured it, thinking that it was nothing. After a few moments of deliberation, we wrapped my toes so that they would not bleed across the entire church floor.

I will never regret that pain, or the hours it took for the local doctor to remove the pebbles surgically. What happened in the church that morning was miraculous, a morning I could never forget. We took our seats in the back, in the section labeled "Coloreds". My family sat a few pews away, with the other whites. I did not see it fit to sit with them, however. I would be a rude guest then, in addition to my skin being a rich, bright red!

The expressions on the peoples' faces are still fresh in my mind. Horror, fury, blatant shock. Someone even cried out that "the coloreds shouldn't be forced" to sit with me. The pastor was outraged by my presence.

"A demon should *not* be allowed onto hallowed ground!" he cried, picking up a metal bowl and coming toward me with it.

People stood, shouting their approval and glee.

"That's it, splash it with holy water! That'll teach it!"

"Don't hurt him! That's my son!" screamed Mother, being restrained by Father and Ethan. If she attempted to aid me, she would have been attacked by the entire church. "You can't hurt my son!"

That is the most frightening thing to experience, that I have witnessed. When you are surrounded by people who would love nothing more than to torture you for evil you never committed, and to know that no one you love or trust has the power to protect you. You are at the mercy of these hateful people—all equally blinded by their prejudice—and when you think you will be murdered in cold blood, you know the worst of what is to happen is only beginning.

I cried. As I understand it, crying in front of anyone is an extreme act of trust, yet that still did not halt them. They only grew angrier. The pastor splashed me with the cold water, then pulled out a crucifix he wore around his neck. He pressed it to my arm. I assume he expected me to be burnt and cry out as I revealed my true nature at the holy symbol's touch. I did not. I continued to cry, staring down at the man in terror.

The Smiths kept their heads down during this, avoiding the encounter. I saw that they were all ashamed, but I could understand their aversion. It was why I avoided the day as well as the people. They were unstable and would have attacked anyone who would think to help me.

"I came in peace, please let me be in peace," I sobbed to the pastor.

He jumped back in shock with a gasp, "It speaks!"

"I am no animal that cannot speak or feel, sir, only misinterpreted as one," I laughed shakily. This idea seemed alien to the pastor. The number of times I would have to explain that I was not a monster were endless.

"What evil trick are you?" he demanded, crucifix held out to fend me off.

"My name is Cory Charles Lawrence, sir," I explained, standing still. My toes were burning and all of me ached to sit to relieve the pain. "I have no recollection of being evil as you accuse, nor of Hell or the Devil. Please, treat me as you would any sane person, for I am sane as well as a person."

"Don't be fooled, pastor, it's a devil from the fiery pits of hell!" shouted someone.

"It's cursed and will bring along its evil!"

"Kill it before it can kill our children!"

"I would never harm children!" I cried out, aghast that they would think me so cruel. "Never!"

"Now it lies! Blasphemy in the Lord's presence!"

The pastor stared at me, blue eyes the darkest and coldest things I had ever seen. "All are welcome in the Lord's house, so you may stay. If you practice any of your demonic ways in our town though, we'll burn you back to where you came from."

I nodded, smiling nervously. "Thank you for being so gracious."

I took my seat with the Smiths, heart thumping and hands shaking from the encounter. I sighed quietly and wiped my tears away. Katelyn took my hand, squeezing it and smiling at me reassuringly. I smiled back, still alive.

The pastor took his place at the head of the church and started off by apologizing for the disruption, saying that today's service would be different than how he had planned. He asked us to relax, to forget the tensions between people and be together as a family under the Lord.

I am not Christian, nor do I follow any religious path. I find that it would be unproductive with how I look to attempt to follow any religion. It would also be irresponsible. I have considered practicing a faith, but I always come to the same conclusion that it would only create unnecessary dramas. If I—an image in many religions—followed a specific one, that religion would then be likely to claim itself as the true faith or be accused of falsehood. Chaos would only be the result, and I am not in such desperate need of hope that I would be reckless like that. After all, I am uncertain any deities exist at all, since time as I understand it is, in itself, an entity. I do not think that any being could possess such cosmic powers as described, nor would they aid us mortals with them.

It was when we came to the songs that I was stumped. Jasmine insisted that I sing with them, and I insisted that it would be a mistake. She gave me a threatening look which I cringed from, but followed her instruction.

I knew the songs from my sister, Lisa. In earlier years she would come home from church singing, and from that I knew every word and tune. I had never before attempted to sing them however, as my voice is too deep and rough to make the words sound as light and free as Lisa had.

Within a minute, the rest of the people singing fell silent. I petered off sheepishly, keeping my eyes down as I mumbled an apology. I could frighten a snake half to death by my face and silence a room faster than a rabid bear. It took me a moment to grasp what they were murmuring.

"That can't be…"

"It sounds like an angel."

"That voice…"

"Sing again," whispered Jasmine in wonder. Katelyn nodded enthusiastically at her mother's words.

I was nervous. I had the attention of all present and they were staring at me as others began to repeat Jasmine's request. I breathed deeply, trying to steady myself. I sang, and no one stopped me. They all held their breath, eyes wide. Some of them had tears in their eyes by the time I finished with the song. It was silent for a long moment afterward. Mother was crying with a smile, Father was holding her. Lisa was grinning at me while Ethan was astounded.

"How...?" faltered the pastor. He wiped tears from his eyes. "Are you an angel?"

I shook my head, stunned as well as any of them. "I do not know what I am, sir."

"What else do you know how to sing?" he asked, eyes filled with wonder.

The remainder of service, I sang while all of the faces turned to me were frozen, enthralled. My voice began to crack by the end of it, somewhat sore, as I rarely spoke to begin with. The pastor sent a woman to warm some water for me to drink, after which he concluded the service and dismissed us. Nobody moved until I stood and limped out of the building.

My eyes adjusted to the sun easily, to my relief. The bandages on my feet were soaked through and leaking black across the pale, bleached wood. My feet throbbed in pain, too, but I stood and stared at the blue sky, watching the birds fly from tree to tree.

People were chattering excitedly as they came out of the church, smiling at me as they passed. Mother, Father and Lisa surrounded me, congratulating me. Ethan stayed away, put out by the sudden acceptance I had at least temporarily gained.

"That was quite the performance, Cory," said a man. I turned to see the pastor smiling at me. His blue eyes were knowing. "How would you feel about coming to sing for us every Sunday?"

I was uncertain of what to say, and when I could

speak all that came from my mouth was a pained snarl. My feet were burning, the pebbles rubbing against my nerves so much that it was difficult to focus on anything but the pain.

The pastor leapt back, some of the passersby rushing to stand between me and him. Some were shouting at me, something that sounded like "Burn him!".

Jeff and Katelyn hurried over to me. I was wheezing, fighting to keep from expressing my pain any other way as I leaned against the porch railing to relieve my feet of some of my weight. They helped me to sit and I sighed as the pain eased.

"What's wrong with him?" demanded the pastor, pushing by the people who stood between us.

"His feet started bleeding, but they're just scratched," explained Katelyn. None of us knew any better that seven of my claws had collected stones that were cutting into me.

"May I?" asked the pastor, hand hovering above the bandages on my right foot. I nodded, wincing and hissing quietly when he agitated the pain. He studied the black covering my toes for an instant before commanding someone to get him water.

When I gave him a questioning look he explained, "I'm the doctor as well, Paul Ericson. You have full claws on your toes?"

"Yes, sir."

"Mm," was his reply, a deep frown crossing his otherwise youthful face. He appeared to be in his late twenties, with pale blond hair.

When a man returned with a pitcher of water and Paul rinsed away most of the blood, he discovered the problem and demanded that someone help me to the back of a truck. It was amusing, three grown men straining to lift me over to the vehicle. I would have shown them mercy had Paul not very sternly insisted that I must not walk until the stones were removed.

I thanked the men who carried me, feeling awkward. They were all out of breath, shaking their heads confusedly. The truck started when Paul was seated in the back with me. He began checking my condition, explaining that an infection can hit at any time and he wanted to make sure that one had not begun with me.

He frowned after taking my pulse and murmured, "Seventy-three beats."

It took only a few minutes to arrive at his small blue home. I was carried again, this time to a rather empty room. It had two beds, two chairs and a small table on wheels. There was a desk with several drawers on one wall. In one corner, I saw a worn leather bag. I had read of but never seen a town hospital. I was amazed by how bare and clean it was.

I did not fit on either bed, of course, and so sat back on propped up pillows against the wall. I cringed at the black liquid that spread across the starched white sheets. It seemed criminal to disturb anything that looked so perfectly peaceful.

Paul was quick, collecting bright lanterns, alcohol and sedatives. He pulled over a chair and the table, setting out some tools he may need. Scalpel, mirror, tweezers. I was embarrassed for being so…careless, and such a burden to transport. I apologized after voicing these to Paul.

He laughed and said, "You certainly are the strangest creature. Apologizing for accidentally injuring yourself on your way to a building filled with people who hate you? What word do I want...? Unique. You're very unique."

I nodded slowly, watching him bring out a needle. He injected the anesthetic and waited a few minutes, watching me carefully. I felt nothing, no changes in my condition or senses.

"Are you feeling drowsy or numb?" he asked hopefully. I shook my head honestly and he sighed heavily, picking up a glass bottle of whiskey. "Alright, we're going to have to improvise. I thought you might not be affected by the anesthetic, but I hoped. Here, drink that."

I drank the burning alcohol quickly. It tasted strange, alien, and it hurt down my throat. Paul instructed me not to cough, that it would only make it worse. I sighed after a few minutes, dizzy. I cannot recall much after that, other than distorted aches being translated by my groggy nerves.

It was a very strange experience. Black covered my vision, I remember. I know that I was frightened by the blood. The unnatural color made my heart throb in fear and I know that through the haze I was aware of myself sobbing that I hated what I am. It did no one any good, I only caused fear. I was overwhelmed by the alcohol's effects, admitting truths I never thought I would speak aloud.

I woke the next morning with a throbbing skull. My feet were mildly sore, but not near as pained as my head. My body felt heavy, like I had not slept enough even though I had slept through a day and a night. Someone placed a cool cloth on my forehead. I moaned and blinked my eyes into focus.

Mother was in a chair beside my bed, a bowl in her lap and a cloth in hand. She smiled at me as I began to stir and look around. Katelyn was sleeping on the spare bed and Paul was taking a seat at the end of my bed to change my bandages.

"I'm glad to see you made it through the procedure just fine. How do you feel?" asked Paul without looking away from his work.

I winced as his finger brushed my sensitive skin. "Different. Almost wrong."

"That would be the alcohol," he explained quietly. "And I do apologize, ma'am, for giving your son whiskey without consulting you or your husband. I felt it could quickly turn into an emergency, however, should there be any delay in treating Cory, and the anesthetic didn't work."

Mother nodded, smiling gratefully. "I understand. Thank you for caring for my son."

I remained at Paul's home for two more days, to ensure that my feet would not be put under any unnecessary stress. I was back in the fields after a week, happy as a clam. My life was turning to the sun. I could see Kate whenever she had the time. I was also the first member and inspirational founder for our church to form a choir.

Cory paused, seeming hesitant. "Do you know what a wonderful accident is, sir?"

Robert considered his words for a moment before nodding. "Yes. Why?"

"That is exactly what happened at church that day. When I crashed my first time, that was also a wonderful accident, because it caused me to meet Kate. Have you lived enough to comprehend exactly what a wonderful accident does?" asked Cory, glancing at the door.

"No, I'm afraid not." Robert shook his head, following Cory's gaze. "What are you looking at?"

"Oh, I apologize. Dinner should be soon and I am quite famished. Hence my impatience. I find it amazing, however, that a man wearing such a snappy suit would be able to set aside any hubris he may possess to speak such a humble statement. Bravo, sir," applauded Cory and he gave a slight bow of his head.

Robert frowned slightly, unsure of whether this strange creature was being condescending or genuinely congratulatory. "Thank you. What does a wonderful accident do, then?"

The demon chuckled and sighed, "It dictates what happens to one's life. The best any of us can do is enjoy wherever we are, whenever we are, however we can."

"But I thought that we all had control over what happens, and we can do whatever we want to," replied Robert, trying to be polite. He gave a slight smile.

Cory startled him by bursting into raucous laughter. After a moment, Robert heard the bitter undertone to the sound. "No, no, good sir. Although, that is a rather humorous theory. No one average person can do *anything* to shape their lives. Those who can are by no means limited by such a simple title as 'average.' They have a strong, durable character that can make a king's palace from sand or the finest wine from pathetic and rotted berries."

Robert scowled defiantly, unwilling to admit such a huge weakness in his life. "Everyone has character, though."

"Only the illusion of, sir, and I do not say this to insult anyone," replied Cory evenly. "True character is as unstoppable as Nature herself. I have seen the glimmering potential for such a rare gift in many people, though it has always been crushed before it can fully blossom. Sadly, when one's character is destroyed, that person then seeks to dominate others' potential."

Robert was frozen by the honesty and beautifully laid out thoughts that this visually savage man provided. "Why are you telling me this?"

"So that you might make use of the wisdom when you return home to your family, and see your wife and children in a new light. Maybe you will be able to nourish their abilities and they you in return, or maybe you will be horrified by the notion and crush whatever they have. I am unaware," finished Cory with a wave of his tail. Robert was amazed by how the demon could emote—physically and linguistically—with a certain gentlemanly manner that he had thought imaginary.

"Huh...So, wait. No one has control of their life, except those with character?" asked Robert, his mind on the verge of grasping some grand new concept.

"I do not recall having said that we do not control our lives," murmured Cory, eyes distant again. "We cannot control what happens in the world, unless we have character. We always have control of how we live, however. We can live happily in the mud, or be dissatisfied in a mighty castle. That we can control, if we have the awareness of our power to do so. What *happens*...Can you control when you become ill?"

Robert nodded. "Yes, with vitamins."

"Oh?" Cory smiled slightly and looked up at Robert. He leaned forward to rest his elbows on his knees. "You can take a vitamin to remove illness and another to cause it?"

"No, we can take vitamins to make sure we don't get sick," said Robert slowly.

"Ah, see there—the difference. You use caution and preventative measures, but you do not genuinely have control, do you?"

"No...I guess not." Robert frowned at this new thought, writing the base concept in his notes. "What are you saying?"

"That without character you cannot control what happens, only what you do with it. You can be happy when ill or not, that is yours to control. Whether you fall ill is not yours to control, in fact, but some nameless cosmic coincidence." Cory grinned, startling Robert. He barely reigned in a cry of fright at seeing the monster-like teeth in Cory's mouth.

Robert recomposed himself. "Erm...My apologies. I didn't expect you to have such sharp...fangs."

"Oh, no, the fault is mine. I have grown so accustomed to people not being frightened by the sight of me. I was rude." Cory closed his mouth, glancing at the door again. "Also, sir?"

Robert lifted his head in interest. "Yes?"

"A little secret," said Cory conspiratorially, smiling knowingly. "Anyone has the capacity to create their own character."

"Would you continue your story?" asked Robert, desiring to know what happened after the incident at church, making mental note to remember Cory's words.

Cory began to nod before faltering, a deep frown saddening his face. "I would, but ah..." He laughed, the sound ringing falsely while tears touched his eyes. "I cannot recall what happened next."

Humanity

Robert Smith sighed heavily, smiling quietly to himself as he slid the papers across the table for Beth to sign. "Here you are. I can't tell you how happy it makes me to know you can't refuse."

Beth returned his smile, shaking her head slowly. After interviewing Cory recently, Robert had to wonder if it was a difference between generations or if he truly was naïve.

"You are such a child, Mr. Smith. A child," she hissed, glaring at the papers with more malice than Robert had ever witnessed previously. "As such you are quite ignorant to the delicate situation we have handled here for decades."

"Oh, I am well aware of the finesse required for torture, Mrs. Lawson," ground out Robert hatefully, all but slamming a pen down for her to use. He narrowed his eyes, refusing to display his shock that the old woman never flinched. "I am also aware of the laws that now protect that man from people like you."

"Researchers? Scientists?" she questioned skeptically, her smile returning. "Or is it that you cannot even admit to yourself your raging curiosity?"

"Just say what you mean," he snapped, irritated

further. He did not know what this woman had done or allowed to happen to his patient, but he knew that it was enough trauma to have Cory refuse to remember.

Now Beth laughed. "You stupid child. We never tortured him because of what *he* is, don't you understand? We know what he is, inside and out, no pun intended. We poked, prodded and gutted to learn more about what *we* lack, to learn of *humanity*."

Robert's glare hardened cruelly. "Now you're insulting."

"No, I'm being honest, but I suppose you're too young to know the difference," she sighed. "Regardless, we learned very little of what we are, or even what we are not. Although, I can say one thing for certain."

"Would you like my professional opinion?" demanded Robert, prepared to spit daggers.

"If I would, I'd never ask," she replied lazily. She shook her head slowly. "No, Mr. Smith, we learned something that perhaps poets have known and have been trying to teach us the entire time."

Robert paused, confused. "What?"

"You see, in part we were assigned to Mr. Lawrence to dissect whatever he is, discover where he or his kind originates. Same planet as us, roughly the same time as well, but how they have remained hidden is beyond us. Regardless, that was only a—how shall I put this?— footnote of our purposes here," she explained slowly, and Robert had the feeling of being a child receiving bad news. Why was Beth being so...gentle with this?

"And what was that?"

Beth sighed, her age apparent when Robert looked her in the eye. "This was a test, Mr. Smith."

Horror was all that managed to climb up his throat, so thick he had to pause to keep from gagging. "Damn it, spit it out!"

"As a whole and as individuals, we are driven to discover what we are by finding what we are not, Mr. Smith," she said sharply. "The last forty years, and even before that when Paul Ericson first reported Mr. Lawrence's existence to us, it has all been a test of the humanity we so desperately seek, Robert, in myths and legends."

Robert choked a moment, uncertain of which emotions were reigning and tearing through him. "You mean...you've tested on him...his entire life?"

"That's the good news," she told him, a strange look filling her eyes as she lifted the pen from the table and signed the paper with a flourish. "The rather horrible news is that this was our test, and we failed it."

Demon *Rising*

<u>Homo Demonicus?</u>

Late on the Thursday evening of July 22nd, the species discovered 41 years ago was named. 30 years after being declared sentient, the monstrous humanoids have been crudely named demons.

Countless demon supporters are outraged and claim that the name causes many cruel assumptions as to the creatures' natures, and may even create needless stresses between humans and demons. All officials questioned have stated that a politically correct term may be instated should the name cause too much tension.

None of these reportedly violent people—a loose term, as they share more characteristics with animals than humans—have been seen in twenty years, since the last "rampage" in January of '90, when a demon burst into the rural home of an unsuspecting family on a skiing vacation. Rumors are spreading now, however, that the N.S.I.S.D. research facility that has been studying this species has a specimen in custody that may be released shortly.

Chapter Two:
Freedom Rings

First Week Under Protection

Sunday

Has my luck turned for better or worse?

Recalling the past month, I had to think that the storm was nearly over. None of the over-eager individuals or teams here had examined me in nigh three months, though I had been expecting it of them. I am certain the reason behind this is that they had wanted me in at least a semi-presentable condition for our guest, Robert. My savior, more or less.

Three weeks. Had it been so short a time or was it that long ago? Time inside these walls confounded me. I could never tell exactly what was quick or slow. What seemed unbearably long was commonly such a short count of hours that I felt too confused to think.

When first I had heard that this man was coming, I was curious as to why but did not consider this. Yes, the *possibility* of being freed, but the probability? Ha!

Nonexistent, from all that I knew.

Two weeks ago, he sent his diagnosis. Beth had stormed about in a rage—something wholly unthoughtful of herself, considering her age. Oh, Helen was thrilled. She had been the one to tell me, against what I assumed were Beth's desires to keep me uninformed. That woman did love to watch my pain, it seemed. Oh, but she would have none of it now!

I was to be released.

Joyous day, I was going to be free! To see the sky again, to feel the wind, to return home. Home...A place that I would likely need to scour the world for. The years would have torn it apart as they had myself. Sadly, home cannot recover so easily by the sound of its liberation.

Oh, and I *heard* the shackles clattering against the floor. It was the sound of final measurements being taken, the feeling of last minute blood tests. It was the smell of that stale room that was mine melting away to the tantalizing scent of the outside that always lingered near the exit.

That was where I stood, frozen with my shock. Robert was there to escort me out, Beth to fume and seethe and spit fiery daggers for words at me bitterly. Finer details of Robert's conditions for my freedom were still somewhat vague to me. The only one I knew was that he was to become my permanent therapist while I adjusted to my new life.

My old life in new garb, I corrected myself. I had known freedom before. The difference now would be the world and not me. *Or could it be a new life, in fact, wearing the old trappings?*

"Well, what are you waiting for?" demanded Beth

sharply. She motioned at the door angrily. "You've got your freedom!"

I smiled nervously, nodding. "Yes...I do."

Robert stood at the door, waiting to open it for me. "Let him take his time with this. It's been awhile."

Over forty years. My heart was beating erratically with both excitement and terror. I motioned to the door handle that Robert held. "May I?"

He nodded, stepping back. "Whenever you're ready."

With the cool metal in my hand, I half expected to be yanked from the door and forced back into my room. I had no possessions with me other than a thick envelope that Beth had given to me that morning. All I had to do was step out that door, with nothing to bring with me from this place and nothing to hold me back.

So I opened the door.

The first thing I felt was the sun on my skin, warm and gentle. Shirtless as I had been years ago, I could feel the joyous sensation everywhere. The light was bright and hot, sharp enough to make me wince for a moment before it began to fade. For the first time in decades, I laughed without bitterness or sarcasm. A genuine, bubbling laugh that made me feel twenty again.

The next thing I noticed was the world around me. Green—so vivid I began to cry while I laughed. Pine trees surrounded the complex, the glorious green framing the open blue sky. The hot pavement beneath my feet did nothing to make the moment less. To the contrary, the burning against my sensitive skin was a wonderful relief from the cold metal and tile I had grown accustomed to.

A light breeze crossed my face, so softly it could

56

have been a caress. I stretched my wings wide to feel the wind against my membranes, laughing loud with more joy than I thought possible. I could smell the sweetness of August, and it was strong enough in my mouth that I thought I could taste it, as well.

Too overwhelmed to notice anything else, I turned my grin toward the people still standing in the doorway. Robert was startled. Beth's glare sharpened. "Excuse me a moment."

I sprinted in a straight line, dropping the envelope in my hands as I jumped into the air. My first down stroke was awkward and strained, but it pulled me away from the earth. Two more strong, steady beats and I was airborne. My membranes burned from lack of use, as did my muscles. That unnamed emotion of flight filled my chest, and for a moment I felt close to home.

I circled the complex five times before I thought I might fall from the sky. Lowering myself to the ground slowly, I landed with a thunderous boom as my weight left my wings and my feet hit the pavement. I looked around at the humans that gaped at me.

"I...That...Wow," managed Robert. He walked toward me, picking up the package I had dropped and handing it back to me. "I have a temporary living arrangement ready for you, Cory. Whenever you want to go, we can."

My eyes strayed to the building with the woman who had starred in many of my nightmares. I took a deep breath of relief as I relished in my freedom. Turning back to Robert, I grinned down at him. He started, but grinned back.

"Now. I want to see the world now," I told him

honestly, even as my heart pounded with excitement and terror. He motioned to a large vehicle for me to board.

When we were both inside—my wings and tail cramped and shoulders hunched inside the relatively small space—the vehicle began to move. I kept myself from starting, surprised by the abrupt motion. Where was the bellow of the engine? I listened, frowning when I heard the too-smooth sound.

"You need your seat belt on."

I glanced at Robert. "I beg your pardon?"

He pointed to a strap on my right. "For safety."

"For safety's sake..." I shook my head to rid myself of my father's echoing voice. With a quiet sigh, I worked to maneuver around myself and strap the belt around me. I groaned, unable to find a way to settle into my seat. Outside the vehicle, the world was racing by in a blur.

"Thank you, Robert." The motion of the car made me mildly ill, moving at such a pace without physical effort. How disconcerting. I noted him frowning at my words. "For transporting me and acquiring my lodgings. You had no reason to aid me, so thank you."

He sighed. "You're welcome, I guess. Before we go to the house, would you like to get some clothes?"

I chuckled at that. "I have no money, and where would I purchase anything my size, or for my specie? Have they shops for that now?"

"I was just thinking..." He glanced at me, then back at the road. "Never mind. I'll have my wife take care of that later."

"You mean to imply...Sir, do you intend to help me more than you already have?" I asked with mild guilt. I had no way to repay him or properly thank him for his assistance. In all of my memory of humans, this Robert character certainly was acting kindly.

"Of course! One of the conditions I had for when you were released was that I become your therapist for a minimum of six months and that you live with me for two weeks to start, to make sure you get the help you need," he explained. He seemed to feel as awkward as I did at that moment.

We were quiet for a minute while I mulled over his words. One of *his* conditions for my release? That implied that the facility was wanting to be rid of me and required his permission. I had been told it was quite the opposite, or had at least come to my own understanding that things functioned as such. Perhaps I was the only one who needed permission at all whilst the rest of them did as they pleased.

"How is it I was removed from that...*place*?" I asked, keeping my phrasing as polite as possible. I could think of more than a handful of vulgar terms that—bitterly—I considered using.

"Oh, just a couple generations of hippies fighting for demon rights," he sighed, then laughed. "I used to think they were nuts, but...Apparently, they knew a bit more than me on the matter."

I turned back to the window, reigning in my excitement. "Rights? I have rights?"

"As of two months ago. Congratulations," he added, his mirth dissipating slowly. "Did no one tell you?"

I shook my head slowly, then stared at my hands in amazement. *Rights.* Legally, I was now a person worthy of acknowledging my power to choose. Was this a dream? Had Beth tested a new drug on me, something that caused euphoric hallucinations?

"No, I never thought...Truly? I have full rights, like you?" I asked, looking at him trustingly. He glanced at me quickly, face sad.

"Yes, full rights. I read through them myself. You need to go through specific branches if you want to do something like adopt—and some loans are trickier to get—but hey. Can't complain, right?" he ended, smiling again.

"No," I chuckled, grinning. "No, indeed not. I must find some way to repay these hippies, as you say they were."

"Support oil or something," he suggested with a smirk. "Maybe everyone will flock over to green energy."

"Ah...No, thank you for that...idea," I phrased delicately. Robert's smirk turned to a grin. The vehicle began to slow. I looked up curiously. "Why is there a *riot* on the road?"

Robert frowned deeply, still slowing the vehicle. "It's not a riot. See the banner? It's a welcome to the outside. I think," he added uncertainly.

"I will dutifully walk the path of paranoia and say that those people are rioting, Robert, and we should find a way around them," I replied, more than willing to avoid a beating my first day free of my cold, concrete cage.

The vehicle was nearly stopped, some hundred or so feet from the commotion. "You know, I was never told that there would be reporters. I hope the car's ready," he muttered, unstrapping himself with a sigh.

I stared at the numbered vehicles and the individuals near them. "Reporters? Oh, dear. Like a black cat..."

"Well, when life give you lemons," he said to me,

leaving the saying half finished.

I smirked and unstrapped myself. "Make grape juice."

He frowned in confusion. "What?"

I chuckled, then stopped myself from exiting when I caught sight of my arm. I looked about in a panic for anything to cover myself with, only able to retrieve the envelope from Beth. "Do you have a spare blanket? Or perhaps a tarp?"

Robert shook his head. "I knew I forgot something. I'm sorry, no."

I sighed sharply, defeated. "Right. Off to the media, then."

We left the vehicle. After a few strides towards the excited group, Robert swore under his breath. He said in answer to my questioning glance, "It's channel seven's girl."

"Is this unfortunate?" I asked, finding myself unable to breathe properly. My tail lashed and curled the air nervously. The world would see me once a story was published or televised. Again, I cursed my visage.

He nodded, face somber. "Yeah. Don't make eye contact with her, whatever you do."

"Of course," I muttered, unable to focus on any one person. There were too many that were bustling about at once. One woman was speaking to a camera, glancing over her shoulder before making her way to where Robert and I were attempting to pass quietly.

"Sir, sir!" It took me a moment to understand that she was calling *me* "sir". She stepped into our intended path rudely, eyes tightening to say that she would not accept no as an answer for whatever her demand was.

"Could we get you to answer a few questions?"

I hesitated, unwilling to reject her completely but liking Robert's proposal of evading these reporters. "No, please, I only want to make it home and begin adjusting."

She continued as though she had not heard my words, in spite of my knowledge that I had spoken clearly. "Are you a male or female demon?"

Robert was kind enough to step between myself and the woman. I stepped back gratefully, glancing around in the hopes of finding an escape. "Miss, please leave my client alone. It's an exciting day, but he really does need some space."

"You, who are you and how are you servicing this demon?" she continued relentlessly. I winced at the reference to myself, noting how sharp her tone was when pronouncing the word.

"That is my own business and I'm helping him to get by hounds like you," he snapped, glaring at her. My eyes settled on the camera lens for a moment and my heart began to pound harder when I recalled that there were thousands of people who could be watching me, *seeing* what I was.

Turn the camera away, I pled silently, averting my gaze nervously. My bland, cold room was very comforting in my mind at that moment, if it meant that these staring eyes would disappear.

"So you're his lawyer?"

"Madam, what would it take for you to allow us passage?" I asked, keeping my voice soft to avoid alarming her. I wanted a quiet grassy yard where I could enjoy the sun and the sky in peace.

She smirked. "Just answer a few questions?"

Robert interceded, looking up at me with concern on his face. "You don't have to. It's your choice, remember?"

"Will she desist any other way?" I asked quietly, hoping the woman could not hear. By the felled expression he then developed, I understood that this was the only way to pass, much to my discomfort.

He turned back to the woman. "Fine. If I feel that the situation is becoming too stressful though, I *will* have you removed."

She smiled too sweetly, and for the first time I noticed the armed and armored men scattered in the crowd. All of them were watching me carefully, then scanning the area before coming back to me. I knew that it was sad that I was too used to seeing men such as them, but I wondered now if they were there to protect me or the humans I was surrounded by.

"Of course. Now, were you male or female?" she asked again.

I linked my arms behind my back, an old habit to restrain and comfort myself. "I believe that I am quite obviously male."

"What's your name? No one knows and it's been a big mystery for the past few years." Her laugh sounded hollow.

"Cory Charles Lawrence." My eyes darted across the faces around me swiftly to check for any signs that I would be attacked.

"Do you have a family? If so, what specie?"

"Human," I replied quietly, eyes stinging as again their memory burned in my mind. "My parents have passed, I believe that my sister is doing well, I do not know how my brothers have fared and—Well, I suppose not..."

She caught my words of avoidance. "Yes?"

"I had a fiancée. I would rather not discuss in detail anything that happened regarding her," I added to deter her, too stressed to wonder how I had even temporarily forgotten being engaged, or when such a thing had happened. My shoulders were stiff with my tension and I kept my eyes focused on the ground, though I knew it to be rude. I did not feel as though it would help anyone if I met her ruthless gaze.

"Do you take part in any satanic practices? Rituals, sacrifices—"

"Madam, I beg your pardon!" I interrupted sharply, offended for the first time that I could recall. I stared at her, aghast that she would be so blunt. "I do not appreciate such generalized assumptions of my appearance and actions going hand in hand. No, I do not practice *any* religion, nor do I sacrifice or devour children. Likewise— to avoid further questioning of such topics—religious artifacts affect me as they would you, I do not collect skulls or chains in my attic, and I take no pleasure in torture! Now, I do apologize for reacting in such a temperamental fashion. You were merely doing your duties, however I would rather avoid any other questions based on fictitious writings or assumptions," I finished, my abrupt flare of irritation dying slowly. The woman was staring at me in shock and a silence stretched on for a few moments.

"Well, I think that this was a wonderful adventure, but that we can be done for today. What do you think, Cory?" asked Robert, not waiting for an answer before leading me gently by the arm past the woman. I followed willingly. "Okay, next time you're under national protection, maybe they can do a better job about keeping the media away."

"National protection?" I questioned, eyeing one of the armed men as we passed. He nodded at me curtly but did not move or speak.

"Yeah, endangered species mixed with wanting to make peace with the first nonhuman people we meet, I think. Where on earth is that car?" he muttered, scowling in frustration. He walked up to one of the men. "Where's the transfer car?"

"Over there, sir." The man pointed but never lifted his eyes from me. The weapon he held would have made me nervous had I not been so accustomed to them from within the confines of my captivity.

"A chauffeur?" mused Robert, frowning. "Not very discreet."

"It's what was sent, sir. Don't worry, either. The home is under protection," added the man, businesslike. He glanced behind us. "You may like to hurry. We can keep the media from following you."

"Oh, finally, thank you!" sighed Robert with a grateful smile. He waved farewell to the man. "Come on, Cory. Off to get you settled, hm?"

I nodded, sighing in relief when I saw the vehicle that would take us away from the noise. "Yes, that sounds wonderful."

"How are you handling?" he asked, striding ahead of me to open the door for me.

"Ah, thank you," I said as I found a way to force myself into the small space. I strapped myself in, leaning to rest my elbows on my knees for comfort. "I have been free barely over an hour and already the world has me exhausted."

Robert sat beside me, buckling before closing the door. "Not too surprising. It's going a hundred miles faster than you remember."

"Oh, dear," I murmured to myself, frowning. I turned to the window on my right to see the world outside. Again, the car began to move without rumbling, though I could identify the quiet sound of the engine this time.

Outside, another car arrived at the site we were just leaving. An older woman stepped from the vehicle, richly colored skin glittering slightly in the sun. She wore a yellow shirt and blue jeans, making me frown. Even at a distance, I could identify her features. The vehicle began to move, the woman slipping from the sight of my eyes.

"Kate...?" I breathed, leaning in my seat to keep her in my view longer. The confusion faded swiftly to recognition and a sharp urgency to see her. My heart beat faster, excited by the sight of my old friend. "Stop the car. Stop the car!"

Robert was confused. "What? Why?"

"I saw Kate!" I cried out. She was out of view now, image burned into my memory. "Had that reporter stalled us a minute longer..."

"I didn't see her." He frowned at me worriedly. "Cory, are you feeling alright?"

I nodded. The vehicle began to turn in on its path, so that she was visible again. I pointed, barely keeping myself from leaping from the car. "There she is! Robert, we must stop this vehicle immediately! Please, she's standing right there...Do you see her now? I can see her crying..."

Robert nodded. "I see her, but we can't stop. I don't

think it would be wise, especially with how much you've already been through today. I want to get you to a calm, stable environment."

"What?!" I hissed unintentionally, my claws catching on the seating. I paid no mind to them, vision blurred. She was gone again, lost to me. "No, this was a random happenstance! It cannot be so perfectly lain out again, nor will I allow her to slip between my fingertips when I feel that fate is handing her back. I say again, stop the car!"

"No," he sighed tiredly, shaking his head. The cloth made a sharp ripping sound as my claws tore through it. My chest felt as though it was cracking in two as we drove farther from her. "For reasons like that seat. You're obviously wound tight and distracted, so things like that are more likely to happen. I won't allow that to...For Katelyn's safety and your better interests, I don't want to tempt fate. If she's so close, we'll find her in the phone book or she'll find us again. If she's really coming back to you, nothing can stop it."

I stared out the window longingly, my tears falling to my lap. I nodded blankly and spoke in a whisper to keep from breaking, "Yes...I understand. I will manage myself more closely around your family, so as to not injure them. And I apologize for defacing the furnishings."

Robert shrugged. "Don't worry about it."

I nodded to myself silently, continuing to gaze out the window. The drive stretched on in time quietly while an odd tension settled about us. I hoped that Robert's romantic idea could be true, although I strongly thought otherwise. The universe as it had been presented to myself of late was cold and unkind. Kate was too precious an angel to be allowed near me, I supposed.

Eventually, the greenery outside melted away to buildings of earthy monotones that dulled my mind. I lost track of where one place ended and another began, apathetic of the matter altogether. Why would it be any of my concern what the outside world looked like? If I stepped out the front door, I was likely to be trampled by a mob. I had rights, yes, but respect or human treatments were things I could not hope to receive until an oak was given enough time to dig its roots into my grave. Then, I may be enough to have a small myth written about me.

Oh, but I was being dark, and only barely managing to keep myself from acting macabre. How could I return so easily to brooding on my day of freedom? The day I discover that I am legally a person, no less. I should have been smiling and humming a merry tune, as I would have when I was not yet twenty. Even after twenty, but before thirty. That was the year my optimism died.

Could I regain my innocent belief that all things ended well? I mulled over the thought as the car began to slow. Looking around in confusion, I saw that we were on a rural, dead road with not another soul around. I scowled in confusion.

"Robert, why—?" I began to ask.

"We're switching cars. It's just a precaution. This car is going to be driven elsewhere while we take the car that *wasn't* on TV back to my house," he explained, unstrapping himself and opening his door. He slid out, then ducked back in to retrieve the envelope. I smiled and thanked him before exiting as well.

I groaned and sighed, stretching my wings to their fullest. As the joints were pulled out, relief made me smile.

The feeling was wonderful, and to have the space to spread my wings completely made me want to laugh again. Too many years, I had sat in a small room with limited movement.

The chauffeur said nothing, though his eyes were wide with surprise when I pulled my wings back in. I followed Robert to the next vehicle, a simple white van with dark windows. He opened the back door and motioned for me to enter. I stared at it hesitantly.

"Ah...Must I?" I asked uncertainly. A forgotten, buried memory struggled to resurface with rain and horror. If I entered, where would I exit?

Robert was frowning. "Don't worry, I checked everything myself. It'll be safe."

I paused a moment longer before clambering in. The seats within were wide and much more suitable to my size. To my relief, Robert followed me into the van and sat across from me. He smiled as he buckled himself in. My returning expression was tentative.

The vehicle began to move and I tensed, tail smacking the floor loudly. Robert frowned. "Whatever's wrong, Cory, there's no need for it. This is just so that no one is suspicious, for safer transportation. We don't want anyone following us home."

I nodded in understanding. "No, of course not."

Again, my tail hit the floor. "Alright...So, tell me a bit more about everything. How are you doing?"

"I am very overwhelmed. There are so many people," I murmured thoughtfully. "So many sounds..."

He was nodding. "Yeah, I know. You're safe, though."

"You seem very certain of your words," I noted,

easing slightly with the distraction of conversation. He noticed, smiling again silently.

"I am," he agreed, grinning now. The vehicle turned left, making me lean. I was only glad that the sky outside was blue and sunny, not dark or stormy.

An awkward silence settled between us; I was not eager to break it. Rather, I enjoyed that it was silent. It was a lull, a peace in the stormy sea that was this day. I was gripping my seat nervously, nearly choking on my pounding heart. Questions whirled through my mind mercilessly.

Where was the house that I would be staying in? Did Robert's family know that I was coming? More importantly, did they know what I was? How would they greet me? Weapons or smiles? Could it be that they would smile and then find some way to rid themselves of me? My eyes widened at that thought, and I considered that my customary caution was approaching the line of complete paranoia.

Surprisingly, the van stopped not ten minutes later, the silence breaking as the back doors were opened loudly. I started, taking a slow breath to steady myself. Robert left first, patting my hand reassuringly on his way. I made to climb out but hissed and retreated as soon as my eyes were in the sunlight.

My skull throbbed sharply, eyes burning from the sudden brightness. Outside, Robert and the chauffeur were staring at me in surprise. Then Robert's shock melted to pity. I focused on the floor of the van, waiting for the pain in my head to cease.

"Are you alright?" asked Robert after a moment.

I nodded. "Yes, the sun only hurt my eyes. I will be

fine once I recover."

"Take your time." Again with those words? Did he genuinely mean them or were they trained? The chauffeur certainly seemed impatient, but Robert's face was calm.

I was glad when my head no longer pounded after a few minutes, and I attempted to exit again. This time, the sun was bright but it did not attack me. I blinked while my eyes adjusted, enthralled by the odd sight before me. A row of similar houses lined either side of the street. They were dull or earthy in color with a black, white or silver vehicle in the drive, if there was a car there. Otherwise, they all seemed empty. No one was outside, save for on the front lawn of the house we were parked in front of.

When I saw the people on the lawn, I jumped back skittishly and eyed the weapons they were equipped with. I counted seven men, all fully armored in black. Two of them held their weapons drawn. The guns were familiar, as well as their suspicious glares.

Robert looked from the men to my wide eyes, glaring at the ones who were ready to shoot. "Put those away, will you!"

They seemed surprised but lowered the weapons sheepishly. Robert sighed and smiled at me apologetically, motioning for me to follow him down a small cement path to the door of the house. He opened the door and entered.

"Come on in, Cory, it's alright," he said, and I relaxed a mite.

I ducked through the door, sighing quietly in relief that the ceiling was tall enough that I could stand erect. Robert led me through the foyer to the kitchen, where a small red-haired woman was working by the stove. I was brought into the spacious room, much to my discomfort.

"Honey? This is the patient I told you would be coming to stay with us," said Robert gently. "We've had an exciting day."

The woman turned, blinking in surprise when she saw me. By her otherwise cool manner, I assumed that she had been prepared for my appearance. She smiled uncertainly at me.

"Right, um...Cory, was it? Congratulations," she said awkwardly with a glance at her husband.

"Ah. Thank you," I mumbled, feeling awkward as well. We stared at each other in silence before Robert graciously cracked the icy stillness.

"Right, so, the girls should be home from the party in a few minutes," said Robert slowly, looking at his hands for focus. "When will dinner be ready, Anne?"

"Five-thirty," she replied quietly, looking away from me with relief. It was nothing I was unaccustomed to, anyway.

"Great," sighed Robert, clapping his hands and startling us all. We fell back into the silence for a moment.

The front door opened loudly.

"Dad! You'd better say that it wasn't you I saw on TV at Cindy's today!" shouted an irritated, youthful voice. I glanced behind me to see a young woman who looked very much like Anne glaring between me and her father. She huffed a sigh. "Okay, that's it. I'm going to get emancipated, because *this*—" she thrust a finger at me "—is the last of your stupid straws!"

He stared at her patiently, asking quietly, "Vanessa, what's that button for?"

"It's 'Humans Forever', an anti-demon activists group that was formed at school last year," she replied coolly. A girl I presumed was her sister, though she did not look like either of her parents, stepped up behind her.

"Yeah, you have to have a crippling case of rectal-cranial inversion in order to qualify for entry," she added, making Vanessa roll her eyes. The new sister then appraised me and took a step back. "Whoa."

I looked between the two, incredibly confused and somewhat stunned by their whirlwind entry and presence. It was much to my grief that I realized a peaceful first day would be out of my grasp, and was rudely relieved when Vanessa stalked away.

Then the sister took her place.

"Hi, I'm Bailey, my dad's non-bitch daughter." She smiled at me serenely.

"I do beg your pardon, but your verbiage is incredibly vulgar for a young woman like yourself. Such language is far beneath your capabilities, I am certain," I replied, keeping my words polite and mindful.

She blinked in surprise and looked at her father. "Is this guy for real?"

"Yes, now go clean up, please," replied Robert. When I looked at him, he appeared reserved and deathly calm. I frowned in concern. "And tell your sister I would like to speak to her before dinner."

"Weather's predicting hurricanes. Gotcha," sighed Bailey, following the direction of her sister.

Anne sighed quietly. "Be nice."

"Yeah. Look, Cory, I'm sorry for Vanessa's bluntness." Robert seemed to choose the word carefully, saying it slowly.

"Ah," I muttered, worried more for what may happen to his family than myself. I shook my head slowly, struggling to clear the turmoil from it. I sighed in defeat after a moment when a sudden wave of exhaustion made my head heavy and knees weak. "I hope none of you would mind if I passed on supper and rested instead? If there is a place where I could rest."

"Oh, yeah, yeah," replied Robert, as though it had not occurred to him that this was a possible ending to the day. He glanced at the clock and laughed, "Well, four hours outside *would* be more exciting than—Anyway, let me show you to your room."

Four hours? My, I had forgotten just how differently time moved on the outside. What had happened in four hours I could have been fooled would happen in four days. Freedom, an interview, that long time in the van. Meeting Robert's family even seemed like a task for a single day.

Robert led me from the kitchen to a half-flight of stairs just past the foyer and kitchen. At the end of the first half-flight was a landing, then another partial flight. When we arrived on the second floor, we strode down a small hall with a door on either side into a room that appeared to be a study. There was another hall on the left wall to us, so we traversed still deeper into the complex that was top floor.

The next hall was longer with four doors, two on either side. Bailey was standing in the doorway of the first room on our right, talking with a smirk on her face.

"...told you not to join that stupid club." She glanced over and saw us, straightening abruptly. "Gotta go. Later, Van!"

"Stop calling me that!" yelled Vanessa from within the room as Bailey hurried down the hall, slipping into the second door on the left.

Demon *Rising*

Robert sighed. "Going at it again. Okay, this is the bathroom for this floor, which you're welcome to use," he said, motioning to the first door on our left. "You already see which rooms are the girls', I hope. And the final one up here on our right was the guest room, but it's yours now as long as you need or want it."

"Thank you," I said gratefully, stepping into the room. There were two made beds lined against one wall, pushed together at the head and foot to create something long enough for me to sleep on comfortably. On the opposite wall there was a small dresser, a desk and a door to what I assumed was a closet. Above the bed, there was a broad window with curtains pulled back, a gorgeous and full view of nothing but sky making me feel welcome. It was everything I needed and more that I had not considered asking for.

I smiled to myself and turned to Robert. "Again, thank you. This is very welcoming and gracious of you and your family to house me."

"It's the least we could do." He waved it away, pausing a moment to think aloud, "The kitchen's open all hours, but dinner's generally around five-thirty or six, breakfast at seven or eight. If you need anything, you can find Anne or myself or, if that fails, you can just holler. The walls are a little thin and the acoustics could make a DJ jealous."

I did not understand what he meant by his last sentence but continued to smile. The feeling of acceptance he was emanating was warm, making me think that we could have spoken entirely separate languages and I still would have understood that he was being kind.

"Thank you." I repeated the only thing I could

think to say.

"Right, well, I'll leave you to rest now and see how Vanessa's doing," he said, smiling tightly before leaving. I closed the door gently behind him with a relieved sigh. Solitude was something I knew all too well, and now I craved the comfort of having no one near while yearning to see or hear other people. Nothing but confusion could greet me when I set the envelope I had been holding—for what I realized was near an hour now—on the desk. Then I went to the bed to lay myself down, body relaxing tiredly.

It was not a moment later when sharp, angry words came from through the opposite wall.

"...how you could support something like this when you *knew* that he would be coming here!" said a voice that sounded like Robert.

Vanessa was quick to reply, "I joined when the group was founded four months ago, and protested against *it* having rights and being unleashed on an unprepared public. How do you know it won't eat us while we sleep?"

"Because he's the most respectable man I've met, and I have thirty years on you, Vanessa."

"Fine, but if it's staying here, I demand a steel lock on my door and pepper spray."

"No. You will quit this disgraceful phase along with that group, and you will behave as if Mr. Lawrence is..."

The conversation quieted so that I could thankfully no longer hear. Guilt settled heavily on my chest. Was my presence already creating catastrophes among this innocent family? I only had a brief moment to wonder before fatigue drowned my mind in sleep.

Demon *Rising*

~~ * ~ * ~ * ~~

Monday

When I first began to stir, I knew something was wrong. There was no light in the room aside from a faint, glittering silver that poured in from yet another wrong incident—a window. I started, gasping wildly in fear. The scents in the room were unfamiliar, and far too rich to belong to the facility. The room was warm and not icy cold to my exposed skin.

Most importantly, when I fell from the bed, carpet met my hands and knees.

Suddenly, I could recall where I was and how I had gotten there as the previous day returned to me. I sighed and shuddered, pushing myself from the floor slowly. I glanced around the room on a cautious impulse, shaking my head.

"Silly old fool," I muttered to myself, pausing. I looked around the room again. What did I do with myself, now that I was rested and felt prepared to face another few hours of a free life?

The envelope on the desk caught my attention. I had yet to open the package, so I snatched it up and sat on the bed before peeling back the sealed flap carefully. The mystery was suddenly intense to me when I pulled the contents out and spread them on the bed. I frowned then, realizing that I had yet to turn on the light.

I stood and did so, relishing that it was my own whim that lit the room and not the procedures of others that left me forever without power. I returned to the bed and the papers there, frowning when I saw a small black rectangle. Lifting it from the bed, I inspected it curiously.

My name had been printed in raised silver lettering on it, just above several sets of four numbers. A photo of myself sat in the upper right corner. The only other decoration were the words "No expiration," which made my frown deepen. What was this? The card was thick and felt like plastic.

Confounded, I set it aside and forgot it when I saw the next papers in the stack. A birth certificate proclaiming unknown parentage—though stating Mr. William C. Lawrence and Mrs. Eleanor V. Lawrence as my adoptive human parents—and in bold lettering stating my species: **Demon**. Attached by a paper clip was a red social security card with my full name, my species again and a single digit: 1.

I laughed quietly to myself and shook my head, too amused to be disturbed by the clear distinguishing that I was not human. I felt giddy and triumphant, like those who had treated me poorly had lost what was a long and tolling battle. The thought that the war was still raging did not bother me, either. Knowing that I was a person lifted my spirits too far for me to care.

Sifting through the remaining papers, I found my thoughts straying too far to care about the finely printed wording. It was a Christmas morning and I was seven, unable to consolidate my scattered focus long enough to finish reading a sentence.

First to distract me was the sky that was paling outside. I had not realized how long I had been awake until I saw the broad and beautiful rainbow spreading its wings from the horizon. I smiled. The sun should be risen in less than an hour, the first dawn I would witness since my liberation.

After a moment, I collected the papers and replaced them on the desk before turning the light off. Again, I returned to the bed to happily and patiently watch the sunrise blossom warmly in greeting to the world and day to come.

It could not have been more than twenty minutes later that the sun first peeked over the horizon. Its golden light flitted across the sprawling land beneath the sky and touched my face. A quiet laugh escaped me, tears of the most precious joy filling my eyes. My palm pressed against the window as the sunlight began to slowly warm my face.

The gnawing hunger in my gut did nothing to spoil the morning. It only made me smile broadly and leave to tidy myself in the bathroom before I ventured downstairs.

The vivid red reflection in the mirror did not startle me. What did surprise me was the size of the room and how I did not need to keep my wings tight to my body. My tail even had space to curl around the air. I noticed these things while I washed my face and rinsed my mouth, then stared helplessly into the mirror and mulled over the predicament of clothing. I had only that single pair of shorts, and this was no issue to me from my upbringing. The scars were what made me shift nervously, but I had no shirt to cover at least most of them with.

I sighed, turning to leave when I started. Bailey was staring at me sleepily. She yawned widely and raised one eyebrow at me, as though this was an ordinary morning and I had lived there years.

She pointed behind me. "You done?"

"Ah, yes," I mumbled awkwardly, shimmying past

her easily. The door slammed behind her with a startlingly loud bang that made me jump again. I sighed quietly and shook my head, thinking it must just be me and my erratic nerves. I made my way through the study and the remaining hall. Downstairs, I could smell the richness of breakfast being prepared and wandered into the kitchen to see if I might be of assistance.

Oddly, it was Robert I found in the kitchen, spatula in hand. He turned when he heard the light scratching of my claws on the cool tile floor. He smiled and—like Bailey—created the illusion that this was a morning of no coincidence.

"Good morning, Cory. How would you like your eggs?" he asked naturally, turning back to the skillet to rearrange strips of bacon.

"I have no preference. Is there anything I might assist with?" I asked, gazing around the large kitchen for the first attentive time. Everything was rich wood, polished stone or unnervingly bright metal. It was a room from a science fiction novel, making me smile with the childlike wonder and curiosity I had when reading such pieces.

"Get out some fruit?" He motioned to a monstrous silver icebox. Controlled by the practices my mother had drilled into me—and the thought that it may be punishable to smudge anything so pristine—I washed my hands before touching the appliance.

I paused when I approached it and took a step back. "Ah, Robert?"

"Yeah?" He turned and smirked at my confusion. "The right one's the fridge, left one's the freezer."

"Of course," I muttered, opening the right door.

"Sorry, I just realized that this must be something

out of a science fiction story for you," said Robert, catching my previous thoughts. Then he added, "Grapes are in the top drawer with the strawberries. Could you pull those out and wash them?"

"Yes." I did as instructed, running water into the sink. "Fruit with breakfast?"

He nodded. "Not all too uncommon. Why, what would you have?"

"When fortune would allow? Applesauce, from Katelyn's orchard." I smiled, suddenly yearning for the ambrosial treat. Was the orchard still there? Had the recipe survived the years? I examined all that was being prepared. "No potatoes?"

A snicker from behind me made me glance over my shoulder. Bailey was yawning again as she retrieved a glass from a cupboard. "That word's funny when someone like you says it. Heh, potatoes."

"Don't mind her. She's always this loose until she has breakfast," commented Robert offhandedly.

She went to the icebox, placing the cup into an indentation in the door and pressing a button. Water began to pour into the cup. I frowned. Science fiction, indeed.

Bailey's eyes widened suddenly and she grinned at her father, chirping, "Hash browns! Cheesy hash browns!"

"Your hips are going to end up as big as your head if you keep up with the cheese obsession," stated Vanessa, entering the kitchen to mimic her sister and get water.

"Girls, it's too early for this sort of thing," sighed Robert. "Go ahead and make hash browns, Bailey."

"Wheee!" squealed Bailey, the high sound of glee making me both smile and wince as I rinsed the strawberries.

Demon *Rising*

"Mommy, Mommy, Lisa is after me!" I screeched with laughter, hurrying to one side of Mother to evade my little sister's grinning face.

She laughed cutely, round cheeks puffing with her grin. "Mommy! Cory tickled me, Mommy! Tickle him back for me!"

"No fair! No fair!" I giggled when Mother whirled on me to capture me in a hug and tickle me. I squirmed chaotically before eventually collapsing into a fit of gasped laughter. "Air! I need air!"

"And Lisa..." Mother turned to my sister. "Needs to be tickled, too!"

"Ah! No! Help me, Cory—Ha-ha!"

Bailey materialized on my left, setting two large bowls on the counter. "Here ya go, someplace to put the fruits. Ooh, grape. Snatched!" she giggled as she popped a grape into her mouth and grinned.

"Okay, okay, out of the kitchen, girls! Go clean rooms, shower, etcetera. You know what day it is!" he called after them as they left the room, tromping up the stairs loudly. Robert was laughing quietly to himself, shaking his head.

I frowned slightly. "What day is it? I seem to have lost track."

"The ninth," he replied absently. He found a large plate and moved the bacon from the pan to the plate. He placed a new set of bacon to cook, coming to the sink to rinse his hands.

"Of which month, again?" I asked, stepping aside to provide him room. July could not have come and gone already, could it? Was it the day I thought it was?

"August. The summer's going by quickly," he

commented, speaking my thoughts.

I nodded. "Yes, indeed."

Through the remainder of the meal's preparation, I thought silently. There was nothing particularly significant about aging another year, not anymore. It felt right that I should not be contained any longer on my birthday, however. I considered the title of the day, and also found that it was apt. The birth of something new, as well as a celebration of surviving another year. A perfect gift and I could ask for nothing more.

Breakfast was a quiet and somewhat awkward affair. Vanessa refused to acknowledge my presence while Bailey spoke endlessly with a flawlessly chipper attitude. Robert had been right, as well. After a few minutes, she began to calm down and speak in a much more controlled manner. Anne was absent.

"She's shopping," explained Robert when I asked if she was well. I glanced at the window and the post-dawn light that glowed outside.

Vanessa voiced my question unintentionally, "This early? She normally waits until noon."

"She's picking some things up for Cory," he replied, narrowing his eyes at her when she began to protest. She sighed sharply but said nothing.

I was blushing with embarrassment and guilt, feeling myself an impedance. "What for? I am not in any desperate need of anything, and I can acquire things myself so as to not burden your family further."

"Oh, no, don't worry about it. Besides, you do need some things to go into stores to, well, *get* what you'd need. Shirt and shoes, for example."

"Ah." I glanced down at myself, blushing deeper. I

abruptly felt incredibly awkward and somewhat ashamed of my scars. I wanted some way to cover them so that no one could see.

Bailey rolled her eyes. "What Dad's not saying is that we get compensated for whatever money we spend on you or whatever, so it's really nothing. Oh, and before it gets really weird, you're his only patient right now, so he's staying home to be available 'round the clock for ya! Feel special," she added, voice commanding.

Robert was shaking his head slowly in disapproval. "Bailey..."

"What? Better just get it out there now rather than dance around the subject for weeks and dramatize the situation," she defended herself, making me laugh. They all looked at me, startled.

I quieted myself and smiled apologetically, mumbling, "Wisdom worth holding onto."

There was an odd silence that made me uncomfortable. I had spoken out of turn, and I cursed myself for it. I averted my eyes shamefully, so that they knew I was remorseful.

"Can I make a protest?" asked Vanessa, voice sounding particularly loud in the quiet. "About being fully dressed before coming downstairs."

"Vanessa," sighed Robert tiredly. "Not now. You know why today is an exception."

I glanced up to see Vanessa glaring at her plate. I looked at my own empty one, mumbling again, "Please excuse me."

No one protested when I stood to clean my dish, in an attempt to escape the bristling atmosphere. It followed me to the kitchen, however. After setting aside my clean plate to dry, I cleaned the skillet and spatula, as well as the baking pan for the hash browns. It was only once I was finished that anyone entered after me, but I was evasive and so crept upstairs shyly.

I retreated to the room I had been allowed to use, wanting to hide away from the alien people and the sharp hostility that at least Vanessa exuded. When the door closed behind me, I slid to the floor in relief.

How long had I lasted this time? An hour? Two? Glancing out the window, I wondered if today would be as overwhelming and twisting as yesterday. Time was dragging hideously. Would the day ever end? How much longer until I could sleep again? I groaned, closing my eyes against the world tiredly.

"Has it always been this difficult to be with people?" I wondered aloud. I was surprised to feel hot tears rolling down my face, even more so when I began to shake with sobs. I was clueless to the reason why I was crying, but I felt the need to release myself. I cradled my head in my hands, at the very least keeping myself quiet. I was uncertain that I would be able to answer if anyone asked me what was wrong.

The tears never seemed to stop. My sobs quieted after awhile, somewhere near noon telling by the light that poured in through the window. I stared around the room through watering eyes and sighed, thinking that I might be ready to face the world again, when there was a knock on the door. The sound startled me, and I hurried to stand and move away from the door.

"Are you alright, Cory? It's been three hours since I last saw you," called Robert, concern heavy in his voice.

I sighed. "As fine as I can be, I suppose."

"Can I come in? I need to get some measurements for Anne..." He sounded hesitant.

I opened the door and stepped back for him to enter. By the change in his expression, I was sure he noticed the moisture on my face. He did not question it, however, seeming to read my nervousness.

"Turn around? Alright, I need to measure the space between the wings and then..." He sighed heavily. "Would you feel alright coming out to the study so she could see everything? She's bound to need to know more than I can say."

I nodded. "No, I would not mind. Just...Allow me a moment?"

He stepped back outside into the hall. "However long you need."

The door was closed behind him, giving me privacy. I dried my face and took a deep breath to calm myself. I caught sight of my tail and the precise scars that stretched across it, suddenly enthusiastic about something to cover myself with.

I left the room, a conversation wafting down the hall to me.

"...think you should have gotten something green. I mean, then he would be all Christmasy. Instead of being a roulette table, what with all the black." I recognized Bailey's voice.

"Well, the options are incredibly limited for his size," defended her mother, sounding playful. They both quieted and looked up at me from piles of clothing and sewing materials when I entered.

"Robert said you needed me," I explained, not knowing how else to banish another silence. I was finding their relentless numbers tiring.

"Ah. Right," said Anne slowly, as though just recalling what she was doing. She looked at a dark brown shirt she was holding. "I need to know where to cut on the back of the shirt and where to put the buttons."

I blinked back more tears, though now they were grateful. "I know most of my measurements, if you would like my assistance."

"Okay, but you have to forgive her fashion sense," replied Bailey with a grin, holding up a black button up. She made a face. "I told her green."

I smiled and sat near them, finding a measuring tape and pins. "I do not mind. Thank you, Anne, for helping me."

Her smile said that she understood that I meant more than the clothing. Bailey remained clueless. "You're more than welcome, Cory."

We were quiet for a minute while I began to mark where to cut on a rather attractive blue shirt. Bailey cried out in horror, holding up a strangely printed dual colored shirt of black and white. She turned to Anne in disbelief.

"Mom, Hawaiian shirt?" she gasped, glancing between me and the article fervently. "He's a demon, not...not...Not!"

"I think it'll look nice on him," she commented calmly.

"Hawaiian shirt?!" Bailey continued to speak as though I was not present, making me smile quietly. "Nuh-uh. Ew. Bad. Leather jacket, good. Button up, tolerable. Hawaiian print? Old tourist guyish! Bad!"

Anne and I laughed, amused by her joyfully defiant youth. Anne cleared her throat, smirking. "Get the tags off of it and set it in the pile. Cory, have you got that shirt ready?"

I nodded and relinquished it. "That should fit once cut. The neck appears open enough for my horns to fit through."

She scowled abruptly and glanced at some of the shirts. "I hadn't thought about that. Oh, well. We'll just have to do extra work on some of them."

Bailey groaned, but I was content. I had done this with Mother before and enjoyed the task of stitching hems and attaching buttons. It was familiar and comforting to me, even amusing when the two women helped me into the shirt. They had me test the range of it, and Anne beamed proudly when it was declared to fit.

"Where could you find anything my size?" I wondered aloud, pulling it off as commanded.

Anne handed the shirt off to Bailey. "Wash that and then put it in the dryer, please. Plus sizes store," she added, in answer to my question.

"I see." I glanced at another shirt and began to measure for that one.

"Oh, wow, it's late," sighed Anne, looking at her wrist. "Well, at least the shirt should be done on time."

"On time for what, if I may ask?" I reached for pins to mark my measurement.

"Dinner. We were going to go out tonight..." She faltered, frowning.

"Burger place, very tasty. Accepts demon patrons," added Bailey brightly, sitting beside her mother again. Her mother sighed quietly. "Honesty, Mom. Total, brutal honesty."

I smiled to myself but said nothing as my frayed

nerves failed to react, continuing my work patiently. It was sometime after I handed the shirt to Anne to cut that there was an obnoxious buzz. Bailey jumped up and bustled off, then came cackling back in almost as short a time as it took to blink. She gave me the blue shirt we had finished. I held it, surprised.

"It is so...warm," I said, pressing the warm fabric to my arm.

"Dryers tend to do that." Bailey sat beside me, grinning. They both seemed amused by my total fascination with the warmth.

I laughed quietly. "It seems Mother was unable to halt the conversion."

"Conversion?"

"She insisted upon hand washing and line drying," I explained, righting the article in my hands. I stared at it for a moment before Bailey crawled over and helped me into it again. The warmth of the shirt was soft and comforting.

Anne turned her head this way and that. "I think the color suits him."

"Well, he doesn't look like a tourist." Bailey shrugged. "He makes purple instead."

Vanessa entered the room from the direction of the stairs. When she saw the clothes strewn across the floor, she glanced at me and made a face of disgust. "Mom, I have three words: Walking roulette wheel. Anyway, Dad called in, we've got a reservation for six. So, chop-chop, people."

She left back the way she had come, all of us staring after her silently. I glanced at Anne, who appeared wounded by her daughter's words.

"I am grateful and rather fond of many of your

choices," I reassured her quietly, smiling and lifting a deep maroon shirt with long sleeves.

They both began to laugh while I was cleaning our work space. My smile was broadening, even while the shirt rubbed strangely against my skin. I felt content, although I was anxious as well about going into public. At least I was covered, shielded partially from the narrowed, judging eyes of humans.

"What's taking everyone so long up here?" called Robert, entering as the last of the sewing supplies were placed neatly aside. He blinked and frowned. "Wow, uh...Nice shirt. What's with all the black...?"

Anne sighed while Bailey snickered. "I thought it would match, and don't you dare say anything about a roulette wheel! Come on, let's go."

Bailey hopped to her feet easily, watching her mother and I move more slowly and carefully. She paused and frowned. "Wait...How are we going to fit in the car? I mean, yeah, five seat belts, but it's a *really* little sedan."

I shuddered subconsciously, dreading being confined in another small space just yet. Robert noticed and sighed, frowning as well.

"Um, well, I was thinking that you could fly over the car, Cory," he suggested. "If you feel comfortable with that."

"Wait. Fly?" Bailey looked at me with wide eyes, gaping. "You can fly?! Right, wings. Wait. No. I don't think he'll be able to keep up with the car. Not with you behind the wheel, Dad."

"I can keep pace," I assured her, relieved by the proposal that kept me outside of a small vehicle. "And yes, Robert, I feel quite comfortable with flying."

90

He smirked. "Right. Sorry about the abruptness of the plan. Would you rather stay home?"

There was that word, *home.* "Oh, there is no issue. I would like to adjust as quickly as possible."

He smiled. "Right. Shall we go see if Vanessa's hot wired the car yet?"

Bailey gazed at him gravely. "Don't give the universe ideas."

Following after the silver vehicle was simple and exhilarating. Chasing the Smiths made me laugh, though the sound was lost in the wind that rushed around me. The speed at which we were traveling made me heady. My muscles and membranes burned from the effort to keep pace and stay airborne. Yet every second I could only cherish the hot pain, as it meant that I was flying and free.

When they pulled into a lot dotted with other cars, I circled in search for a place to land. There was a convenient grass strip across a small road from the lot, so I began to lower myself as I slowed from the blitzing speed I had flown to follow them. In spite of my precautions, my landing was still clumsy. Perhaps I was getting too old for such excitement.

Glancing about to ensure the way was clear, I strode across the road to the lot. Robert waved with a welcoming smile while his family entered the building. He met me halfway, keeping stride with me with slight trouble. I slowed my pace, finding myself pleasantly winded from the flight.

"So, you're ready for this?" he asked uncertainly.

"As ready as I believe I may ever be," I replied, opening the door for him politely. I motioned him through, but he hesitated and watched me with concern. I smiled kindly. "Yes, if I find myself without proper restraint or overstressed, I will remove myself from the situation."

He relaxed some. "Alright."

I followed him through, needing to duck through the door. Inside, the ceiling stretched high above even my own head. My tensions eased, knowing that we were in a relatively open space. Robert approached a young, heavy set woman behind an eclectically decorated desk. Her back was to us as she organized what I could only guess were pamphlets.

"Hey, Chris, could we get private seating?" asked Robert. The girl behind the counter turned around, her eyes going wide when she spied me.

"Robert, what are you doing?" she hissed with a glance at me. I shifted awkwardly, knowing too well why she stared. I did not have *acceptance.*

"What? I called ahead of time, like you asked!" he replied in a hushed voice. He smiled to me apologetically.

"Yeah, and I thought you were kidding!" She sighed, looking up at me with a cringe. "Well, I guess we've gotta...But you, Robert, if I get fired you owe me."

"Fine and thank you, Chris," he replied, relaxing. He noticed the large pamphlets she was grabbing. "He's a senior, by the way."

She groaned, but replaced a pamphlet. "Okay, everyone, this way."

"Oh, right..." muttered Anne, halting mid-stride before we approached the full entry into the dining area. She pulled sandals from a large purse she carried and gave

92

them to me with an apologetic smile. "I almost forgot."

I returned her smile and slipped my feet into the simple design while refraining from wincing. I enjoyed feeling the ground beneath me, but I was more concerned for the poor materials that were sure to be destroyed in just this wear.

"Thank you, again."

We followed after Robert and Chris to a closed off alcove with plenty of seating. I sat furthest in and I assumed that this was to reduce the likelihood of strangers viewing me, although it was far too late for that. Anyone we passed by through the restaurant stared, conversations dying no matter where they were and the instant they thought I was out of earshot they began to whisper furiously. I heard one man swear that the manager should be called so that I could be removed.

When we were all settled, Chris hid a wince. "I'll go get your waiter."

Robert sighed when she left. "Well, it's still going good so far."

"I think they should have rejected us," said Vanessa stiffly, throwing a narrow-eyed glance down the table at me. She was seated as far from me as was possible, on the other side of her father.

Robert turned to her and I was sure he meant for me not to hear his next words. "Remember what we talked about last night, young lady?"

She smiled tightly. "I'm just being honest, like Bailey."

He sighed, and when his face was visible again it appeared as though he was forcing himself to calm down, relieving his features of a threatening expression. He

93

smiled again, clearly attempting to lighten the mood when a young hazel-skinned man appeared at the alcove. His expression was hesitant but friendly. It was clear when he saw me, as his eyes widened in shock.

"Uh, hi. I'm Elijah, I'll be your server this evening," he managed to speak clearly. He smiled politely and avoided staring at me, though he still cast curious glances at me. "What can I get you to drink this evening?"

"Lemonade!"

"Ew, um...pink lemonade."

"Which is lemonade dyed pink," muttered Bailey with a smirk.

"Whatever cola you have," said Anne. This seemed to be nothing more than habit for all of them.

"Root beer." Robert looked to me with a questioning expression.

"Ah, water please, Elijah," I replied, softening my voice and features as much as I knew how to. Still, he jumped slightly when I spoke.

"Right. Water, lemonade, pink lemonade, cola, and root beer," he recited easily, smiling at us all. "I'll be back in a few minutes with your drinks."

Vanessa turned on Bailey the moment he was gone. "Pink lemonade is not just dyed. It's sweeter."

"Read the ingredients list," countered Bailey. "Yellow five in one, red forty and bleach in the other."

"Girls, behave," interrupted Anne quietly, giving them each a stern look. I felt awkward and intrusive.

Bailey's attention was quick to turn, and she looked at me with a grin. "So, what's it like to fly?"

Her parents seemed to tense at the question, but I was thankful for her natural innocence. "Wonderful.

Incredibly...peaceful but invigorating. I think it is a pity that others may never experience it."

My words were met by cold silence, clearly exuded by Vanessa. Bailey and Anne stared at me in confusion. Robert appeared to be the only one who understood my meaning.

"Okay, pink lemonade." Elijah materialized from nowhere, setting an iced glass with pink liquid in front of Vanessa, distracting her glare. He set a bubbling pop in front of Anne, again iced. "Cola. Root beer. Lemonade. And water," he finished, coming to me last. I could smell the light tang of fear in the air but he did not shy away from me just yet, maintaining a polite and welcoming atmosphere.

"Were all of you ready to order?" he asked, voice strained. He looked at us all for at least a moment each.

"Bacon cheeseburger, medium well, add guac," chirped Bailey, first to announce her words.

"Again with the cheese," muttered Vanessa. "Um, chicken salad, Italian dressing."

"Just a regular burger. No pink." Robert's choice suited him, in my mind.

Anne sighed thoughtfully. "Chicken sandwich, no onion."

Elijah looked down at me expectantly. I stared at the pamphlet in front of me, grasping that the menu choices were there and that I should have been considering my meal while he was fetching drinks.

"Ah..."

"Bacon cheeseburger, medium well, add guac," a stage whisper came from my right.

I glanced at Bailey hesitantly. "I do suppose so..."

Demon *Rising*

"Great! It'll be a bit, but I'll be back to check on you," said Elijah before hurrying away. With the sharp scent he was creating, I was guiltily glad when he left and the air began to clear.

"What exactly is 'guac'?" I asked, the word queer in my mouth.

"Guacamole!" She grinned at me. "Avocado plus salsa equals yum."

"She's never been the best at math," chuckled Anne playfully.

"Ah..." I remained quiet while the family bickered playfully, hopefully melting back into the shadows behind me. None of them seemed to notice my silence either, for which I was grateful. I could collect my thoughts and assess my condition.

I had never been to a restaurant before, even before I had been taken. Stepping outside during the day was not too strange for me, however. There was a vague sense in my memory that it had been acceptable and perhaps even common for me to be out in the day. With all of the strange people I knew were surrounding me, I felt weak and vulnerable, however. Out of place among all of these humans. Although Elijah was a comfort, with how he struggled to treat me as human.

"Oh, yeah, Cory." Robert turned to me, disrupting my thoughts. I glanced over, frowning curiously. He grinned at me. "Happy birthday."

I blinked in surprise. "What?"

"Happy birthday!"

"Happy birthday."

Vanessa was glaring at her glass silently. I wondered if there was anything one of us could do to lighten her mood, knowing one of the simplest ways would be my leaving. Would my absence cure the bitterness? From how she spoke to even her family, I thought not.

Her father was watching her expectantly. "Vanessa?"

"I'm not going to encourage another one of your mental failures," replied Vanessa sharply, barely glancing at me.

Robert suppressed a sigh, clearly annoyed by her persistence in stating her dissatisfaction. "There's no mental illness involved this time."

"Really? Last time I checked, your motto was still 'there's a pill for everything'." Her own words seemed to bite her hard, making her purse her lips against obvious tears. She took a deep breath to calm herself.

He was torn suddenly between defending himself and his work or comforting his daughter. I cursed him silently when he did not choose his own child. "Vanessa, you're not being—"

"And you've got those 'national security' guards doing crap like dressing up like citizens so they don't cause a riot at a restaurant!" she cried out in frustration, interrupting him. "But you know what? I think they're really here to protect the rest of us from it, not the other way around and it's one of the first things I've seen go right in a long time."

"If I am intruding, I can wait for all of you outside, so you may have privacy," I said quietly, keeping my eyes down in shame and guilt.

"No, Cory—"

"I think that's a great idea," said Vanessa snidely. Without looking, I knew she was expressing happiness at the idea of me leaving. "If you could never come back that would be better, but I'm not too demanding."

"Vanessa!" scolded Anne sharply. She placed her hand on my arm for comfort. "It's alright if you stay. We'll just have a talk when we get home."

"No, now's fine with me," offered Bailey lightly. I sat back in my seat, pulling as far from the anger as I could. "As long as Dad and Vanessa can stop bickering for five seconds, we should be fine."

Robert narrowed his eyes at her. "That's enough of that, young lady."

I stared between the faces of the family sadly. I could not recall my own family having fits like this where we would antagonize and be angry with one another. With a sigh, I stood and set my napkin on the table.

"Please, excuse me. I require fresh air," I muttered sharply, turning away quickly so that none of them could see the unbidden disappointment I felt on my face.

Weaving between tables was of no difficulty, until an unobservant woman in heels clipped my tail. I groaned but continued forth, sighing in relief when I was able to breathe in the outside air. It was heavy, of course, and smelled putrid but was oddly still more refreshing than the too-clean gas indoors.

For a moment, I was rendered immobile by absolute grief for that little family. I knew it was inevitable that people would be angry or aggressive with one anther, but within one's own family? With only the future of worsening over time, like an infection in a wound. It was no difficult task to understand which part I played while I wondered if the wound could heal without any outside influence. Or had it been cut too deep and left to sit too long?

I shook my head to clear it and ambled off to one side of the entrance to sit, barely hidden by bushes. People still passed, staring or making a point of ignoring my existence. I thought on what the girl Chris had said about losing her job by servicing me. Perhaps she was right in fearing that. After all, who in this world could stand to tolerate a demon, *without* substantial payment? The idea brought me back to the scientists...

Sighing heavily, I shook my head in disbelief. Had it truly been little more than a day since I left that place? Was the world out here always simultaneously unbearably short and agonizingly long? Looking up at the darkening sky, I was glad that the day was ending. It meant that my ever-loyal companion of darkness would come to shield me from the stares and bring me dreams, beautifully sweet dreams of what I might do with my freedom.

Kate...

There was a light breeze that rustled the leaves of the bushes beside me, and it seemed to whisper her name. The leaves as well, and my heavy breath. Everything spoke of her to me. I knew deep within myself that she was where I needed to be. I knew that what Robert had said about injuring those around me was both right and wrong.

I was tired, my restraint weak with it. If I could go to her—see her again and maybe hold her—it felt as though I might finally rest at ease. I would be capable of controlling my strength properly then. I could be free of these constant stresses...

Of course, what if Robert was indeed correct? What if I was near mentally shattering after all this time of enduring? It had to happen at some point during my time, and today was my 68th birthday. Perhaps it was too soon. Should I risk waiting? Should I find her now?

Oh, the cruel choices placed before me.

"Cory?" Bailey peered around the bushes at me. She smiled shyly, made-up eyes wide. "Uh, Rob—Dad sent me to see how you were doing."

"Ah." I patted the space beside me for her to sit, leaning forward to rest my elbows on my knees. "I need longer to recover. Sit, if it would be no issue."

"Oh. One sec." She was gone into the restaurant for a moment and returned just as swiftly. "Okay, they know we'll be a few."

"That was rather...speedy," I commented offhandedly. She sat beside me and I moved my tail to my other side so as to not disturb her with it.

"Yeah. I've been wondering. Um, if it's not too personal, does your tail *ever* stay still?" she asked in a forward and childlike manner that made me laugh. "What? Oh, sorry, was that offensive? Is there a politically correct term I should use or something?"

"'Politically correct'? Oh, dear. No, calling my tail what it is was not offensive," I assured her, smiling to myself that she would even consider it such. An amusing young woman. "To be honest, I have never paid mind to it. It is as much a part of me as your arm is a part of you."

She stared at me with a strange expression for a moment. "I don't get what you mean."

"Are you always consciously aware of whether your arm moves, or is it instinctual for the most part?" I asked, motioning to how she was now picking a hole in her jeans without seeming to notice. She froze, glanced down at her hand and then shook her head. "Similarly with my tail. If I think it may become a nuisance, then I move it aside but then do not mind it."

"Oh...Is it the same with, erm, those?" she asked, pointing to my back awkwardly.

I shook my head, smiling at her. "Not quite so much, no. My wings are much larger limbs, after all. It takes a bit more concentration to keep them in check."

"Oh." She bit her lip and then stared at her hand as though it was the most fascinating thing she had ever spied.

"Your questions are not intrusive, Bailey," I told her with a chuckle. "Contrarily, I find them relaxing. If I recall correctly, only three other individuals have ever asked me these questions."

"Really? Who? When?" she asked, looking at me with wide eyes again.

I laughed and shook my head. It was wonderful to see such an insatiable curiosity. "Another time, I do believe. We have kept your family waiting long enough."

She stood with me. "Okay. What are you turning today, anyhow?"

"Sixty-eight." I held the door for her to enter.

"Wow, you're old."

I chuckled, ducking inside after her. "Yes, and you are very young."

Bailey grumbled incoherently and led the way back to the table. Anne was smiling cheerily while Robert and Vanessa both bore repentant expressions. The remainder of the evening passed uneventfully, though I again flew over the car. The air was much more palpable at night. It was also incredibly enjoyable to fly with the cool air whipping against me, the nameless emotion of flight swelling and filling me. There was plenty of laughter when we arrived back at the house, and we all departed to our rooms for sleep. Thankfully, I was again able to rest easily.

~~ * ~ * ~ * ~~

<u>Wednesday</u>

The adventure of the morning took place in the bathroom after a shower, when I struggled to find a way to don one of the new modified shirts. The trick that I had difficulty in discovering was how to not cause my crippled right shoulder pain, removing many of my former methods for dressing. Thus, some half hour later, I finally left the bathroom fully dressed to be glowered at hatefully by Vanessa before I slipped back into the room.

Staring out the window, I found myself yearning to be outside. I made for the bottom floor, passing no one. Truthfully, I was relieved that nothing stopped me from reaching the back door and stepping out.

I smiled when I breathed in the fresh air and felt the cool grass beneath my feet. The sun was halfway up its climb to the middle of the sky, smiling down at the world patiently. Its warmth on my skin was exuberant, as well as the happiness it caused me. I stood and felt the breeze for a long while, humming to myself absently.

Sometime later, I laid myself down on the grass with a content laugh to myself. Birds were chirping back and forth to one another somewhere nearby. I stretched my wings out beneath me to rest them on the ground and warm in the sun. There was a foolish, youthful grin on my face while I stared up at the soft blue sky in wonder. Clouds littered the vast expanse of open space, cottony or misty in nature.

I closed my eyes against the world and breathed deeply. Thoughts and images dance behind my lids playfully. It was only a moment later that I was caught up by them and engulfed in the past.

"Momma, look at the baby!" I breathed, eyes wide with wonder. The little eyes in its round face stared up at me. I giggled.

"She's your sister, Cory. Her name is Lisa," said Mother with a smile. I grinned.

"Wow. So she finally came out...Hi, we were waiting for you," I told the baby. She closed her eyes and I looked up at Mother to shush her. "Shhh, Lisa wants to sleep now, Momma."

Mother laughed quietly and made room for me to clamber up onto the couch beside her. I cuddled into her side and she wrapped an arm around me warmly. I yawned widely, falling asleep with Lisa.

My smile was satisfied, like myself.

"Mother, you said once that all people have soul mates and guardian angels," I hedged quietly, staring at the fairytale book in my hands. The story about the evil devil being slain to save the princess had me in a fright.

She looked over at me from her cooking, smiling softly. "They're the same thing, Cory, guardian angels and soul mates. But yes, everyone has one. It's impossible to not, like the day existing without the night."

The notion that she was proposing was romantic and hopeful. I stared at my hand and memorized the color of it. "Do you think I could have one, in spite of what I am?"

Mother paused, setting aside the spoon in her hand to kneel in front of me, meeting my gaze. "Yes, Cory, of course. And what do you mean, in spite of what you are?"

"A devil, Mom," I whispered tearfully, keeping my eyes downcast. I sniffled. "I'm evil, the book says so."

"No, no, no, honey, you're good," she contradicted, taking me in her arms warmly. I trembled while I struggled to reign in my tears. Why was I crying? The devil never cried. "You're good. It doesn't matter what you look like. Inside, you're a perfect little angel. And the world's learning, Cory. Someday, you can go out with the rest of us and the only reason anyone will look is because you're adorable. You'll even have your own princess to rescue from the real villains."

"Mom," I complained, embarrassed. I grinned at her telling of how the world could be. She kissed my forehead and returned to the stove. "Thank you."

The sky above me was still clear and flawless, so I allowed myself to drift again into memories. They were distant but sweet. Lush but simple.

Katelyn sat beside me near the pumpkins, yawning widely. It was unsurprising that she was tired now, when my day was just beginning. The moon was low on the horizon, just rising for the evening. I motioned to a full plate that she was welcome to partake from. It was my lunch.

She lifted a carrot and snapped off a piece, setting the larger portion back on the plate. "Sorry I haven't come by in awhile. Paul believes that as a choir member I should know where every song originated, memorize the music, and is an overall pure follower of the Homework Faith."

"Blasphemer," I muttered with a smirk. She smacked my arm playfully, nibbling at her carrot. I retrieved an apple from the plate, staring at it a moment. "So, your excuse is too much homework?"

"Yeah, what's yours?" she asked, grinning at me.

"Can I pretend I broke my leg?" I bit into the apple, savoring the flavor.

She shook her head. "You used that last time."

I nodded in acknowledgment, thinking. "Has it truly been two months since last visit?"

"Yes, it has," she sighed, that sad look crossing her face. I remembered the porch swing, wondering how often she thought of time and its countless instances of grief. She was the one to distract herself this time. "You look different. Did you grow again?"

I stiffened, blood chilling. I set the apple back on the plate and stared at the ground, shaking my head slowly. "No."

She frowned, watching me carefully. "Hm...Are you getting hooves or something?"

"No." Again, the single word to avoid the matter. I wished she had never noticed in the dim silver lighting of the half moon, slowly rising higher in the sky. She was far too observant.

"Can you tell me?" she asked after a long moment of silence. The world had quieted at some otherworldly instruction that provided an ominous silence.

I breathed in deeply, glancing at her. The passion

inside me was dying, realizing that there would come a time when she would no longer return to the farm. She would move to a city and likely marry a human man while I stared out my window, alone.

Still, she had given me a few years worth remembering.

"My face has gotten worse again," I relinquished reluctantly, not wanting to look at even the moon. Nothing could console me while my chest felt hollow.

"What?" She moved nearer me, shaking her head slowly. "I don't see it."

"The plates, slits down my cheekbones, my nose— My face!" I repeated sharply, pulling my legs close to me. "The entire thing is just vile."

Her fingers traced over my face but I did not stop her. I loved feeling her skin against mine, and her touch was so gentle that I thought I might fall asleep. When I knew she had to leave soon, I was more eager to experience her, as well. Her fingertips ran over the indentations I had told her of, the thin and precise slits in my very bones that had developed of their own will.

She smiled at me. "It's not that bad. You could be growing fur."

I laughed once, amused abruptly by her statement, then I paused. She was indeed correct. I frowned deeply. "I hope that never happens."

"Don't worry. I won't care," she assured me quietly. For a moment, I wondered if she was sincere in her statement. But then, even if she was she could only see in time that her future was better not entangled with mine.

~~ * ~ * ~ * ~~

Demon *Rising*

I moaned and stretched as I woke, blinking and sighing deeply. Had I genuinely fallen asleep? Yes, it seemed so. I was cold, as well. I looked about, blinking in disorientation when wet droplets began to fall on my face and body.

Then I saw the dark sky above me, a grin spreading across my face easily. I laughed and settled in for a storm, stretching my wings as far a I could. Rain droplets tickled my membranes. From within the house, I heard the Smiths wondering as to my whereabouts. They would find me sooner or later, meanwhile I would enjoy my first rain in too long. All I had been allowed were cold or boiling showers. This would be a natural event where I would not be pressured for time.

I would savor every second of my freedom to be soaked and mud-covered once again.

Which is precisely what I did. As the rain became heavier, the yard became wetter and the mud was easy to press between my fingers. The substance was rich, thick and moist. Nothing could have felt better, I thought. Nothing available to me at that moment, at least. But the cool water in my hair and running across my skin was wonderful. I was in a great haven.

I do not know how long it was before Robert opened the door, standing in the space and staring at me. He laughed incredulously, shaking his head slowly.

"So, Cory, felt like being ten again?" he asked, still inside. The rain was pouring, allowing me to rinse the mud from me easily.

I grinned at Robert, laughing again. "It is a glorious rush of liberty to stand in the rain. I have always loved—"

Demon *Rising*

A clash of thunder cut off my words and made me start violently. I reeled back before falling to the earth, clutching my left shoulder. I was gasping, the memory of a different thunderstorm making my faded scars burn uncomfortably. I stifled a hiss of pain. What on earth was wrong with me? What unknown memory caused this?

Before I could regain control of myself, Robert rushed out to my side. "What's wrong?"

I shook my head and groaned, righting myself awkwardly. "Nothing, nothing. Only the thunder. It startled me."

Again, the terrible force boomed overhead. I shuddered as the memory drew nearer. I bit back my irrational terror, telling myself that there was nothing around to fear. Even so, my shoulder continued to burn.

"Is your shoulder okay?" he asked in concern, examining it as though he could see through the shirt I wore. "It looked like you were in pain."

"Just a memory," I gasped, making my way to the open door. In my mind, I could see eyes staring at me and only me. I kept myself from falling too deeply into that mirage.

I succeeded in stumbling through the doorway, dripping generously onto the living area's carpet. Robert followed me inside, closing the door behind himself. I stayed where I was, uncertain of whether I should continue further into the house while I was soaked.

Robert called for Anne to bring us towels, looking at me with a frown. "It's alright, you know."

I nodded slowly, relaxing enough to drop my hand from my shoulder. "Yes, I am aware. I was surprised, and it seems that my body is as skittish as I am, with an even

108

sharper memory."

"Well, let's see what we can do to help, hm?" Robert smiled and Anne came back to us with a large bundle of towels. I smiled back tentatively, but a sure feeling filled me even as the thunder rumbled and shook the house again. I was beginning to believe Robert that eventually I truly could be *safe* here.

~~ * ~ * ~ * ~~

August 22nd, 2010

Today marks the end of my second week outside. Soldiers still stand out on the front lawn, where I am now. It is not so strange or threatening as it first was. Rather, I have found them to be quite cordial and welcoming of conversation. Although, when Henrickson is on shift all are in agreement that if we annoyed him with our idle chatter he may become...How had Santos phrased it? Trigger happy.

Not because he is an overall disgraceful or bitter man, but Henrickson is older than the others, appearing to be just a few years my junior at youngest. I imagine he is seeing the similarities that I see and they stir disturbing memories for him.

Regardless, the last two weeks are a blur in my memory, although as I live through even today the events are long and tiresome. To think that the days to come may very well still be high in number is exhausting. I find it difficult enough to struggle through this moment. How will it be next week, or next month? Not easier, certainly. Oh, it is rather pointless to expend my energy thinking on this

109

now, though. What comes, comes. The only thing I may do is endure it.

And thinking of enduring, I have been told by Robert that I am doing extremely well thus far. I am uncertain that I feel so confident, but I do suppose that I am finding my balance, at least in the days' schedules. My erratic moods have calmed some as well, which saddens Bailey. She enjoyed calling me manic-depressive and claimed that it could work for a catchy opening to her show and tell performance, when she would bring me to class. Robert denied her permission to do so, of course.

Which reminds me of Vanessa. She is still bitter and somewhat vindictive, although now I am curious as to who she is attempting to hurt. If she is as hellbent as she displays, I would have been murdered in my sleep already. An unnerving notion, but a very true case according to some of her increasingly sharp glares. She only verbally assaults me when another of her family is present, however. It makes me think that something occurred—or did not, as the case may be—that has left her wounded or scared.

I wish I could help. Truthfully, even though I am technically the patient, I do believe that this family could benefit from an outside voice. All of them hold one thing or another in the dark, out of sight from the others so that they will not see. The behavior creates tension. Even the sweet, open-minded Bailey is hiding something. What, I am unable to tell, but it is apparent only when her parents are near.

Is this genuinely my business? Am I intruding further? Even if I am permitted to aid them, am I capable? I cannot tell when I am going to fall to pieces. I suppose it would be unwise to begin deciphering when others will. I will allow things to play out for now, but if I am asked for assistance I will find a way to give it.

~~ * ~ * ~ * ~~

<u>Thursday</u>

Robert smiled at me invitingly as I took my seat for our weekly formal session. I sighed heavily but was otherwise able to relax.

"How have you been this week, just to check up on you?" asked Robert, smile taking on a slight hint of irony, likely at the fact that we did live together.

"Reminiscing," I replied quietly, lost in thought. "I have found that things I could not recall before are becoming quite...vivid."

Instantly, Robert's attention was rapt. "I see...Well, are you ready to discuss any of it?"

I focused on my hand, nodding slowly. "Yes, I do suppose I am."

"Whenever you're ready, then," said Robert gently, waiting for me to begin.

I smiled slowly. "Of course, of course...Well, I remember that my sixteenth winter was the coldest I had ever known. The ground was frozen against my feet, but I continued to tend the fields for the winter crops. I regretted that I had no warm shirts that fit properly while Mother was busy knitting me things to keep me warm. I remember that the moon was clearer in winter than in any other season, and at times I would stop my work to stand and stare at it..."

111

Chapter Three:
Gathering Wisdom

Late in November, I developed an illness. Everyone assumed that it was a cold and that I would be well inside three days. I continued to sing at church to the best of my abilities, but my symptoms only escalated. Soon, it made me nauseous only waking up. I had a fever of 106 and my resting heart rate was 83 beats per minute, 26 beats faster than usual according to Paul and his later tests.

Everyone was concerned about me. People would come by with soups and stews and wishes for my well-being. Paul commanded that I take no visitors, in case my illness could be passed. Normally, I would eat enough to feed two grown men in a day. When it came about that I was barely finishing a bowl of watered-down stew in a day, then later regurgitating it, Paul requested to live with us temporarily to easier care for me.

Only he, Lisa, and Mother were permitted to enter my room. Paul worked to ensure that I would never be without a caretaker. He did a fine job as well, rarely leaving my room. When he did, it was for the most basic of reasons. He slept on a cot placed by my window, which had been covered by heavy drapes so the sun would not

112

disturb my rest.

By the end of the first week of my illness, I had difficulty breathing properly and Paul was near insisting that I be taken to a city hospital. We waited three more days in the hopes I would get better, and for fear of what other people who did not know me would do to me.

Nine days after I fell ill, my breathing became easier. On the tenth day, I was able to eat in peace with minimal nausea. I asked for more than just the watery soups, but Paul refused to permit me anything more until he was sure I was fine. As a result, during the next two days of recovery I sat with constant pangs of hunger in my gut. It frightened me, too, when I began to see those caring for me with a different eye. As you would look at a chicken, perhaps, I was beginning to appraise Paul. I requested as many books as possible then, so that I could keep my focus elsewhere.

I was more than relieved on the thirteenth day, when Mother and Lisa came in with food for Paul and I. Then Katelyn was permitted to enter, bringing one of her get well baskets. I was forced to wait in bed a few more days to recover, but when Sunday came around I was out of my room and stretching my legs happily.

Then, my common mode of transportation was flight. Paul joked that I would freeze in the clouds so that I would not be bedridden from pebbles again.

It was one week from Christmas. Paul instructed me that I would be practicing carols this week, in front of the attendees. I discovered, however, that it was not only carols that I was performing it was a whole narration for the nativity scene! Ha! Imagine such a sight, a demon performing in a church and narrating the birth of Christ.

The idea is still amusing.

Freshly recovered from illness, when I entered the church the people cheered and applauded. I blushed deeply and smiled sheepishly. Paul grinned and waved me up to the front, where the five other choir members were gathered. It was a small choir to be sure, but the voices were powerful like no others. Jasmine and Katelyn performed in the choir with me, as well as Lisa. The two others were men I was unfamiliar with but had helped on occasion.

Paul opened with a short sermon and then allowed us to begin with our practice. I stared at the paper in my hands uncertainly, looking at Paul pleadingly. He motioned me urgently to read, so I did. Those present fell victim to a ghostly silence, their eyes and mouths wide with wonder as I spoke. I had enthralled each one with my natural cadence, and later I was told that it sounded as though I had sang my words the entire time.

I loved that Christmas. The warmth and acceptance was joyous, overwhelming and beautiful. At the official performance, Paul asked me to kneel and close my eyes. I did so with a frown, and stood to find that he had affixed a halo to my horns using wire! Oh, everyone laughed, myself included. The spirit was light and lively, as it ought to have been every holiday where family, friends and strangers gathered 'round as equals to spread the peaceful times. Well...

The next spring, Katelyn invited me to a dance, requesting that I be her date. She gave me quite a start when she first proposed this, of course. I was comfortable now with performing before the church, but never came out in the day outside of Sundays.

"It's going to be starting late—at eight—so it'll be dark already," she tried to comfort me. "We could even make you up if that would make you feel better."

I chuckled nervously, shaking my head. "No, no. My appearance is not my concern. I, ah, feel...out of place. Among others our age you see, I am awkward. I am unaware of how to act."

Katelyn pursed her lips. "Oh, alright. I really would love it if you came, though."

I sighed quietly in regret. By then, she was fourteen and developing quite gorgeously. I was finding my eyes straying to her softly curving hips or...Much more often than my polite tendencies could stand. I looked her over then, jaw dropping slightly in my amazement.

At that time I had identified what the strange new emotion was. It was not love. No, I knew love from a much younger age. It was passion, a physical passion. Any time I even thought of Katelyn by that point it flooded me. Oh, that passion still pains me any time it comes. It pained me then, because I never thought that such an emotion could be felt by anyone for me. Now, I despair that I have known such pleasures and cannot share them with anyone.

I wanted to cry from how I was torn. I caved to Katelyn's whim in the end. She was thrilled, dancing about and chattering happily that she had a dress already, a flattering blue one with a flower print. While she was speaking of how wonderful she looked in it, I half wondered if she was taunting me intentionally. I yearned to see her in it. My passion felt as though it would leave my control if it got any stronger.

Mother was overjoyed that I was participating in

social activities. She bustled about in the two weeks preceding the dance, rushing to get me an outfit. Ha, it was more than amusing to me. I even asked her why I could not just wear my pants, as I always did.

"Because this is a very special event," she told me with a motherly grin. "It deserves special measures."

So, when I arrived at Katelyn's home to pick her up, I was blushing in my embarrassment. I wore a trim black jacket over a deep blue vest and starched white shirt, with black slacks. Much to my embarrassment, Mother also had me wear a black bow tie. My sharp appearance stunned Katelyn when I knocked on her door to meet her before the dance. She gaped at me, depthless eyes wide as she took in my odd clothes.

"I thought you were just going to wear pants," she admitted with an awkward shrug.

"So did I. Mother thought otherwise," I chuckled, looking to the floor bashfully. My eyes had strayed from her face to her gracefully curving self. The passion was a physical pain for me then.

The dress was a wonderful blue that accented her luscious skin perfectly. It also fit her curves and hung in such a way that it was teasing, floating about her legs but never quite folding over her body in any way that would satisfy. Everywhere, her skin was naturally smooth and hairless, making her nearly glow in the sun's dying rays.

"Do you like the dress?" she asked, making me look up. I watched her twirl and curtsey. I smiled, heart pounding in my chest so that I thought she must have been able to hear its spirited gallop.

I nodded nervously, barely reigning in my emotions. "Yes, you're lovely. I mean—it's lovely. On

116

you."

She smirked knowingly and nodded. "Thanks. It cost my last three months' allowances."

"Katelyn, aren't you going to the dance? It's going to start without you if you're not off soon." Jeff came to the door, smiling at his daughter. When he saw me he blinked in surprise. "Wow, Cory, you look…sharp."

"Thank you," I mumbled shyly. I felt strange dressed the way I was. It was too proper and fancy. I was much more comfortable in my battered cut-off jeans, stained with mud. They were easy and familiar.

"Kate, did you need a ride or will Cory be able to fly you?" Jeff asked Katelyn. She turned to me questioningly.

I faltered, uncertain. I had never flown anyone with me before and was unsure of my own strength. Katelyn looked so fragile, too, that I was concerned the force of the wind alone would damage her.

"I…have never tried," I admitted, suddenly tempted by the idea of holding Katelyn in the clouds. I was grateful that no one recognized when I blushed.

"Alright. Kate, I'll drive you," said Jeff, eyes knowing when he looked back at me. I nodded in agreement with his plan, thinking myself untrustworthy at that time.

I flew above the automobile impatiently. My passion was rampant within me, making me wish it were gone so that I could be a proper gentleman. As it was, when I landed and took Katelyn on my arm with a half bow, it was all I could do to keep my composure. I was tempted quite thoroughly to brush her with my tail and many other improper, rude things my vulgar mind could imagine. I was relieved when we were into the light and near people. It forced restraint upon me.

The dance was held at the church, just like every other town event. The children within were stunned when I entered. Some gaped, some glared. A robust, pale young man met us inside, a few steps from the door.

"I think you don't want to be here, *Cory*," he sneered, motioning to the door pointedly. He was roughly a foot shorter than I was, making his threat strange when I was the one staring down at him.

"No, I would very much enjoy being here, thank you," I contradicted politely. I gave him a smile as well, in the hopes he would understand I had no desire to fight.

That was a lie, though. My heart was already pounding in excitement from Katelyn's touch. At the mere thought that I would fight, my blood began to boil in my veins, a snarl building in my throat. A fight was a way to relieve the passion in me and give me time to recover from the monstrous flood of it in my system.

Three more built boys came to stand behind the first one, who then smirked. "You really don't want us to embarrass you in front of your girl, do you?"

A growl broke from my control. It was deep and threatening, even to my ears, rolling into an angry snarl that made the boys jump and tremble. I felt no pity or guilt at that time for whatever distress I caused those boys. After a moment, all that they had said was realized by my distraught mind.

I composed myself, "I apologize. Strictly speaking, Katelyn is not 'my girl', nor is she anyone's girl that I know of."

The lead boy shook himself from his shock and

chuckled menacingly, "Come on, let's take this outside."

"I do not wish to fight!" I snapped back, eyes narrowing. I had never before been this aggressive towards anyone. It was liberating to stand up for myself, though it was likewise painful to feel violent while doing so.

"Leave us alone, Richard," said Katelyn quietly. I glanced down at her in surprise. There was rarely a time when she did not feel a need to make her thoughts known. To my shock, her eyes were downcast and shy. Her hand on my arm shook slightly.

The boy she called Richard ignored her. "Well, we'll have to use some forceful persuasion, won't we boys?"

Katelyn shrunk back as the boys stepped closer to me. She hid behind me, clearly defining for me what was wrong. My hands curled to fists as the fiercest, hottest anger flashed through me. Gently, I led Katelyn outside with me. The boys followed us and I guarded her while I guided her back inside.

"Pardon me, Katelyn, I will not be long. Please socialize without me for the time," I told her kindly with a smile. Tears were in her eyes and she looked behind me concernedly. "I will be fine, I promise you."

Others came out to watch the supposed fight about to occur. Katelyn was pushed next to a rail while I went to meet Richard in the front grass. He was laughing to another one of the boys with him.

"Don't worry, guys, I've got this. A couple little rocks crippled him, remember? I'll be doing more than that," he chuckled, eyes glinting with malice.

"Do you truly desire to brawl with me?" I inquired. I was furious, thinking that these fiends had acted in ways that frightened Katelyn. Flooded as I was already with physical needs, violence was conceivable to me then.

"Yeah." He eyed me as though I were something queerer than I was. "Right."

He held his fists up, lurching forward to hit me. I stood frozen where I was when his fist connected with my middle with a hard thump. I stared down at him as he pulled back, wincing and shaking his hand in pain. Something powerfully invigorating to my self-worth occurred to me then, my need for violence abruptly ending with it. I was no demon, I was more than anger or other brutish behaviors. I was what I made myself to be.

"Understand that I could harm you," I told him quietly, so that no other ears would hear. I narrowed my eyes. "Also grasp that you did not injure me. I *choose* not to strike back. However, if you continue to frighten anyone I *will* act against you and your cohorts with more than a song in my heart."

I stretched my wings luxuriously to intimidate him before striding proudly back to Katelyn, through the throng of chattering people. They gaped at me in amazement. Richard and his band of villains did not follow me as a cheer erupted from the teenagers about me.

"Why are they celebrating?" I asked Katelyn, feeling awkward.

She grinned at me. "You stood up to Richard and his gang! *Without* getting beat up. It's a first."

I nodded, noticing Ethan run out to meet Richard and begin conversing. My temper was calmed, leaving a somewhat hollow ache in its place. "I believe they will leave all of you be for a time."

Little had I known just how disturbed the children

Ethan associated with were. A few days after the dance, he returned home late from school. His face was bruised and bloody, clothes torn and bloodstained as well. He never told Mother or Father who did it, but I knew and he gave me a pleading look. Against my better nature, I honored his wishes.

The dance, though. Oh, it was joyful. Frequently, the player would be reset by children who had brought with them their own records for amusement. There was dancing—fast and slow—to far too many genres, some of which never should have come into existence.

I do believe there was a span of thirty seconds when I had enough space and curiosity to dance. Katelyn cringed away from me and shook her head disapprovingly. What were her words?

Ah, yes.

"Ooh, that's painful."

"The twist?" I asked with a grin.

"Was not meant to include wings or tails."

I laughed at that, thrilled by how I was enjoying myself with these strangers. Better yet, how these strangers seemed to not mind me. I was ignored or treated as everyone else.

Mm, longingly I recall the one dance I shared with Katelyn. It was slow and soothing, with her resting tenderly against me. She barely was able to reach my shoulders with her stretching hands. I was content to have my arms around her and even the passion subsided, calmed by her touch. We were all living happily.

Then, as she yawned sometime around 9:40, I smiled and suggested we return home. We walked back, and I did tread carefully upon the rocks. Once we were out of sight of the church, Katelyn took my hand to hold the entire walk home.

I estimated that it was 10:30 or so when we arrived at her home. It was picturesque suddenly, my walking her home from a wonderful evening out. I felt almost human. Normal and human. Not fully mind you, because I was still incredibly socially awkward, but it was enough to make me smile broadly.

Walking her to the door, I was reluctant to leave or say good night. I wanted to sit on the porch swing with her all night long, to drag on the glorious hours until we could stand not one more second. Time is fast, though, and it raced by while I stared at her wonderful face.

She asked me to bend down, smiling as she did so. I bent and offered her my ear as I assumed she meant to share a secret. Her next movement was one so beautiful it would be impossible for me to forget my glee in that moment.

She turned her face just right, guiding mine with a hand that materialized from nowhere.

Katelyn pressed her lips to mine gently and it was all I could do to keep myself under control. I can still vividly recall the taste of her, how warm she was. The sensation was sweet, tingling. My chest constricted as my passion doubled, filling me abruptly. Tears sprung to my eyes as the seconds stretched on, capturing me in her.

To be honest, for a brief moment a part of me wondered if life could be a fairytale. Part of me wished that the evil witch's spell had been broken, that I was free of my face. In some ways, I believe I was. Thankfully, I was never disappointed by the strange workings of life.

When the kiss ended, I came back to myself to see

Jeff raising one brow at me in disapproval. I bowed my head in apology, feeling ashamed that I had so rudely taken advantage of Katelyn.

"Come on in, Kate. Cory, can I talk to you?" asked Jeff, Katelyn entering their home and shutting the door behind her.

I nodded. "Yes, sir. I apologize for kissing your daughter."

"Yeah, that's not it," he sighed heavily, shaking his head. "You've had your eye on her for a long time."

I kept my eyes down as I wiped away my tears. "Sir?"

"I'm not going to worry that you kissed her. It was coming, I knew it." He waved that thought away, frowning as something else concerned him. "You stand up for Kate a lot, I know. I should be thrilled. I don't think she could end up with a better man. But..."

I looked up in shock. "A man...?"

"Well, you're not able to do much that anyone else can. I'm not sure how good that would be for Kate, you know," he explained. I nodded in understanding. I had long since accepted my life on the farm. "I don't know, guess I can't stop her if she's determined to be with you. Just take care of her, alright, Cory?"

I nodded, a sense of honor settling around me. Jeff trusted me, not a year after meeting me. "Yes, sir. Thank you."

Jeff nodded, eyes still thoughtful. "Hm. Thanks for taking her out tonight. Well, good night, Cory. Have a safe trip home."

"Good night, sir."

I flew home from there and when I arrived I was

surprised to see my parents still awake, waiting for me. They were both smiling proudly. Mother greeted me with a hug, Father with a pat on my shoulder.

"How was the dance?" asked Mother. Her eyes were moist though she was smiling with joy.

"Wonderful," I replied, and found myself with tears of happiness also. Life was turning around at last.

Mother led me to the couch in the living room, sitting beside me while Father took a chair. "Why don't you tell us about it?"

So I did. Everything they wanted to know, I told them. Frequently, it was even things they wanted to hear that I was able to say without lying. "Nobody stared", "I was not attacked", and "I was not screamed at" were the truths that they were most gleeful over. I never mentioned the fight. Finally, I told them about Kate.

"Oh, I'm happy for you, Cory!" exclaimed Mother, sure to wake the entire house with her laughter. She hugged me again.

I saw Ethan at the doorway, half in shadow. "He's not as good as you think."

"What?" demanded Father, frowning. He waved to Ethan. "Come in here, Ethan, so we can see you when you're talking."

He did, face hard with some bitter emotion. I imagined it was jealousy, with how often he would watch Kate when she visited. "He got into a fight with some of the football team and won. Cory's as bad as he looks."

I stared at Ethan in shock. "I never hit that boy. You saw. Everyone saw that he was unharmed!"

Father glanced between us. "Alright, both of you, tell your sides. And they'd better be believable," he added with a hard look at Ethan.

I gave my side, even explaining what I had told the boy who had challenged me. "But I never hurt him. I walked away after that."

Father nodded. "Okay. Ethan?"

"Richard asked Kate for a dance, but Cory got mad. They went outside so that they wouldn't cause a fuss in the building, and then he hit Richard. I saw him do it. Everyone else that saw was just too scared to stand up to him or tell anybody," finished Ethan solemnly.

Father looked back at me. "Would you let Richard dance with Kate, even though she kissed you tonight?"

Ethan's eyes went as wide as saucers. "She what?!"

"Yes, if she wanted to and he would not hurt her," I answered truthfully. A small part of me felt a twinge of selfishness and jealousy, but it was easy enough to deny.

"Your room, Ethan, now," said Mother sternly, eyes narrowed. Her expression was one of disappointment. Ethan stood quietly, glaring at me spitefully before exiting.

Father and I sat in silence for a few minutes awkwardly.

"So...your first fight, huh?" he asked to break the silence.

I nodded, abruptly ashamed of myself. "Yes."

"You only got hit the once..." He paused, frowning deeply. "And you didn't hit him?"

"No," I replied quietly. My eyes dropped to the floor. I looked back up when he started laughing.

"I'm proud of you, son," he said, beaming at me. I smiled tentatively. "You talked your way out rather than, well..." He motioned to me as though it must have been obvious, then continued to explain, "You could knock

125

anyone flat, easy as ever. But you didn't. I'm proud."

Sometime shortly after that, I began to muse over how my parents—*human* parents—could ever have been proud of me, no matter what I did. Likewise, I wondered why they had taken me into their home instead of butchering me as a harmless, demonic babe. Both were likely inconsequential now, but still I was intrigued by the answers.

I asked at some point I know, though I cannot recall the circumstances. Mother replied that I was her child so she would always be proud, and that from the moment she first saw me she had known that I was hers. Father...He answered me with his own questions.

"Why *wouldn't* I want you as a son? For that matter, why wouldn't I be proud to *say* you're my son?"

For the first time, I felt directly appreciated and wanted. I had always known that my parents cared for me on some level. Whether it be out of pity or their own goodness had never been made clear until then. They were proud to call me theirs.

Cory halted suddenly, tears in his eyes and on his face. Robert watched silently, the longing and desperation in Cory's eyes making his heart heavy. He thought again on what Beth had said about their tests of humanity, finding himself like a statue as he witnessed the man sitting before him.

He cleared his throat to keep his composure, and Cory looked up curiously. Robert smiled and asked gently, "Can you continue?"

He watched Cory pause to think a moment before nodding, still apparently distracted. "Yes, yes, I can."

"Will you?" he asked, still gentle.

Cory nodded again, seeming to collect himself for what Robert could only imagine as torturous recollections of long lost wonders. "Yes, I will. The next two years passed wonderfully..."

After the dance, Kate and I began to kiss more frequently until it became our common greeting and farewell. I never minded the custom. In fact, I enjoyed it more than I ever admitted to anyone then. I was relishing in many things I had never thought I would. My passion returned to drive me mad.

I had earned acceptance from the town. My nineteenth birthday, Paul even organized a party for me at the church. My family was ecstatic that I was finding a place for myself; I felt more complete than I ever had.

That summer was bittersweet, entangled with too many realizations. A threshold is a wonderful descriptor, a threshold to a new stage of life. I suppose it began roughly a week after my nineteenth birthday, sometime after Kate returned home from vacation.

Sixteen now, Katelyn was more beautiful than I ever could have imagined. We had planned a picnic and I had chosen the location to be back behind the corn fields, for privacy. I requested that someone send her when she arrived, so I sat there waiting.

Propped up on my elbows, I watched greedily as Katelyn crossed the distance between the corn and the shady tree I had set up beneath. I could hardly believe that this was the tiny girl that had come to me five years ago. Her face was still gentle, but angled now in the most attractively exotic ways.

The yellow dress she wore fit her nicely, her curvaceous self filling the cloth in every right way. Even as the dress came to the knees of her long legs, I wished it shorter. I could see the smooth skin of her calves glittering faintly in the sun, and like an insatiable beast no amount of time to admire her could ever satisfy my hunger.

"You grew again, didn't you!" she accused as she flopped down beside me with a grin.

I grinned. "Three inches."

"That's not fair," she laughed, laying down beside me.

"Not fair? You were the one who left for two months on vacation. That, my dear, is not fair," I countered firmly.

She looked down guiltily, pouting her full lips in a way that only made my craving grow fiercer. "Can you forgive me?"

I smiled gently and chuckled, "Of course, Kate. You know I only jest."

Kate's eyes flicked up to meet mine—to trap me— and she threw herself onto me playfully. I wrapped her in my arms, winding my tail around her as well. Relief washed through me and I sighed as an unknown tension left me.

"Oh, it's wonderful to have you home," I murmured happily. I stretched my wings out, resting them on the warm grass. The sun was being kind, granting the world a peaceful, lazy heat to bask in. Kate's weight atop me was welcome and light. She was soft, resting against me and listening to my heartbeat.

"You know how to pick a picnic spot. It's very quiet back here," she commented, her tracing fingers on my arm sending shocks of pleasure through me.

"Mm. I wish you could be here at night. It is very much loud and alive then," I told her, smiling contentedly.

Kate began shifting, and I stared up into her eyes just inches from mine. As always, my heart began to race and pound in my ears when we kissed. Two years of her kisses and hugs and they were just as new as the first time. Every time, my monstrous lust crushed my chest.

Ah, yes. We were alone, my gentlemanly ways overpowered by my passion-thrown body... Heh, well, a gentleman never speaks of anything as such, even to another man, and I am a gentleman now even if I was very ungentlemanly at that time. I will say that it happened quite some time later that we were both nude and allow any matured minds understand what I mean.

Kate was curled beside me on the sheet I had brought for the picnic. I held her close, heavy thoughts on my mind now that I was satisfied for the time being. Gazing at the foliage above me, I frowned deeply while I wondered what her parents might do when they discovered I was not as well-mannered as they had perceived. Even my own parents, when they found their son had been raised improperly somehow.

As an adult now, I know there is no "proper" way to raise a child. There are bundles of improper, unsuitable ways to be sure, but no completely proper way. Proper varies child to child, while improper remains roughly the same for every one. Looking back, I know that both Kate and I had incredibly open and accepting parents, particularly for the times. Which is why I am very grateful for the punishments we received, seeing how they were not near as horrific as they could have been.

We remained as we were for some time before dressing and partaking of the lunch I had prepared earlier that day. An incredibly fulfilling day, I had thought—until the time for Katelyn to go home. We carried the picnic supplies back to the house before I walked her back to her own home.

The trip was peaceful. Frogs and crickets had begun to sound their nightly melodies in the final hour of the day. We held hands, the small contact comforting to me. Relief was still with me then, as well as a new adoration for Kate, though I did not know how I could possibly come to love her more.

Her father was waiting for us when we arrived and thought nothing of it when we shared our evening kiss. I hoped we might be able to slip past our parents' notice with this.

My hand slipped confidently and traitorously to Kate's waist, as it never had, cuing to Jeff of the day's happenings.

He said nothing until Kate was inside, keeping his voice low and avoiding looking at me. "I'll let you know when you can come see Kate again. Have a good night."

I was choking on guilt and terror, ashamed of my actions like I had never been. Mother noticed my dark mood when I returned home, but had no chance to question it. I ducked past any of her inquiries, eating swiftly before turning my exhausted mind to my evening chores.

It was not until eight days later that my parents

became privy to all that happened and was weighing on me. Mother had woken me sometime around noon with a worried frown.

"Jeff called, he said that they're at Paul's. He wants you to meet them," she told me, giving me a shocking fright. I rushed from my room, down the stairs and out the front door without a word. Not six yards from the house, I was jumping into the sky and flying as fast as I could to the other end of town.

I recognized the Smiths' automobile in front of Paul's home, making me even more terrified. It was not a vengeful prank, it was real. I found myself wondering why I had never considered my actions more seriously before this, why I had been so youthful and ignorant. Ignorance can aid us to grow, however, so I cannot forsake it.

As soon as I landed, I was dashing into the home breathlessly. Paul looked up at me in shock. Jeff was sitting in a chair in the entrance hall, keeping his eyes on his feet and refusing to look at me. My panic forced my throat shut so that I could hardly speak.

"Jeff...You called?" I managed to croak.

He ignored me, Paul speaking in his stead, "Yes...He did. Now, please understand that we're all men here, so we *do* understand how you're feeling."

His words only made my heart pound as—impossibly—I became more frightened. "What happened?! What's wrong?!"

Paul sighed. "Jasmine insisted Kate be brought in when she complained about not sleeping well for the past several nights. She's badly bruised and required four stitches between three separate and rather deep *cuts* on her back. Luckily, there are no infections. Jeff said you would

131

know what happened."

I flinched and stumbled back in shock, feeling as though I had been slapped. "Stitches…?"

"What happened that Kate needed stitches?" demanded Mother, behind me. I was in such turmoil that I had not heard her enter, though I should have known she would have come to Paul's.

Jeff looked at me accusingly. "Ask your son."

Mother came up beside me, worried. "Cory, what happened to Kate?"

"I…We…My hands…claws…" I sighed heavily, covering my eyes with one hand. Guilt was the only thing I could feel more clearly than my own…*dislike* of my naiveté.

Mother gasped in understanding after a moment to grasp my words. "You…? What?!"

"We don't think she's pregnant and nothing was broken," consoled Paul. It was a small thing, but it still relieved me some. Oh, a curse that I should worry over breaking those I loved.

"Oh, Kate! Are you alright?" asked Mother concernedly. I pulled my hand away, looking over to see Jasmine and Kate entering the room. Jasmine gave me an icy glare. Kate smiled at me shyly.

"I am sorry, Katelyn," I apologized formally, feeling that it was not my place to act familiar with her at the time.

"Don't speak to my daughter," ground out Jasmine, eyes narrowing.

"What you did was irresponsible," my mother told me quietly. I nodded, feeling claustrophobic from the emotions pressing in on me.

Demon *Rising*

Kate scowled defiantly. "It wasn't just him, you know! It took the both of us!"

Her defending me only made my guilt worse. I thought that I was a horrid man, betraying the trust of our parents. Worse than a man, in fact. I was the demon I so resembled, enjoying the time spent while I had injured Kate. My guilt blinded me from seeing that I had no intention of hurting her, nor had I any knowledge of such. Oh, the woman had hidden it from me as well as her parents. I understand why she did.

"Katelyn, please, you need not defend me," I barely ground out, eyes on the floor.

"I told you not to speak to my daughter!" snapped back Jasmine, stepping forward and slapping me. My skin stung, to my surprise. I began to cry silently, thinking I may never see nor speak to Kate again. The idea was brutal but realistic in my mind. A just reward for the monster I had somehow become, though I had no knowledge of *how*.

In retrospect, I know we did nothing wrong. At the time, however, we were evil. Myself in particular for taking advantage of her willingness, I do suppose. Now though, I half think that she was in fact the villain. Time and time again, I have learned that she may appear innocent, but…Well, she never has been the perfect lady, only the perfect woman. If you understand the differences between the two that I am referring.

It was a moment before I realized that I should do my best to keep my tears rather than shed them. "My apologies."

"Please! Control yourselves in my home," commanded Paul, stepping between Jasmine and I. He checked that I was alright before he continued, "There's also no need to assault Cory. He behaved as—"

"A demon," snapped Jeff.

"—a man," finished Paul lamely, staring at Jeff incredulously.

Mother was silent, eyes averted from me.

"I would rather defend Cory as a man indulging in sin than stand by while he's beaten unjustly and accused of being something he is not!" Paul tried again sternly, near shouting.

Everything was too much for me to bear. I snarled unintentionally, body wound to the point where I thought I might lash out. Whirling, I rushed from the home in a panic. Just as I was beginning to run to take flight, someone grabbed onto my hand and shouted my name. I threw them off of me, half-turning to see that it was my mother.

"Oh, no," I groaned, guilt welling up inside me. I looked up at Paul pleadingly before continuing with my cowardly escape. Jeff shouted angrily after me and I felt that he was justified. First Katelyn, then Mother...

I flew. I do not know how long, just that when I finally landed the sun was arcing back toward the horizon. Beneath me, there was a forest. I saw a small clearing and landed. I stood for a moment in confusion before my anger, terror and guilt overwhelmed me again.

I screamed and wept. I am unaware of when I stopped or if I stopped, only that I then began to destroy everything I saw, hoping to find some solace in it as my mythological brethren had. I only fell deeper into my pit of despair, eventually sitting on a tree I felled and staring at my bloody, splinter-filled arms. The black liquid was hot, so that it felt like it should have been acid.

Night fell, but still I stared at my hands. I am not certain I was even thinking, only ignoring the growing pains of hunger in my gut. Some time during the night, too, I recall a doe having come near me as she sniffed delicately for plants to feed upon. When she took in my appearance completely, she shrieked and bolted in the opposite direction from me. I began to cry again.

I slept through the next day, waking to again destroy what I could. My body felt worn as I pushed it to its farthest—that I had explored, in any case. It amazed me that I was still conscious when dawn broke again, the glittering rays of the sun blinding me painfully. I groaned and blinked against the light, deciding I should return home then.

I forget how much of the journey I walked and how much I flew, only that it was also blurred by my desire to be numb. When I arrived on the edge of the farm, I heard people shouting. Lisa came to my side with a relieved grin and I am somewhat guilty now for selfishly not considering how worried she must have been. I know that I walked past her—past everyone—going to my room to be alone. The worried faces only brought back the emotions I had spent days ridding myself of.

That night I cleaned my blood from my arms, ate and worked in the fields. When my chores were finished, I flew back to the clearing to destroy more trees before returning home around noon.

The next two weeks continued in that pattern so that I could keep myself from facing the reality I loathed to know existed. One day, I overheard Mother on the telephone with Paul.

"...coming home with his hands covered in his own blood...Yes, thank you, Paul...Thank you."

I entered the kitchen to find Mother wiping away tears from her eyes. She tried to smile, turning away abruptly to the counters to continue preparing supper. I stood in the doorway, not knowing what to do with myself.

It had not occurred to me that anyone else would be feeling my suffering. To the contrary, I thought they would all be glad that I was paying the price for what I was, and their worried faces were only masks. I hoped it had made them happy, since it was causing so much pain to myself.

"Why were you crying?" I wondered aloud, startling Mother. She stayed still for a moment before smacking the counter.

"Damn it, Cory, what's wrong?!" she demanded, shoulders stiff. She turned to face me, eyes glistening. It still causes me grief to think that I had worried her so much. "Why do you keep hurting yourself? Why won't you let anyone help you?"

I was confounded. What did she wish to help me for? "Why are you crying?"

She sniffled, struggling to compose herself and failing. "You're my baby, Cory. No matter what you are or how old you get, you'll always be my baby and I will always love you."

Her words threw me into confusion. I stared at my bruised and scabbing hands, feeling like the scared little child I had once been. "...Mom? I never meant to hurt anyone."

I slid to the floor, still staring at my hands. Mother hurried over, sitting on her knees to hold my head and stroke my hair, to comfort me in ways only a mother can.

Demon *Rising*

It was the first time since I was a child that I had been consoled by her. I had been stumbling about blindly, foolishly thinking that my parents would not guide me when I was lost.

"I know, Cory, I know," she told me, kissing my head. I hugged her back, caving to my fright, guilt and grief.

Mother...Oh, how I do miss her. I have not seen her in forty some years, as you well know. Just a couple of weeks ago, just before I was released, I called the farm to see how everyone was. The first call in a decade. Well...Lisa answered the phone, and she sounds so very wizened now. Her voice has become thin and frail. It is frightening. She told me that...Mother and Father had died seven years ago. It was not unexpected, to be sure. I merely wish I had been able to hug them one last time and tell them I was grateful to have them for my teachers. I apologize. Please, allow me a moment to collect myself before I continue...

"I don't want to lose Kate. I love her," I sobbed brokenly. It felt as though I had already lost her again, the world ripping her from my desperately grasping fingertips. That was when I had my crushing revelation.

Every man has this moment, I am sure, whether he be a boy or old and dying in his bed. The sudden, terrifying understanding that you have no power over your life's desire, the thing that gives your breath a purpose. The shattering second where you must cling to faith in yourself and your commitment, no matter where you come from or how you look. It is the mortifying, sharp moment of thought that makes you tremble as you know beyond any certainties that you cannot keep your desire close or capture and own it. You must set it free so that it may own itself and all you may do is be kind so that it may stay beside you.

When this occurred to me while being held by my mother, I wept like I had never wept before. I thought I had sacrificed enough of my life—my future—to the world for it to be satisfied for centuries to come. Now, it seemed as though I would have to relinquish my reason for a future, for my very life to continue and be worth anything. I know, you stare at me aghast like I am surely insane for tangling my life so heavily with another's. I think so, too, sometimes. I imagine my thoughts may be an alien concept for you, particularly from this cruel face with a supposedly wicked tongue. But, oh, onward with the story, I do suppose.

I could not bear to work that night, going to the tree behind the cornfields instead. Sitting beneath it and listening to the nighttime symphony, I searched for the crescent moon with questions weighing on my mind:

Where had I come from? Why was I here? What was my purpose? If it was to sow hate and pain, could I bear not to? Oh, so many things I still wonder now. Mother followed me through the field, though, and gave me a letter.

"It was with you when I found you," she told me. "The angel said that when the time was right, I should give it to you. I hope it helps you find what you need."

With that, she left me. I stared at the old letter with a frown, moving it this way and that. My heart began to race in my chest, thrilled that I may begin to understand at last how it was I appeared in the field. Then I paused and frowned, thinking that it did not matter.

Demon *Rising*

No, not thinking it. *Knowing* it did not matter. Whatever I was, I could rise above it. Whoever I was, I could always make myself who I wanted to be. So I folded the letter neatly and put it into my pocket, smiling to myself at this new revelation. I understood what I needed to do next.

The night was still young—the moon not yet risen—so I flew to Kate's home. It was a short flight, and when I landed on the lawn Jeff was standing on the porch, arms crossed as he glowered into the darkness where I was. I was wholly unsurprised. My wings make a thunderous noise when I fly, after all.

"I thought we made it clear that you could only visit when we said you could," called Jeff. I could see his eyes narrow slightly.

"Where is she?" I asked, keeping my voice low. It would be unproductive if Kate heard me, when I meant to speak with her parents in private.

"Inside. She's just about finished healing up after what you did," he added, making me cringe guiltily.

"Good," I murmured. I took a deep breath and let it out slowly. "Is Mrs. Smith available?"

Confused, he frowned but nodded. He entered the home, leaving me outside in the night for a few minutes. The abruptness of my actions was settling in around me, my blind courage beginning to fly away. When Jeff and Jasmine finally stepped out onto the porch, my tail was flicking the air while my heart began to pound anxiously.

I pushed all of that aside so that I could speak.

"I would like to start by asking you to understand that I acted only as any other human man would, but I do not intend to use that as an excuse. In fact, I would like to

139

take full responsibility for my actions," I told them honestly. I could feel my guilt and darkness leaving me slowly as I began to speak what had been troubling me.

"Then what's the point in saying that?" demanded Jasmine, cocking her hip and glaring at me as she had certain rights to.

"So that you might listen to what I have to say, as if I were human," I replied slowly and quietly, imagining what it might be like to look the part. "I wanted to say that I am sorry for whatever stress you have been put under and thank you for caring for Kate even when I was the one who injured her, and so should be the one to take responsibility there."

They stared at me for a long, agonizing moment. Finally, Jasmine broke the silence. "Was that it?"

"No," I sighed, settling into the new environment easily enough. "You must also know that the only regret I have for my actions is that I hurt Kate. If she had remained uninjured and our parents had reacted in the same manner I would have no regrets for what I did. I am sorry that you have been impacted so heavily, but I am not sorry for what I did. If you are going to be angry or hate me, then do so. I will not deprive myself of my life to please others and protect myself from those who do not approve.

"Also, I apologize for evading facing you two," I added. My heart was calming as I came into a rather peaceful acceptance of the situation, my life, and myself. "I realize that wallowing in guilt and self-pity was not aiding anyone but myself, since I needed to allow myself to experience and release those emotions. If you would permit me to apologize to Kate, as well, that would be wonderful. If not, then I am ready to be on my way and

140

leave you all in peace."

Jeff turned to Jasmine with a sympathetic expression. "I think we should talk in private for a minute. Excuse us, Cory."

They went into the house again. A short moment later, the door opened and Kate peered outside warily. She must have seen me, because the grin that lit her face was one I had never seen before. She crept out of the house, closing the door gently before charging off the porch and across the lawn toward me. It was a swift moment until she was in my arms and embracing me.

"It's about time you visited," she sighed. I could feel how stiff her arms were, as though she were trying to hold me as tightly as she could. Thinking of that and the healing scabs on her back, I was frighteningly aware of just how fragile she was.

"I am so sorry, Kate. I needed time to myself," I told her softly, rubbing her back carefully. A warm happiness began to spread through me. "Oh, glad as I am to see you, I am afraid you need to go back inside."

"You're not trying to get rid of me, are you?" she asked, trembling slightly.

"No, no. Your parents are inside discussing whether I might be able to visit you, so I would rather be respectful to them and their wishes," I explained, pulling her gently away from me. Her black eyes were captivating and tear-filled, making my heart ache with guilt. "If you would like, I could meet with you some nights."

She nodded, pouting. "Yes, please, if it's not too much of a bother..."

"Of course, it is never any issue. I love you." The words came naturally, and I felt they would comfort her more than anything else I could say. Oh, and they were so right and so honest I wanted to laugh. I never thought that speaking anything could send such a harmonious sensation through me.

Kate's expression was one of shock. She gasped quietly, backing away slowly. She was terrified—there is no other word to describe her wide eyes and gaping mouth. Spinning 'round on her heel, she hurried back inside before I could do anything more.

I refrained from following her, instead standing still in my rejection while I waited for her parents to return. With all the power I could muster, I pushed back the pain to remain calm. I was somewhat confused at that moment, and only wanted to focus on finding something to progress my life for the better.

Jeff and Jasmine came out again. Jasmine seemed petulant, eyes narrowed at me, but most of her hostility had vanished. Jeff—kind and open man that he was—wore half a smile, relaxed. He was nodding slowly.

"It's fine if you talk to her. Just a few minutes though, since it's a school night." He stood there for an awkward moment before adding, "We'll go get her."

I only had to wait for a moment before she came out again. Her parents allowed us privacy, so I stared at her longingly and fought to keep myself from crossing the distance to her. She stayed on the porch—in the light—as far from me as she could be.

"They said you wanted to apologize," she said quietly, not looking at me.

I nodded. "Yes."

"You already did that," she hedged, still quiet. I could see her edging toward the door.

"Yes," I said again, voice shaking slightly. It felt as though the lawn were a chasm that was growing wider every moment.

She scowled at the swing. "What do we do, then?"

I knew she was referring to what I had told her. I winced. "I...I don't know."

She glanced at me quickly when she heard the pain in my voice. "Are we still friends?"

"I hope so," I replied, shifting my wings nervously. I desperately wanted to hold her. "I can...I can set aside what I feel, if you would rather maintain our current relationship."

"I don't know," she answered honestly. Her face was pained, so open and vulnerable...I thought I might break there and beg her to tell me what she needed.

We were silent again for a time. She slowly turned to face me completely, eyes wide and trusting. Her slight frame trembled, tears rolling from her eyes.

I hurried over to her and took her in my arms. "I'm sorry, Kate."

"We were never going to be just friends, were we, Cory?" she asked quietly, still shaking. I felt her hot tears on my skin.

"Would you like me to be honest?" I rubbed her back gently. She nodded and looked up at me. I shook my head slowly. "No. I felt more for you than just a friendship, since I first saw you."

She pressed her palm to my abdomen, then pulled away sharply as though the contact had burned her. "I'm confused about what I feel."

"However long you need, I can wait," I told her. I only barely noticed that my pain had vanished while

143

standing beside her. "In the meantime...I believe you need rest for tomorrow."

She groaned. "Remind me about my math test..."

"Good luck," I murmured, stroking her hair with a smile. "Sleep well, Kate."

She nodded and smiled back. "Sleep well."

I turned and began walking away, feeling at ease with myself. Everything I had needed to say to Kate and her parents was said. I also felt confident that no matter what happened, life would continue to be enjoyable.

I was at the edge of the lawn when she called my name. I turned around swiftly, a new joy blooming within me when I heard her say my name.

"Um...I think I love you, too," she said shyly. She hurried back inside and my smile broadened.

That morning at breakfast, I told my family what had occurred the night before. I also apologized for my recent behavior and all the grief it had caused them. They accepted the apology, glad to see me happy again.

Kate and I continued our relationship preceding our...adventure. Even so, it seemed so much richer and genuine. Our parents never let us be alone for extended periods of time, of course, and for some time after my depression had ended I had a suspiciously drastic number of chores to complete, so that I had roughly ten free minutes between them, eating and sleeping. My punishment for being a hooligan, I do believe.

That Christmas was also unforgettable. I was relieved from chores the night before and so slept from late morning of the 24th to early morning on the 25th, exhausted after three months of extra chores. I awoke in the morning, sore as always from my too-small bed. I tidied up and went downstairs for breakfast, wearing a buttoned shirt that Mother had modified just for the holiday. In honor of the holiday's colors, the shirt was forest green.

The morning meal was light, so that we would all be prepared for the feast to come. Mother began to cook some dishes to bring to the church for the annual Christmas party, where I would be narrating and singing again. While something was in the oven, we went into the living area where the tree was shedding its needles on the floor. There were some presents beneath it, as always. One for Mother, one for Father, two for Lisa. I frowned that there was nothing for me, but was unconcerned. I thought I was still paying the price for my misbehavior months earlier.

When we arrived at the church, everyone was shifty around me. They glanced at me in fear, staying away when they could and avoiding conversation. At one point, I found a mirror to confirm whether I had sprouted an extra horn or some other horrible thing. Nothing. My face was as devilishly ugly as it had always been.

I went through the narrations and carols somewhat numbly, only consoled that Kate was not avoiding me. She stayed close to me and I to her, as we generally were when we could be together.

As soon as the retelling was over, people began to leave. Fled is actually a much more apt description. Before Kate's parents left, they said that she and I could visit one another the entire day—a Christmas present, of sorts. So Kate and I walked back to my home alone. I was careful on the road and made it home without any injuries.

When we arrived, Kate announced rather loudly that she wanted to sit in my room and read with me. No one present made any fuss of it strangely, though I considered it to be because of the holiday. So we climbed the stairs and opened the door to my room.

"Merry Christmas!" came a chorus from several people within the room. Kate's parents, Paul, some of the men that I would help from time to time.

I blinked in surprise, looking around in shock. I was unable to even wonder how they had all fit into my room without standing on one another. "What?"

Kate pulled me over to a giant bed that took over what must have been half of my room. "You have to try it! They've been working on it for months!"

"Working?" I mumbled, going over to the bed numbly. Everyone was staring, waiting for my response. I laid down on the bed and I wanted to never move again.

"Thank you," I laughed, staring at the ceiling with a grin. "Thank you all!"

They burst into laughter while I stretched. The bed fit my entire length, plus a good foot extra to make for growing space. Kate laid down beside me and then Lisa piled onto the bed, from where I do not know.

I fell asleep there easily, my body not having had such peaceful rest in years. When I woke again, Lisa was gone and Kate was nestled into the crook of one of my arms with my tail wrapped about her. It was nighttime, the moon still shining brightly outside. Sighing contentedly, I stayed awake to watch her sleep.

Cory chuckled. "I do suppose that last confession could be considered unstable."

Robert shrugged, unconcerned. "Everyone watches

their loved ones sleep at one point or another. I'm curious about something, though."

"Please, you may ask me anything," replied Cory with a small wave of his hand. He seemed to have collected himself some since his earlier upset.

"You're telling me what seems to be the biggest moments of your life," said Robert slowly, composing his thoughts. "What was your average home life like? How did you normally interact with the other town members?"

"My home life?" murmured Cory, pausing for a moment. "Well, most of anything we did was in a common area, such as the living room. We would read, converse, listen to the radio shows. Lisa and I would help Mother cook now and again. Average life, I suppose."

"And with everyone else?" he prompted.

"I saw and spoke with them at church. None of them made any sizable impact on my life, however, so I remember none of their names," he answered slowly, examining one of his hands. "When someone required the assistance of brute force, I was called upon. For a short while, my nickname was 'The Tractor,' since whenever one was needed I was there instead. Otherwise, just the same as anyone else who lived in a small community."

Robert took his notes, nodding to himself as he did so. "And did you and Kate ever become...active again?"

"Ah...Yes, the eve of her eighteenth birthday she seduced me," he replied, frowning as though he only relinquished the private information because it was required for the session.

"Did she force herself? Not to be rude or intrusive," added Robert quickly, seeing the defensive irritation on Cory's face. "It's just standard questions."

"It was a willing act by both parties, sir, and I mean that she *seduced* me," he said with a sharp sigh to punctuate his words. "I apologize. I do not wish to speak of such personal matters without the express permission of the other person."

"Right." Robert looked at his notes. "Well, then, how does the story go from there?"

Cory smiled. "Quite unfortunately, that is again all I can recall."

Robert's face fell sympathetically. "Right. Well, do you feel like you've gotten anything this week?"

Cory's smile broadened and he nodded. "Yes, yes I do, Robert. I do, thank you."

Demon *Rising*

Dear Diary,

Today has been nothing short of wonderful. This morning I awoke beside Cory. It was an accident, really, but I suppose I can't feel guilty or ashamed since no one woke me up to go home last night.

It was overwhelming when I opened my eyes to find him watching me. It was not so much that he frightened me, rather it was the way he watched me. I think the word I want is with reverence. He smiled and tried to hide something from me, though, and I can't help but wonder what that was. From the glimpse I got I can only imagine that it was pain.

From then, though, he took me to the window and the chair beside it. I sat on his lap and we watched the sun rise across the farm. I must admit, though, I watched Cory watch the sunrise more than the actual event. It was beautiful. He seemed enraptured by it, but he also looked a little sad. I think it was an unconscious movement when he put his hand to the window, almost like a poor animal that wanted out of its cage. He held me close after that.

I can only wonder how he can bear to live such a limited life so passionately, seeing everything through his window. How can no one else see it? He's good and kind, but I'm finally understanding that he'll never be able to live like the rest of us. I think...I want to live with him, in spite of that. I want to wake up with him again, I want to watch him watch the sunrise again, and I want to see his hidden pain heal so that he can smile completely.

I think I'll always love him, since I don't think I'll

149

Demon *Rising*

ever leave.

Sincerely,
Katelyn

Chapter Four:
Open Wounds

Third Week Under Protection

Wednesday

I sighed and averted my gaze as I caught sight of my reflection in the window. The cool day in late summer allowed me to wear a full-sleeve shirt, but that did not remove the precise *disgust* when I glimpsed my face. My horns, while in better condition than when I had left, still stung on occasion and were filling in the surgically removed pieces missing from them.

The revulsion of my scars had not begun as quite so intense, nor so limiting. Like any disapproval one would have with themselves, it began by stares. Then the murmurs I overheard whenever I left the house. Or perhaps it was the children who would flinch from me, call me a monster or cry. Men hated me. Women hated me. Children trembled in my wake. I suspected the only reason the men on the lawn or the Smiths felt comfortable near me was the ever-present reality that if I attacked I would be shot. Lethally, with the number of guns that surrounded us.

Still, I sat on the porch without much worry. After all, Henrickson was not on shift until seven in the evening.

151

Demon *Rising*

So Santos and Thompson were sitting on the porch, enjoying a glass of lemonade with me.

Thompson was staring at the glass with a content smile, shaking his head slowly. "Man, not even my mom makes lemonade this good."

"If Henrickson found out, *he'd* be jealous," agreed Santos, speech hinted with a slight, fluid accent. He turned to grin at me. "You'll make a very lovely wife someday."

I laughed. Male jibes had not changed much, at least. I was not in a mood to continue the jest, however. "No, no...I believe that I am already bound, if I can recall correctly."

"Ooh, a lady friend." Thompson frowned, endearingly dull and young. "Or is it a man friend? Santos, were you serious about the whole wife thing? Is there something I don't know about?"

Santos chuckled to himself but did not answer. It was only a minute later that I thought the boy might genuinely be incapable of understanding, and so relieved his confusion.

"A woman, Thompson. Not a lady," I corrected, sipping my glass. I smiled proudly that I could recall Mother's recipe even after the years. They misinterpreted my expression, laughing raucously.

"A? Singular? Now I'm disappointed," gasped Thompson between fits of laughter. "I was under the impression that demons got around."

Santos jabbed Thompson's glass with an elbow, unconcerned when the drink spilled across his companion's front. "Please excuse the young man to my right. Apparently, he's still a sophomore."

Thompson was grumbling incoherently as he

152

brushed his front futilely. Scowling, he glanced about as though looking for something, then stopped and stared at the remaining sip in his glass. His shoulders hunched with a heavy sigh that made me wonder if the sun had suddenly died out.

I chuckled quietly. "Nothing to be ashamed of. Honestly, I envy his youth."

Thompson started. "What? I'm envied?"

"Not by me." Santos shook his head with a superior smile.

"Isn't that a good thing?" wondered Thompson, frowning at the grass.

"How did you make the team, again?" asked Santos playfully, although sounding genuinely curious. Before he could receive an answer, the front door opened and Robert stepped halfway out, crossing his arms at all of us sternly.

"Alright, ladies, the latest news is that Henrickson's on his way now. Back to your posts. Leave the glasses," he added, seeing Thompson attempting to slip more lemonade into his glass. Both flowed easily back into their unyielding masks, watching to ensure nothing could sneak past them.

Robert took the two glasses they left behind, smiling at me. "Having a good day?"

"I believe so," I replied distantly, frowning as I stood. I took the pitcher with me as I returned indoors. The house was quiet and empty. Anne was cleaning somewhere in the massive domain of her bedroom and the girls were off to school. With a glance at the clock, I was relieved to know that they would be home within an hour.

"You don't know?" asked Robert, helping me to clean the dishes used and store the remaining lemonade.

"Not fully, no." I placed the rinsed dishes in the washer, still bemused by the device. Yet another object that had not existed on the farm.

"Can you describe it?" A strong portion of Robert's method was handling occurrences for me as they presented themselves, rather than chasing down my traumas and beating them from me. At that moment, I did not know which practice I preferred.

"Restless. Lonely, although that may merely be the unbearable silence," I listed, staring at the startling contrast between the black polished stone counters and my vivid red skin. My claws were nearly imperceptible against the counter, while my skin only became brighter. The scars were also accentuated, so I looked away yet again. "Pitiful. Useless. Ashamed..."

My words saddened Robert immensely. "What do you feel would help you?"

I sighed quietly to myself, considering. In the last two weeks, I had been working diligently to adjust to this new place, life, *time*. My thoughts strayed instead to what I wanted desperately, what I dreamed of having once I had control and the days were not quite so dizzying.

"My family." It was only once I had spoken that I realized that my whisper was as loud as my voice would dare become. Why was that? "To see my home, my sister, my brothers..."

The name I neglected to speak was one that Robert noticed. He did not question my reasons, however. He likely already knew that I kept her from my mind intentionally recently. After all, the idea of seeing her was tormenting, particularly when I had to wait for an unknown time before I could.

Demon *Rising*

"You sure are a quick one to recover," noted Robert with a slight frown. I wonder, was he concerned by this? "Most patients take months, sometimes years to go back home. Are you sure you're ready?"

"Yes, I know I am," I replied readily. Sitting about waiting for myself to emotionally heal by the will of someone else was beginning to turn me insane. I told him this, then continued, "I would like to take my recovery into my own hands. This includes rushing into the excitement of where my old life collides with the new, as opposed to fretting over whether or not it would be wise to do so."

Robert blinked in surprise and stared at me. "You're not human."

I chuckled somewhat nervously. "Yes, Robert, I do believe this truth was already established some time ago."

"No, I mean that you...There's no good way to put this, is there? The way you've thought through everything, I've never seen another patient do that," he explained, shaking his head in disbelief. "Very unique."

I smiled, Paul's words from years ago repeating in my mind. Then I started as I realized that he had spoken them to me a little over fifty years ago.

Half of a century. I considered how much time had passed, yet how little. The world had left its mark on me, but I had not left my mark on the world. I may never be allowed to place my signature on history, yet I was not disturbed by this. Only quietly submissive and tiredly accepting of my place.

Robert sighed but smiled at me. "Well, then. Shall I arrange things for you?"

I started, smiling slowly. "That would be wonderful and very generous of you, Robert."

He shrugged. "A few phone calls, finding something to rent that'll fit you. I'll let you know what's happening and when."

"Thank you." He left and I wondered just how I would manage to find a way to thank him and his family for helping me in all of the ways that they had.

~~ * ~ * ~ * ~~

<u>Friday</u>

"Anne, you said that this...*card* holds my compensation for the last forty years?" I asked again, baffled by the idea. What an advanced and strange age! Water coming from iceboxes, ovens that supposedly cleaned themselves, televisions as thin as books, and now all of my finances being held on a thin piece of plastic? I would be unsurprised when pigs began to fly alongside me.

She nodded. "That's what the letter said. Forty-one years' compensation as well as monthly payments for compensation, some demon organization and disability, even though you look fine to me."

I smiled slightly. Apparently, between Robert and myself neither of us had told her of my arm. I was somewhat surprised to be paid because of it, though. Aside from it, I could function perfectly well physically. Like I had when I was thirty, even.

"Thank you for your reassurance, Anne. Here, though." I handed her the card. "I suppose it is well past time that I contributed and thanked you for your assistance. You said you would be shopping for groceries sometime this evening? That should well cover the bill."

She stared at it in shock. "Cory, this really is unnecessary."

I paused. "Ah, yes. Bailey mentioned something about this...Well then, is there anything else I might be able to help with? Laundry, cleaning, cooking...?"

"You're not one to sit still, are you?" she asked, returning the card.

I chuckled and shook my head. "No, much thanks to my parents."

She sighed, nodding slowly. "Well, I guess you can do the cooking..."

"Thank you." I was genuinely relieved and grateful, not wanting to stare out the window and thinking I would not possibly be able to stand another day of sitting and reading. My hands yearned for some task to fulfill.

"That's a first," she laughed, shaking her head. I thanked her again and replaced the card in my room. Such a strange adjustment, as well—*my* room, in their house. Yet day by day, it was slowly becoming a place for me.

"Wait, you can cook, too?!" gasped Bailey in shock. She was rinsing the tomatoes as I had requested, setting them aside as she finished.

I chuckled quietly, peeling an onion carefully so as to not collect any beneath my claws. "Of course. I would help my mother before I began working in the fields. Even after taking up the fieldwork, I found it pleasant to cook with her."

"Wow. We don't normally do much cooking, not like this," she clarified, motioning to my preparing the onion. She sniffled, the wafting oils making her teary. "I think I know why now."

"A little onion never harmed anyone." I smiled quietly to myself, amused. As I lifted the knife, I forced back the fear I felt of the object in my hand and began to chop the bulb methodically.

Bailey frowned. "Hey, wait a minute. Why aren't you being affected by the onion?"

"I am immune." I tossed the chopped onion into the pot, grinning as I turned back to my station. Bailey cried out, stumbling back in shock. I straightened my expression instantly, focusing on my cutting. "My apologies."

She composed herself quickly, returning to my side shyly. "That was...kind of freaky."

I sighed quietly, retrieving the washed carrots from the back of the counter to chop. Again, I forced back my fear. "So I have been told."

"Does it freak you out?" she asked quietly, rinsing the next of the tomatoes. Her demeanor was skittish, even as I turned away to place the carrots in the stew.

"Does your own smile disturb you?" I replied, keeping my eyes down, somewhat guilty for frightening the poor girl. The scars on my arm only shamed me further.

"No." She was rinsing the third tomato.

"Why would I be frightened by mine?" I began slicing the celery with meticulous focus.

From the corner of my vision, I saw her shrug. "I don't know. Maybe you don't see it very often and you're used to our human looks, so yours are a little...um, sharper than ours."

I smiled, wondering how it was the young girl was able to think so clearly of others. What was it that made her so drastically different from her sister? What were they hiding that changed them?   Again, I could not help worrying for this little family's future.

Fourth Week Under Protection

<u>Monday</u>

Time.   Did it mean anything anymore?   Was it always so...spontaneous? So long, so short, so sharp, so dull? No, no, it meant nothing. Nothing left to struggle with but oneself in endless loops, nothing left to yearn for but to sleep long enough to dream.

In spite of my purposelessness, I was still glad to see the sky again. The beauty of it was relieving after too long of artificial lighting. I spent most of my time out of doors in the back yard, alone sitting in the cool and gentle grass. That was where Robert found me.

"Pretty sky," he commented, sitting beside me. I nodded, vaguely aware of the rather thick stack of printed papers he set aside. He smiled at me broadly. "I have some good news for you."

I smiled, feeling dark. What good news could there be anymore? My life had at last reached its peak, leaving me longing for the lower places on the mountain.

"What of?" I asked to humor him. I did not want to aware him of my recent decline in mood. He would not understand if I could not. Perhaps another week or so to begin comprehending the source of the emotional shadow...

"Well, okay, good and bad news," he relinquished

159

reluctantly. "Lisa said that she's up for a visit on Thursday. Your brothers are busy with some stressful things, they said. But I gave them the number so that they could get back into contact when they were ready."

"This Thursday?" Ah, good news, indeed! My little sister Lisa, how had she fared? Was she still as cheerful and bright as I could recall? I hoped so and refused to imagine any other outcome of events that resulted in her bitterness or despair.

"This Thursday," he echoed, smile fading slightly. "If you're up for a bit of excitement. I know not much has actually been happening, unless you count the occasional accident in the kitchen."

"None of them fatal, thankfully," I laughed, shaking my head slowly. Robert was right. Excitement was something that had been lacking of late and something that made me curious about the future. "That is very good news, now. I have not seen Lisa since the Christmas of '68, when she was visiting from college. Dustin visited with his children and wife in '66, but I do not recall having seen Ethan since he left home..."

He hesitated. "That's not all."

I chuckled. "You would make a lovely jester."

"I have a list," he said slowly, lifting the stack and handing it to me. I glanced at the front page, the same name attacking my eyes repeatedly.

Katelyn Smith.

"I made it so that we can start looking," he explained. Was my face horrified? Was it joyful? Was it as stunned and baffled as I felt? I am uncertain even Robert could make heads or tails of what to say or do. "I thought, since you love having something to do, this would definitely keep us busy for a few weeks."

"Us?" I echoed, latching on to the first thing my mind could make sense of.

"Of course! I wouldn't leave you alone to do this." For the first time, I saw him with a new light that I rarely saw in humans. Dedication and loyalty were the names of his strengths, and I guessed that he was so true to them that he made himself a fool. "I've got routes planned out. Santos and Thompson are ready to take outings with you. Everything's ready, if or when you want to start looking."

It was only when a wet drop appeared on the paper that I realized I had tears in my eyes. "Thank you, Robert. You are too kind."

"Just helping you out." He shrugged off the comment easily, receiving the papers from my outstretched hand. "On a lighter note, we were thinking of doing breakfast for dinner tonight."

I laughed, mildly grateful for the distraction. "Sir, you are absurd! Breakfast for dinner? What does this entail, exactly?"

He stood and offered me his hand. I took it and allowed him to aid me, though I required no assistance. His eyes widened as he nearly toppled over from my weight. I laughed again.

"Pigs in a blanket, this time," he replied in answer to my question as we started indoors. "Last time we had cold cereal, insistence of Vanessa."

"What about next time?"

His reply was drowned out by my thoughts as I followed him inside. Things were falling into place. I was going home to the farm. More than that, I was at last going to put my mind at ease and answer my questions.

Demon *Rising*

~~ * ~ * ~ * ~~

<u>Tuesday</u>

I was reading in the living room when Bailey first approached me. Robert had lent me a thick, dusty volume of poems with which I could entertain myself by memorizing and reciting the cadences under my breath. She had a pen in one hand, paper in the other, and bore an earnest expression.

"Can I ask you some questions for an article that Supernatural Supporters is doing for the school paper?" she asked quietly, voice as somber as her face. I could not help but smile at her method of pursuit as I set the poetry book aside.

"Supernatural Supporters?" Vanessa scoffed vindictively. "Right. *That* pro-demon group."

Bailey ignored her. "So, what do you think?"

"I would be more than happy to acquiesce," I replied, following her cue. She sat in the chair beside the couch, grinning.

"Okay, this is so cool! It's like an interview." Her child-like enthusiasm was like that of a four year old at Christmas. "Alright. First question...No, we don't need to know his name, that's already all over the press...Oh! Hometown?"

"Ah..." I frowned deeply, shaking my head slowly. "For the life of me, I cannot recall. I am unsure I ever knew."

She stared at me with a mixture of disbelief and pity. "Right. Um...How has life been as a demon?"

162

"It has been worthwhile," I murmured reflexively, barely noticing my own words.

Robert looked up from the book he was reading. "That must be the fifth time you've said that."

"What, like it's trying to prove something?" scoffed Vanessa rudely, sneering at her father. I reigned in my shock and disapproval.

"I suppose I may be attempting to convince myself more than anyone," I told her evenly. She started and looked at me as though she had just noticed my presence there.

"Why would you?" she demanded, cruelty faltering. I saw that she was struggling to keep her face from revealing whatever weakness frightened her so terribly.

"Why would I not?"

She blinked quickly, eyes tearing up while she glared at me. Standing abruptly, she spat, "I hate you," and stalked away. I heard her footsteps thudding on the stairs as she fled to her bedroom.

I was quiet for an uncomfortable moment. "Should one of us not comfort Vanessa with whatever troubles her?"

"I don't know," admitted Robert with a sad, fatherly glance at the stairs. He sighed. "Ever since th—*she* hit her teens...I don't know what happened, but she's not my little girl anymore."

Bailey left silently, and I understood then that he was not speaking simply of Vanessa. Sometime in the history of their family, they had all changed and no one had noticed.

"May I propose something?" I asked quietly, turning my attention from the stairs to Robert. Would I be speaking out of turn in this instance or could it be acceptable? Regardless, I felt a familiarly creeping darkness when I considered letting this be, a hideous knowledge that I would be damning and denying myself.

He looked at me tiredly, eyes dim and cast into a hopeless shadow. "What is it?"

"Treat them as your daughters, but respect the bright women they are becoming."

He only smiled, unsurprised at my referring to them both. "I'll try that."

Robert stood and left as well. I sat in silence for some time, though I did not feel uncomfortable there. The sun was pouring into the room through the large windows that looked out into the back yard. This was the first I had witnessed Robert acting with his family from a different place than the usual throne many individuals mistook for their seat above others. He was capable of much kindness and expressing equality with anyone, so I was only mildly surprised when he and Vanessa returned downstairs, chattering idly. I realized then that I had been expecting to hear shouts above me, the sounds of them arguing as I had heard my first night here. What startled me most was her smile—as I had never seen it untainted by scorn or spite.

When she genuinely apologized to me, I understood that time did still have meaning to others, if not to me. I lifted the poetry book to continue reading, feeling more than content.

~~ * ~ * ~ * ~~

Thursday

Demon *Rising*

Robert managed to find a car to rent for the day that was not too small for me. Again, when I thanked him, he merely shrugged and said that he was only helping a man, not saving the world. If he had been as insightful as Bailey, would he have understood that he was saving *my* world? The likelihood of that occurred to me then and I only smiled, thinking that he was an endearingly obtuse person at times.

The drive to the farm took four hours. We stopped every hour or so to stretch, much to my glee. Although, I was disoriented in learning that the trip was so short. All those years, I had felt worlds away from home when in fact if I had flown a couple hours east I would have been there. So close, yet so far...

When we arrived, time became a blur. I could not recall leaving the vehicle or walking the distance from the street to the house, the fields stretching out around it bare and empty. I was in another time entirely, when the crops were always rich and the home was not peeling paint or looking so rotted. Even Robert did not exist beside me in this mirage, yet when I took the first step onto the porch I was shocked back into the now and had to wonder if *this* was not the illusion.

I stood on the porch of the old farm house in sheer confusion. The place was familiar, yet it felt wrong to return. Mother and Father would not be waiting to greet me after a night of chores or a day at the church. They would never be greeting anyone in their home again.

Lisa now lived here, having inherited the house in my place. What did she look like now? Surely not the adorable little sister I had grown up with. Would she look like a grandmother or just a mother by now?

Taking a deep breath to steady myself, I knocked on the door while I attempted to keep myself from shaking in fear. I jumped when the door opened to a small elderly woman with graying hair. She had the same sweet smile my sister had always worn. When she saw me, she gasped in shock.

"Cory?! You...You're really back?" she asked in a voice as frail as she appeared.

"I told you that I would be permitted to leave," I replied awkwardly. Too long, I had been gone from home far too long. It was alien now, the scent of it horribly changed.

"You told us that a lot thirty-seven years ago," she said quietly, sounding bitter. She appraised me for a minute. "If it weren't for the skin color, I'm not sure I would have recognized you. You've collected a few scars since I last saw you."

I looked at a particularly nasty scar on my arm. There were several other, smaller scars that crossed every which way. They were all vicious, ugly purple things that marred my already hideous appearance. I understood what she meant, as I had seen my reflection earlier that day.

"Dear, Cory, your *face,* too," she gasped in horror. "What did they do to you?"

I looked away with a sigh, shaking my head and forcing back tears. I wanted to finish a happy visit before I began to delve into all that had genuinely happened. Slowly, I realized that the joy had left this place. "I apologize. I would rather not discuss any such things at the moment. How have you been? You said you had grandchildren now, when last we spoke over the phone?"

She nodded, smiling and allowing me to relax into

166

this strange new environment. "Yes. You remember I had a daughter?"

"Yes, I do. How many children does she have, then?" I inquired politely, keeping the conversation casual.

"Three girls," she smiled, laughing lightly. "My granddaughters are gorgeous. You're sure to meet them this weekend, too."

"This weekend?" I asked uncertainly, thinking that I would not be staying here long. Already, the gloomy atmosphere had begun to press in against me. What had happened here that left such a sad mark?

"Well, of course. You do want to use your room again, don't you?" she asked sincerely, motioning for me to come in. I ducked inside, keeping my head bowed under the short ceiling.

I laughed quietly. "I forgot how small these rooms were."

"I don't do so well on the stairs anymore, Cory, but your room's still there, in almost the same condition you left it in," Lisa told me, pointing up the stairs. I nodded as I began climbing up to the second floor, nostalgic.

When I opened the door to my room, my memory said that Kate should be waiting for me with a smile. My hopes were bruised with disappointment when she was not there, but I knew that she would not be. Family was one case, expecting Kate to have held on was foolish and greedy.

Lisa was right. The room looked exactly the same. My things were in the same corners, other than the wicker basket Kate had first given me. There were letters stacked within it, all addressed to me with no stamp. It was Mother's handwriting. I wept to think that she had written me so often, giving me the letters the only way she could think to. I could imagine her coming in here, sitting and waiting for me to come home. How heartbroken she must have been, when so many seasons passed without word of me.

Closing the door behind me gently, I then went to sit on my bed. I remembered the Christmas that it was placed in my room and chuckled sadly. There were traces of my old world everywhere here, but it was all so far gone that I never could have hoped to touch it.

Robert knocked quietly before stepping into the room. He looked at it in wonder, as though he had witnessed a fairy tale come to life. He smiled at me. "So, this is where you grew up?"

I nodded and smiled back, wiping the tears from my face. I pulled the wicker basket onto my lap, picking up letters and staring at them. Some of them were dated on the envelope.

"Yes, this was my home. Although...That window is new," I commented with a frown. "Otherwise, it look— My mistake, the records and player are missing. As well as some books. Oh, a pity, but after so long I cannot expect it all to be just as I left it..."

My eyes strayed to the top of the wardrobe, and I paused with a curious frown. I stood and lifted the photographs gently, frown deepening as a sorrowful, distant recognition swirled in my mind. Robert came to my side.

"What are those?" he asked, squinting to make out the images. I wiped the dust from them and offered them to him. "Engagement rings? Why do you have photos of engagement rings?"

I chuckled, shaking my head slowly. "I cannot recall. I assume that I was going to purchase—"

"Will you marry me?"

"—one," I faltered, the strangest images of a bright hospital room flashing in my mind's eye.

Robert smiled slowly. "They're all silver with topaz."

"Only the most beautiful for Kate," I replied, then started when I realized that, vaguely, I could remember this. I sighed quietly, shaking my head. "Silver is an unappreciated, gorgeous metal, like the moon is neglected in favor of the sun. Topaz...Kate's favorite color was yellow."

"Why not get a gold ring, then?" wondered Robert, not seeming to have noticed my momentary disturbance, or the strangeness of my remembrance.

"Because it is a vain color and rather unattractive, in my modest opinion," I replied. Robert was rifling through the photographs curiously. I stopped him on the most familiar of them, drawn to it by some buried force. "That was her ring."

Robert stared, transfixed by the simple yet breathtaking design. Seven little stones were set into the metal to form a heart. Carved into the metal on either side of the heart were tiny, delicate roses. I sighed, wishing that I knew more. What had she said, had I even asked her?

"I will gather my things and meet you downstairs shortly," I said quietly, collecting the photos from him and placing them in my basket.

He gaped at me incredulously. "Aren't you going to stay, like your sister offered?"

I shook my head, finding his disappointment sharp.

"No. I cannot."

"You're home, though..." He sounded sad as I began inspecting the room for anything else I may still cherish.

"Sir, this is not my home. It is the hollow husk of a place that I cherished when I was young, but it no longer holds any of its former powers or safeties. So I will leave this farm and allow my sister to continue as though I had never come. It will be a dream to her, as these last years have been to me, and life will move ever-dutifully onward."

Robert was stunned. "Right. I'll be...downstairs."

I nodded curtly. When the door closed behind him, I took a deep breath to steady myself. This place was torment, staring at me from every corner and surface with blank, unblinking eyes. I could not stand how small the room was, how hot it felt or how the sky looked as though it was falling from its perch amidst the clouds.

I had to leave. My old life here was driving me mad! I could see the specters of my old self and the shadows of my loved ones, moving about in memories too long dead to bear. No, this place was too full of everything I had once desired—that I still wished I had had the opportunity to expand upon—to think of staying much longer than an hour. I paused.

One lonely hour, trapped between the night and the day...

"Leave me be!" I hissed to the forsaken echoes furiously as I finished with everything. I halted when I found my hidden niche with the photos of Kate and her old diary. Then, as I lifted those gently from their place, I saw my own journal. Blue and worn, the poor book certainly held more than should ever be asked of any instrument. I opened it carefully and glanced at a passage, heart suddenly racing. What forgotten treasures could it hold?

August 9th, 1967

> *I am watching Kate sleep as I write, and now I mark the thirty-seventh month of her stay. It feels paranoid and obsessive to count, but I cannot help myself. After seeing Lisa leave home, I keep expecting Kate to do the same, with no warning and only a note to tell me where she has gone.*
>
> *But here she is, not an arm's length from me. I think she may stay here with me and never leave. I hope she will, but I worry for her. If she stays—and the thought of her leaving is very unpleasant—then she will have been greatly limited in her life. Has she experienced enough to know that this is the choice she wants to make? Ah, a question I fear asking her.*
>
> *Of course, I cannot say that we are young. Others just our age are already married or have children. Should I propose? Looking at her face, I can never understand what I should do. Does she want me to wait?*
>
> *Maybe creating a family with her is unwise. ~~If she marries me~~ If we have children, will they look like me? Could we dare, knowing what they will have to endure?*
>
> *Well, as torn as I am between my wants and worries, I suppose only time will tell.*

I closed the journal with a wistful sigh, enjoying that I had a way to understand as I placed it in the basket. The weight of the treasured items was comforting and all I needed from this place, all I wanted. I left the room,

171

ignoring the shadow memories of Kate sleeping in the bed or the demon child staring out the window longingly.

As I was hunched climbing down the stairs, I heard Robert and Lisa conversing.

"...me when the last time he saw you before being taken by the N.S.I.S.D. was?" asked Robert, voice muted and coming from my right. Ah, the kitchen.

"The N.S.I.S.D.?" asked Lisa. There was some clattering. "Tea?"

"Oh, no thank you." I could imagine him waving away the cup. "The National Science Institute for the Study of Demons, N.S.I.S.D."

"I didn't know it had a name," she replied. "I hadn't visited since the previous Christmas, though. I stopped by the hospital from time to time when I heard he'd been shot, but every time I came he was asleep. Let me tell you how disorienting it is to see Cory out cold at *night*," she added with her giggling laugh. She had not changed as much as I had perceived.

"Gossiping?" I asked playfully as I entered. The thought of leaving so soon abruptly felt awkward, twisting inside me.

Lisa smiled. "I am about that age now, aren't I? Although, this young man seems to be entering the stage early."

Robert frowned. "Oh, that's right..."

It was unsurprising to me that he had forgotten how much younger he was.

"Why don't you sit, Cory? You look like you're ready to bolt out the door," commented Lisa with a keen gaze. "Or were you already prepared to leave again?"

Her words stung but I did not feel undeserving of

them. "I want to visit you, Lisa, just not here. This place...It feels wrong."

She nodded slowly and I guessed that she saw the same phantoms that I did. "Right. Well, I have your number, so I know we can make a date again. One thing, though. Mom and Dad are out by the old tree. They didn't want to be too far when you came back. Visit them before you go?"

I nodded, feeling strange with how she spoke of them, as though I might see them standing out there when I went. "Thank you, Lisa. I will miss you."

"I've missed you, too, Cory." For a moment, I was her elder brother again and we were lunatic children, chasing one another through the house. "Take care."

When I left the house, the air was chilly and the sky was dark with clouds. The smell of coming rain was odd without the crops to accentuate it. I strode around the house, spotting the tree easily. It captivated my attention and made me lengthen my strides.

Its branches were weathered and creaking but they still hung protectively. The leaves covering it were beginning to yellow, while the occasional brown one fell to the ground, overeager.

I pressed my palm to the bark of the old tree, smiling sadly. The ghosts of my memory were there, and I could see me in my ignorant youth with Kate, sprawled out on a blanket. The sun was warm then, the world was kind...

The light rain on my shoulder was cold and kept me from completely losing myself to the phantoms. I felt like I could reach out and touch them, the children there. If I could warn them, maybe they could avoid this cruel fate.

"Was this the tree...?" asked Robert in a quiet murmur that could easily have been lost in the breeze. He came up beside me, touching it with wonder.

"Yes," I choked, then sighed as I forced my grief away. I allowed my smile to remain and wiped silent tears from my face. If only there could be a day when I was not falling into tears. "This tree...There, I carved that for Kate when she asked me to. We were, oh, eighteen and fifteen?"

Robert's fingers traced the delicately carved lettering. The tree had begun to regrow the bark, smudging it somewhat, but it was just as gorgeous as it had first been. My own claws had carved it. I had never quite believed that my hands could craft anything so graceful.

"Wow. You never mentioned it," he said, stunned. He continued to admire it.

"If you stride through a forest, every other tree is marked in a similar fashion. It is nothing particularly remarkable," I replied coolly. I sighed sharply, looking back the way we had come. "I believe I am ready to leave now."

He turned to me, eyes watchful. He smiled slightly, and I sensed that he was attempting to comfort me with the gesture. "We can come back again."

"No," I said quickly, sharply. The rain was coming down harder while the sky darkened slowly. "No, I would rather have the unfamiliar world than ghosts haunting me everywhere I turn."

"Right. Where are your parents—Ah." His voice trailed off weakly as we caught sight of the two headstones not forty feet from the tree. Robert was frozen while I strode over slowly to kneel between the two graves. I stared at the stiff lettering, the rigidity of the reality settling around me coldly.

Here lies the woman who could love me as her own and the man that could call me 'son'. My mother and father. I reached out to touch the coarse stones that were wet now. I knew well that the parent passed before the child; it was common and natural. What they had endured to reach these quiet, modest graves was harsh and cruel.

"I'm sorry," I whispered, forgetting Robert's stoic presence. I wanted to believe that they could hear me, that the heaven they had known as reality existed and they were happy there. "I'm home too late, and not to stay."

Robert's hand brushed my shoulder. "I'm sorry we couldn't get you out of there sooner."

"No," I sighed, standing tiredly. My body was only worn because of my mind's exhaustion, I knew. I wanted to sleep for days, hoping that the excess rest might be able to heal my hidden bruises. "No, those who cared did all that they had the power to do."

When I turned around, the guilty expression that Robert wore told me he had been an individual set against my freedom. For the safety of young children or the purity of the world. Whatever his reasoning, I did not fault him for it. It would be foolish of me if I blamed all who spurned me.

"Well..." he mumbled awkwardly, glancing back at the way we had come. The fields that had once bore fruitful crops were barren now, allowing us to see the vehicle sitting on the street. He sighed, making his way in that direction.

Wistfully, I hesitated a moment longer in the rain before following Robert. glancing over my shoulder at the old house that was familiar and strange, I waved farewell to

Lisa on the porch. The communication we had was silent but allowed us the closure we had been needing. Whether we would visit again, I did not know.

As I found my way into the confines of the car, I knew that I would sleep easier tonight. I felt more complete, more like myself after seeing my sister. I stared out the window and watched my old home disappear from view without remorse.

"I'm sorry for acting out of turn," said Robert quietly after a few minutes of driving. I continued to stare out the window, heart aching when we passed Paul's old broken down home. "I've been forgetting that you're my patient and not my..."

"Uninvited guest?" I murmured. The town was behind us now. I looked over to see him scowling at the road.

"Friend," he corrected, startling me. He glanced at me and sighed. "Yeah, I know, it's bad for a therapist to get attached. If you'd feel more comfortable switching to someone more competent, I would understand."

I took a moment to compose myself. "No, no. I am confident in your abilities, only...A friend?"

Again, we were victims of silence while we each thought. The rain continued to barrage the car thunderously. Some hour or so later, when we stopped to rest and stretch, Robert cried out abruptly in anger. I looked over at him curiously, concerned about his well being.

"Robert, what is the matter?" I asked, all too aware of the strange glances passersby were giving us.

He sighed heavily, shaking his head slowly. "I've been played. We've *both* been played!"

Demon *Rising*

"How?" He was wringing his hands and beginning to pace. I watched with a frown, disconcerted for a moment while I recalled that the man having what I could only recognize as a breakdown was my therapist.

Robert stopped in front of me, sneering. "There are hundreds of people who would do better at my job. The N.S.I.S.D. *wants* you to be considered a threat and come back, they *want* me to screw everything up and I'm doing a damn fine job of it!"

I nodded slowly, his realization making clear sense. After all, Beth had allowed me to leave without any defiance. Even as old as she was, that woman never backed down without a fight.

"And you agree," he noted with a sigh, sitting heavily.

"Not at all. Robert, you are a good man and, while I do believe that I require assistance with my faculties, a companion is much more useful than paid assistance. In my experience, at least," I added, seeing his incredulity.

He sighed again, not seeming comforted or convinced. "Sadly, the world's changed from what your experience was. You get more if you pay someone sometimes than you can from a friend."

The rain was slow, a soft mist compared to the storm earlier. "Well, since you are both my friend and being paid, I do suppose I am still better off than with one of those other individuals you seem so overshadowed by, hm?"

Robert laughed and shook his head. "You're nuts."

"The reason I need you, no?" I grinned, lifted from my sympathetic gloom when he smiled in return. "Shall we continue homeward?"

Demon *Rising*

~~ * ~ * ~ * ~~

August 28th, 2010

My imagination or my age must be melting through my mind. The days have gotten shorter now, less difficult to drag through. This is something that Robert told me may happen after a few months—not weeks. Now he tells me that I must just be one who is swift in recovery.

I have begun to feel otherwise. I have begun to feel...tired. The days are shorter and easier, yes, but I am numb now to it. Most of me wants to be numb. Seeing Lisa helped nothing, and my brothers are unwilling to visit me just yet. They are both in difficult positions, and I would not be of any aid but only be an impedance.

Hope is not all lost yet, I suppose. I do not want this hope, though. It is sharp and bright, but would be painful to lose. The old window to the outside, my long lost childhood hope for a brighter life. A life I could call my own and perhaps children who could call me father. A wife, my fiancée...

Robert has created a list of all Katelyn Smiths in the city. If lain out from paper to paper, it might stretch the length of the front lawn! How had I never noticed just how common her name was? Or has it become more prevalent in recent years?

We begin searching next Monday, at eight in the morning. He will take a picture of her with him so that he will know her face and we will embark to search the city for her, address by address.

The very thought of a successful venture has my

Demon *Rising*

heart racing even now! But I am still wary. After all, she may yet live, but how does she live? For or against demons? Alone or...wedded?

Broken

Robert Smith rung the doorbell, impatient while his concern continued to rage within him. He sighed heavily, checking his watch with a frown. Cory should still be out searching for Kate. Robert still had an hour before he met with the demon for lunch.

"Come on, come on," he muttered, rechecking the address he held. He glanced at the numbers beside the door. This was the place.

"Are you sure this is the right place?" asked a dark-skinned elderly woman beside him.

Robert nodded. "Yes, I'm positive, Kate. She should be here."

The door opened to an annoyed, withered woman. She glared at Robert. "What are *you* here for? And who on earth is she?"

"This is Katelyn Smith, and we're here with some questions for you, Beth," replied Robert, given up on appearing sharp or commanding with this woman.

Beth shrugged and opened the door. "Well, then, won't you come in?"

Robert nodded and lead the way, glancing behind to check that Kate was following. Beth closed the door before guiding them to a clean, decorated living space. She motioned to an attractive sofa before sitting in her own chair across from it.

"Please, have a seat," she said, and Robert thought she sounded rather dry. "What answers do you want?"

They took their seats, shifting awkwardly before Katelyn spoke first. "I need to know what happened to Cory at that place. Robert told me that you were an employee there."

"He's too modest. I was the head of operations," replied Beth, meeting Robert's eye. He felt a weight on his shoulders, a guilt that told him they never should have come. "Exactly what events would you like to know about?"

"You...experimented on him." Robert heard how difficult the words were for Kate, and he wondered for a moment how she even managed to speak them. "How?"

Beth laughed quietly. "You don't want to know that."

"I have to," said Kate, tone sharp. Robert leaned forward with a quiet sigh.

"She may be taking Mr. Lawrence into her home soon, with her two grandchildren. We need to know triggers, events, things that will be coming up so that we can also prepare for how to help him," explained Robert, meeting Beth's gaze. She nodded with a smile.

"So you came to me? I'm touched, truly." She sighed and stood, motioning for them to follow. "Everything you want is in my study. This way."

Following Beth, Robert kept his eyes out to see what kind of woman she was. He was surprised to find wedding pictures on the walls, images of children and families. What startled him most was when they came upon her study, and beside thick envelopes was set a picture of what he presumed was her granddaughter.

"Let me see..." She shuffled over to a filing cabinet and began pulling out folders. "Images, test results, theories. They're all organized by date."

Katelyn rushed forward to take the folders from Beth and set them on the desk to flip through. "Thank you."

"Don't thank me yet, girl." Beth took her seat at the desk, pulling out a particularly worn folder. "This was the first year. Here...is the first test."

Robert came over, skimming the page. "It was just a blood draw."

Beth laughed. "Yes, I know. Would you like to see what Mr. Lawrence did to us for that little draw?"

She flipped a page to show them the photographs. Katelyn gasped sharply while Robert felt his stomach churn in horror. He flipped through all of the images, bile rising in his throat.

"Oh, God," he managed to whisper, shaking his head slowly. "I can't believe that Cory would ever..."

"I love that picture," commented Beth, apparently ignoring both of their reactions. "You see that? That there was what was left of our steel chair that we designed to hold him. Worked about as well as wet paper. And that stallion still refused to break for another twenty years."

"What...? Why...?" Robert could not find himself to finish his questions.

Beth turned her response to Katelyn, who stood trembling with tears in her eyes. "You wanted to know what happened to the poor demon. What we did while experimenting? Torture, easily enough dealt with comparatively."

"Speak clearly, Beth," commanded Robert, still somewhat faint. He was managing to find control, pushing his devastation aside for the moment.

Beth looked between the two of them, her words condescending. "You still don't understand, do you? The worst, most defiling act was the first one. Can you even imagine that?"

"You're a monster!" spat Kate.

"Yes, I'm well aware, but at least I can understand his nightmare," retorted Beth, narrowing her eyes slightly. "We took everything from him. Imagine that, just that. He began in a room, and when he lost everything—think, *everything*—he found himself again in a room. Do you honestly believe that whatever else we did makes any difference? Oh, poor boy has a fear of sharp, shiny objects. Easily acquired without our assistance."

Robert's heart sank. "Everything he ever wanted."

Beth laughed, the sound cruel to Robert's ears. "Worse, boy. Everything he needed."

Chapter Five:
Embrace

Fifth Week Under Protection

Monday

I landed on the front lawn, tucking my wings in. I shook my head, cursing how silly I had been in thinking that finding Kate would be as simple as knocking on a few doors before the woman I had chased for so long stood in front of me, ready to welcome me home.

No, I had not anticipated the day. When Robert and I had started out, we had both been hopeful. Then, when we met for dinner, while we were not quite as enthusiastic we both still had hope. Now, seeing him waiting for me on the porch with a drawn face, I knew he had succeeded more than I only in that people did not scream and slam their doors when they saw him.

"No luck?" he asked.

"None," I sighed tiredly, following him into the house. The smell of supper after the long day was intoxicating, making my mouth water. I was far too worn to care what it was or identify the scent.

Bailey and Anne were in the kitchen cooking, and they both looked at us hopefully when they saw us enter.

Demon *Rising*

"Did you guys find her?" asked Bailey, face transforming slowly from her smile to a look of total despair. "You didn't find her."

"Please," I said quietly, backing out of the room slowly. "No more mention of the topic tonight."

Before they could stop me with words, I hurried to the back door. Where no armed soldiers were waiting for me, I found a place at the edge of the light to sit and contemplate. The darkness shrouding me was comforting to my mind only briefly, but it was enough of a reprieve.

Think, now. What happened today? I questioned myself, following Robert's advice to inquire as to what was upsetting me. What happened that caused the emotion? When did I begin to feel this way?

After the twelfth woman had screamed at me to leave her be. Or perhaps after the fifteenth can was thrown. Was it the countless stares and insults? Maybe it was the restaurant that had refused to serve "my kind" unless it was medium rare.

"Momma, what's wrong with me?"

"Nothing, honey, you're a perfect little angel."

Had she lied? Had I lied to myself by believing her? I pulled my body close together, hunching as I felt as though the world was closing in around me. I wanted her guidance again, as well as Father's. I wanted them to hold me and tell me that all would be well. Was I weak for that? Was I dumb, childish?

The sound of the door opening behind me startled me.

"Hey," greeted Bailey calmly, sitting beside me. She stared up at the sky with me.

The moon was gorgeous and full, glittering in the

185

night. The air was crisp, making the sky even clearer to my eyes. Briefly, I wondered how the night would look to the human girl beside me. Was it as precious and rich as I saw it? Oh, and richer still because it shrouded me, all of my ugliness in scars and inhumanity in features, because I was embraced by the place that had protected me faithfully for years.

"So..." Her voice broke the silence, making us both jump slightly. "Who is this Katelyn person?"

I smiled at the stars, recalling the first time Kate had sat beside me beneath them. They had not changed terribly, which made me glad. "She is...*was* my fiancée. We were going to wed in the spring of 1970 if not for...an accident?" I finished uncertainly, the memory on the verge of breaking through to me. I shifted uncomfortably, unnerved by the dark sense I had from the forgotten past.

"Oh. Wow, that was a long time ago..." she stated plainly.

"Ah. Yes, it was," I agreed warily, allowing an awkward silence to ensue.

"So, um, I'm going to guess that you noticed I hide something from my dad?" she asked suddenly. What on earth was the girl doing? Or saying? She had certainly succeeded in confusing me and capturing my rapt attention.

"Yes."

"Well...um...that's because I—I like girls," she rushed, then paused to take a deep breath and steady herself. "And, you know, it can be kind of hard sometimes."

I paused, frowning deeply. A heavy sigh escaped me unintentionally and I closed my eyes. "I apologize—"

"Look, I don't want any pity—"

186

"No, not pity," I interrupted swiftly, words harsher than I intended. I opened my eyes and smiled down at her gently. "Bailey, I do not understand why you are telling me...this."

"There's a pill for everything, in Dad's words. I'm kind of surprised that he's actually searching with you. So, you know, you looked down and I wanted to say I know it's hard, but don't give up," she explained, staring up at me oddly. Her face was honest, leaving me awkward again.

I looked away again, listening to the distant sound of cars. While her thought was endearing, it made me seriously consider what I was actually doing. Kate would have her own life now. Her own home, her own family. She may well not wish to see me.

"Thank you, Bailey." I nodded to myself, rearranging what I should do with myself. Perhaps I could travel, like I once imagined. I could have no home, nothing to be tied to but the sky.

Bailey smiled. "Cool. When are you going to start searching tomorrow?"

"I will not be searching anymore, Bailey. I will look for ways to...move on," I tried the phrasing, but it did not feel quite right, like betrayal on my tongue.

The small girl bristled. "You can't do that! Just take whatever you and Kate had for granted and then toss it away!"

"It is none of your concern—"

"Fine! Move on. But I know plenty of people who would be lucky to have the opportunity you have right now, you overgrown shoulder devil!"

The door slammed shut behind her, making me sigh. I would be unsurprised if no one understood my

187

intentions. Already, I had discovered my home and town tattered and half-ruined. The farm was going to be sold; that place was long dead.

I had seen my family and how they were fairing. I phoned my brothers and neither had wanted to visit, but all was well with them. Ethan had sounded strange and old, very meek compared to how outwardly hostile he had been before. Dustin was mourning the loss of his wife, as she had passed some three months ago. Lisa was happy with the family she had raised, and I was satisfied after visiting my parents' graves and saying farewell to them.

The final item on my list was to find Katelyn. If I found her, I would see how well she was. I hoped that I would find home with her but it was a fool's dream, and I was not young enough nor a dreamer to imagine that she was unmarried or otherwise unengaged with someone. But I would seek her out, if only for one last glimpse of her.

Would there be a life after this for me? Could I find some other desire to urge me onward? Or would I go to a hell and serve a purpose too cruel to think of? Where did demons go when they died?

I stared at the moon longingly. I wanted to stay forever in the sky, with the moon and the stars. The ability to be in the daylight and look down on the vibrant colors of the world would also be a wonder, but I had to be in the sky. Always, the enchanting sky.

"But that would be wrong," I murmured to myself, shaking my head slowly. My tears fell delicately onto my arm, diamonds in the moonlight. "There is no rest for the wicked."

Sighing heavily, I brushed the tears from my skin and returned indoors. Supper no longer smelled appetizing.

Demon *Rising*

I slunk past the kitchen to the stairs, not wanting to encounter Robert or Anne, who were talking quietly in the kitchen. When finally I reached the safety of my room, I found paper and pen to relieve myself through words.

Tuesday

"This is taking too long," sighed Robert at dinner. Thankfully, the place of choice had an outdoor patio and the sun was warm on the final day of August.

"It would be terribly convenient of her to step around a corner into view somewhat spontaneously, as she did last time," I agreed tiredly. Four hours of searching in two separate places and still, nothing. If anything, I thought we may have been taking steps backward.

Santos and Thompson were seated on either side of me, not bothering to dress casually. They were both enjoying the meal, as well, and I imagined that this was a wonderful reprieve from standing and staring at the same dull-colored street every day.

"This lady sure is hard to find," commented Thompson as he finished his meal in what could have been mistaken for a single inhalation. For some curious reason, the boy thought eating was a higher priority than breathing. Curiouser yet, his face had not turned blue.

Santos was taking his time with his soup, however, scowling at Thompson. "*Woman*, Thompson, there's a big difference, and women are far more preferable."

Thompson just shook his head. "I don't get it."

"You will," added Robert. He pushed his half-eaten plate of food in Thompson's direction. "Still hungry?"

"Am I?" He dug in happily.

"So, are we calling it a day or continuing?" asked Santos, looking only at me.

"Continuing. The faster we work through these blasted lists, the faster we know if she even lives in this city," I replied, against all odds finding a new well of determination to draw from.

Thompson grinned, already finished with the second plate. "Woo-hoo! I am all for not standing around again."

We all stared at Thompson, and I was glad to have his light mood handy. It would certainly help me to keep what little sanity I had left in the days sure to come.

～～ * ～ * ～ * ～～

September 1ˢᵗ, 2010

Nothing. Still, all we find is nothing! It is as if we have begun to search for a needle in a haystack, but the needle has gotten bored and left us to our futile treasure hunt. If that indeed is what we are doing, treasure hunting. Or are we just looking to confirm all of the atrocious suspicions and what-ifs that we have all thought what must be a thousand times now?

No, it cannot be pointless. It cannot be hopeless. There has to be something left to hold on to. There must be, because I feel as though there is nothing left.

190

Demon *Rising*

~~ * ~ * ~ * ~~

Thursday

The fourth day now, and at last the weather had begun to mimic my darkening mood. Clouds had settled in sometime after dinner and I had donned a beautifully sewn cloak that I had crafted, so that I would have protection over my wings from the rain.

After nightfall, I had asked Thompson and Santos to allow me to wander alone. It was unlikely that anyone would genuinely recognize me with the dark material pulled about me and covering my face, wings and tail. Not in the dark, at least. They had assented with little protest, leaving me to myself in the cool night on a dark street corner, the words on the paper making little sense to my weary eyes.

With another glance at the street sign to confirm what I had read, I began to make my way down the lonely and rainy sidewalk. My enthusiasm was spent after days of searching for the correct name and house, so my strides were shortened and slowed to postpone the coming disappointment. The rain was becoming heavier, transforming from mist to a light shower before I was four houses down the lane.

A yellow vehicle drove past me slowly, catching my eye. Of course, it had to be her favorite color that I saw this depressing eve, only minutes before fate slapped me again. I watched it pull into a driveway some five homes away. Across the street was a booth with a phone, and I considered calling Robert without confirming or denying the final address. I was tired and in no mood to be spurned

191

yet again.

"...have any of the soda because you'll never get to sleep tonight," said a hauntingly familiar voice, down the street. I looked back at the yellow car and the woman retrieving groceries from it. There were two children revolving around her with flitting movements. I stared in wonder, disbelieving of the sight until I saw her sure walk.

I frowned, half-reaching a hand to her instinctively. Did she not see me? Could she not recognize who I was? My heart twisted before I recalled that I was intentionally covered by a cloak. She did glance down the street toward me, but the expression on her face was wary of me. Still, her eyes caught and held me for a moment where I could not breathe.

"Come on, inside and no more arguing about the soda. In, in," she repeated when she opened the door to her home, ushering the children inside. I nearly called to her to stop, to come to me.

"Kate," I murmured softly, the name nearly lost in the beginning rumble of thunder overhead. I hurried over to the phone, a new course of action mapping itself in my mind. I could walk not a hundred feet, knock on that simple door and see her, the woman who had once brightened my dark room.

Suddenly, I realized how weak a will I had when she was a temptation, and I was glad for it. I needed someone from the past in a place without ghosts, where we could be unbound by what we could recall happening in the room from years gone by.

I inserted the required amount of coins before dialing and waiting impatiently. Every second that blazed by felt too long, and I knew that it brought her a second closer to her bed and sleep. Every tick of the clock meant that I may have to wait longer—*hours* longer—to see her.

Finally, he answered his phone. "Hello?"

"She's here, I need to go but don't worry—"

"Cory?" he asked sharply, sounding stunned. I was surprised as well by my rush of words and zeal.

"Yes?"

"Try again, but slowly."

"I found the home. I found her," I told Robert, nearly choking. Was my lack of breath due to excitement or fear? I did not know. I spoke slowly and meticulously, so as to keep my voice level and my mind calm. "I...I need to see her, to know that she is happy..."

"Wait for me, Cory. If you have a nervous breakdown—"

"No, that will not happen," I said firmly. Some powerful, deep part of me knew this. Similarly, it knew that I was where I needed to be and that everything was right. Through the scratched, filthy panes of the booth I could see the lights of her home. My heart was too loud in my ears and it felt as though my chest should not be able to contain it.

Robert sighed. "Fine. Which address is it, so that I know where to find you?"

"The final one on today's list. If I do not call you when the visit is over, please come by in the morning to see that everything is fine," I requested, terrified. The emotion that had my tail twitching and hands shaking was raw terror. Forty years. How much had changed? Worse yet, had she forgotten me?

"Of course. Cory?" He sounded awkward and apprehensive.

193

Demon *Rising*

"Yes?"

He sighed again, defeated. "Good luck."

"Drive safely and good evening, Robert. My regards to your family."

I placed the phone gently back, stepping out of the booth and into the rain. I kept myself hidden as I crossed the street, fists clenched.

"Will you marry me?"

My memory stirred, enchanting and horrifying.

"Yes."

As I approached the door, the rain became heavier. I sighed, watching a silhouette moving about in what I thought would be the kitchen. I knew it must have been her. I could feel her presence as I came closer, walking up the small path to the doorstep.

"Do you mean that?"

The years apart...What had they done?

"No. I...I just need to see you."

There was a strong sense that everything that had occurred had brought me to stand at that dark door, on that rainy street, scarred halfway beyond recognition. I could recall all that had happened to me, and now I was walking forward toward a future I could never anticipate. My knock on the door was loud and firm, sure to be heard even over the growing sound of the rain. I was nervous as I had never been before.

I assumed she had married like everyone else I had known, so it was no surprise when a small child answered the door.

"Is Katelyn home?" I asked gently, not wanting to frighten the young boy. He should not have been able to see me with how well I had concealed myself beneath the cloak, but my voice would have done the trick just as well as my face.

He smiled and nodded. "Yeah, just a minute. Lemme go get her." He ran off, leaving the door wide open and calling out loudly, "Grandma! Grandma, there's a man for you at the door!"

"Oh, there is? Okay, okay, I'm coming," she laughed. I sighed, a wave of comfort overtaking me at the sound of Kate's voice.

When she came into my view, I was surprised. She did not look as old as I had thought she would. Her face had aged, a few strands of her hair had turned silver, but she appeared no older than her mid-forties, with a smile I wished I could have seen so much sooner. Her eyes were still near black and depthless, catching me off guard for a moment and trapping me.

All of the love that had gone neglected during the testing flooded me. It was all I could do to keep from going to meet her in a hug as tears sprung to my eyes and a sob escaped me. I could see that she was well, and now could not find the will to turn and leave.

I never should have come. My place in her life, in what once was my life, had long since vanished and been filled with other things. Her children and grandchildren, her husband. I choked on that thought.

"May I help you, sir?" she greeted me as a stranger.

"Kate," I managed to sigh, pulling back my hood enough for her to see my face, keeping hidden the worst of my scars. She gasped and stumbled back in shock, eyes wide. "I apologize. I should not have come."

"Cory?" she breathed, eyes watering. She stepped out into the rain with me, touching my hand with hers. She

195

fell forward, wrapping her arms around me, shaking with violently sobs. "Cory!"

I held her. There was nothing else I could think to do. I did my best to keep her dry, and then I began to cry with her. When she touched me, the world shifted from the nightmare it had been the last few decades. , back to a night that never should have gone awry. I wanted to stay, to share life with her as I had planned. My chest was crushed from the grief.

"I missed you," she sobbed brokenly, shaking harder. "And you stopped calling. I've missed you!"

"I know, and I am very sorry for that," I told her. It was righteous judgment that I felt her pain now, when I had been the one to cause it many times over, no matter how I did or did not remember it.

"I thought you'd died." She pulled back and stared up at me, face contorted in pain.

"No, no, no, shh, I'm fine. I promised you, Kate," I choked. The porch swing felt like it had happened in another lifetime as I echoed dully, "I promised you."

"Grandma, who is that man?" asked the little boy who had answered the door.

"He's really ugly," a girl whispered to the boy. I laughed at first, amused by the honesty of youth, and then had to fight back more sobs. That was what had caused my entire life to unfold as it had: the way my body looked. I was an outcast for it, a science experiment.

Katelyn turned around to face the two children, ushering them in again. "Kyle, Sarah, go inside and get ready for bed. Now."

"Yes, grandma…"

Katelyn took my hand and led me into the home,

glancing behind at me with concern. I closed the door behind me, falling into my older rhythms, mindful of my claws and grateful for the eight-foot ceilings. Kate took me to the living room where toys were scattered across the blue carpet. There was one of those new televisions, as thin as a book, set on a stand across from a deep blue sofa.

She released my hand and motioned to the sofa, "Maximum capacity's 800. You should be safe. I need to go tuck in the little ones."

I nodded and took a seat, sighing heavily. Why had I come here? What was the purpose? I waited anxiously for either Kate or her husband to walk in.

"No, no stories tonight, you had them last night and I'm visiting with my friend." A pause. "Yes, tomorrow night." Kate sighed. "And I'm sure Cory will be here in the morning, you can talk to him then. No, no more questions. Sleep tight!"

She sighed when she came back into the living room and stood by the couch awkwardly. She looked anywhere but at me, wringing her hands nervously. Why?

"You should be able to sit on the couch safely. I am not quite that heavy, you know," I said to break the silence.

She smiled and nodded. "How much are you nowadays? You look like you grew again, of all things."

"Seven feet four inches, twenty-two foot wingspan and 344 pounds. The way the scientists put it was I 'fully matured' at 30," I half-chuckled, thinking again of my freedom and the small victory in it. Katelyn's expression cut me off sharply.

"How can you still laugh? I read the papers, I know what ungodly things they did to you!" she nearly shouted. She took a deep breath to calm herself. Her eyes began to

197

water again. "I cried myself to sleep every night. I still have nightmares of when they...I heard when you got out, but I didn't know where you were!"

I did not know if it was my place to stand and comfort her, so I buried my head in my hands. "I know. And I can hardly recall half the things they did to me. I tried to stay together for you, so that when I got out—"

"What? You could come back and see if you still had something left of your old life? Dustin and Ethan hardly missed you!" she snapped, tears soaking her lashes when I glanced up. "Lisa gave up twenty years ago. I'm the only one who's held on this long, Cory. I can't hold on any longer. I'm alone most of the time, and it's all been because I've waited for you."

I stood then and took her in my arms. "I'm sorry. I never wanted...I hoped you had someone to be there with you. I wished it was me, but anyone kind would have sufficed if it meant you would not have to be alone."

"I wanted *you*," she sobbed, shaking in my arms again. I wrapped my tail around her as well, praying that it would calm her some. "No one else...Just you."

"Sh, I know," I whispered, loathing myself. I wished I had been cruel and evil, that she could have seen me with clear eyes and moved on to someone else who could have given her so much more. Her children and grandchildren. This home, perhaps.

All of the things I still wanted to give her but would never be able to.

"I love you still." As if those words could replace everything I had not done.

She sobbed harder. "I love you, Cory."

Those words made the night all the better, as though

it would be stars in the sky rather than stormy rains. Alas, the time was weighing heavy on my mind and I began to pull away gently. Her hands caught me firmly and she stared up at me with her enthralling black eyes.

"Will you stay tonight?" she whispered, and I wondered if she could bear to speak any louder.

She could have persuaded deities with those eyes.

"Where will I sleep?" I asked her in a beaten tone. She had won; I was at her mercy.

"With me in my bed, if you're still interested," she said with a small smile. At my puzzled stare, she added, "I'm not married. Never have been." Her smile fell suddenly, and she frowned as though something had just occurred to her, "Cory...Your face..."

I bent my head lower and allowed her to trace over the scars on my lips, eyelids, jaw. After the years of being cut and studied, her gently stroking fingers were a relief. She wiped tears away as she had decades ago, bringing more of them to my eyes. I dropped to my knees and pulled her close, pressing my cheek to hers carefully. She wrapped her arms around my neck and we stayed there for some time, refusing to release one another.

"What did they do to you?" whispered Kate after awhile. I could feel her beginning to shake with what must have been a fright.

I gave her a reassuring squeeze. "A few scrapes and bruises. I can tell you another time..."

She flipped back the hood of my cloak, gasping in horror. "What...?! Oh, Cory, what did they *do*?!"

"Just a few tests...Experiments," I relinquished unwillingly, desiring to spend a night in peace with her at long last.

"What are you hiding?" she demanded, stepping back and pulling back the cloak covering my front and arms, gasping when she glimpsed the skin revealed there. Her face contorted in anguish and she met my eyes in terror. "Why didn't you tell me?"

"If I said anything, they would revoke the phone privileges that Paul worked to get for me," I told her, wishing to keep my other reasons private for the time. My memory was on fire, things coming to me with a horrifically natural flow.

"That's not all of it. You can't lie." Her hand traced the blemishes across my arm, distracting me for an instant. Her eyes were grieving, tears overflowing. For a moment, I was glad for the shirt that hid the worst of the marks.

I sighed regretfully. "They were people with families, Kate. You know I would never dare to endanger whatever they had."

She glared at me hatefully, startling me. "They did the same thing to you! They took you away from us, for no good reason! They took everything away from you, from all of us."

"I know!" I cried out, beginning to sob. "I would never want their children or spouses to have to suffer that. I mourn that the rest of you lost what you did, and every day I wish that there was some reward for what I sacrificed in there, but none exists! The only thought that consoles me is that their lives are still worth living."

She stared at me in despair as I allowed myself to finish breaking. So many years that had gone unsaid, "their lives are still worth living." My sobs ripped from my chest, sounding unbearably loud to my ears. I forced myself to quiet, recalling briefly the young children in the other room. I caught myself on one hand to keep from falling to the floor, covering my face with the other while I grieved.

No matter the freedom I had miraculously been granted, they had won. I was broken.

Kate pulled my hand from my face gently. She pressed her lips to my forehead softly and looked me in the eyes as she sat on the floor beside me. She was crying, as well.

"Your life has always been worth living," she whispered, brow furrowing with her distress. "I've never met anyone as loving or gentle as you. I never will."

I ached terribly with a muddled combination of painful emotions. "In these past years, I have come to wonder just what I am anymore."

"You're Cory," she laughed in a whisper, taking my hand in hers. "You're my—my angel of 54 years, and you're home...You're finally back home."

"Can I be?" I asked, seeking permission to be home. Why did I? Why did I feel so inadequate and undeserving now, when I sat beside her? Was it guilt? Whatever it was, it brought tears to my eyes again.

She nodded slowly. "You can be home."

I wrapped my tail around her waist, smiling with an odd relief at her words. Again, as in younger years, I wondered how even a human man could possibly have deserved her. "Thank you...Thank you."

"You're always welcome." She yawned then, reminding me of just how late it must have been. Kate sighed tiredly, gaze drowsy. Then she smiled at me meaningfully. "Have you ever not wanted to be tired?"

"Come now. Let's get you to bed," I said quietly,

helping her to stand. I smiled at her gently. "Shall I carry you to your bed?"

"Mm..." She shook her head, steadying herself. "It's upstairs."

"An easy journey." I lifted her carefully, beginning the trek up the stairs. I chuckled. "Oh, I have missed this."

"Mm..." she murmured, eyes already shut. At the top of the stairs, there was a small open room that looked down over the living room from behind simple railing. There were two doors—one so close to the wall I assumed it was a linen closet.

I opened the door on my right to a dark bedroom. Lit dimly by light from the street, there was a bed with the head of it against the farthest wall. To my right when I entered, there was a wardrobe against the wall. I strode to the bed and pulled back the coverings, laying Kate to sleep. I replaced the covers, tucking her in tenderly.

Returning downstairs, I switched the lights off before going back to Kate's room. I was torn between my exhaustion and excitement. A portion of me was also mortified of sleeping, lest I wake alone.

When I closed the door quietly behind me and set myself on the bed beside her—dominating more space than could possibly exist on the mattress—Kate stirred slightly with a startled, sad moan. I wrapped an arm around her, pulling her close to me.

"Sh, sh," I hushed gently, not wanting her to delve into any distressful memories. "Rest now, Kate, I am here. Everything is fine now."

She nodded drowsily. After a few minutes, her breathing evened out to the distantly familiar pattern I had buried in the deepest parts of my memory. It was comforting and disorienting to hear. I was accustomed to a lonely room and an empty bed to share with myself. Holding her close to me brought back the years when I could recall the shadows of a yearning to propose, when we had even lightly discussed children...

Our ages put all of that out of reach now.

With a yawn, my thoughts settled into a numb hum in the background of awareness. I was warm beside Kate and loving where I was and how I was, even as I could not sleep. Anytime I began to doze, I would start awake with a shock of fear, but the warmth of her against me and the sound of her breathing calmed me easily. Sometime in the night, I wrapped my tail over her, smiling even as I watched the sky outside beginning to gray with the morning light.

Soon now, I thought slowly. Oh, and how beautiful it was to remember her face in the morning and know that I would see her soon. Exhausted, I somehow found a small burst of excitement at the thought of her morning smile.

As Kate began to stir beside me I sighed quietly, tiredly. The light from the window was gray and pale, rain pattering against the pane gently. I stared at it, brought back to the farm house for a moment. The chilly days in the fall when Kate and I would lay beneath the warm blankets on my bed, content to be just where we were, as we were. So young, we saw time and the world as endless creations that could never possibly hurt us...

I found myself in tears again, my palm pressed gently to Kate's cheek as I began to understand where I was. She was there beside me and warm against my side— my window into the world I could not touch, and my safety now that I was in that world. The missing piece I had dreamt of when I was younger, the woman that had taken to liking a monster. Oh, were that I could give her the world to do with as she pleased, then I could be content with myself at last!

With a groan and a sigh, Kate's hand found mine on her face, a small smile of comfort brightening the room considerably. "Mm...Good morning."

"Good is far too bland a word. Spectacular may do the job," I replied with a smile, shifting onto my left side so that I could view her fully. With a content sigh I murmured, "I missed you."

She nodded before catching the double meaning of my words. "Were you awake all night?"

"I was afraid of sleeping," I explained quietly, dropping my eyes to the sheet sheepishly. With her free hand she began to trace the scars across my face contemplatively.

"So was I," she admitted, then paused for a moment. Sounds from downstairs came through the floor, muffled. She sighed. "Kids are up. That means I am, too."

"Would you prefer to continue resting?" I asked, sitting up slowly. My body felt worn from lack of sleep.

Kate laughed. "And you'll what, Mr. 1960? *I* can hardly keep up with today's technology."

I paused but refused to become fazed. "Oh, I should find a way to manage. At least in entertaining and feeding children, if not coordinating my way about highly glamored technology boxes."

She frowned at me. "Are you talking about a TV, microwave or computer?"

A *what*? I sighed. "I will see to breakfast."

"Mm...I haven't had your cooking in years," she

murmured, sitting up and throwing her legs off the edge of the bed. I did the same, standing and stretching as best I could with my physical limitations. Even so, my right arm flared, making me hiss quietly. I chuckled at her words regardless, turning to face her while rubbing my crippled shoulder.

"What's wrong?" she asked, furrowing her brow in concern.

"Ah...My arm is permanently injured. A side-effect of a particularly unpleasant surgery, I am afraid," I replied. Something crashed on the floor below, making Kate and I jump.

Her eyes were wide. "They're trying to get into the sugared goods."

And, with a manner so familiar to me I could have been fooled that these were our own children, she rushed downstairs to keep them from whatever sweet treats that she had made recently. Chortling softly to myself, I retrieved my cloak before descending into the lower premises. The two children were sitting on the couch, staring at the television with strangely shaped remotes held between their hands. I frowned.

"Children, what on earth are you doing?" I asked, glancing at the alien screen, intimidated. I had a sudden yearning for the church and the seasonal gatherings with a radio.

"Video games," replied Kyle hurriedly without looking at me.

"Ah..." I was uncertain as to what he meant by those words. My frown deepened. "Would a book not be a better suited activity for a stormy day such as this?"

"Good luck trying to get them to read," called Kate

from the kitchen, behind me. "They're not interested when they have the TV."

I shook my head in disbelief as I joined her in the kitchen. "Where are your books, if I may ask?"

She smiled at me. "You may. I'll show you in a minute, just let me get their breakfast ready."

I waited patiently, observing her while I had a lulling moment. She wore flannel pants and what appeared to be a spare shirt for her evening clothes, as she had on occasion years ago. Amazingly, time had been as forgiving to her as it had been cruel to me. Her form was as enticing as I last recalled and her skin was still smooth and glowing, interrupted only by the laughter or sadness lines around her eyes and mouth.

Had it in fact been that karma was kind to her to atone for the carelessness taken with me, I never would have thought to change it. She was meant to be beautiful, as I was to be ugly, and I would bear scars enough for us both if it kept her in such perfect conditions.

"You know, it's rude to stare," she said quietly, breaking my trance.

I shook my head with an incredulous laugh. "Of course, it would be you to remind me."

She served eggs onto plates with jam toast, placing them on the table between the living room and the kitchen. The children rushed over to the table eagerly, as if summoned by some magical force only apparent to their ears. I smiled, my own stomach protesting at my lack of food. After the years, however, food was not as exciting as it had been in youth. I was more intrigued by the books, and discovering all there was in this new life of mine. And this did feel more like life than the recovery time at

206

Robert's.

Kate led me to a small hallway at the other end of the living area, where there were three doors—one on the left, right, and direct center. Opening the door on the left, she stepped inside.

"Um...When it seemed like you weren't coming back, I took a few of your things to hold on to. Reminders, I guess. I'm sorry," she added, sounding somewhat guilty.

"I do not mind at all," I assured her, entering the room. It smelled of old texts, which I could see placed neatly on several shelves. In one corner, there was a chair positioned beside an old record player. Beside that, there was a box full of albums, some of which I was unable to recognize.

On the wall directly across from the entrance, there was a window that revealed the world and the gray clouds outside that covered the sky like a blanket. I turned around and noticed the piano sitting beside the door, dusty and unused, like a child's neglected toy as they outgrew such simple things.

"Sarah calls it the Old Thing Room, and I think it suits the place," said Kate, leaning against the door frame.

I smiled and nodded, comfortable in the warm space between books. "It is very enjoyable. Is...Is that the old book of fairy tales?"

I knelt by one of the shelves and pulled out the battered book with its yellowed pages, feeling nostalgic. Opening the book, the spine groaned quietly to tell me that it had not been viewed in quite some time. The page I saw had a picture of a stately prince, sword brandished at the evil devil that was guarding the princess. I shut the book immediately, chest constricting as a strange terror overtook me. I felt Kate's hand on my shoulder.

"Are you alright? You normally didn't slam books shut like that." Her voice sounded at a distance while bright lights and glinting knives were inches before my mind's eyes, my screams echoing in my ears.

Nausea was at a threatening proximity and I suddenly felt as though I had chills. "I need to step outside."

She helped me up and out of the room. The children were laughing with each other when we walked through the living room, jelly and egg curiously crushed in their hair. I groaned, fatigued and ill with it, though I gently pushed Kate away from me.

"I will be fine, although the children appear to require some assistance in their coordination with utensils," I told her, waving toward the table. I managed to keep my balance on my way to the door; when I exited, the stench of the city only made my churning stomach worse. I hurried back inside and shut the door, leaning against it with my eyes shut tight against the house I loathed to see. All I saw behind my lids were their masks spattered with black as their little knives cut me. The prince with his sword pointed at the devil...

I groaned again, swallowing back bile. It felt as though the world was constricting around me, trying to choke me with its unforgiving fickleness. I removed my cloak, gasping as it seemed that the air was easier to take in with it off. I reopened my eyes to the entrance way of the home, gazing at the stairs tiredly while I listened to Kate scolding Sarah and Kyle for "making such a mess."

Sleep. That was all I needed, to rest my weary mind. I mumbled some incoherency or other when Kate watched me climb the stairs. My sleepless night was catching me swiftly, making the sight of the open bedroom door welcome indeed. I stumbled through, not caring to close the door behind me.

Sitting on the bed, I lifted Kate's pillow slowly to my face. It smelled richly of her, and I wondered again what she had done to hold me close when I had been taken. What *had* she done?

Tired as I was, my mind blurred as I struggled to solve the riddle. My body eventually coaxed me to lay myself down and close my eyes to sleep at last.

~~ * ~ * ~ * ~~

Voices came to me from a distorted distance.

"Let him sleep. I can stay or come back later."

"Are you sure that won't be any trouble? He used to just pass right out again if you woke him up to ask him something."

"Well, this is probably a very exciting time for him...Besides, I think he's more than deserved a bit of peace after the past few days."

"What's happened?"

"Just...a lot of stress while searching."

I groaned, realizing that I was returning to awareness. The voices hushed for a moment, then continued in a whisper.

"How was he last night?"

"We were both up and down, but I think he did well after all the time."

"Good. That's good..."

"Who...?" I blinked my eyes open, squinting up at

the unfocused figures.   As my vision righted itself, I recognized Kate and Robert's smiling faces.

"Morning."   Robert frowned to himself. "Or, afternoon."

I sat swiftly, glancing between Kate and Robert in bemusement. How long had I slept? Why had Kate not woken me sooner to...leave.   Suddenly, I wished that I could return to last night and say everything I should have said, all that I had held so close for so long. Setting aside my distractions, I focused on now.

"Robert." I was surprised, though I had known he would be coming. I had asked him to last night, after all.

"Cory, uh...Kate, could we have some privacy?" requested Robert, frowning worriedly. She nodded and left, closing the door behind her. "What happened? You look terrible."

"If I tell you, will you prescribe me medications or have me placed in a home?" I asked quietly, staring at the carpet. My illness seemed to be fading slowly in spite of my rest, and I felt a droplet of sweat sliding from my brow. A strong indication that I was in poor condition.

Robert shook his head, leaning against a wall. "No, Cory, I know that would only make things worse. But so will not talking about what's got you like this."

"Extrapolate, please. I am afraid I do not know what you mean," I evaded, uncreative. That prince and devil!

He saw through my thin guise. "You've had your visit. I think we should go, maybe come back next week if she's available."

I looked up at him in shock, shaking my head slowly. "No, no, I will not leave here. It is the closest to home I have been in decades. And, oh...Did you see her? She is so close..."

"And you look like you saw a scalpel," he countered sharply, making me flinch. He sighed heavily. "Sorry, but it's true. You don't look like you'd last another day here. I mean, you seem more unstable now than when I first met you in that facility."

"What would you do for your family?" I demanded. His expression melted to one of exhaustion and he shook his head for me to stop before beginning. "I had more than anyone should rightfully ask for. That woman you saw, she was going to be my wife. She waited for me, Robert. As a friend *please,* help me. Because I will not willingly lose my home again."

Robert nodded, eyes watering in sympathy. He came to sit beside me, sighing again. "As your friend. As your therapist, I'm going to need you to call me every day so I know you're...Well, you know the details. I'll need to have a session with you at least once a week to start... You're sure you're ready for this?"

I sighed, releasing the breath slowly. "No, but I am uncertain I will ever be until I act."

He groaned, rubbing his temples as though this was paining him. "Let's see how she and the children feel, then. If any of them express the slightest discomfort, you'll have to stay with me."

"Reasonable," I agreed, looking up at the door. "Thank you, Robert, *thank you.*"

"I still need to talk to you about how you've done so far," he said, shaking his head. "Do you want to do that before or after we ask them?"

"After," I replied swiftly. My exhaustion was

beginning to slow my mind. My commonly precise control over my body was slipping, feeling clumsy and uncoordinated. I stood with a groan. "I need to know—"

"Whoa, Cory." He helped steady me as I stumbled and swayed. "Maybe you should keep sitting."

I glanced at the door and imagined what was waiting for me behind it. Sighing, I sat back beside him. "Very well. You wanted to know how I fared last night, correct?"

Robert smiled in encouragement. "Yes."

I mulled through my thoughts, wondering how to piece together the previous night. None of it made sense after I had asked to walk alone. Everything blurred, or the emotions were too fresh for me to organize them clearly.

After a few minutes, I sighed and shook my head tiredly. "I cannot say. I myself do not know how I have managed."

"Kate said you didn't sleep," he mentioned offhandedly, intertwining his fingers.

"No, no, I did not," I muttered, stifling a yawn. As it was, I was prepared to return to a pillow.

Robert was quiet for a moment, thoughtful. "Well, why don't I go see how Kate and the children feel, then. I'll wake you up again if you need to go, and if you get to stay, well...Be sure to call me in the morning."

I glanced at him, shaking my head slowly. "How I ever doubted that karma would return to me with good like you, I will never know."

"*Why* was completely understandable. Anyway, sleep well, Cory. Oh, um, I think I'll have the boys keep watch for awhile longer. On the street corners, at least."

I nodded in understanding, watching him stand and

stride to the door. "Thank you again, Robert. For everything you have done."

He barely glanced over his shoulder. "Thank you for teaching me to do what I think is right."

With those words, he exited and closed the door behind himself quietly. Righting myself, I laid myself back down on the mattress. I stared up at the ceiling a few moments before doing the only thing I could think to— dream.

~~ * ~ * ~ * ~~

September 4ᵗʰ, 2010

The last three days have been a spectacular treat that both Robert and I are glad for. Kate continues to tell me about how she has been these last years. Some of her news makes the word 'surprising' far too mundane. Astonishing better fits the description.

For example, it was in the winter of 1972 that she gave birth to her only child, a daughter who was the mother of the two children I had met the first night. This daughter, whose name Kate has neglected to mention, died not a year ago in an accident. Just last month, Kate won the custody of her grandchildren from the father, that she has said is a poor influence whose only good acts were creating Kyle and Sarah.

After everything, it is of no surprise to me that such an individual exists. Many of the scientists working for the N.S.I.S.D. had families, including Beth. Although, it still baffles me to even consider that woman being a mother.

The soldiers that once stood on Robert's lawn now

guard the street corners and the backyard dutifully. I would wonder why I am still being protected, or think that these precautions are pointless, but I know that it is their very presence that has warded off potential attackers thus far. The longer it is that no one comes to maul me, the likelier the event becomes. After all, only those determined enough will hold on to their hatred beyond the initial wave of horror since my release.

Life with the humans around me has become somewhat easier, now that the thought occurs to me. Why, just yesterday I was accepted into a bookstore without complaints or a manager being called. To the contrary, the manager found me to say what an honor it was to be able to begin accepting demons at his store. I wonder, should I fear him more than the ones brandishing their weapons? Faithful to my paranoia, I will keep the children from him.

Oh, the children! They are delightful! Although, they have rather harsh tendencies of shouting, swearing and violence towards one another. Kate tells me that they have calmed some, that they would be much more vulgar or harmful. I wonder, how is this possible? All she will say is that their father is to blame. I believe that she does not want to say what he has done to his own children.

Those thoughts aside, I am beginning to adjust to interacting with them. A great portion of myself is thrilled! The only child I can recall speaking to or playing with was Lisa, too long ago to genuinely count. It may be too early to tell, but...Could this be a true second chance at everything I had nearly had? Roaming in the day, moving from home, possessing friends, being Kate's husband, perhaps even fatherhood? Could this be true karma, coming back to me at last?

Demon *Rising*

Whatever the reason for this, I cannot help but rejoice. I am here, I am free, and my life is again filled with those who care. What more could I ever desire?

My next visit with Robert is Thursday, the 9th. I hope that I may have nothing more than joyous things to share.

First Week Outside

<u>Monday</u>

"Grandma, how do you know the demon man?" asked Sarah quietly, glancing at me warily.

Kate smiled at her granddaughter, amused. "He's my very good friend since I was just a *little* older than you."

"How much older, Gramma?" breathed Kyle, eyes wide as he bounced enthusiastically in his seat.

"Oh, a few years."

"Wow, you must have been so old!" Kyle was grinning. I smirked secretly, glad to see that I was not alone among the "old" people.

"Yes, yes, now finish your breakfasts so that you're not late for the bus to school."

They groaned but obeyed, some twenty minutes later being escorted out by Kate to meet the bus. I remained seated on the couch, watching the sky gradually being lit by the rising sun through the kitchen window. A hulking yellow vehicle came and went before Kate returned indoors, appearing tired. She smiled when she saw me and came to sit beside me.

"I have to get up and start cleaning soon," she grumbled tiredly.

"Oh, I can take care of that for you," I offered, then grinned mischievously. "Since you are such an old woman."

She smacked me playfully. "You haven't changed a bit, have you? Poking fun at my age..."

"Of course. However, those dishes must be too difficult for someone your age. I'll go tend to them," I added, bending to kiss the top of her head out of buried habit and pausing before I did so. I stood smoothly, chuckling when Kate narrowed her eyes at me, then huffing when I continued onward to the kitchen.

As I began to wash the dishes, I paused when an abrupt realization shocked through me. Not even a week after being reunited, Kate and I were already falling back into our older habits and rhythms. I smiled quietly to myself and said nothing, though I was certain she had noticed this as well.

At that moment, I knew that with only time and the kindest efforts we could recreate home here.

~~ * ~ * ~ * ~~

September 7th, 2010

Could all of this be real? Is it possible that I am dreaming, even now? Kate has accepted me back openly and graciously. Kyle and Sarah have expressed a liking to me, even if it is only as an individual to play with, or rather on.

Demon *Rising*

But this is home. I feel it everywhere. The rooms are bright, warm and welcoming to me, the opposite of the N.S.I.S.D. Every morning I wake beside her, I recall that I am nearly in the place I have always dreamt of having once again. Without my parents, childless and still working through my scars, but all of those are nearly forgivable when I consider that originally I had never thought that I could wake in any way but alone.

I have friends, as well. Genuine friends, not humans who befriend me falsely to their own gain. No, Robert enjoys aiding me. He is my friend, as well as Santos and Thompson to a milder degree. Bailey and Anne claim to enjoy merely conversing with me. Just this morning, while speaking with Robert over the phone, he mentioned that they are missing me. Oh, how good it is to be missed!

Many of Kate and I's old habits—such as morning kisses or brushes of the hand—feel somewhat awkward now. I am not all too surprised, but I wonder if it is that the other of us has changed so much as it is ourselves worrying over how the other will accept our affections. Time will tell, and I cannot wait for its answer!

The colors of fall are beginning to appear in the trees in the backyard now. They are so very vibrant and glorious! It makes me sad to think that they will fall and leave the branches barren come winter, but I do suppose all I can do is enjoy the beauty while it lasts. Of course, spring is also not too terribly far away. New blossoms will greet me for the first time! Oh, so many countless joys around me, I cannot grasp at which ones I should revel in first!

However, I believe that a wonderful beginning would be to no longer waste this day writing of what I long to experience, and rather go to live it as I never have.

~~ * ~ * ~ * ~~

Thursday

"Ah, Cory, welcome back," sighed Robert, smiling when he saw me. I returned the expression, cherishing how welcome I felt here.

"Thank you, Robert. I hope I am not too early. The flight was much shorter than I had anticipated," I explained, following him to the living room. My favored room, seconded only by my fascination with the advanced appearance of the kitchen.

He shook his head. "Don't worry about it. I was hoping you'd be early, actually. It hasn't been the same without you," he added offhandedly.

My smile broadened. "I am uncertain of whether I should rejoice or apologize."

"The first one." Robert laughed and grinned, waiting for me to seat myself. I took the coveted and comfortable leather seat, relaxing into it easily. "You visit once a week. Once we get used to it, we'll all settle down."

"We?"

"The entire family, Vanessa included." He sat across from me, on the couch.

My eyes widened. "I'm glad she seems to have calmed some. How are your children?"

"Bailey's doing very well. Apparently the, uh, Supernatural Supporters are getting attention. As she puts it, the pro-demon movement is on," he laughed again, but I noticed the worried tightening of his eyes.

218

I kept my smile in place. "Well, so long as she is not injured in any...extreme situations, hm?"

"Indeed," he agreed. He was quiet for a moment, face thoughtful. "But Vanessa's no longer participating in Humans Forever. In fact, she's suggested a couple things to Bailey for the Supporters."

"Really?" I laughed, grinning now. "Well, congratulations, to you and to them. It seems a great deal can occur over the short course of a week."

He nodded. "Indeed it can. I believe that's the reason why we met...?"

"Ah, yes." I thought for a moment, donning a frown slowly. "How do we start this, exactly? All of the aid you have given me thus far has been far from this...formal."

"Oh, right. Um..." He frowned as well. "How about I start you off with a question?"

"I say that would be excellent, Robert. Was that the question?" I asked, smirking.

He ignored my poorly orchestrated humor. "How have you been this last week?"

"Splendid. I have actually been questioning how real all of this is. I find that it must be impossible for anything to be so...gay," I chose the word easily, smiling broadly as I did so. I could share my happiness, and I would as I knew how.

Robert smiled in return. "Good, that's good. Um...Has anything bothered you, or have you had any questions that you feel need answering?"

I hesitated a moment, glancing out the large window to the brilliant green of the lawn and the soft blue of the sky. "One."

He waited a moment. "Yes?"

"I wonder...how she had her daughter. Who the father was, how she felt toward him...Those children you saw, they are her grandchildren," I told him, feeling wistful. The originally bright atmosphere was thick now, darkening with things I had gladly not thought of. "The daughter passed last year, and their father is absent, so Kate has custody of her grandchildren."

"Daughter?" asked Robert. I nodded. "I see. How does that make you feel, knowing that Katelyn had another person's child?"

I thought for a moment, envy weighing heavily on my chest. "Many things."

"Can you tell me what they are?" asked Robert gently. I glanced at him with a worried frown, uncertain of myself. Could I truly be so selfish to wish such things? "Whatever it is, it's alright."

I sighed heavily, looking at my hands. My chest constricted painfully. "I am jealous of the man that gave her that; I still wish it was me. I want to recall raising that daughter with Kate, but cannot. I want to mourn her as a father, not a stranger. Kate was alone for all of that...I want to remember that I was there with her, a good husband for her, but all of those years I only see blurs of what happened in those damned rooms!" I took a deep breath to calm myself. "My apologies for my vulgarity."

"Don't apologize. You were saying how you felt, and I thank you for that." I looked up in surprise at Robert's kind smile. He took his notes, then frowned at me. "Do you feel better after saying all that?"

I nodded slowly, the weight on my chest lifting. "Yes. I still feel confused, though I expect that shall lessen in time."

"It will. Can I ask you to do something when you go home?" asked Robert.

"Yes?"

"Ask Katelyn about who the father was and if she has any lingering attachments to him," said Robert. My heart raced in panic at the thought of knowing. "It should help some to know where you stand in her life, compared to who you might view as your rivals."

"I see. Well...Thank you again, Robert, for aiding me so willingly," I said with half a smile. He reminded me of Paul at that moment.

"Have you considered taking up a hobby?" he inquired, turning the conversation from the heavier subject.

"Not yet, no," I replied, shaking my head. I was careful to ensure I did not damage the leather with my horns. "There is too much to do and appreciate already."

Robert nodded with a smile. "I know, but it might help to ground you so that you're not so erratic or overwhelmed."

I paused, grasping the sound sense behind his reasoning. I laughed to myself. "Well, then I suppose I shall find a hobby."

He grinned. "I suppose so."

~~ * ~ * ~ * ~~

September 12th, 2010

After Robert's suggestion to take up a hobby to practice, the piano within the Old Room has inspired me. I believe that learning to play the instrument may be the perfect device to ground myself. Although, there is one puzzle I have yet to find a way around—my claws. If I learn to play, they will damage the keys, no matter how gentle I manage to be. This will require some consideration.

<u>Forgotten</u>

The demon watched the children playing, a smile on his lips. After all of the years, it seemed he was at last home. Beside him, Katelyn was reading silently, the occasional brushing of a turning page reminding him of how brilliant the day was.

A warm sensation surrounded him, and for a moment the demon was foolish enough to believe it was mere happiness that caused it. As the warmth spread and was accompanied by the distinct feeling of recollection, he slowly realized that it was more than joy, it was a memory of it.

Tears came to his eyes when he heard the echo of an angelic voice in his mind. He saw the stars set against black velvet through a window, a window of a place he knew was safe and wonderful. There were faces, godly faces, all guarded by an army of gorgeous, graceful people.

As the memory faded he found himself trembling, agonized while he was trapped by the mortal coil. Cory felt Katelyn's hand on his, heard her voice calling to him concernedly.

"I remember..." he murmured in a daze, tears falling to his lap. He stared at them on his hands in confusion. When had that happened? When had everything begun to feel as though his soul had been ripped from his body?

Katelyn stiffened, watching him with grief in her eyes. "What do you remember, Cory?"

He frowned, looking at his hands with disbelief. So scarred, so demonic...What happened? "I remember...From before. Before you knew me, before I was ever here..."

He heard her stifle a sob. "...Hell?"

He felt numb, sick with the truth. "No, worse."

"What was it, Cory?" she begged, and enough of him was aware to have his heart twist at the pain he heard in her voice.

He turned to look at her, more tears in his eyes. Silently, his gaze turned back to the children laughing as they played. He shook his head slowly as the horror settled like ice in his heart.

"Heaven."

Chapter Six:
An Honest Wound

Second Week Outside

Tuesday

"Kate, who was the father?" I asked in a murmur, watching Kyle and Sarah play in their bedroom through the crack in the door. I smiled in amusement, seeing the floor littered so heavily with toys.

"You saw him," she dodged, still behind me. I did not reply, staring silently as I waited. She knew what I meant, sighing softly, "Memory gets a little fuzzy at our ages..."

"Did you feel for him?" My smile slowly turned to a frown as something about Kyle's face appeared disturbingly familiar. Not the eyes but the smile, the way it seemed more like he was grinning.

Kate scoffed. "Oh, no. No, no, no. I didn't like him much, actually."

I scowled. Why was it that he looked so familiar? "Then why bear his children?"

She did not speak. Instead, her slim and delicate fingers touched my arm gently, as she might touch glass. I looked over at her to find that she bore a guilty, heavy

225

expression.

Tears gathered in her eyes. "I...It was dark, a couple years after you were taken. I recognized them by how they laughed, Richard and his gang."

Horror was sinking in slowly, out of place as I listened to the children giggling. In my mind, I could all too clearly imagine where they would have chased and cornered her. I could remember Richard's face...Yet even as my pain for her bit me deeply, I could not bear to look at her.

Suddenly, she was even quieter, voice the softest murmur. "But it wasn't any of them. Your brother..."

My mind was numb, so I took her close without feeling any relief for myself. I acted with the vague, dreamlike thoughts that I could shield her from that past and that I could protect her from it now, from the fact that his grandchildren were playing just beyond the door.

"Ethan...?" I choked. I prayed that I was mistaken, that this pain could have been an overreaction, imaginary, unnecessary. But she nodded, betraying the dark secret.

Slowly, the cold and metallic numbness began to melt away to molten fury. Still in my arms, Kate felt too fragile as I unwillingly envisioned what he would have done. I pulled my arms away from her and linked my hands behind my back, hoping that the action may restrain me. I kept my eyes on a wall while I glared, swallowing back the hideous, beastly sounds of anger I could feel building in my chest.

Kate was trembling but silent as I strode past, leaving through the front door. I needed time to think, outside with the open sky above me so that I would have some way to escape if it all became too much.

Demon *Rising*

The sky was painted with twilight, granting enough light so that all who saw me could cringe, scream or blare their horns in anger. I ignored them all, walking past and along the street without thought. It was the movement that mattered, that released some of the boiling hatred I could feel torturing me from within. In spite of my wishes, a low growl constantly escaped me, startling those who strode close enough to hear it.

The air bit at me, its all-consuming maw icy. That was relieving, as well. The frigidity of the air gave my rage a purpose in warming me. I could see my breath, and for a moment was confused that this was only early September. I had been away from the seasons too long, it seemed.

Ethan. Unbidden, the name came back to me, sounding foul and evil. My chest constricted painfully at the thought that he had touched Kate, that he had—I could not bear to even think it.

A new, darker loathing for that facility crashed through me. It was because of them that I had not been there, either to protect her or help her through the aftermath. It was *their* fault that we were here!

I halted my thoughts before they could continue through the thorny path they were crafting. Oh, I could not blame any man who's name I did not know for that accident. I desired someone to blame though, someone I could hate and hate and *hate* for everything that had happened. Yet there was none, so my anger simmered without a target while I searched for some way to release it.

Dark fell too slowly while the day fought to remain. It prolonged the sweet freedom that came when not a soul could see my face, and the blissful light of the moon's silvery grace.

Demon *Rising*

While others could recognize what I was they struck out verbally, in some cases throwing an object at me. Even so, I refused to bow down and flee back to the safety of the indoors. This was my world now, too.

Finally, finally, the sun vanished and the sky was dark, although not even that could break through my anger to calm me, not while the streets were still lit with orange or white lamps.

I snarled in frustration. Why could they not allow me my freedom of darkness?! Where would I find that solace, that bittersweet wonder the empty fields had possessed when I was a child? Must I fly from the city and go for miles before finding that there was no place left? No haven that I could bring to Katelyn and her grandchildren?

A shrill cry broke my thoughts, slapping me back to the empty and dead street beside which I walked. The person cried out again just a block or so ahead of me and I was able to understand that they screamed for help.

I surged forward instinctively, my raw feet burning while my claws scraped against the concrete. I turned into the alley I presumed I had heard the screams from, freezing. Three dark-clad men were stalking after a smaller, willowy figure I thought was a woman. In the center man's hand, a knife glinted; the other two held metal baseball bats. None of these were what halted me and made me tremble. It was that I spoke and drew the attention of these men unto myself.

"What are you doing?" My voice resonated in the stillness, and the frozen air felt like thousands of needle points pressed against my skin.

They all turned to look in surprise. The man with the knife grinned and shrugged, pointing at me. He muttered something to the man on his left, laughing when he did so. The man on his right took a threatening step toward me, brandishing his weapon eagerly.

"We were just going to help this MTF along, give 'im a free surgery and make over. Out of the goodness of our hearts, right boys?" said the center man with a chuckle. The woman whimpered, stumbling back deeper into the alley.

I did not understand the man's words, but his manner and menacing tone were clear to me. I stepped into the alley tentatively, heart beating painfully in my chest. They terrified me with their weapons and cruelty, but leaving the woman to be victimized was unfathomable to me. I had to help her somehow.

"Please, just...Leave now and I will do you no harm," I said slowly. The words were awkward even to my own ears. The men laughed with a haunting, quiet humor that made me shudder.

"Look, the demon's giving us a chance. Sammy, why don't you go and thank him properly?" asked the man, nudging the man on his right. Sammy nodded and came at me, bat held back to swing.

I barely caught the icy metal with my left hand, changing my stance to guard my right shoulder instinctively. The man grunted, yanking the bat from my grasp. He aimed high, bringing the weapon across my face. I growled deeply, eyes narrowing. My face throbbed with an odd warmth as I felt the skin beginning to bruise slightly.

I swung my arm, catching Sammy with the back of my forearm and pinning him against a wall. I grabbed his jacket and lifted him with a groan, catching sight of a large

229

trash container. I placed him inside of it, jamming the lid so that I could take him to the authorities when I was sure the woman was safe.

When I turned back, one of the men had her pinned against a wall. The man with the knife smiled with a disgusting pleasure. I started towards them, making the men pause. The one with the knife sighed, turning to face me with an annoyed expression.

"Again, release her and you will not be harmed," I said, weighing my luck to my options. The knife terrified me, making every one of my scars burn with recognition of the malicious object.

The man laughed, seeing my hesitance. "What's wrong, big wolf scared of the bunny? Well, we can help with that. Just as soon as we finish with the tranny, we can fix you up and make you look a little more human, if you're patient enough."

I choked at his meaning, glancing at the woman. I could save her from these men. All it would mean for me was another scar or two. The knife in his hand was more like Death's scythe in my eyes.

Before I could think my actions foolish, my hand shot out to shove the man back against his own wall and pin him there. The man holding the woman cried out, tossing her aside and lifting his bat from the ground. My heart was in my throat, my pulse a thunderous drumbeat in my ears.

The one I had pinned struggled, lifting his knife and cutting my forearm. I hissed, my blood hot as ever against my skin and steaming in the cold night air. The man with the knife exclaimed in shock, staring at my blood with wide, horror-filled eyes. I heard the knife clink when it hit the ground.

A cold, sharp pain blossomed across my wings. I cried out in shock, but the other man was already hitting me again. The woman was crying out for him to stop. I heard a smack and saw her fall to the ground at my feet. I bellowed on instinct, making the assailants freeze with fear and begin trembling.

The bat hit the ground next with a sharp and painful clatter. I grabbed the former wielder's jacket to pull him forcefully with me. I shoved both of them against a wall, narrowing my eyes at them.

"Will you obey now when I tell you not to move?" I demanded, a cruel edge to my voice. They cringed back into the wall, terrified of me. I turned to the woman, allowing my expression to soften. "Are you uninjured, madam?"

She lifted herself shakily, nodding. "Yes, and thank you so much for saving me."

The man who had held the knife glared at her hatefully. I growled threateningly and he averted his gaze instantly. She edged toward the exit, avoiding the men lined up against the wall.

"Madam, I do realize that you would relish returning safely home. However, if you could direct or lead me to the nearest police station?" I requested, fetching Sammy from the garbage container. He gasped and struggled against me pathetically. I frowned, confused at how simple it was to maneuver the man in spite of my age and lacking in my previous physical prowess.

"Oh. Right, yes. Um...This way." She began to walk in the direction I had come from.

I waved for the men to walk ahead of myself. "I will

carry any one of you who attempts to flee."

Eyes downcast in fear and the air rank with the scent of it, they trudged after the woman. I followed behind, wincing. The ground was cold enough that my raw feet stuck to it, pulling the skin with every step. Where I had been cut was burning with the chill of the air, the skin around it searing as more blood leaked from the injury.

Not two blocks later, there was the station. The woman opened the door for the villains to enter, watching them warily. I ducked through last and managed to dodge the ceiling by hunching slightly. A woman in a green uniform tensed when she saw me.

"Did it hurt any of you?" she asked tersely, hand poised over a small rectangular device on her belt. Sammy and the man who had held the knife nodded silently. She pulled the device from her belt, holding it ready before addressing me. "Put your hands where I can see them, now."

I held them in front of me, trembling.

"What are you doing?" demanded the woman from the alley. She released the door, stepping up beside me. "He's the one that saved me from them!"

The officer started, then turned to the three men. "What?"

"Tranny whore, narcing on your own species," muttered Sammy crudely. I scowled down at him.

"Okay, okay, so *they* attacked you?" asked the officer, pointing to the woman, who nodded. "And *it* just happened to be in the area and felt like saving you?"

"I guess. I don't know why he did, he just...did," she replied awkwardly, glancing at me tentatively.

"Okay, we're going to need to—What's that?!" she

232

cried out, pointing to my blood on the floor. Where it had hit was hissing quietly and smoking, the black substance having burnt through the carpet, making its way through the concrete beneath.

I gaped at the dripping black as it continued to corrode the floor. "My blood. It has never done that before."

When I glanced up, I looked to every pair of staring eyes, pleading that none of them saw. Stronger yet was a desire that none of them could remember, so that only I could hide the event. Just as I looked back to the floor, all activity continued as though nothing had occurred, skipping backwards a few moments in time.

"Larry, help me process these guys, will ya?"

"Sure." A man helped her to escort them away. When they returned sometime later, the female officer aided the shaken woman to a chair, speaking gently. The male officer stared at me for a moment. "Sandy, what's the protocol for situations involving demons?"

"Depends on the demon," called the female officer, glancing over her shoulder at us.

"Last name?" he asked me.

"Ah, Lawrence. Is there anything I should do?"

He ignored my question. "It's the Lawrence one, Sandy."

"He's protected, so don't bother with anything yet. Just have him call someone to pick him up and leave a contact number, in case we end up needing him," sighed Sandy, shaking her head and returning to the woman, who was smiling at me in thanks.

I smiled back, earlier stress forgotten in the relief that an abhorred act had been prevented. The man led me to a desk with a phone, motioning toward the object. He watched while I dialed and waited patiently for Robert to answer.

"Hello?" He sounded confused.

"Good evening, Robert, I hope I did not disturb you," I greeted, staring at the ceiling. I felt awkward being watched by the officer, a mouse in the eyes of a hawk.

"No, not at all. What did you need?" he asked, attention captured.

"Would you happen to be in the vicinity of the station on..." I turned to the officer, hand over the speaker. "What road is this?"

"The southern end of St. Louis."

"St. Louis, it seems," I continued to Robert, nodding to the officer in thanks. "The southern end, I am told."

He was quiet for a long stretch. "What *kind* of station, Cory?"

"Police station," I replied, a sense of guilt beginning to creep up my spine from my tail. "It is far from what you may think, Robert, I assure you."

"Alright. Why are you calling, then?" he asked, voice strained. Was he cross?

"I am unfamiliar with the region and require aid in returning home. Some minor council might not be taken with a grain of salt this evening, either," I added hurriedly. "However, if you are currently engaged or otherwise unwilling, I am certain there is a service I would be able to utilize."

Much to my relief, he did not question why I would not phone Kate for my need. "Alright, alright. I'm about ten minutes away, alright? Just stand outside and wait for me if you can."

"Thank yo—"

The line disconnected, silencing me. Sheepishly, I replaced the receiver on its cradle and turned to the officer. "May I wait for him outside?"

"Yeah. Sandy, I'll be back in a few," he called to his coworker. She did not glance up from her conversation with the woman.

When I stepped out into the night air again, it was viciously frozen against my skin. I had no rage to warm me this time and so shivered slightly from the cold. It was a wonder to me how it was I could stand even colder temperatures when I was younger. Then again, in that once upon a time I had been working diligently, keeping warm through activity.

The officer did not speak, standing stoically as far from me as he could. I was not offended, though I wondered if I should be. It would not change anything if I was, however. Nothing but my being emotionally distraught, in addition to being unable to cure the discontent within myself.

To my dismay, there were no stars glittering against the velvet night, the only perceptible light artificial. The moon above was not full, smiling down on the world thinly instead. It brought me no happiness or peace. Where it was placed, where I stood to view it, everything was far too cold to make it as warm or breathtaking as it once was.

Thankfully, it was not too much longer that my mind had to wander listlessly through tiring thoughts before Robert's familiar silver car pulled up beside the station. He stepped out, face blank as he nodded to the officer, then to me.

"Was there anything else you needed before I can take him home?" he asked the officer politely.

"Oh, yeah, a number to contact him at, in case we need him," said the officer with a sudden start of recollection. He found a paper pad in his pocket while Robert materialized a pen from what I perceived as thin air.

Without a word, Robert wrote his personal number on the paper offered, smiling and nodding again at the officer. He opened the door to the car, seating himself before I was able to stride to the other side to begin clambering in. Once I had managed to curl in around myself, the engine sparked to life quietly. Robert pulled out into the road smoothly.

Neither of us spoke, but I sensed the anger he did not voice. It was sharp in the air, intensifying my own guilt. But why should I regret anything? I saved a woman from three hostile men and what could have only been a terrible fate. Should I apologize for such a thing? Was it a crime now to aid a fellow person, if not of the same specie? Or could I not in my lacking of apparent humanity?

"Would you mind telling me why I'm picking you up from a police station?" asked Robert quietly. His voice was loud after the silence.

"The media is sure to tell why in three different ways. You are bound to favor one of those stories," I replied just as quietly, keeping my focus on the window. My chest was tight with guilt and fear.

"I want to hear it from you, Cory." The tone he used when he spoke my name made me feel like a child being reprimanded. Had I done something so wrong? Saving someone, was that a shameful and punishable offense now?

I sighed heavily, watching the lights turn from red to green. "I was taking a walk and heard someone scream for help. I found them, saw that a woman was being attacked, so I removed her attackers and then turned them over to the police."

"Damn it, Cory!" he shouted suddenly, making me jump. I stared at him in shock as he glowered at the road. "You should have let everything be and just kept walking!"

"I apologize, Robert, but what small pieces I possess that anyone can call human will not go neglected by me," I replied swiftly and firmly. Why was it terrible?! What corruptions of society had taken place so that I was scolded for saving a woman?!

"You're walking a fine line, Cory, no matter what you were doing! As a demon, if you're involved with *any* violence, they can send you to any number of places, the N.S.I.S.D. being the most likely!" he snapped. He pulled up to the curb in front of Kate's home slowly. With a sharp movement, he turned the car off and dropped his hands to his lap. "Damn it..."

The door opened and Kate walked out, hurrying over to the car. Robert rolled down the window on my side so that she could speak to us without him setting me free.

Kate's face was worried. "I saw a story on the news. What happened?"

"I—"

"He saved a woman by manhandling three men and dropping them off at a police station. Thankfully, the woman was willing to stay and vouch for him, by the looks of things," interrupted Robert. "We might want to find a good lawyer that supports demons."

Kate was horror-struck. "What?! Cory, why?!"

"Because it shows more 'mental and emotional stability' to help someone in need rather than walk by and allow them to be injured, possibly killed!" I retorted, unsnapping my seat belt and unlocking my door to escape the cramped car.   Kate stepped away so that I could clamber out of the tight space, then came forward and grabbed my hand firmly in hers.

She looked up at me with wide eyes. "You've only been out six weeks. Please, be more careful."

I heard Robert's door open and slam, then he began walking over towards us. "Yes, do be more careful. I'm not about to let you go anywhere, but there's also only so much that I can do."

I sighed. "I would rather be thought violent than silently proven heartless."

"And that's one of the reasons why we can't replace you," said Robert, then blinked in surprise as if he had not meant to speak those words. He shook his head slowly, motioning back to the house. "Let's get you inside and patched up."

"Patched up?" echoed Kate with a frown. She saw the black smeared on my arm. "How did that happen?"

"One of them had a knife," I muttered, eyes focused on my feet as we made our way to the door. I held the door open for Kate and Robert to enter.

Robert froze just inside the home. "A knife?"

I nodded, stepping inside but not moving beyond the linoleum flooring. My feet were raw and smearing a small amount of blood, claws rubbed to the nerve from the concrete. I sighed quietly and shook my head. It seemed symbolic to me that the ground injured me when I walked into the hateful world. It was the physical manifestation of the hostility and anger, a constant villain that whipped me to make me run back to my cage.

Kate whirled on me, tears in her eyes as she shook her head slowly. Her words were a soft whisper, "Don't *ever* do this again, Charles."

"I was unaware I would find someone being attacked while I took a stroll," I mumbled, stepping into the kitchen for paper towels. I moistened them and dabbed at my arm.

"Stroll? You stormed out!" she cried in distress. I heard her come into the kitchen after me. "Calmly, I'll grant you, but for you it was storming."

"I was upset, Kate, and I apologize, but I needed to move free of the home. I was worried I may harm your or the children if I stayed," I confessed, wincing when the cool water made my cut sting mildly. I glanced at the black smeared across the linoleum from the entrance and through into the kitchen.

"You still didn't need to get involved with that fight!" She put her hand on my arm and forced me to look at her.

"And allow the poor woman to be beaten?!" I cried in shock. I shook my head furiously, turning away so that I could brace my hands against the counter. Again, my body felt like fire was in my veins from boiling anger. "Not after what you told me earlier. I could not risk that happening to another, not with Ethan on my mind."

"I don't care! If she was silly enough to go wandering around at night with how things are today, she deserved it!" Her hand was on my arm again, trying to turn me around. "Look at me, please, Cory!"

"I CAN'T!" I yelled, forcing myself to stay where I

239

was and keep my tail from attacking the air. If I hurt her in my anger—I cut the thought off, glaring at the sink. "I can't. I'm sorry, Kate, I *am* but I'm afraid I'll hurt you. I don't care what that woman was doing or why she was attacked, but you never deserved it, you never deserved anything like that!"

Something escaped me. It was a deep, guttural sound that was purely demonic, strangling off into a horrible animalistic snarl. As my voice died away, I heard Kate's hushed sobs behind me.

"He gave me my daughter," she hissed, defending my traitorous sibling.

"Which is more than I ever have, I know." There was a rustling and I knew that she had left the room. A few moments later, I heard the door to the bedroom upstairs slam shut. Only when I knew that she would not hear did I allow myself to weep.

The distinct clack of shoes against the floor alerted me before I felt Robert's tentative hand on my shoulder. "It's alright, Cory. What happened earlier that caused you to leave the house?"

"Ethan," I ground out, trembling more with grief than anger now. "He raped her. He's the father."

I felt him stiffen beside me. "Ah..."

Time blurred by in my eyes as the tears fell freely, spattering into the sink. Somewhere, I finally remembered the blood on the floor. I grabbed more towels, kneeling and wiping the mess away. When I was finished, I stared at the black substance hatefully before throwing it in the garbage. I cleaned my feet, then went to the couch to sit in silence. Robert lingered near the kitchen hesitantly.

"I'm an animal, Robert, not rabid," I spat bitterly,

motioning a clawed hand to the spaces on either side of me. "There are plenty of seats to spare."

A tiny voice answered instead, "Cory? Is everything okay? I heard yelling..."

"Not now, Kyle, please," I sighed without looking at the child. I knew he would be terrified and I could not stand to see that.

"Is everyone okay?" he asked again with a sniffle.

I nodded stiffly, wishing that I knew how to care for him in that moment. "Yes. Everyone's okay...Please return to your room, Kyle."

His feet shuffled away and the door closed quietly, the latch of the handle sounding incredibly loud. Robert took the seat offered on my left. Out of the corner of my eye, I saw him watching me carefully for a long time.

"I'm going to go see how Kate's doing," he said finally. I nodded numbly, still staring at nothing. He stood and left for the upper floor.

I turned my attention to my hands. Scars lined each finger, surrounded every claw because of the studying. My claws...Black and inhuman. In that moment I wanted nothing more than to *be* human. A man that could live in peace, that could hold a loved one without the fear of maiming them.

I glanced at the wall to the room where the poor children were, no doubt in need of comfort that I could not give right then. If I could have the weapons removed from my fingertips, the red taken from my skin and replaced with anything more natural. If I could have been born human...

My fingers curled to make fists. I could find some compromise, though. If I filed my claws, then there would be less risk of injuries. I knew that I could not rid myself of my horns, since they bled profusely once cut too deeply. My wings? Would I willingly cut those from me, along with my tail? The equivalence would have been removing my arms or legs...Could I hate myself so much, or want to be something other than a demon that profoundly?

"Yes," I told myself, glancing up at where I knew Kate would be sitting on the bed. Had I been human, had I been a man! That would have been my daughter, those would be my grandchildren, Kate would be my wife. My family would want me and I would not have been ripped from them. Nothing would have...

The sound of footsteps above me brought me back to the current moment. I sighed quietly and relaxed my fists. The door opened upstairs, the muted voices of Kate and Robert becoming clearer as they stepped from the room. I waited until they were at the bottom of the stairs and coming to sit beside me before I looked at Kate.

Her face was aged and tired, eyes reddened while her cheeks glistened faintly. My chest constricted with guilt. Had my yelling done this to her? Was I still proving myself a burden and unsafe? Even as I felt my heart twisting with the pain of my thoughts I kept my face calm and my eyes focused.

They both sat before Robert spoke. "Cory, I would like to talk to you and Kate, together. How do you feel about that?"

"I do not mind," I said slowly, struggling to recreate my natural speech in spite of my inner turmoil. I felt Kate's cool fingers slip into my open palm, dwarfed by my hand as it curled to hold her fingers gently. My face remained placid, to my amazement.

"Good, good," he murmured thoughtfully. "Now, Kate, Cory told me a bit about the relationship you two used to have. Just from what he's expressed and what I've seen tonight, I think having sessions with the both of you might help salvage some of what you had. What do you two think? Kate, would you like to join us occasionally? Cory, how do you feel about having shared sessions?"

Her fingers tightened around my hand. "Yes, if he's fine with it."

I considered this for a moment. At times, this would mean that she would glimpse the thinnest slivers of what had occurred inside the N.S.I.S.D., things that I was loathe to share with even Robert. Others should not have to carry those things in their minds. Could I stand to allow Kate to witness such horrors? Or rather, could I stand the alternative of never being comforted by her, never hearing that everything is gone and well now?

"I would like that," I murmured, wondering if I should be cursing myself for this. What would she see if I showed her the marks I could feel coming closer to the surface? Could I stand to allow her near that pain?

Kate sighed but smiled satisfactorily. "I'm going to make tea. Would you boys like anything?"

"Tea's fine," said Robert, smiling. "Thank you."

"It's no issue. Cory?" she asked gently, catching my attention. I met her eyes for a moment, relieved by them.

Everything will work out. "No, thank you, Kate."

She nodded and left the living room.

"I need to apologize," said Robert, looking over at where Kate was working in the kitchen. "For getting upset like that in the car. I'm worried that things might be set

243

back because of what happened...I think it might be in your better interest if you changed therapists. I keep allowing my friendship with you to come ahead of my job to you."

"I phoned you asking for a friend, Robert," I replied slowly, reluctant to start anew with a stranger. He knew my story already and I felt comfortable speaking with him. "That aside, I would still prefer to remain with you."

He shook his head, smile saddening. "You're kind and accepting to your own detriment sometimes."

"Or perhaps you do not see yourself so clearly," I suggested to deter his rather saddening case of self-thought inadequacy. How incredibly hypocritical of myself.

"How is it you can stand to be like this with everyone?" he wondered quietly, so that he might have been speaking only to himself. Regardless, I replied.

"Would you like me to tell you something romantic? That I felt myself the beast from the fairytale, or imagined myself an unfortunate prince and began to play the part? No, Robert, my personality has been as it is since I can remember. My parents used to be amazed by its full, rounded formation at such an early age, as well. I have habits and paranoid tendencies, mind you, but nothing spurred me to be kind or unthinking of myself other than a burning desire to see those around me happy and be content with that."

He stared at me incredulously, giving me a moment to feel the odd chill shiver down my spine. My thoughts strayed to what had occurred earlier. I hesitated only a moment, glancing at Kate still occupied in the kitchen as she watched the kettle heating.

"Robert...I am frightened of what I may become after this," I said quietly, staring down at the carpet distantly. The anger I had felt earlier, the violence I had willingly stepped into. My body was changing as well, blood turned to acid one moment while it was safe the next. I did not want to begin considering how not one person seemed to recall that I had been cut earlier, or the acidic blood that had eaten into the floor.

He nodded. "Would you like me to answer as your friend?"

I frowned and nodded slowly after a moment. "Yes...I suppose that may help."

Robert smiled kindly. "I think that you'll be fine, because you have plenty of people who will do whatever they can to help you."

I looked up at him, smiling. "Thank you, Robert. I hope that you are correct."

"I know I am," he replied, grinning and reaching out to accept a steaming cup from Kate. "Thank you very much."

"You're welcome," she said quietly, taking her seat beside me. Glancing between them, I knew that I would be more than safe in their capable hands, if only to restrain the dark, violent creature I could feel lurking within me. There was one question in regards to earlier that burned my mind for a moment before I went to comfort the children, however.

What is happening to me?

~~ * ~ * ~ * ~~

Wednesday

I picked up the file, scratching the counter with my

245

claw as I did so. I stared at it for a moment, strangely excited and awkward about what I planned to do. Seeing the door open in the mirror, I turned and shut it. I locked it as well, embarrassed by the thought of Kate seeing this.

Holding my hands over the sink, I rubbed away the sharp claw point of my left thumb. It felt odd and alien when I touched the dulled claw to my skin. Regardless, I did the same with the remaining claws of my left hand.

I tested my new grip, disoriented when I did not need to work around the dangerous points. The object—my comb—slipped from my grasp too easily. I sighed, frowning deeply as I considered how I would adjust to trying even harder to be human.

A knock on the door made me jump. "Cory, are you okay? You've been in there awhile..."

"Ah, yes, just fine!" I called back, beginning to file my right hand. Her rattling the doorknob had me filing too quickly, rubbing to the nerve on my index finger. I exclaimed in shock as the wounded claw burned at the contact to the air. Blood hurried from the wound and collected in the sink swiftly; my heart pounded anxiously.

"That doesn't sound fine," she countered. The knob rattled again. "Why did you lock the door?"

"Ah, that smarts," I hissed, running warm water into the sink for my claw. "Erm, privacy, Kate! You have no need to worry."

"No need to—Cory, I heard you shout a minute ago! Can you please unlock the door and explain what you've been doing in there?" she asked tensely.

I winced as I placed my claw beneath the water, then sighed as the pain began to ease. "I...I suppose."

The knob rattled. "Cory..."

"Right." I reached over with my left hand, unlocking the door reluctantly. After a moment she entered, examining me quickly. She caught sight of my hand under the water, though my claw had stopped bleeding.

"Why is your hand in the water?" She looked at the sink more carefully. "Blood? Cory, why were you bleeding?"

I turned off the water with a sigh, praying she did not notice the filer with its fine traces of my claws smeared across it. "I accidentally nicked myself on my claws."

"Uh-huh. Why's the filer out?" She raised her eyebrows at me in warning that I was caught and would do better to not evade the truth.

"I..." I groaned, glancing at my hands guiltily. "I thought it would be better if I reduced my risk of injuring anyone."

"Reduced...?" Her eyes flicked to my left hand. She reached for it, examining the dulled claws and touching her fingertips to them with a frown. She dropped my hand like it was a snake. "Robert's hearing about this."

"It is an irrelevant matter what I do with my claws, like it is with one's nails," I muttered defensively, blushing deeply with shame. I fought to hold on to the thought that had me act to start with.

She left the bathroom and I followed her, wanting to stop her from phoning Robert. Why? What did it matter if he knew? Was this such an ordeal? Did I feel as though I had disappointed him?

Him or myself? "Kate, please, why are we informing him? Why is this so important?"

She trumped down the stairs with a huff. "Because

247

for how many years have you not done this? Why do you suddenly care?"

"I am tired of worrying over whether or not I may injure someone," I explained, attempting to work through my own thoughts. It was not helpful that it was at that moment I wondered if she would have cared if I were human. I pushed the idea aside for the moment. "I want to be safe..."

She calmed somewhat, changing her course from the phone. She watched me and sighed, picking up one of my hands. Running my fingers down her forearm gently, she sighed. "Fine, if that's all."

"...and human," I relinquished in a mutter I hoped she could not hear. Kate narrowed her eyes and tossed my hand away again. Her annoyance flared, but I caught a glimpse of something else in her eyes.

"Oh, great. Cory, you're sixty-eight! Could you be a little less immature?" demanded Kate exasperatedly. She sighed, stalking into the kitchen to begin cleaning dishes.

"Immature? How?" I questioned, following her as far as the living room entrance to the kitchen. She stiffened when she heard me so close, throwing an irritated glance over her shoulder.

"I don't know," she snapped sarcastically. With how recklessly she was cleaning the knife in her hands, I was anxious for her safety. "Worrying so much about how others think you look, filing your *claws* to be something else? Not even starting about how you act with the kids."

I cringed at her harsh words. "Kate, I apologize. I matured in response to what happened in that place, memories and habits I would much rather leave in the past, not the present. I only have twenty-seven years' worth of experience to work from then, and I never had the chance to be a father! You have been a mother and a grandmother for years."

She dropped the items in her hands, whirling on me. "So, what? I'm being unfair?"

"Yes, actually!" I half-laughed, more bemused by her behavior than amused. Her features shifted abruptly, brows furrowing as she sniffled. I hurried to her side, kneeling to meet her watering eyes. I held her face gently between my hands, wiping away the droplets that raced from her eyes as I hushed her in a murmur. "Oh, Kate. Kate, my dear, there's no need to be sad. If I upset you, I'm sorry."

She trembled slightly. "It's your fault for not fighting hard enough...and it's mine, too. And Eleanor's—"

"Hush," I interrupted softly. I shook my head slowly, keeping my eyes on hers. They were brown now, and sad enough to have the sun vanish. "It's no one's fault. What happened was no one's fault. No one could have known, no one could have stopped them...But it's okay. You're fine, we're okay, *everything* is okay."

Kate placed her hands atop mine, miniscule in comparison. Her breaths hitched as her lips began to quiver. "No, none of it is okay. Nothing's okay. You could still get taken, people don't think the kids should be living with you...*Nothing* is okay."

"Hush," I said again, wrapping my tail around her carefully. "I'm right here and I will demonstrate that your grandchildren are safe here. And come three o'clock, they will walk through the front door, forgetting to put their shoes and backpacks away as usual. In three hours, that's all. Until then, you're able to stop worrying about such heavy thoughts a moment, sit down and allow me to take care of you like I haven't done in far too long, and like you have not relaxed in longer."

She nodded meekly, tears slowing. I kissed her forehead gently, disregarding my hesitation at last. She did not protest, also allowing me to guide her to the couch. When she was seated, I cradled her face in my palm gently. She smiled slowly.

"Thank you," she murmured.

I kissed her forehead again. "It is the least I can do for you. Now, what would you like me to do first?"

Kate glanced at the seat beside her, then at me pleadingly. "Just...stay with me for awhile?"

"Oh, of course," I sighed, taking the seat. She nestled into my side once I was comfortably adjusted. I embraced her, brushing her hair gently with my trimmed fingers. A few minutes later, her breathing was soft and slow. I smiled and closed my eyes, loving where I was.

~~ * ~ * ~ * ~~

September 15th, 2010

Today has been eventful, and oddly fulfilling. It feels as though Kate and I have genuinely seen one another for the first time since my return. She allowed me to care for her and I believe that she may continue to permit me the honor. I hope she does.

My claws are now filed and blunt. I suppose now I may be able to learn to play the piano downstairs. My grip is off and wrong, but I still feel safer now. Just an hour ago, I was able to hold Kate's hand and brush her face without concern. I can apply pressure now without cutting skin. It is a rather brilliant sensation that makes me heady. It is almost able to counteract the heavy sense of betrayal I feel deep within myself, toward myself.

~~ * ~ * ~ * ~~

<u>Thursday</u>

"Are you feeling better than Tuesday?" asked Robert to begin our session.

I nodded. "Yes, yes I am. Yesterday was exciting, but I am certainly feeling much brighter."

Robert smiled, relieved. "I'm glad. What do you mean by exciting?"

"I filed my claws," I told him, ignoring my embarrassed blush. Caring for Kate was our own memory to keep to ourselves, as it used to be. Her distress was also something of hers, nothing of mine to share.

His eyes widened and he glanced at my hands in shock. "Well...What's your reasoning?"

I took a deep breath to calm myself. I was in safe company. Why was I disappointed in myself? "To remove some of the risk of injuring others. And...I feel...as though I might be somewhat more human."

He frowned deeply. "I see."

I saw that he was keeping his deeper thoughts to himself. "I know that my reasoning is unstable at best, but I do feel better now. I feel safe."

Robert nodded slowly, face saddening. I could see that he understood. "Well, if it helps you adjust, then at least for now I suppose I'll leave it be. That aside, what else have you done? How have you felt?"

Allowing myself to be distracted, I smiled. "I...I believe that I am still doing better. Time has taken on the meaning I have missed."

"Which is?"

"It only passes so quickly because it is enjoyable." I smiled, and the remainder of the session passed by in a blur. Before I realized it, I was standing on Robert's front porch bidding him farewell before I took flight.

I glanced at the sun in the sky as I turned to fly homeward, keeping my beats steady. At last, I had a spare moment to myself to think of what to do with recent developments.

My mind immediately turned to my acidic blood and the amnesia those around me had suffered. Without another thought I changed course, searching for the alley I had been cut in. I remembered quite vividly the sound of the knife clattering to the ground. Had no one returned to collect it? Would they?

It was not too long that I had to search before I found the alley and a clear patch near it to land. By now I was far too accustomed to the commotion people made by my abrupt appearance. It was simple to ignore, involved as I was in unraveling this mystery. I just nearly was hit by two cars as I crossed the street, aiming straight for the dark alley.

As I expected no one was in the alley, making my task much easier. Thankfully, it only took a short moment of searching before I found the blade's handle—connected to a melted, useless lump of metal.

"What on earth...?" I muttered, for a moment thinking that I had found the wrong object. Then I saw the black that had dried and crusted on a particularly sharp piece of the mess. I looked at the ground where I was more than certain I had pinned the knife's wielder, touching my fingers to the edges of many small holes where something had eaten through. "Oh, God."

Then I looked at my arm where I had been cut and the scabbing there. With a deep breath to steady myself, I took the sharpest part of the warped blade to it and cut, biting back my pain and fear.

With a hiss, I pulled the metal away to watch my blood drip onto the pavement harmlessly. I looked at the unrecognizable blade again, then at the holes in the ground.

"What am I becoming?" I wondered aloud, while on the fringes of my memory I heard angels sing a haunting melody and for a moment I had the frightening thought that they had sung it for me.

Third Week Outside

<u>Thursday</u>

Robert answered the door, smiling broadly when he saw Kate and I waiting there patiently. "Oh, come on in. Anne's in the kitchen, Cory, if you'd like to say hello."

I nodded with my own smile, ducking inside after Kate. He closed the door behind me. I peered into the kitchen, laughing when I saw how frantic Anne appeared when using so many pots, pans and knives.

"Anne, hello! It has been near three weeks since

last I saw you and here you are, hiding in the kitchen and slaving over a hot stove?" I chuckled. I motioned to Anne. "Kate, this is Robert's wife. Anne, may I proudly introduce Katelyn."

Anne came over, smiling. "Oh, so you're Kate? I've heard a bit about you. Cory would mention you sometimes while he was staying with us. He hasn't eaten you out of your home yet, has he?"

Kate laughed, sounding a mite nervous. "No, not yet. Believe it or not though, he's practically a bird compared to when he was in his twenties. He didn't say too much about me, did he?" she added with a narrow-eyed glance at me.

"No, not at all. And don't worry, all men talk. There's no helping it," assured Anne with a look over her shoulder. She sighed tiredly. "Well, back to the job. It was wonderful seeing you again, Cory, and lovely meeting you, Kate."

I led Kate to the living room, hoping we might converse in the large and open space. Bailey and Vanessa were sitting there, homework splayed out on every surface, and looked up when I entered. Bailey grinned, dropping her pencil to rush over and hug me. I hugged her back lightly before releasing her.

"Hello again, Bailey," I greeted with a grin that she did not flinch at.

"Cory! I thought you might not come back again!" she cried out, craning her neck to look up at me.

"Three weeks is not very long, you know," I told her. I gave Vanessa a small, silent wave that she returned, to my astonishment. "Bailey, Vanessa, please meet Kate."

Bailey looked over at Kate, holding out her hand.

"Oh, wow. So you're the famous Katelyn. You're so pretty!"

Kate shook her hand with a smile, glancing at me again. "Yes, apparently I am famous. You're Bailey?"

"Yep. Oh, that's a gorgeous ring. Where'd you get it?" asked Bailey, admiring Kate's right hand. I looked at it curiously, not having noticed previously.

I started though, my grin fading. The tiny gemstones glittered in the light, the carved roses barely faded in spite of the years my memory told me it must have endured. On the edges of my mind I could see that ring in the palm of my hand, could see it being slid onto her finger...Oh, it was beautiful when it graced her hand.

"Cory gave it to me. It was our engagement ring," she said, holding the ring up to study it more carefully. I paused. I could vaguely recall this, and I found myself struggling to retrieve every last moment from my memory.

Robert strayed over, instantly intrigued. "Really? May I see? He showed me pictures but—Oh gosh, that really is a breathtaking ring."

Only the most beautiful for Kate, I thought, recalling when I had told Robert this. She was blushing deeply, enriching the vibrancy of her cheerful expression.

"Wow," he sighed, shaking his head. Then, as if it were just occurring to him, he looked about at the room. "Right. Shall we start?"

"I'll move out and help Mom in the kitchen." Bailey left with a wave and a smile, collecting her homework beforehand. Vanessa did the same with a wary appraisal of Kate.

I took a seat on the couch beside the large windows that overlooked the back lawn. The sky was a brilliant blue, the grass a vivid green. I smiled to myself; it felt good to be free.

It was a moment before I noticed that Kate had taken a seat apart from me, in the velvet chair that sat across the coffee table from me beside Robert's leather one. Her back was to the beauteous wonders outside, her face focused on the task ahead as she turned to Robert on her left.

"Alright, what do we do?" she asked, glancing between myself and Robert.

"Converse, primarily," I replied, bringing my attention back to the room. The world outside beckoned to me, but I kept my yearning to myself. I would be flying again soon enough, once it was time to leave. "About our troubles. Oh, that is a poor explanation. Robert?"

He nodded, sitting there not as my friend but my guide. "Having multiple people in a session is awkward at first, so I have some questions just to break the ice. After that, it's a fairly natural flow. Whatever's troubling you, stopping you from doing something, frightening you, all you do is tell me and I help you to deal with it however it needs to be dealt with."

"Right..." Kate was unsure. Always the believer in her own inner strength. Oh, I admired her personal power. "Well, not to sound too rushed, but I only have three hours until the kids no longer have anyone to watch them."

I smiled tenderly at her, then apologetically at Robert. "Your questions, sir?"

He nodded in understanding. "I think one of the important questions for both of you that needs answering is how you felt when you fell out of touch, whenever that was, however that was. What was the impact? How did you feel? What did you do?"

"*It's Wednesday, Mr. Lawrence! What would you like to eat today?*"

I glared despairingly at the tears on the photograph of my family. "*Just whiskey.*"

The server started. "*But, Mr. Lawrence, you need something to eat with the whiskey. Paul says—*"

"*I'm in pain and I'm nauseated. Please just give me the whiskey.*" *I hoped she did not notice the lie in my words. I was averse to being lucid for awhile after the phone call yesterday. My resolve was beginning to crack already. I needed something to get me by until time made her voice stop ringing in my ears, time enough to recover from losing half of my hope for returning home.*

"*Mr. Lawrence—*"

"*Whiskey!*" *I shouted, turning my glare on her. She jumped away, the smell of her fear rank in the stale room. I kept myself from baring my fangs.* "*Please.*"

Trembling, she reached into the cart and pulled out a shot glass. She grabbed the amber liquid next, moving to open it. I shook my head slowly.

"*Just leave them. I'll manage,*" *I said with a heavy sigh, looking back at my photo. I heard her set the objects on the bedside table before rushing from the room. At last, I could have a temporary indulgence from this constant ache.*

"Cory? Cory, are you listening to what she's saying?" asked Robert, jerking me from my dark memory. I looked about in confusion for a moment.

"I apologize, I seem to have lost myself. Please, continue," I said quietly. My throat was constricting with grief, the room too small for a sharp second.

257

"It was hard," she said with a pointed look at me. I wondered if she was irked for my lapse of awareness or something that I had no recollection of doing. "The calls were all we had to hold on to, aside from a few pictures. I stayed in his room after the—he was taken, and even when he stopped calling. Charlie, my daughter, stayed with me in the room. Sometimes Eleanor would sleep in there with us. Heaven knows the bed was big enough, with space to spare..."

I could not look away from Kate. I had stopped calling? Why? The reason was near my grasp, close enough that I wanted to flinch away from the pain.

"And what did you think had happened?" asked Robert quietly. Could he see the torment in her eyes as clearly as I could? Could she see my guilt as clearly as I felt it?

"I thought he had died," she replied almost silently, expression wistful. I flinched at her obvious pain. She fingered her ring. "Eleanor refused to believe that. I continued to live with the Lawrence's another year before I moved out with my eleven-year-old daughter."

Robert was nodding slowly. "Why did you name her Charlie?"

"Oh," she laughed, blushing slightly. The change of topic seemed to lighten her mood for a short moment. "Cory's middle name. At first it was to keep him close, but the older she got...It was like he had left an echo of himself that was raising her. She would read all of his favorite books, stare at the moon, listen to his albums endlessly..." Kate looked up at me shyly. "I really think she was supposed to be yours."

My hate for Ethan vanished in an instant, startling

me. I could not bring myself to even be angry. Kate's love for her daughter was too strong for me to deny. I nearly wanted to thank him. Her influence was not quite that powerful, however. I was able to break away from her gaze with mild effort and turn my attention to the sky outside the window to think.

Charlie. Three weeks with Kate and she had never told me the name of her deceased daughter. A daughter she had named after me...

If I had been human, I thought again. Even so, this daughter could have been raised by me, according to Kate. I wondered idly what Charlie had been like and wished that I could have met her, my mourning for her becoming more personal the more I learned of her.

"Well, thank you, Kate. Cory?" asked Robert.

"Yes?" I looked at him reluctantly. The topic I knew he would return me to was painful.

By his gentle expression, I could understand that he saw my pain. "What happened for you?"

"I love you, Kate." I took a shaky breath to steady myself, tears soaking my face. "More than anything."

"Cory, are you okay?" she asked, sounding worried.

I nodded to myself, savoring the sound of her voice while I could. After this, I would only have fading and smeared images. "I only wanted you to know."

"Well, you know I love you. Oh, coming, Eleanor!" she called to my mother. My heart twisted inside my chest. "I have to go, Cory. Will you call again tomorrow?"

"I don't know," I whispered, thinking of some way to give her the truth. "I may be scheduled for something already."

259

"Oh. When next you can, then," she said hopefully. "Bye, Cory."

"Goodbye."

I listened to the dial tone for a minute before placing the phone back on the cradle. I wanted to cry out and express my grief in an animalistic, primal mourning. Still, I stared at nothing numbly and allowed myself to experience the loss in defeated silence.

"I took to drinking on occasion, when I could not sleep from missing her," I replied, keeping my honesty vague. My habits with the whiskey went deeper than a sip to help put me to sleep. The first two weeks, when the memory of her was strongest, I had maybe hours when I permitted myself sober awareness. After that first period, however, she faded away into memories and photos, so I no longer drank even for the pain of the operations.

"Drinking? Alcohol?" asked Kate in disbelief. I nodded absently, glad to see her sitting across the room from me. Her presence eased the anguish of the past and made the present worthwhile. "Why didn't you call if you missed me that much?"

I smiled—a strained action—and replied quietly as the reason finally came back to me, "To give you the chance to live in the world, without me. It seemed unfair to continue as we had and ask you to...I wanted you to have everything you deserved. I could not give you anything, and I knew you would never let go otherwise. Apparently, my plotting was overthrown by your determined genius yet again."

She sighed heavily, releasing the breath slowly. Her eyes slipped shut while her expression appeared as though she was trying to hide something. "That decision wasn't yours to make alone. You should have asked me what I wanted."

"You never would have agreed," I murmured, grasping at where she meant to go with her words.

"Damn straight!" she snapped sharply, glaring at me with tears in her eyes. "There's a point where your altruism can turn into raw cruelty!"

"Kate, please calm down," interjected Robert hurriedly, holding out a pleading hand to her. My hand relaxed from the subconscious grip on the couch's arm. I took deep and steady breaths to sooth my heightening tension.

A tentative knock at the entrance to the room caught our attention. Bailey waved, wide-eyed at the darkness I knew she sensed in the room. "Hey, um, did you want us to bring dinner to you?"

"Dinner?" echoed Kate with a frown. She glanced at the watch on her wrist uncertainly.

"It's old person speak for lunch," she clarified with a playful grin. "Steak, and a veggie mix with green beans, mushrooms, onions... Anyone want some?"

"Yes, please, if no one would mind my eating in this room," I said with a glance at Robert.

He smiled and nodded to his daughter. "I'll have a plate, thank you."

"No, thank you, Bailey." Kate glanced at me, then hid her face as a tear streaked across her cheek. The thought that I could not wipe away her troubles with that tear was as painful as my guilt that I could not rid her of either, yet had caused both.

Even so, I could not help myself calling to her quietly, "Kate, come sit by me?"

Without ever revealing her face, she moved in an instant to my side. I wrapped my tail and arm around her, hoping that it may help her some. She took the flat of my tail in her hands lightly, fingering it silently as she used to. I smiled timidly. The contact felt wonderful. Did she feel similarly?

Bailey appeared before me with a plate and utensils wrapped in a napkin. I set the plate on my lap with my free hand and took the napkin, thanking her quietly though I felt somewhat awkward dining away from a table. She glanced at Kate in my embrace, awkward for a moment.

"Here, Dad," she said quietly.

"Thanks, honey. I'll bet it's as good as it smells, just like everything else cooked recently," he told her with an apologetic smile and glance in my direction. She understood and left.

Robert waited a moment before smiling at me and unwrapping his utensils. "Now, Cory, would you mind continuing with complete honesty?"

I laughed to myself. So he had noticed. Removing my arm, I mimicked his actions. I cut myself a bite, frowning thoughtfully as I ate. A few minutes later, I nodded to myself.

"You caught me, Robert," I sighed guiltily. The sun from the window was warm, a slit of it dancing on my arm. "I drank to keep myself from phoning. It kept my resolve, well, apathetic until...your memory faded enough that I could stand the emptiness without it. I remember once, with Paul..."

I laid on the table, wondering what part of me they would cut next. Seeing some of the tools lain out on a nearby table, I had to wonder if this would be a particularly bloody affair.

"It had been roughly a week since...There was something—Blood. I know that black covered so much..."

Paul moved to set aside his scalpel. I saw the neat thread and needle he was reaching for, and I cried out in panic. I was still mildly intoxicated, head and thoughts dizzy with whiskey.

"NO!" I yelled, staring at him with wild eyes. "Listen to me, Paul, LISTEN! Don't save me...Just let me go. I have no family, no freedom...Don't save me."

"I asked him...I begged him..." I murmured distantly, eyes seeing things years dead. "He had a knife, a scalpel...I was on the table for another 'examination' and he was the one to perform it..."

Staring at the bright object in my hand, I gasped with horrified realization at what I was holding and dropped it. The sharp knife fell to the floor with a clatter. It was a snake in my eyes, a vicious and venomous thing that would only bite me. I set my plate on the coffee table and stood in the same movement, shaking uncontrollably.

"Air," I gasped, stumbling over to the door. "I need air."

The door opened too smoothly and I fell outside, dragging myself over to the grass. Feeling its coolness beneath me, I looked up at the vast blue sky dotted with clouds. I was still free. I let my wings fall to the ground and stretch across the grass. The sun was on my face, soft and warm. *I was still free.* The slight nausea that had begun to twist my stomach was fading slowly as I breathed deeply, safe beneath the open sky and unchained by walls.

I heard people behind me, and Robert placed a hand on my shoulder for comfort. "It's alright, Cory. We put all

263

of the knives away."

"Oh, thank you," I sighed tiredly. "Thank you. I do apologize for my reaction, but I cannot—Not while speaking of—Air. Ah, the air is good."

"It's alright, it's fine. Take your time, Cory," he said, keeping his tone soft. I sighed again, feeling like a timid animal. "Is there anything we can do that will help?"

I paused and thought for a moment before nodding slowly. I kept my focus on breathing, speaking in a hushed volume to keep myself calm. "Kate...and may we continue to speak out here? The walls are confining, maddening...I need the sky above me. Nothing but the sky."

He nodded. "We can do that. Kate, can you come here?"

"What is it?" she asked, voice coming closer as she spoke. I smiled slightly, her presence easing the pain and panic somewhat. On my other shoulder I felt her hand, soft and small.

"He requested you," replied Robert quietly. He patted my shoulder. "I'm going to go take care of things inside, alright? I'll be back in a couple minutes if you're comfortable with that, Cory," he added. I nodded numbly and his hand vanished. I heard activity inside before the door was shut.

Kate sat in the grass beside me to see my face and all the hideousness that resided there. After a moment she asked, "What happened? What was wrong?"

"The knife." I watched her expression change slowly from confusion to the beginning lights of a dawning realization. "It reminded me of the scalpels. Anything that is silver or glistens as sharply as those tools...those tools and the harsh lights...Thank you for being with me, Kate. It keeps me from going too deeply into the memories of that place."

She nodded, face pained. "They did more to you than what was said in the papers, I'll guess."

"They did more than I can remember," I murmured distantly, seeing the scars on my bare arm. Against my greater desires, the day was oddly warm for October, barring my ability to wear anything with long sleeves to cover me. All of my wounds were bare for the cruelty of the world to see.

I watched her fingers move to the marks on my right arm. Her fingertips trembled as they traced the angry violet scars lightly, sending shivers of sensation across my skin. Tears of shame came to my eyes, so I pulled my arm away slowly, gently so that she could understand that it was all my own discomfort. I wanted to revel in her touch, but it seemed wrong to ask her to feel the demonic and inhuman thing that was me and my burdens of time.

Kate stared at me tearfully. "You were so handsome..."

The door opened suddenly, startling us both. "Are you doing any better?"

"Yes, Robert, much better. Thank you." I did not respond to Kate's wistful words. Instead, I shifted to sit comfortably, pulling my wings in to provide space for the others to sit.

We were quiet for a moment as we listened to the world. The breeze was cool and gentle, a peaceful transition from my horror only minutes ago. I closed my eyes to the world so that I could be blind to all of the beauty that failed to mask me. I could not bring myself to yearn for darkness, however. Not now that I was in the sun without fear, not when I had spent my entire life lit only by electricity or stars.

"Where did we leave off?" wondered Robert absently. I imagined that he was like myself, lazing because of the sun's warmth.

I heard Kate shift beside me, her hand touching my arm tentatively. "Paul. It was an operation, you were asking Paul for something...?"

"Nothing," I sighed, shaking my head slowly. I reopened my eyes to see the glorious blue sky. I forced the words to stay within my mind, thinking what it would do to Kate. Or Robert, the poor youth. "Nothing."

Her hand pressed against my arm gently. I glanced over to see her concerned brown eyes. "Alright."

Again, none of us spoke. Kate had a hold of the flat of my tail and was turning it this way and that. Robert was watching with a curious smile.

"So, Kate...Why did you keep the ring?" asked Robert lightly. The silver band was bright and glistening in the sunlight. I smiled, flicking her hands with my tail gently.

"I..." She sighed, brows furrowing slightly as she thought. It was an excellent question and I found myself holding my breath as we awaited her answer. "Honestly, I can't remember. I think it was to keep Cory close...I'm glad I still have it, anyway."

"As am I," I murmured with a smile to myself. Seeing that she had held on as long as I had was enough to banish the sharp memories of the nightmarish past. I lifted her hand to me using the flat of my tail, holding her fingers tenderly as I examined the gorgeous contrast between her gold-glinting skin and the silver. "It is still beautiful on

266

you."

She smiled and removed her hand gently. "It's a beautiful ring."

Robert nodded. "It is."

Again, silence overtook us too easily. A few minutes passed again beneath the sun and surrounded by the soft breeze before the door opened.

"Hey, Dad, we got everything cut." Glancing over my shoulder, I saw Bailey peering around the edge of the door timidly. "I'm not disturbing anything, am I?"

"Well, there was a very nice silence," teased Kate with a smirk. Bailey smiled slowly, seeming to understand her humor.

"Take two on lunch, then?" asked Robert, glancing between Kate and I.

"Now that I'm actually hungry..." She sighed and nodded, standing stiffly. I followed their leads, curiously the most fluid of us in movement.

Robert entered after Bailey retreated, but Kate hesitated at the door, looking after me uncertainly.

"Will you be alright?" she asked concernedly.

I paused to consider before nodding, for the first time in too long believing the words when I spoke them. "Yes. I will be fine."

~~ * ~ * ~ * ~~

September 25ᵗʰ, 2010

I have found a tutor to teach me how to play the piano yesterday. The first seven that I phoned told me that they had no more room for students, though I suspect they were reluctant to have any relations with a demon. My first lesson is next Wednesday, on the 29th. I am excited and jovial. Although, I do not suspect it will be anything of too much excitement, particularly after these past two months.

Has it been so long? If I look at the calendar, then it will tell me that only a week more will complete the time. My, has the time passed swiftly. It has been incredibly fulfilling, however.

I wonder...would I change anything in the past, knowing now where I have found myself?

Chapter Seven:
The Wax Lullaby

Fourth Week Outside

Saturday

The glorious orb in the dark sky pulled my eyes to toward it, making it impossible for me to move. I remembered winter on the farm, when the skies were clear and the stars vivid...I sighed, imagining those wonderful nights; in my mind, I could see my old home.

"Nice to know you still stare at the moon." Kate's even breathing was a gentle sound in the calm when she entered the dark room, nearly silent in her movements.

"I had no windows to do so for too long," I replied in a murmur. I turned to look at her and motioned to my lap for her to sit. She did so, leaning back against my chest. I could feel her tiny, fluttering heart and wondered if it always beat so fast or if mine was merely slow. "Everything is always so new and exciting, like I am a young child. I still feel grief over everything lost, however."

She nodded, pulling her legs up onto my lap and tucking them beneath her. She laid the side of her face lightly on my chest. I entwined my arms around her,

269

cradling her lovingly. We were quiet for a time.

"I've missed this," she whispered. Delicate and small, her hand rested inches from where her head was. Her fingertips tapped against my skin in time with my heart, making me smile.

I began to hum an old melody I knew from before I could remember, a nameless tune that felt as old as the stars, allowing my eyes to slip shut for a moment. When I opened them again, all I could see were Kate's eyes. They enveloped the world around us as she came closer. My heart did as it had when we were young, pounding in my chest. The emotion of flight burst through me abruptly, making the kiss that much sweeter.

The first kiss in too long a time to remember.

I sighed contentedly when we broke apart a moment later. I gazed at her, smiling gently. "I have been craving that more than you know."

She smiled as well, settling against me again. She was warm in my arms, the sweet smell of her wonderful in the evening. "Mm..."

"Rest well, my dear," I whispered, kissing her hair gently. Laying my head back to watch the moon, my eyes slipped shut as I was overtaken by warmth and safety.

Sixth Week Outside

<u>Sunday</u>

"Your hair's getting long," noted Kate absently over breakfast. She smiled. "It's always grown so fast."

270

I chuckled quietly. "Those nice gentlemen at the Center kept it well trimmed to my scalp. I may grow it so that I can pull it back again. It may take attention away from the scars some," I murmured to myself distantly. I smiled, though. I could choose what I did to my own hair again. It was certainly an empowering feeling.

"Wait..." She stood and came over to me, disbelief in her smile. Her fingers were gentle, touching something near the base of my right horn, with a laugh. "You're going silver, mister."

"Oh, *now* I feel like a senior," I laughed. Sarah snickered. "Is it a pretty silver, at least? Something that flatters reds and browns?"

"Stop that," she chided playfully, returning to her seat. "I've had grays since my forties. It's hardly fair that you got to wait until you were almost seventy."

Her words made me pause. "Seventy? That is right, only two years left to this decade...My, I do feel aged."

"Wait until someone tries to help you cross the street," she warned me. This time, Kyle was the one to snicker.

I smiled, shaking my head. "I will be panicked the day that happens, and watching for large vehicles."

"Why would you do that, Grampa Cory?" asked Kyle innocently, turning Kate's horror-struck gaze from me to him. His face was too innocent and he had spoken his words doubtlessly. I turned my smile to him.

"Did you just call him Grandpa?" asked Kate, smiling slowly in disbelief.

"He's not our grandpa, Kyle," whispered Sarah severely.

Kyle shook his head stubbornly. "No, I didn't call

271

him grandpa. I called him Grampa. He is our *grampa*, Sarah," he whispered back loudly, making a face.

"Refrain from squabbling at the table, children," I chided gently, looking between the two. They seemed to forget their bickering, turning to me simultaneously.

"What does that mean, rethrain?"

"No, not rethrain, *retrain*," his sister attempted to correct him.

Kate and I stifled our laughter before I began to explain the word to them. Neither flinched when I grinned, but instead grinned back at me as they repeatedly struggled to pronounce "refrain."

~~ * ~ * ~ * ~~

<u>Nightmares</u>

13th week outside

<u>Thursday</u>

Robert sat across from the demon, both of them staring anywhere but at one another awkwardly. The hands of the clock reached after the numbers eagerly and still, silence reigned. Finally, Robert cleared his throat and looked Cory in the eye.

"So, where shall we start this week?" he asked, genuinely curious.

Cory shrugged but did not flinch at the question. That Robert could see, at least. He had to remind himself that the man he dealt with was altruistic and—much to the disagreement of others—thought himself to be a true

272

demon.

"Well, perhaps you could tell me about the facility," suggested Robert gently, and he saw the panic in Cory's eyes. He leaned forward, keeping his voice soft. "Just a little, or none if you're not ready yet, Cory. Whatever you feel comfortable with."

In spite of the panic that Robert could still clearly see, Cory smiled and waved it away. "No, no, of course I can discuss that...place."

What happened there? Wondered Robert for what he thought must have been the thousandth time. The apparent strength that Cory possessed seemed to dull in the shadow of this past, when he had otherwise stood readily against every obstacle that others struggled with for years.

"Whenever you're ready," replied Robert, prepared to wait. Much to his surprise, Cory took a deep breath to begin speaking.

"The first thing that comes to mind is a time when they...They were testing a new anesthetic. I remember how frightened I was when they strapped me down that time, how terrified I was that I may not wake up again. The needle bit me, I remember, and then the world blurred in my eyes...

"When next I woke, there was a bright light in my eyes, a glaring light that pierced my skull painfully. I was confused, my vision coming into focus slowly. I felt...pain, in my chest, though it was blunt and ebbing. I could hear voices, and one of them sounded like Paul. Some of them were hushed, others were panicked and urgent.

"'We need more anesthesia. Now, Victoria,' said Paul.

"'I'm more intrigued to see how it reacts,' replied a

woman, and when I turned my head to look, I groggily recognized Beth. Her eyes were alight with curiosity, smock and mask spattered with my blood.

"I moaned, finding myself with limited movement. I tried to glance at where I was, but a mask that covered much of my face kept blocking my vision. The people were becoming more urgent now, and I saw someone with a needle coming towards me.

"I struggled to see now, lifting my head with great effort. I remember that I tried to scream but that the sound was muffled, a pipe in my throat blocking it before it could escape. Trapped, all I could do was stare in horror at my gaping chest. Where I had always seen vibrant red, abyssal black dominated my vision.

"There was the pinch of the needle, amplified in my panic, and I was falling. Out of time, out of actuality, out of my body, I was only falling. I recall also when I woke in my room after that operation. My body...I could not move for days from the pain, and I could barely stand to breathe without crying. I couldn't..."

Cory faltered, eyes locked on a nightmare from another time. Robert had to take a deep breath to stop himself from trembling, shaking his head slowly as he struggled to understand what he had just been told. To Robert's surprise, Cory continued to speak even through his tears.

"But I wonder if I deserve everything that has happened," he whispered brokenly, meeting Robert's eyes. He had the strangest feeling that Cory was begging him to confirm or deny his words, if only to finally understand. "I remember heaven. I remember hearing the voices of angels and feeling the warmth of joy. But I can't remember what I did—whatever heinous act *I did*—that had me removed, sent here...like this. I can't remember."

With any other patient, Robert would have immediately thought them delusional, but the uniqueness of this situation had him believing Cory's words.

Later that evening, after uncertainly finding a way to reassure Cory, Robert found himself sitting in his study staring at his patient's file. He scowled at the name there, deep in his thoughts.

"Come on, Robert, why is he talking to you in the first place?" he muttered to himself, shaking his head slowly. He sighed heavily, flipping open the file to look at images that the N.S.I.S.D. had supplied him with. Perhaps he could find some answer in his history. Robert would have continued on for hours, he was certain, but he paused on one of the first images.

Frowning, he rummaged for a magnifying glass in his drawer, placing it eagerly over a curious birthmark in one image. At the base of Cory's skull, Robert was able to see the apparent shape of a crown with three points. Three small symbols resided there, one atop each point: a small crescent on the right, a star in the center and a sun on the left.

"What the...?" he murmured, flipping to another image where the birthmark should have been visible, but he froze. "Where is it?"

"Where is what?" asked Anne from behind him. Robert shook his head and sighed, leaning back in his chair.

"I just...Oh, long day, I guess. I'm so tired I'm seeing things," he laughed to himself, but even as he replaced everything on his desk, Robert could not shake the feeling that there was something very wrong about all of this. As if the Fates were proving him right, when he went to investigate the picture with the birthmark the next morning, the marking was no longer there.

~~ * ~ * ~ * ~~

December 27ᵗʰ, 2010

I have not written in months now. Oddly, I have not missed the act, nor have I required it. Robert has moved our visits now to every other week with tentative plans to make the adjustment permanent. I am rather partial to this idea, as it permits me yet more time to enjoy life with Kate and the children.

What is there to even write of? Christmas was enjoyable, I know. Kate had all but forced me into a forest green sweater with a reindeer on the front, claiming that it would demonstrate my holiday spirit. I did so to entertain her, although I felt ridiculous.

Ha! I have just realized that I would much rather be downstairs with the family that I hear laughing than sitting at this dank desk writing.

~~ * ~ * ~ * ~~

February 16ᵗʰ, 2011

I am sitting at the table downstairs now, as it is by all technicalities the seventeenth of the month. The clock proclaims that it is three in the morning, and by how exhausted I feel I have no doubts as to its accuracy. Ah, my body rather smarts. My skull and eyes are sore from my lack of rest this evening.

Twenty minutes ago, I was woken by the queerest nightmare. I have left the bedroom so that Kate may continue to sleep while I attempt to remove the sequences from my mind by use of ink and paper.

It began with me sitting in a café across from Kate. We were discussing something that I cannot recall before the world froze. I panicked a moment when she did not move, and when I stood to check her condition I found that she was made of wax. In the logic of dreams, I left the café in favor of the streets, where cars were unmoving and pedestrians were halted mid-step.

The world was nearly silent aside from a breeze. I turned around and around, confused and frightened. What had happened to this place?

A crow cawed, startling me. I whirled to see it stare through me with one broad crimson eye. I took an impulsive step towards it, reaching out a hand as I did so.

"Wait!" The severe outcry made me wince and turn in search of the banshee that had wailed. I froze when I spied the elderly, bent woman at my side. Her face was hidden beneath rags for a hood and cape.

"Child," she crooned, gazing up at me with a crooked grin though her eyes did not exist. The sight made me reel back in shock, fear sharper now. "Greatness is your path, I see it in your soul. I see more, too. Death and grief, if you follow the crow. But you must walk on thorns, or else you will face the demise of your rich breed."

The crow shrieked to punctuate her words. When I looked back at the bird I frowned. Had it grown? The woman drew my attention again with a sickly cackle.

"The choice is yours, child. Stay here and turn to

wax with the rest of these creatures, or follow that bird to your purpose and pay the price." She cackled again, pointing a withered hand in the bird's direction. "Go now to the storm or you'll be lost forever, Prince! Fly, fly, fly!"

She vanished, though her voice echoed in the city streets. Again the crow had grown and now it blinked at me once before the entire setting changed. We were in the park near home, surrounded by the night. Kate was wax still, standing near me and staring past me. I frowned worriedly at her before turning back to the crow, crying out in terror when I saw what stood in its place.

It was a foot shorter than myself, with mixed proportions that were wrong and nightmarish. Its face was human aside from the bulbous, blood-colored eyes with slits for pupils that stared at me in misery. The size of its ribcage was that of mine, but some sadistic power had attempted to affix it to the body of a normal man. Like its ribs, its arms were disproportionate, thick with muscle and hanging to the knees of its otherwise human-sized body. It was a hideous thing with skin so thin and pale that I could see the muscle beneath the supposedly protective layer.

It sighed, the sound so soft it was more like a hiss, while it stretched its ebony wings out behind it. A frightening smell came from it like nothing I have ever known. It reached a claw-like hand to me, beckoning me with its delicate, hissing voice, "Follow me. The angels are waiting to be slain. We await your command, Prince."

From behind me, I heard Kate begin singing, "Death rolls, Death rolls...The stars are all Death rolls...His hands are a child's, his face is a man's, his heart is a god's..."

I awoke there, on a hauntingly familiar note that I

278

have never heard sung by anyone. I am uncertain the note exists outside of my dream. Oh, and that song, that lullaby...I know it from my youth, but I know that I have never heard it in my ears before!

Those are not what frightened me in my dream. Not even that horribly disfigured creature is what had me stifling screams as I woke. No, no, I think what should horrify me more is that what the old woman was proposing felt right. Following that crow felt more real than even sitting here, writing. The entire dream still rings with the truth and finality that some of my premonitions have had.

"Prince," they had called me, and the angels were waiting to be slain. Oh, what was that? Could it have something to do with the instant when my blood had turned to acid? Or my memory of heaven? Is that why I was banished? Because I was—or am—a traitor?

Living as a human has begun to feel like turning to wax on occasion, as the woman had spoken. Curiouser yet, the strangest sense that there is something that I must do that I have forgotten about creeps upon me at times. I think that either I am having an overactive imagination, or there is indeed something that I have forgotten. What could it be, though? What is the purpose that I have neglected to remember?

~~ * ~ * ~ * ~~

March 14th, 2011,

Recently, I cannot help but think of my nightmare some month ago. Anytime I step outside, the world is frozen even as people rush through their lives at hundreds of miles a second. No, as in the dream I see them as wax figures that barely move.

Am I imagining things? A great deal of myself hopes that I am delusional. After all, it is not just the humans that I have seen as wax, of late. My own reflection is seeming to be taking on a rather strange appearance, almost like...wax.

$$\sim\!\!\sim * \sim * \sim * \sim\!\!\sim$$

(April 3rd) 28th Week Outside

<u>Sunday</u>

"Happy birthday, Kate," I whispered, pulling my hand from her eyes. She gasped, staring at the room with wide eyes. Yellow flowers decorated every surface gorgeously, making it seem as though it was the sun that had taken perch on the sill rather than the moon. Petals were tossed across the floor and bed in a picturesque reality that smelled sweetly of beauty.

Beneath the bed, I had set a music player with a disc I had requested Robert to create for me. I pulled the remote from its hidden nook behind a vase and commanded the music to begin, as Robert had shown me how to do. Kate beamed at the room like it was fairytale magic, then at me.

The woman I saw was not tired or aged. She was filled with the glory and determination of her youth. The lines on her face seemed to vanish, time releasing her from its villainous clutches so that she stood before me with all of the perfection of her self from decades ago.

"When did you do all of this?" she asked

breathlessly. Her eyes glittered brightly with glee.

I smiled, replacing the remote, closing the door with my tail so that I could continue watching her. "I do believe that there was a film I did not see at the theater..."

She laughed joyfully and I reveled in the sound of it. "Oh, it's beautiful, Cory!"

"Check the bathroom," I murmured quietly, nodding my head toward the door. She hesitated before taking my hand to bring me with her. I followed willingly, heart warming that she loved this gift.

Within, the rich scent of apples and chocolate made her sigh calmly. Placed in the bath, there were lavender soaps with a freshly cleaned robe and towel. Beside that, there was a blue flower print summer dress similar to the one she had worked for when she was fourteen. On the counter was a large basket with her favorite apples and chocolates set behind a smaller wicker basket. It was worn and somewhat battered, with marks from my claws on the handle, but she still seemed to recognize it.

She stepped forward in a dreamlike trance, hand reaching out to touch the yellow journal. I had arranged the three photos she had given me in the basket. In the center of them, a fourth image taken from the dance was carefully placed, surrounded by the three other standing artworks.

"You kept them all?" she asked, lifting the photograph of the dance from the basket.

"And have an addition to the collection," I replied. From another hidden space, I retrieved my thick old journal. Its binding was a simple, deep blue. I gave it to her, brushing her hair lightly with my empty hand. "I hope it might begin my atonement for my absence."

Kate looked up at me in surprise and set aside the

281

photo. She opened the book to a random page and read aloud, "'July 27th, 1961. Kate has been gone near two months now. I believe that the world misses her as much as I do.' I remember that trip," she laughed to herself.

"'The frogs and crickets have not sung since she left, and the moon seems to have dimmed.' Didn't you tell me that it was loud by that tree, though?" she murmured to herself thoughtfully. She looked at me with a frown.

I grinned sheepishly. "Once you were home, everything sang again."

Kate smiled and nodded, still very young and vibrant before me. She glanced behind me. "I'm going to lay down with this—And this," she added, grabbing the wicker basket with a grin. She flew past me, crawling onto the bed with a mad fit of childlike laughter.

I chuckled and followed her, sitting on the mattress with more care. She lay on her stomach, book in hand with a look of intrigue making her eyes wide. I settled in to watch her read, smiling to myself happily.

Home.

Even as the past was smoldering as ashes, I was in the place that was closest to nothing less than bliss. My siblings were complacent to visit with me while I lived with my fiancée and her grandchildren. My grandchildren as well, when Kate and I would finally wed. Although, the date was still uncertain.

Now before me was solid and profound evidence that I could share joy again. With Katelyn laying close enough to touch, her scent filled the room to mix with that of the flowers too perfectly. I had my family, my friends and all of them said they were glad to be with me. I was not a burden but a companion.

The melody playing brought me back to myself slowly and I began to hum with it clumsily. It was an unfamiliar song, one I assumed Robert had added. Kate looked up from the journal with tears in her eyes.

"I haven't heard you sing in years. Just the once a few months ago," she explained quietly, setting the book aside. She sighed, closing her eyes and smiling peacefully.

"I have not sung in years, but for that once," I replied, wrapping an arm around her. For a gorgeous moment I forgot what I was to the world and was only myself, unscarred and human.

"Please don't stop," she whispered sleepily, holding my hand close to her face. I was glad then that my claws were filed and could not harm her.

I continued my awkward humming willingly, the warming season taming the air to a comfortable temperature. Kate's breathing slowed after a few moments, and the heartbeat that I could feel was calm. I chuckled to myself, standing and going about turning off the music and lights, glad again that the Smiths had been able to care for Kyle and Sarah this evening.

Before I turned off the final light, I paused to watch Katelyn sleeping. I smiled warmly. "Rest well, my dear."

~~ * ~ * ~ * ~~

30th Week Outside

<u>Sunday</u>

"Sir! Sir, can you help me?" called a voice to my right. I glanced over curiously, frowning when I saw the small, hunched figure trembling. They were hidden between two buildings and in shadow, where I thought not a soul could see them suffering. I could not distinguish their features.

I stepped into the space innocently, unconcerned for the groceries I still held. "What assistance do you require?"

"Oh, it's dreadful! You see, there's this demon..." The figure straightened, its former guise being tossed away. It was a man just inches shorter than myself, lean and hostile in stature. Hands appeared behind me, shoving me farther between the buildings.

"It's a big problem, could give my kid the wrong ideas," the man continued. Another man came to his side, handing him an iron bar. I glanced about for a way to run, my heart beginning to race in my chest.

"Sirs, please, I only want to return home," I said shakily. Laughter surrounded me, dark and haunting. I whirled around, angry faces everywhere I looked. "Let me go home."

Others held weapons as well. A knife glinted on the edge of my vision. The fear it invoked was not of the object but of the pain it could cause me. I did not have long to evaluate the entirety of my danger. The iron bar came across my back before the remainders of the group understood the signal to begin their assault.

It was within the first few seconds that they brought me to my knees. The blow of a human did nothing to me, but the cold and unyielding weapons were not merciful. I screamed for help that I knew could not hear and would not come. Where the knife cut me my skin burned from the air and my blood.

"Hit it harder!"

Demon *Rising*

"Break its tail!"

I should have stayed home.

"Look! Its blood is black!"

Why had I not stayed home?

"Let's find out how much it bleeds!"

Minutes or hours could have passed until I was left lying on the hard ground choking, and all I could remember was that I had been beaten. I groaned, attempting to right myself but was kicked back to the concrete. My head cracked against it, throbbing viciously.

Someone grabbed my hair, pulling my face from the ground by it. My throat was too sore to do more than gasp in pain. "I wonder if it's some demon practice to have long hair?"

"Cut it and find out."

I felt the tension of the knife pressing to my hair before it sliced through, and my face met the ground yet again. I winced, wishing that I could muster some will to defend myself but unknowing of how to begin. They were laughing again as I felt rough hands grab one of my wings and force it open.

"Should we teach it a lesson about keeping its head in the clouds?"

My skin tingled, sensing the sharp blade hovering above the membrane. My eyes widened in horror and I whipped with my tail at the arm holding me. Blood pounded in my ears and I was standing in a movement not even I understood. Some animalistic sound found a way to summon itself from my raw throat as I bared my fangs at my assailants in fear. Many of them leapt away from me, holding their weapons high to ward me off.

Without a second glance behind me, I fled the

hidden space as swiftly as I could. My body was searing with pain and bruises as I made my way to the sky, chest aching as my heart raced with the sound of thunder in my ears. With heavy, gasping breaths I barely managed to keep myself airborne.

I flew as fast as I knew I could, driving my body to the edge of exhaustion in my rush to distance myself from my attackers. Having flown from the shop only some mile from home, it was not long until I saw my street beneath me. In spite of the car I saw in the driveway, I landed on the harsh surface of the street, stifling my cries as I stumbled and rolled across the concrete, rubbing much of my skin raw.

I righted myself in an instant and rushed for the house. The knob was in my hand barely a second before I was closing the door behind me and hurrying up the stairs. From what I heard, Kate was in the back room reading to Kyle and Sarah while I raced up the stairs, careful to cause little disturbance. It was only once I had made it into the bathroom and begun to clean the blood from my face that I allowed myself to stop.

"Oh, how am I to handle this?" I muttered, staring at my battered reflection as if hoping that it would supply me with an answer. A sob ripped through my shock. I bowed my head to the mirror, resigned. "What am I doing?"

In spite of the earlier downturn in luck, I attempted to act as though nothing had occurred. My hair was now too short to pull back, but I combed it and ignored whatever else happened to it. The most of my worries were the deep, angry bruises that covered much of my body. There were small cuts on my face from where I had hit the ground, as well as lighter bruises. On my back and arms were deeper, violent cuts from from a man who had wielded a knife. More scars for my collection.

I dressed myself with a long sleeved shirt and full pants to hide the worst of everything, burying my soiled clothing in the laundry. I would make certain to perform that chore before Kate had the opportunity.

When I went downstairs, Kate watched me descend silently. The furrow of her brows was questioning but she said nothing as I entered the kitchen to begin dinner. I only wanted to forget the afternoon and continue life without thinking that things would only become more difficult.

I could only continue on in my self-induced ignorance for a few minutes until the sounds of the television started in the other room. I cringed when I was able to make sense of what I heard.

My voice came from the living room, metallic and broken, "Help me! Help! Stop, please! Anyone, please!"

"Can we turn that infernal thing off?" I called, scowling at the tomato I was slicing methodically. I was too distracted to notice at first how fiercely my hands were shaking. Behind me, I sensed Kate's presence.

"What are you hiding and why?" she asked, voice as strained as her patience.

I did not answer. What would I tell her? What *was* I hiding? *Why* was I hiding? Was I ashamed that I had not defended myself before fleeing? I paused. No, I would not have been able to fight back. Somewhere in time, my will and self-worth had been broken.

"...Should we teach it a lesson about keeping its head in the clouds?"

The terrible sound I had made earlier echoed now in the home harshly.

"Why are you trying to hide this?" she demanded, coming to my side and forcing me to face her. Her eyes were narrowed, watching me carefully.

"Why did you hide your cuts and bruises when we were younger? Because I have always known that it was not Paul's homework that kept you from visiting," I countered, far from having the proper patience with this subject. Their laughter still rung in my ears, sharp and villainous. Or was that the recording being played by the news?

Kate crossed her arms, stubborn as she prepared to outlast me. "Oh, no, this is *not* the same!"

"Yes, it is the same! Pro and anti-demon activists, demonstrations and protests! There was even a march last week where people demanded that I be treated as the animal I am and have me put into a zoo. For the safety of the minds of children."

"Demons in general, not just you," she muttered in a defeated tone. Distantly, I was guilty for being so sharp with her.

"Well, where are they?" I demanded, tears burning my eyes as a hopeless solitude surrounded me. "If these laws and activists mean *demons*, then why am I the only one? Where are the rest? Why, day by day, do I find myself *alone*!"

The film replaying the day's event stopped and the voice of a woman took its place, "In other news, rumors say that the NAACP will no longer continue to support demons, on the grounds that—"

"Kyle, turn that thing off!" snapped Kate, rubbing her temples to soothe her tension. Again, my guilt swelled in my chest. "That's just bull!"

"What are the chances that demons aren't supported because there's no evidence that they're people?" I whispered bitterly, tears falling over.

She shook her head. "It's shit. All of this is just shit!"

"Language," I muttered reflexively, glancing at the two children in the living room. They were both frozen and turned to the kitchen with wide, innocent eyes. Oh, they should not have seen that film. I abandoned my station in favor of the children. They both climbed into my arms and clung to me, trembling. I murmured them comforts, ignoring the pain in my body. "The demons. Where are they?"

Kate sighed, following me to the living room. I knew that she was still seething about the channel's gossip but grateful for a distraction, not unlike myself. "They started showing up in the seventies at first. Just here and there. Most of the time they were dead, some farmer or hunter mistaking them for a bear. They became more common somewhere around '77, and only in the U.S., but they were attacked and killed by a bunch of over zealous idiots. A lot of them fought back, which didn't do well for the petitioning for rights. After '83, they stopped showing up. It was like they all died or something," she finished quietly. It was a long moment before I realized that I was staring idiotically at the center of the room, still holding the two children confusedly.

"I never knew. I never knew..." What did I feel?

Numb. Or perhaps bemused was more apt. "I always thought I was alone..."

"I'm sorry," said Kate, sounding guilty.

"No need, no need," I murmured, frowning deeply. A strange sense of completion settled into place around me as I began to comprehend that I had not been as alone as I had perceived. Even if there were no other demons but me at that moment, the thought that there had been others like me nearly made me smile.

"Kyle and Sarah...Help me see that they are alright? They never should have seen...Oh, hush now, hush. Everything is alright, child," I murmured quietly, allowing Kate to take Sarah from me. I continued to comfort Kyle, relaxing into my seat with a sigh of relief. "There is nothing to worry about, hush. Hush."

The children fell asleep in our arms, and it was only once they were safely tucked away in bed that I allowed myself a hiss of pain. Kate helped me to the couch again before hurrying off to find a medical kit. I sat in silence, lost in thought.

~~ * ~ * ~ * ~~

36th Week Outside

I sat at the piano to practice. The instrument was a therapeutic thing to play; my fingers moved across the keys in a familiar rhythm. Robert's suggestion of finding a hobby seemed to help me to adapt to the world, giving me the time to think and process that I needed. I frowned, wondering where I would have ended if not for my good friend.

Demon *Rising*

Life had calmed, my recent attackers had been found and were now being sentenced for their crimes. I was not their first hateful crime, but I prayed that I might be their last. Only the worst of bruises and cuts were still healing, but it would only be another week before I was nearly recovered.

The evening of the incident, I had gone in for medical attention when Katelyn had seen my injuries. It had taken 19 stitches in total to hold me together, but I felt all the better for it. Of course, now the days held a strange, horrible stillness. Like the calm before the storm, I felt something coming though I could not grasp at what. Perhaps it was the waning of humanity's final moments of tolerance for me.

It was a few sharp moments before I realized that my hands had stopped playing, still on the keys of the piano. I stared at them, at my filed claws, and wondered why it was I had done that. So that I could blend in with the human society around me? So that I could perform things I would otherwise be unable to do? Was it personal desire or peer pressure? It frightened me for a moment that I could not recall if what I was doing was what I wanted anymore.

37ᵗʰ Week Outside

__Thursday__

The knock on the door did not startle me. Rather, I had been expecting it. I halted my cleaning for a moment to answer it and welcome Robert in, smiling in greeting.

He appraised me for a moment, smiling as he did so. "Doing better, are we?"

"Yes, yes, much better," I laughed, closing the door behind him. I held up my arm to show. "The bruises have healed."

He was nodding. "That's good. How are your stitches?"

"Removed," I replied easily, finishing what I was cleaning. I replaced the supplies beneath the sink, washed my hands and went to join Robert in the living room. "I feel extraordinary. Almost like I might be able to fly."

Robert laughed and shook his head. "The doctor ordered three months no flight, remember? Nothing remotely strenuous."

"Ah, yes," I sighed, shaking my head slowly. "I suppose I am only growing restless. Too long without my fullest mobility..."

"And you still have another five weeks of it," interjected Robert, smiling at me like I was a child. "Regardless, how have you been? Cabin fever aside, of course."

I laughed and shook my head, slowly coming to myself. I sighed, thoughts deepening. "I have remembered more of what happened that had me in that...place."

Robert's attention was instantly rapt. He leaned forward, face and tone gentle. "Really?"

Nodding slowly, my eyes fixed on memories long passed. "Yes...I remember words, powerful words that lifted the world into a brighter place...What were those words...?"

Chapter Eight:
Changing Tide

I have a dream. Those are the words which ring out with such power only because a man made them powerful, historical. I remember that Paul purchased a television for the church just so that we could watch the broadcasting.

The church was crowded that day, people standing in the aisle and cramming into the pews. I held Kate and Lisa on my lap to conserve space. There was so much connectedness there, even when you could clearly see the separation of people—one half of the church seating whites while the other half held primarily blacks, myself and Lisa being the only exceptions.

When that man's voice sounded in the room, everyone fell deathly silent. We listened intently. I noticed some people closing their eyes, others staring at the floor while they focused. Beside me, Jeff and Jasmine were nodding to themselves, glancing at Kate and smiling hopefully every few moments.

I barely remember the words that became too much for me. In fact, I cannot recall the words directly, only the chilling reality that they opened to me. It was a dark, cold place that I came to recognize as the world I had unknowingly been living in. Where my sense of self-worth and acceptance were based upon my bright skin and the features I wore. Where I had subconsciously accepted that I was less than someone because I was not the same color as my family. The most frightening thing was the mention of children—the possibility of *my* children.

I had never considered before that I might have the gift of heirs. For a moment, I thought of how close Kate and I were becoming and then realized that, *yes*, children were becoming a likelihood in my future. If I was able to reproduce outside of my own specie, of course.

Pure, raw *hatred* shot through me abruptly. I imagined young, innocent children that looked as I had, being sheltered from the world for their own protection from its violence. The scene in my mind made me hideously enraged. Yes, I had not minded the indoors after awhile, but it still made me miserable. Then, seeing others having to be put through similar pains...

It occurred to me at that moment that my parents had suffered with me every day when I was a child.

I needed to escape the tightly packed room with the hopeful words that would never apply to me or whatever family I brought up. "Please, excuse me, ladies."

Kate and Lisa allowed me to stand with curious glances at one another. I made my way through the crowd to the exit and stepped outside. I should have been relieved, but the open spaces only seemed to fuel my emotions.

On the porch, I could still hear the television, so I went toward the edge of the property off near a small patch of forestry. Then back to the steps of the porch, then to the trees again restlessly.

I was angry, pacing across the small lawn in front of

the church. Within the building, I could still hear the muffled speech. I halted a moment to glare at my crimson hands, rich and glittering in the sun. My claws—black and evil and sharp for violent uses—only spurred my fury.

The door to the church opened and closed when cheers erupted from the building. I sighed heavily, shaking my head. I hated that I was *lucky* to be considered a person at all.

"What's wrong, Cory?"

I whirled to see Kate frowning at me with concern in her eyes. "I would like to tell you the truth, but part of that is that I want to be alone."

"Are you...*mad*?" she asked incredulously. She came closer to me, intending to comfort me. "Why are you mad?"

I stepped away from her, out of fear of harming her than actual upset. "Why aren't you?"

She blinked in surprise. "That doesn't answer the question."

I sighed sharply. "We should not have to fight for what others are granted at birth! Not when it is equality or freedom, and *not* for the comfort to know we will not be attacked by some stranger! It is sick and cruel!"

Kate nodded sadly. "I know. It never bothered you like this before, though."

I turned my back on her, hoping she did not notice the tears beginning in my eyes. Anger and despair twisted inside me, barbed and painful. I wanted to be human then, so much that my throat constricted with the desire.

"That's not what's actually upsetting you, is it?" she asked quietly. Her hand pressed against my wing gently, calming me slightly.

Demon *Rising*

"I'm happy for you—all of you—since you seem to be coming closer to social acceptance, but when that happens...what becomes of me?" I asked, wincing at the words. I looked up at the sky for comfort, then turned my head back to the ground. The empty sky was worse than here on the earth—up there, I was completely alone. "Will you stride forward to stand beside the whites as equals?"

"It only makes sense that you finally start thinking about yourself after a speech like that—which you walked out on too soon. You would've liked the ending." She sounded amused, stepping to my side to look at my face. She even took my apparently inhuman hand in hers. "It'll be like always, Cory. We'll all stick up for one another. You won't get left behind, not if I can help it."

I gave her a half smile and shook my head. "If I have children? What cruelty will they face, because of their horns or their eyes? I am lucky enough, but that luck cannot be expected to pass on to my progeny."

"You're worrying too much. Everyone's children are at risk for getting a short stick. Fate's cruel *and* equal," she said with a small laugh.

Much to my odd disappointment, my anger was subsiding. "Yes...Thank you, Kate, and I'm sorry."

She rolled her eyes, steering me back in the direction of the church. "Don't be." There were loud cheers inside. "Sounds like a party. Shall we?"

I smiled. "Yes."

When we went inside the church, we watched Paul removing the "Whites" and "Coloreds" signs from the pews. There was a group of people in the back that were seething at the act. I recognized Richard and his band, Ethan, and what looked like Richard's and the cohorts'

296

parents. Some of them stepped forward, statures enraged and trembling with it.

"What are you *doing*, Paul?!" shouted what looked to be Richard's father. He thrust his finger towards the the signs on the floor. "This is sick!"

"It's called a movement, Will, and a darn good one, in my opinion," retorted Paul firmly, eyes glittering with what must have been triumph. Recalling how good natured Paul was, I know that it must have been a relief to openly demonstrate integration in the church. In fact, that first time we had met I believe he was only acting so violently because of the people present.

"You'll be *mingling* with things less than human!" hissed Will spitefully. I think it sad now that none of us flinched at his words, commonplace as they were. "Just like the Coloreds do with that demon damned by the Lord Himself. They're all as low as him and you'll be going even lower! The lot of you, vermin! Demons!"

Paul's jaw tightened, eyes narrowing. "You chose the wrong *vermin* to single out. If every Colored were only half as good as that boy, I'd still be more than happy to join hands with them over you. Now, in this church all are welcome, as evidenced by that demon. I think it's only right that everyone's welcome to sit where they please, too. Understand, Will?"

The man glowered at Paul. The people behind him were only becoming even more furious. I think the only thing that kept them from attacking was that they were easily outnumbered. Instead, Will spat at Paul's feet and shoved past.

"And, uh, Will? It's peace to all in the Lord's name. Don't cause any trouble here." There was a hidden threat in

297

Paul's voice, but I could not grasp at what it was for the life of me. I am glad I never found out.

From then on, signs all over town were changing. Attitudes, people, places. By 1965, Paul's first actions had inspired the rest of us. Now, snide comments from Richard, Will and the rest of them could not be helped. Nor any attacks, sadly. They were always discreet, so that no one could directly say it was them.

Silently, we all knew who it was, and they became shunned to the edge of our community. Likewise, we could only do so much about violent persons who drove through or visited our town. Everyone did their part to stand up against aggressive behavior though, so that even the worst situations were easily taken care of.

Ethan left home in April of 1964, and that July Kate moved in. The little girl I had known Lisa to be was gone, a beautiful woman with a scholarship standing in her place. Come September, she would be off to college. Times were evolving and, as my siblings were progressing and moving out, I came to understand an even deeper view on how limited my life truly was. Even with its best possibilities, I lacked the freedom to go beyond the town's boundaries. Thankfully, I was content with my simple life and all it held.

Kate acted as a helper for Mother. She would cook, clean or garden where appropriate. My own chores became lengthier as all of the tasks were spread out amongst the four of us. Although, there was talk of hiring extra hands come the turn of the decade.

The next few years passed uneventfully for me. I was a phantom in the world, watching it change and pass me by. Now, some three weeks before the night that has

298

led me here, I began setting things in motion.

I spoke with Paul, since he visited the larger cities frequently enough that it would seem inconsequential when he went again with a camera. He took the photos I requested, and one week later returned with my desired product. Mother and Father saw it fit to fund the project, since I had never been payed for work on the farm and they were highly enthusiastic about what I had planned.

Attempting to be discreet, I asked Kate if we could go on an outing. Somewhere close, of course, but a place to go for a weekend where we could be alone and I could explore the world. Naturally, she grinned and told me "it was about time" for me to go someplace else. Some three days after that, she reported that there was a safe place with plenty of forest, so that I could hide easily. It was a campground as well, where there would be civilized facilities should we require them.

We planned to go the next weekend. She would drive ahead with supplies while I would fly behind once the sun had set—for safety. That afternoon when I woke, my heart was pounding in my chest. I thought she would surely notice or guess at my plans, but she gave no hints to such knowledge. So, at the predetermined time, she had an old truck packed and she drove off.

I was grinning all the while when I returned to our room. I checked my hiding space where I kept everything I wanted safe. Sitting inside the wicker basket—beside the two letters Kate had sent me years ago, her old journal and the photographs she had given me—the small, blue velvet box was safe. I picked it up tenderly to open it and check on the glimmering little ring inside.

The light of the sky said that dark would be coming

soon, but I continued to admire the piece of metal. What would she think? What would her answer be? Could she love a demon but be ashamed to wed one or begin a family with such a monster? Oh, I could only muse. Which tormented me, of course.

After some thirty minutes of sitting, staring and thinking, I finally placed the box in my pocket and stood. This was going to be a night I would always remember, no matter what happened. I was still ignorant as to how unforgettable it would be.

Before setting out to meet with Kate, I bathed to make myself as presentable as possible. Once I was done, I had the strangest urge to wipe the steam from the mirror and see what I looked like. I wanted to look past the horns and the assumption that all demons must be grotesque as a gargoyle, to see if I genuinely was. An absurd wish, I know, but I did. I stared at and studied my face and neck and the way that it connected to my shoulders.

My nose was long, thin with a slight hook and it appeared odd below my heavy brow and between my sunken eyes with their pronounced sockets. My bright green eyes always stood out against my skin—the red that it was—and I realized that my eyes had more to them than just green. There were flecks and spirals of gold, and at certain angles the green darkened to something frighteningly awesome. My cheekbones were so sharp that anyone else would have appeared terrifyingly gaunt, but my square, full jaw made it instead that my face was oddly completed once you accounted the jutting though squared chin.

My full, rounded sapphire lips would seem odd on anyone, yet they only complimented everything else in the oddest ways. The bone plates on the sides—above my cheekbones and beside my eyes—had formed dips and grooves that were startlingly graceful. Even the two formations on either side of my face, that seemed more like I had been gouged with a knife...Those were graceful, too.

I found that my face held a dark, ghostly beauty unlike anything I had ever known, seen or even read described in novels. Not quite like a beast, not human, yet more horrifyingly wonderful than both. I was otherworldly.

With my hair undone and wet, it fell about my face in chunks but...The frame of black hair was horrible. It cast my face into shadow and accented everything flawlessly. I looked like a demon prince, a gorgeous monster with wide, knowing eyes that captivated, penetrated. I wondered if the power I saw in that gaze was my imagination or if it actually existed. Even so, I gazed at the reflection as if it were a stranger I had never met. I had never been attractive, never seemed to have power. In my mind's eye, I witnessed this creature on the other side of the glass bare its fangs at me and I heard it hiss, as if it were saying that what I thought—what I knew—was true.

I shook my head slowly, pulling myself back from my observations. I brushed my hair and tied it back, relieved that the demon prince no longer stared back at me. Instead, it was my familiar face—gentle and gentlemanly, in spite of the harsher features I bore. I preferred the kind face that was powerless and far from intimidating.

Fully dressed in my ragged shorts, I left the bathroom and went downstairs for supper, my breakfast. Mother was still cooking—Father reading after a long day in the fields—so I set the table for the three of us. That reflection kept bothering me, though. The darkness and terror it made me feel...

"Mother?" I asked, frowning deeply. She turned with a smile and set a dish of food in the center of the table.

"What is it, Cory?" she inquired when I said nothing for a minute.

I sighed, thinking it all must have been in my imagination. "My face, does it look any different?"

She came over, turning it this way and that. "Stop frowning and I can tell you. There...Hm, it does. Like it changed overnight. A bit of a late bloomer, but you're handsomer for it."

I started at the word, chuckling uncertainly. "Handsome? Mother, putting false ideas into the minds of children like that."

She ignored my teasing. "Why were you asking?"

I shook my head slowly, frowning again as the image of that stranger's horrible, princely face came to mind. "Just...a trick of the light, it seems. I thought I saw something else."

"Hm," she murmured, then sighed heavily. "Cory Charles, how many times do I need to tell you that you need to let your hair dry before putting it back?"

I blinked in surprise—seeming to have forgotten— and removed the tie from my hair, allowing it to fall about my face haphazardly. "Ah, yes. My apologies, Mother, I forgot."

She smiled, putting another dish of food on the table. "Of course, you did. I don't see why you insist on having it back. It looks good down. Maybe a little long..."

"I am due for a trim," I agreed, taking a seat at the table. Father joined us and we said grace before beginning.

Father noticed that my face had changed, as well.

"Kate's a lucky girl," he told me in that fatherly fashion. I blushed but did not respond. Had anything genuinely changed? *Overnight*, of all things?

After breakfast was finished and the dishes were cleaned, I stepped outside to watch the full moon disappear behind a thickening cloud. I frowned again, an odd feeling of familiarity in my gut, almost as if I knew the moon and would miss its presence. I shook the notion from my head, and, after a running start, jumped into the air. The comforting beat of my wings had my disturbances melting away from me, though the darkening clouds gave me slight worry.

I remember the sense of nostalgia I had when I flew during that storm. The lightning shot and thunder cracked while rain spattered against me. I had a frightening sense that I was flying off to my demise. Oh, and I was, in so many ways I could never have imagined. That night went wrong in nearly every way. It could only right itself with Kate's survival. I thank the universe for that every second I can, that he missed her with that weapon.

No, I landed and hugged Kate tight, memorizing how small she was, how soft and warm. She smelled so wonderful, that indescribable scent only our lovers can possess. Oh, she was rich with it, and it filled me with tears when she began to speak the words of my dream only a decade before.

Before the killing thunder could sound, I turned around to face my shooter. He was hidden—buried in shadows—but as he pulled his trigger and the lightening flashed I could see the ranger's terrified face, drenched from standing beneath a gutter.

Demon *Rising*

This time, after the crack of the gun, the pain exploded in my chest. I choked and gasped for air, but I received it. The gun cracked again, hitting me in the left shoulder. I clutched at the wound, hissing when it burned like I had never known. Falling to my knees, I bellowed in anguish. This was my hell, opening to swallow me whole.

I recall Kate's screams to the ranger. I know he stopped shooting. There was a thunder clap that startled me and I fell the rest of the way to the muddy earth. I pushed myself up to all fours, managing to turn myself over before I lost my strength. I lay there gasping when Kate appeared above me, pressing a thick, warm blanket to my wounds. I remember screaming and sobbing my pleas for some way to make the pain stop. Kate only cried that she did not know how.

There was a moment where everything was horrifically clear to me. I was not going to see Kate again, not for some time. I knew that and it aggrieved me terribly. I knew I had to give her the little box in my pocket, at the very least. I barely managed to, but she just tucked it away in her own pocket.

Her eyes never left me, those eyes...Her face...It was torn apart by stress and sadness so hideously that I was afraid she may never smile again. I felt her pain as though it were my own; I still do. That was by far the worst part of any of the pain that occurred over the next two weeks—her pain. It weakened and wounded me in ways I can hardly describe.

It is only in retrospect that I understand Kate had commanded the ranger to get his truck and a tarp. I had to be put in the bed, since I was far too monstrous in size to fit into the tiny cabin. Kate sat beside me, still applying pressure to the now-damp blanket. She had covered me with the tarp to keep me as dry as possible.

Sometime down the road, I turned to Kate and said, "I love you."

"Don't say that!" she sniffled, checking the blanket. Black splotches were becoming visible where she applied pressure.

"I mean it," I told her weakly. I felt mad, my mind completely broken from shock and blood loss.

She looked like she would die from her pain. "I know. But don't say it like you're saying goodbye."

"I will live for you," I swore before realizing how foolish that was. If I died, it could only break her, and it would be at my hands that she was crushed.

The pain flared then, making me writhe and scream with the brutality of it. I would swear it lasted hours, but I know better now. It could only have been minutes later that I lay exhausted and panting, staring up at the clouds. The sound of a man shouting came to me from a distance.

"Get him inside, NOW!" I could recognize Paul's voice. I blinked, and when my eyes opened there was a ceiling above me. I am unaware of how they got me into Paul's home, only that I had blacked out.

My skin felt as though it must have been on fire. It was too warm inside. My eyes rolled around groggily, taking in blurred images of my surroundings.

"Kate...?" I slurred. My every thought kept turning to her, fighting to complete some unfinished idea. Her face materialized from nowhere. I remember my hand curling around hers and thinking that she was so very small right then.

"Paul, shouldn't we give him something for the

pain?" asked Kate, her tone marred by panic. I cried at her distress, mumbling that she should not worry over me any longer.

Something was strapped over my abdomen, shoulders and both of my arms securely. "Only alcohol works, but that's not a good idea right now. You're going to want to let go of his hand and step back, Kate."

Kate's hand left me and I looked over at her sadly. I wanted her as close as possible while things were muddled and I felt as though I was dying. I understood Paul's words when an object like frozen steel cut into my left shoulder. I screamed and writhed against my bonds, snarling wildly and flailing my tail. My wings were beneath me, held in place only by my weight.

I remember Kate's sobs clearly. They let me know where to look for my hope and a promise of something outside of the pain. Her eyes told me that I could make it through this and we could continue our lives together.

It was not that her eyes lied to me. I lied to myself, telling myself any hopeful story I could think to. I so yearned for a reason to fight to live, anything that was better than the storm's rain beating down on the roof of that pain-wracked room. I was a fool to think that my predicament could have ended so easily. I should have known better from every other situation my life had come to, nothing could have saved the sliver of life we had salvaged together.

~~ * ~ * ~ * ~~

"I apologize," choked Cory, wiping fresh tears from his face. Robert watched in wonder. "I have yet to be able to think of this and not cry. Speaking of it is...distressing."

Robert nodded and pulled a small package of tissues from his bag. He offered them to Cory. "Take your time with this."

Cory declined the offer. "Oh, I missed Kate. Without her...The emptiness and loss of that night has only recently become bearable. I suppose that is why I can remember it again."

"How frequently did you call, in the N.S.I.S.D.?" asked Robert, setting the tissues aside and pulling out his pad and pen.

"Every day until June 2nd, 1983," whispered Cory, face contorting as he sobbed. Sympathy welled up inside Robert, making his own eyes water.

"Did they not want you to call again? What happened?" asked Robert gently.

"They wanted me to call; she wanted me to call. She kept speaking of how the world was changing and what we could do with it when I came home." Cory's face was pained. "When I told her goodbye, I knew I would never call again, for her sake."

"But you wanted to?"

"Every day."

Robert made a note with a twinge of guilt. How much more could he have done for this man? How much had he not done out of prejudice? "Why didn't you?"

Cory sighed and stared at his hands. "That year, I was going to turn forty-one. She was thirty-eight. Everything she told me...She could not call me, so it was up to me to maintain contact. I hoped that she had moved onward with her life, without me. She deserved wonderful children, a good home and a kind husband to wait on her. I could not provide any of that anymore, so I let her go."

Robert swallowed back whatever tears he had been accumulating. "Did you consider what that may have done to her?"

"Please, do not remind me of whatever pain I have caused her!" begged Cory, falling back in his seat and covering his face with his hand. Then he whispered brokenly, "Or of whatever happiness she denies that my absence created."

"I'm sorry." Robert's pen scratched noisily as it raced across the paper. He paused. "You're saying that like you only hinder, instead of making her happy. Don't you think you're being a little hard on yourself?" asked Robert.

Cory pulled his hand away slowly, face hardened with what Robert could only recognize as anger. "I was treated with prejudice even by those researchers, who claimed so *proudly* to take care with me. If indeed that is true, then the average citizen is not expected to look at me as a person but as a rabid beast, as has been demonstrated in weeks previous. I have been seen as a demon and monster before. It is an unkind way to be received. Tell me then, Robert, am I 'being hard on myself' or merely thinking realistically of the world's overall dislike of me?"

Robert sighed heavily, suddenly weighed down by guilt. He thought of his own life and how hard he had considered it to be. He had been such a blind fool. "Would you have stayed with Kate in '69 if you'd have had the choice?"

Do I even need to ask? wondered Robert, already knowing Cory's answer.

"Oh, villain that I am, I would." Cory shook his head with a grimace.

Robert frowned. "I'm not sure I would call you a villain, Cory."

The demon chuckled darkly. "Not a villain? What might I think myself, if not a black-hat?"

"Well," sighed Robert, giving Cory a reassuring smile. "I know that things have been doing a lot better for Kate and the children since you came."

He gave Robert a small, sad smile. "Yes, yes...I suppose, though the overall treatments that I have received...Oh, what else am I to make of myself, Robert?"

Robert's answer was confident. "I know you. You're a good man, Cory, and yes, I mean *man*. Not a demon or horrible omen, just a man who's doing the best he can with what life's dealt him."

Robert could see the change in Cory's smile. "Thank you, Robert, I...There is so much happening now, too many things to think on."

Robert had the feeling that Cory was hiding something, had *been* hiding something. "Would you like to talk to me about these things?"

Cory took a long moment before sighing and shaking his head. "Perhaps another day."

Slowly, Robert nodded his head, worry mixing with his curiosity. "Alright. Would you like to continue telling me what happened, then? Or are you finished for the day?"

In spite of the distraction, Robert could still see the darker thoughts weighing on his friend's mind. "Of course, of course. Time was thin again, and I recall a vivid nightmare of mine that spoke of the future. It was terrifying, like the previous experience. So much in it was alien..."

Demon *Rising*

~~ * ~ * ~ * ~~

There was a labyrinth. A dark, cold and stone-walled labyrinth. I was lost in it, wandering the corridors while my heart raced with my mind. I trembled more the further I went, worried that I was alone. I could vaguely recall what had happened last I was awake, so there was a tingling sense of fear that this was a place of the dead—somewhere I very much did not want to be.

I heard people calling me: Mother, Father, Kate. I heard Lisa screaming and began running in that direction. As I rounded a corner, they came into view. Dark clad men were restraining them and their faces were all distressed, watching me with grief and denial. It was a moment before I understood why. Then the cold metal bar came across the side of my head. The blow made me stagger and my vision swim. There was an instant where there was rain on me, strangely warm for the season before it became icy.

When the world righted itself in my vision, I found myself on the freezing floor of some terribly lit tiled room, shivering and completely bare-skinned. As I looked up and around myself, I found endless pairs of hollow eyes set into white cloth masks. Glinting, malicious knives came toward me, and I recognized Paul's eyes among the dozens.

I started awake then, mortified by the distorted visions I had experienced. They carried the strong sense of purpose my first precognition had. They were overwhelming, making my waking experience disorienting and sharp.

"Where...?" I gasped, confused by the bright lighting and unfamiliar surroundings. It smelled peculiar to me. Kate came toward me from the corner of my vision, smiling in relief. Her face was streaked with old tears and lines marked her face, as though it had been contorted frequently. I imagined that I was dead then, unknowing that I had indeed survived.

One of her hands was holding mine, the other stroking my hair soothingly. "Finally, you're awake."

I groaned, blinking my eyes into a more comfortable focus in the bright lighting. "Of course. How long has it been?"

"A few days," she replied, her worry apparent in her voice. Her eyes seemed too moist, too sad for anything to be right. "We didn't know if you would live at all."

I remember chuckling twice, wincing when that sent shocks of pain from my bullet wounds. "I promised."

"You did." Her smile broadened, lighting her expression like the sun.

My returning smile died slowly as I took in my surroundings. I found that it was not that the room was so much bright as it was that it was just an incredibly pale white, with equally white curtains. The sun shone through the open window. There was a small wooden table beside my bed and Kate had the only chair in the room. In a corner, there were bags of things I recognized: Kate's clothes, some books, a pillow and a blanket from our home.

My throat was dry and sore. My stomach churned with a strange, starving nausea that made my throat constrict. My eyes strayed back to Kate, who was watching me intently. Her worry made me uncomfortable and guilty, as though it had been my fault that she was not content; I wanted her to be happy.

"How many days has it been, precisely?" I asked, sounding and feeling somewhat faint.

311

She looked at her hand still holding mine. "Three and a half. Would've been four if you hadn't woken up until tonight."

I sighed carefully, my shoulder and chest flaring with too sudden of movements. "I see. This would explain my desire for food and water. No, no, only water. I am uncertain I can tolerate any more than that."

She handed me a glass. "Paul gave me instructions. He said you need to drink slowly and you can eat light after three hours if you haven't puked the water up."

I nodded, sipping the cool liquid. It felt wonderful in my throat. I was incredibly tempted to drink the entire glass in a single breath, I was so thirsty. "Where is Paul?"

"Oh, Paul's helping out at the hospital while we're in town. Your father just left for home, since today's my day," she explained. I frowned, curious about her meaning. She noticed and said, "We've been taking turns watching you for Paul. We had to take you to a city hospital.."

"Ah." I shook my head slowly. "It seems I have a knack for requiring all-hour medical assistance whenever I fall ill."

She giggled and nodded. "Yes, you do."

We were quiet for a time while I sipped the water. The occasional breeze through the window brought with it the warm fragrance of early summer. The trees were still bright green and blossoming from spring, and I could smell that rich perfume that can only be from freshly blooming flowers, so soft and delicate. The afternoon was so calm and so wonderfully gentle that the other night felt out of place with its thunderstorms and darkness.

An eager knock on the small room's door startled Kate and I equally. We stared at the door, me wishing I had not spilt water on my bandaging and she with a heavy, annoyed sigh. She released my hand and stood, eyes narrowed as she swung the door open.

"What?" she snapped. A finely dressed woman stepped back in shock, but recovered quickly. I noticed the pen and paper she held as she peered around Kate.

"Oh! It's awake! Miss, please, just a quick interview, since it's recovering," asked the woman quickly, smiling charismatically. I saw a bustling man carrying a camera beside the woman, attempting to look around Kate into the room. "Or maybe just a picture?"

"He's not an 'it', and how many times do you have to be told no?" retaliated Kate rudely. I was amazed by how fierce she was. She waved at the man to put away the camera. "No, no. Shoo."

"Kate? Who are they and what do they want?" I asked, unnerved by these new individuals. My old fears were slowly coming to the surface, making me shy.

"Oh, you two know each other? How?" asked the woman, relentless with her inquiries. I was stressed, with my nerves somewhat strained and fragile, so the alien woman's persistence had my hands balling to fists. My claws accidentally shredded through portions of the sheets and my tail hit the bed with a muted thump.

Kate glanced over her shoulder at me and after seeing my expression closed the door to a crack and said, "Please, just stay away," before shutting it completely.

She stood by the door, staring at it silently for a few minutes. When she turned around, she seemed stressed and tired. She smiled at me, though. An image of her distressed face in the rain came to mind and I was suddenly overjoyed at seeing her smile.

313

"What was that, exactly?" I asked, eyes following her as she came back to the chair and sat. I held out my hand to her, which she then took.

"Damn reporters," she swore, narrowing her eyes at my surprised expression. "Yes, I know it's unladylike, but it's true! They come by every day! Three separate teams, all hounding for a story."

"Be forgiving, Kate," I begged quietly. "Remember that they have never seen me before. You are right that I would rather have privacy, just be tolerant of them?"

She sighed heavily and shook her head. "No. They won't stop coming and as soon as they have a chance, they'll turn you into something you're not. I have nightmares about *headlines* now."

I chuckled softly at that, careful not to irritate the wounds. "Well...I am unaware of what to say to that, then."

We made light conversation for a few hours while I sipped my water. At one point, Paul came in to check up on me. He looked as though he should have been in a bed himself, sleeping. When he saw that I was awake and well, he left again to fetch a light meal.

While he was gone, I recalled the original intention I had left the farm for. I turned my head away from Kate while I found my voice to ask her. The other night, I had been determined. After my nightmare and the rather unfortunate accident, I was afraid to say anything.

So I waited three days until I said anything, while Paul was again off to get food.

"Do you still have that little box I gave you?" I asked quietly, looking away at the curtains. The world outside was cast into a beautiful twilight, sky painted with rainbows of rich color.

314

"Yes." She pulled it out of her pocket and held it out to me, staring at it curiously. "Why? What is it?"

After experiencing the constant media, I was unbearably aware of what I was. I was loathing it, loathing my face. Whenever I caught sight of any part of myself, I cringed and looked away. It was horrible, a curse that only tormented me. All I had desired in life was peace on the farm, peace with humans, and a joyful life with Kate. When everyone I met gaped and stared though, I felt hideous and like I would—*could* only ever be a wretched burden.

"May I see it?" Looking back at her, I held out my hand for the object. She relinquished it easily. Feeling its tiny weight in my palm, I sighed. "I hope you can forgive whatever it is I am, with all of the stares and anger."

"I've never thought you've done anything wrong," she replied evenly, frowning at me concernedly. She put her wrist to my forehead to check for a fever. "Are you okay?"

"I never should have..." I swallowed back the words tearfully. "You deserve far more than anything I can provide, but I suppose you know that already. In any case, I may as well lay out my cards."

"What on earth are you talking about, Cory?" she demanded sharply, watching me carefully.

Before she could say any more, I held the box out to her. "Open it. And please, refrain from laughing."

She grabbed it and opened it cautiously, worry dissipating. When she saw what was within, her eyes widened and she gasped. Kate's eyes—being kind—were only dark brown when she looked back at me with tears in them. Even as I was not trapped, a terrible guilt welled up

315

in my chest when I saw her expression.

"My apologies. I never should have...Just, please, be gracious and let me have some time to think," I said quickly, wishing I could escape the cramped whiteness of the room.

Rejection was the only possible ending. She cared, yes, but no one could ever be asked to bear the responsibility of my presence. Even thinking of the trouble I caused my parents, I wanted to leave them all to their human lives and never disturb them again.

"But...do you mean it?" she asked quietly. I saw her face changing, looking like she might cry. I began hushing her, comforting her as best I could.

"Yes." She did not reply immediately, so I asked the burning question to break the silence, "Will you marry me, Kate?"

She nodded, smiling slightly. "Yes."

For one short, glorious moment I felt human. I thought that my life could have been some imagined nightmare, and the woman I loved more than anything had just told me that she would marry me. I could see us in a home with children, then grandchildren later. I saw us as happy and me as a human man, with the most wonderful woman I could imagine caring for me and allowing me to care for her.

Just as swiftly as my mind thought these things, the images were shattered by a light knock on the door. Kate answered it, allowing Paul to come in with a dish. I was back in that hospital room with my aching and tired body. I stared at the ceiling before allowing my eyes to slip shut, face contorting with grief.

"What's wrong, Cory? Has the pain escalated? Do

you feel dizzy or nauseous?" he asked gently. I heard him setting the dish on the bedside table. He took hold of my wrist, which I pulled away carefully.

"It is incurable, even with medical science," I told him, blinking my eyes open. I sighed carefully at his questioning expression. "I would rather not explain at the moment. Thank you for your concern, and for saving me, Paul."

He smiled and nodded. "There's no reason anyone wouldn't have. You also have my congratulations."

I followed his gaze, seeing the ring on Kate's hand. His smile broadened at my sheepish expression. "Thank you. The proposal went better than I had hoped."

"Better?" scoffed Kate, shaking her head as she took her usual seat. "You got shot twice!"

Paul was nodding. "It's true."

"I would rather not hope for too much from life, you understand," I attempted to explain. Kate seemed to grasp it without my directly saying that I had worried she would say no. She knew me too well, so also understood that I would be heartbroken without her.

Paul grasped my meaning as well, but continued to harass me for a minute before he returned to his volunteering. After I ate, Kate held my hand and sang me to sleep.

Nightmares woke me every night—or day, depending on when I fell asleep. Every shadow was threatening and every time I closed my eyes, part of me was frightened that when I opened them there would be some monster waiting for me—*if* I opened them.

My family switched shifts, just as Kate had said. When Mother was with me, she was always smiling in relief and caring for me as best she could. Father would talk to me about marriage and family—he always said that he had no doubts that I would be a good husband and father—but would read when my eyes began to slip shut from fatigue. Jeff and Jasmine would visit me every few days, concerned for their son-in-law-to-be.

I slept most days away, only conscious for five or six hour stretches. During those, at least once there would be a reporter checking to see if they could get a photo or an interview. The answer remained the same: no.

One night, Mother and Kate changed posts just as I was beginning to drift into sleep. I recall vaguely that Mother released my hand so that Kate could take it seconds later. I smiled faintly when I heard Kate's singing as I fell into the warm embrace of peaceful dreams at long last. But, just as surely as my life flows, that peace could only last so long.

My heart jumped in panic when I awoke to Kate's screams from the other side of the door. I flung myself out of bed, gasping and stumbling across the room as pain lanced through my body from my wounds. The world swam in my eyes as tears easily covered my face, but I had to see that she was safe.

"No! You can't take him! NO!" Her shrill cries became more understandable to my groggy mind the longer I had to process. I was at the door, the meaning of her words sinking in steadily. I thought it must have been another nightmare, and Kate was fighting to keep Death from me. Oh, was I ever the fool.

When I opened the door, Kate rushed over to my side with tears in her eyes. She wrapped one arm around my waist protectively, helping me back to bed. A well-dressed man followed her in, continuing what apparently was the argument I had overheard.

"See that? He's out of bed, which means I can take him after all," the man snapped in a rather impolite manner.

"Please, sir," I panted, laying back in bed with a relieved sigh. My body still felt weak, even after half a month to recover. "Do not speak to my fiancée in such rude manners."

The man's thin face turned red. "What?! No, you two can't wed! And he *will* come with me!"

"Yes, we can and no, he won't. The doctor hasn't released him yet and you have no grounds!" argued back Kate viciously, face fierce.

"It's not human! Only two *humans* can be married and I have perfect grounds, unless you can supply me with documents stating that he's a legal resident of this country."

She glared at him hatefully, standing tall to meet the challenge. "I hope you enjoy disappointment."

He sneered. "He will come with me, girl, and it will be soon."

"Why don't you take your ego and put it where the sun—"

The slap I heard next startled me. It was the distinct, sharp sound of flesh hitting flesh. Kate was frozen with her surprise while the man seemed disturbingly gleeful and obviously considered himself to be justified.

A savage snarl erupted from me. The pain that flared in my chest only made the sound sharper and crueler. The man jumped in surprise at the sound while I pulled myself out of bed again. I pulled Kate close to my side while glowering down at the tiny, cowering creature before me.

319

"Leave NOW!" I yelled loudly, punctuating the words with another snarl. I bared my fangs, the memory of Richard frightening Kate—*my Kate*—raw in my mind. "And you had better pray that I get shot again if you ever hope to come near us safely. GO!"

The man scrambled out the door, his fear leaving a foul reek in the air. I groaned, exhausted and in pain after such exertion. I refused to lay back down in case Kate needed my protection, however. After a few minutes, she finally persuaded me to at least sit on the bed with her tucked securely into my side.

"Are you alright?" I asked for what must have been the twentieth time. Like every other time, she nodded curtly. I stroked her face gently. "You need not worry about him returning. I will be healed soon. We can return to the farm...Everything will work out."

Everything will work out. The same words that Mother had promised me when I was younger. When I said them to Kate, they did not hold the same truth. They sounded hollow and dead, their childhood magic long dried up and used.

Two days later, my torture began.

Father and Kate had come to visit with Mother. The gathering was wonderful. We were all conversing lightly, smiling in spite of the rain pattering against the closed window.

None of us expected the door to burst in, hanging off its hinges. I was already sitting up, so I only stared in horror as five fully armed men surged in. One each went to restrain my family members, two charging at me and wrestling me from the bed. In the doorway, that evil man was grinning.

Demon *Rising*

In a single moment of overwhelming fury, I slammed both men away from me and cried out in pain as my wounds seared. I staggered as I stood, moving to pull a man off of Father. The two I had attacked grabbed my arms with a sudden jolt of force that had me stumbling back, struggling to remain standing.

Using my imbalance to their advantage, they pulled me to the exit. Mother was screaming for them to leave me be, to not hurt me. Father was also shouting at them, that they were all idiots, swearing at them that they were making a mistake. Kate only screamed my name.

"NO!" I bellowed, bracing myself against the door frame as the two men struggled to wrestle me from the room. Kate—still restrained by one—stared at me like I was something she could barely think to lose, as though it might kill her if I was pulled out that door.

My next cries of denial were to her, begging her—all of them—not to care so greatly that it may destroy them. All the same simple word, "No." Her eyes were begging me as well, asking me to fight harder for her, for us. *For my life.*

I was torn, but before I could know what to choose, one of the men pulling me stopped. Instead, I felt his hard fist slam into the wound in my shoulder. I snarled like an animal, just as surely as the kind of creature they thought me to be would react. The other man stopped fighting my strength and joined the first—kneeing my wounds, punching me, later slamming me forcefully into the wall quite a few times.

Vision swimming dizzily, I was dragged from the room. I moaned, fading in and out of awareness for a few minutes. I remember stumbling half-blind through the rain, being shoved into a large van. Chains...the sound of thick, rattling chains as they were used to restrain me, and more screaming. Oh, the screaming...The sounds of what freedom I had being ripped away from me.

It was only after the van rumbled into motion and a few minutes passed in silence that I came back to myself completely.

Understand that it did not occur to me then that I would never have my life again. My mind was shocked by the abruptness of what was happening. For all I knew, I had fallen asleep and would wake up at any moment.

I stared at the smirking man through my disheveled wet hair. Neither I nor my body was aware of how I should feel right then. I wanted to have the capability to become angry and break free of the vehicle so that I might return home. I missed my family and friends already, as I had never been without familiarities at any point in my life.

"Where are you taking me?" I asked quietly. No, I lied when I said I was unaware of what I felt, because I felt subdued. It was as though this man had towered over me with some great, unfathomable power that I could not begin to combat against. Of course, I now know why it was that little man was trembling as he sat across from me, why he demanded there be weapons pointed at me and chains to bind me.

"A research facility."

"Where?" I asked again, the first feelings of the forced separation breaking through the confusion. "Will I be able to visit my home, my family?"

"No, and they're not your family." The man seemed sharply pleased to say this.

I was quiet for a moment, my body's fatigue like a

strangely protective film between myself and the man's apparent cruelty. My wounds were aching strongly, but still feeling much better than when the uniformed men were punching them.

"Why are you taking me?"

"Well, look at yourself," he chuckled, motioning a hand at me.

I did so, then back at him dryly. "I am wearing a hospital gown, sir. Last I was aware, this was not an offense that was treated as I am being treated."

"Not the gown, idiot," he snapped irritably. "The skin, the claws. Horns? We're not going to let a demon walk around like that. We have no inkling of what you'll destroy, and if this is a hoax...Well, we need to teach you a lesson about not making such a commotion."

"Sir, I am what you see, but I do not act in any way uncivilized."

My words were ineffectual. "Are there any more of you ugly bastards out there?"

I sighed, defeated. "No, sir."

"Do crosses, holy water and other religious relics work on you?" he asked, then smiled tightly. I did not trust his next words. In fact, I thought he might do everything that could possibly harm me just to see if I felt pain that way. "So we know what not to do."

"No, sir, those items are useless against me," I replied obediently. Part of me was disgusted by how weak willed I was. Meanwhile, another part was glad that I knew when to stop so that I would not be beaten further.

The man only nodded, and the rest of the journey passed in silence.

When at last we came to a complete stop, I was

blindfolded and led by the chains. I felt rough stone like pavement before a cold, smooth surface made me yelp in surprise when my foot touched it. They pulled my chains harder to keep me moving.

I was taken down several hallways, turning too many times to recall exactly what my path was. I know that I ended in a tiled, windowless room that echoed every sound back to me. They yanked the blindfold off of my face, startling me again so that my tail whipped someone behind me. They beat me to the ground and began to manhandle me.

I was stripped of my clothes—my hair being yanked twice quickly—and then thrown to the cold floor. Before I could orient myself, a powerful stream of icy water seemed to be attacking me, moving across my entire naked body cruelly. My skin stung and felt bruised, although I knew none of these humans would notice. I was crying out in terror and pain for them to stop, but they did not. They continued to do things as though I were a dumb animal that was unaware of how to care for itself.

I was shivering violently from the cold—and somewhat worried about catching cold—when they threw a heavy wool blanket over me. The fabric was uncomfortable against my wet skin, but I was too grateful for some measure of warmth to complain.

I was forced to my feet and all but dragged down a long, winding corridor that was too disorienting to my tired and traumatized mind. When they stopped me, I was then shoved into a room with a large bed-like table in the center. I recognized some of the tools set out on rolling tables from Paul's bag, although some of these seemed much sharper and more threatening.

Demon *Rising*

"Get on the table," commanded a whip-like voice. A slight woman walked over to the tools, obviously expecting me to do as I was told.

"What will you do?" I asked, tears of fear in my eyes, voice shaking equally from cold and fright.

She looked at me, eyes narrowed so that her already sharply angled face seemed to cut me somehow, and I flinched. "Get on the table *now*."

I nodded and sat on the table, shaking horribly. It groaned slightly and I could feel it straining at my weight, cold metal making me cringe. The woman stared at me as though this was my own fault for the table's misfortune.

"Are you completely relaxed, so that the table is the only thing supporting you?" she asked, still unforgiving.

"Not fully, no. Would you like me to be?" I asked quietly, keeping my expression subdued. I was shying from any possibility that might have me being injured any further.

"No," she snapped fiercely. "We'll need a better table. Stand up and follow me."

I did as instructed. She led me through that hall again, and I was suddenly horribly aware of how short the ceilings were. I could stand fully, yes, but with barely three inches to spare. I hunched my shoulders, attempting to make myself smaller for comfort's sake.

I felt wrong and defiled, being forced to go about stark nude and half-frozen, with nothing more than a blanket sized for a human man that hardly fit around my wings and shoulders. I also felt incredibly impolite and so instead wrapped the garment about my waist. The freshly exposed skin on my shoulders felt as though it was being held to ice.

Demon *Rising*

The woman entered a different area, with scales of all shapes and sizes built into the walls or sitting on desks. Many people in the room looked up in interest, their eyes appraising me. The sudden realization of how cattle must feel settled over me.

"Stand there." She pointed to a painted square on the floor and I did as instructed, hearing more metal creak and groan. The square of floor dipped slightly and my eyes widened to think that this was a scale. I was too absorbed by how they must have built the thing to notice what she was doing. "Jesus! Frank, can I get you over here and make sure I'm reading this thing right?"

A short, elderly man with glasses came over dutifully. He looked at whatever the woman was indicating and nodded slowly. "Yes, that all appears to be in order."

"389? Jesus," she repeated, glancing at me skeptically. "It has wings. How does anything stay airborne at that weight?"

"Don't jump to conclusions," said the elderly man hurriedly. "It may be incapable of flight."

"I have been able to fly since the summer I turned sixteen, sir," I replied quietly. He was startled by my speech, likely having assumed me mute or some other ridiculous thing.

The man turned to the woman in shock. "It talks? Nobody mentioned it talked!"

The woman seemed bored, taking notes on a paper pad. "Yes, how fascinating."

He grinned at me as a child might at a parrot, I suppose. "Do you have a name?"

"My name?" The notion that I might be regarded as a person *now*—particularly after the previous few hours—

was relieving but took a moment to process in my mind. When it did, I grinned back and held out my hand to shake. "Cory Charles Lawrence, sir, and may I ask your name?"

I startled the poor man and he leapt away with a cry of shock. Before I understood what was occurring, I was being forced to the ground by guards I had not noticed, their guns aimed and ready. I was gasping, trembling at the sight of the weapons. I had not the slightest inkling of what was expected of me then or what I might do to incur their violent responses.

"Please, I mean no harm!" I begged, half sobbing my words. I wanted nothing more than to be home, or even in that hospital room, resting with my family near me. I wanted Kate's hand to hold and my parents' reassuring words to hear. I covered my face with my hands, rolled onto my side and curled in on myself, rejecting the world around me...

Cory's distant eyes focused on Robert, tears in them again. "I wish I could say that my situation changed for the better. I would lie, though. I have always been scared in that place, even remembering..."

Robert shook his head slowly, aghast. "I can't believe it..."

"Neither can I. The transition was so sudden, I still feel as though I should wake up at any moment." The demon frowned thoughtfully. "Sometimes, I even wonder if that ranger knew what was in store and was trying to do me a mercy. Regardless, I can only wonder and am here now. Oh, I apologize. Here I sit rambling on when you apparently have a thought burning your tongue. Please, share it."

"All these years, they said they were doing humane experiments..." He shook his head, expression contorted in disgust. "Ugh! I'm almost ashamed to be human now."

"Why?" murmured Cory, entwining his fingers and setting his hands in his lap.

"For what they've done!" exclaimed Robert, outraged. This could not be kept secret. Others had to know what had genuinely happened.

"And?" challenged Cory suddenly, startling Robert. "Humans kill one another constantly, yet that does not make you feel shame that the efforts of so many good men have gone to waste? So many men...I am but a random victim, one of thousands. A demon, too, yet I am not ashamed of that. In fact, I am glad for my ability to reason and to be able to bring some other meaning to such a wretched reputation. You—like anyone—could do the same, if you chose."

Robert glanced away guiltily and muttered an apology. "Again, I allowed my friendship...I'm sorry, Cory. Please, would you continue?"

~~ * ~ * ~ * ~~

Roughly two years passed with nothing but terror and painful—although minor—experimenting. Some of the smaller scars I have came from those times— particularly the ones around my horns. They did not have an anesthetic then, so they were limited to not causing pain that I could not endure on my own.

As I said, two years. Then everything changed

abruptly. Paul was there, wearing one of their horrible lab coats. When I first saw him, I cringed away and hissed in terror, shielding my face with my arms.

"Cory, calm down, it's me!" he cried out.

I gasped, taking a few minutes before I recognized his voice. "P-Paul? Paul is that—Is that you?!"

When I pulled my arm from my face, he was there beside me. He grabbed my arm with a fierce scowl of disgust as he examined some of the incisions there.

"Yes. Sorry it took so long, but I had to go through too many unnecessary classes. What have these idiots been doing to you?!" he demanded sharply, turning my arm another way. "You look like skin and bones compared to when I last saw you! And these pathetic 'surgeries' aren't being treated properly. You've got several infections, and you'd think *someone* in here with half a degree would notice that your skin's turning white and oozing green puss! Oh, when I get my hands on the person in charge here..."

I let him rant. I never wanted him to stop. His voice brought back memories of home I had not realized I had forgotten. At some point, he helped me to my feet— exclaiming again that they needed to feed me better and let me have physical activity—and guided me out of the room. Barely two doors down the hall, the sharp voice of the frightening woman—Beth—stopped us both.

"What do you think you're doing, trainee?" she demanded. When we turned to see her, she was just as cruel in appearance as she has always been.

Paul's face hardened. "I'm taking Cory to the medical facilities to get his infections treated. Also, just maybe before he withers and dies, I'll take him out for a walk and give him a decent meal."

She scoffed. "It's not a pet, so don't name it. It also doesn't need walks or 'meals'. It survives just fine on what we've been giving it."

"Would you eat what you've been giving him?" he retaliated swiftly. Her eyes narrowed. "I thought not. I need two steaks, a side dish of vegetables, and a bowl of fruit ready for when I'm done cleaning his cuts. Now, if you'll excuse us."

"You don't take him anywhere without my say, trainee!" she snapped fiercely. I flinched away from her, barely catching myself against a wall before I fell to the ground, my legs weak from misuse and abuse. "I'm the one who does the ordering around here. Now, put it back in its cage."

Paul glared. "*You're* the one? May I start by saying how much I hate you? This man has been poorly treated, most likely since the minute he arrived. Now, not just as his friend but as his doctor I am going to take care of him. *You* won't force me to do anything. You and your people need me—the person who knows what he's doing. So shut up, keep the food warm, and we'll be on our dandy ways."

Beth's eyes were wide, as though she had been slapped. "We don't need you. Put it back or you're fired."

"Woman, I may be a pastor but I'm not above punishing the wicked, so to speak. I've had a bad day, so go away."

He led me off, leaving Beth in utter shock. No one had stood up to her in such a manner, and had I been in better condition I suppose I would have been impressed and surprised by Paul's behavior.

It was painful while he was cleaning the infections, but I felt wonderful afterward. He walked me around the halls until I thought I might collapse. When we arrived back in my room, the food there made me salivate, my stomach claw, and my manners evaporate. Nothing had ever tasted better.

From there, Paul acquired a phone and privileges for me so that I could call my family. As often as I was allowed, I used the device so that I could cling to what small portion of sanity I had retained. He also had my living situation reworked. Before long, I had clothes, records and a player, blankets and a bed that fit my size, and enough books to fill my recovery time with something more than what my life had become. He even had pictures of home brought to me.

It pains me that I cannot recall any but the first conversation with my family by phone.

How did that conversation go? Yes, yes...

Mother answered the phone, "Lawrence residence, this is Eleanor speaking."

My throat felt tight. It was my mother! The first time I had heard her voice in three years. "Mom...?"

Something shattered on the other end and she gasped, crying out, "Cory! Quick, get over here! It's Cory! Kate, go get Will! Baby, oh my baby, are you okay?"

Even her voice and motherly words could not fight the harsh darkness that resided there. I was shaking my head but replied, "Yes, Mom. Paul is here...He said that all of you were doing well when he he got me photographs from home."

"Cory Charles," she whispered, sounding broken. "Tell me the truth, please. I know you don't call me that unless you're upset. Paul says things happen..."

"I know, Mom, I know," I sniffled quietly. I heard

a commotion on the other end.

"Your wife said—"

"Is it really him? Eleanor, please, don't say it's a mistake." The phone traded hands. "Son?"

"Dad," I laughed. It was so good to hear them all. I picked up one of the photographs and stared at it, awkward after so much time away from home. "How are the crops?"

"Three years and you ask how the crops are?" he countered, voice thick. He chuckled quietly. "They're not half as good as when you were tending them, just like the rest of us. The entire farm misses you, apparently."

I chuckled. "I miss the farm."

He was quiet for a long moment. "I love you, son. I didn't say it near enough when you were here, but I do. Yeah, yeah, Kate, hold on. You call again soon, alright, Cory?"

There was some rustling, and then Kate's tentative voice came over the phone. "Cory? Is that—Are you really there?"

"Yes, Kate, I am," I told her quietly. I wiped my tears off of the photograph in my hand. "I miss you."

Muffled voices and noises. "Are you okay?"

When she asked I had to reply honestly, at least once. "No. I am exhausted."

"What have they been doing to you?" she demanded while my defenses were down. I barely caught myself before I told her everything.

"Nothing, nothing," I said hurriedly. Why? Was I protecting these people? Was it too horrific for me to voice? I was unaware, so I told her one of several truths. "The only thing keeping me from sleeping is a nightmare."

"Stop lying," she ground out, sounding angry.

I cringed at her upset. "No, Kate. I would much rather not talk of anything that occurs here."

"Please," she begged. I could hear that she was nearing tears. "I feel useless over here. I can't do anything on the farm half as well as you could, and now you won't let me help you."

"For good reasons, Kate, I promise you," I told her gently. My chest was heavy, being crushed by forsaken and cruel emotions. "Right now, though...I'm sorry."

"I hate you," she sobbed brokenly. I cringed, then wondered if she was right to. Would it do her more good than her love for me? That was the first time it occurred to me that it may be better for those that I loved if they had no attachments to me. They could all live happily without me. "And everyone else. I hate it all."

"...Do you mean that?"

~~ * ~ * ~ * ~~

"I cannot continue, I apologize," whispered Cory. His eyes were distant, his face shimmering with tears.

Robert nodded slowly. "That's okay. You're doing very well so far. Take all the time you need. It's only—" he glanced at his watch and fibbed "—It's still early."

"Oh," he sighed heavily, shaking his head. "Please, allow me to skim over the rest of the...traumatic details. After speaking so much of life before...I cannot continue thinking of this much longer."

"That's alright, Cory," said Robert gently. He motioned to a glass of water beside Cory, then pulled out a tissue. "Go ahead and clean up, get some water. We'll take this at your own pace."

333

Cory nodded, accepting the tissue this time. He used it to dry his face before sipping his water. "Thank you. Oh, thank you..."

The demon stared at the table, more tears in his eyes. Robert watched, heart twisting sympathetically for all of the misfortunes he had endured. He could see the shadows of the scars on the demon's face now, highlighted by their violet shade. Cory's face looked almost like a patchwork creation, reminding Robert of creatures from horror films.

Cory's eyes flicked up to meet Robert's gaze. He blinked slowly, saying softly, "All this time. Oh, so much time...Let me finish, so that you may be on your way home."

$$\sim\!\!\sim * \sim * \sim * \sim\!\!\sim$$

Those who viewed me as nothing more than an animal were irritated by Paul's actions. They became more hostile toward me, sometimes coming into my room to disturb me with their anger. The details are rather doleful, and I would rather not bother with them. However, many of those who were aggressive toward me were the ones who would operate on me, vivisect me, things of equally unnerving natures. My right arm...I am told it was an accident, but I have always suspected otherwise. I cannot move it above shoulder height or I am crippled with pain. Even lifting it halfway is mildly discomforting. A terrible 'accident' during an examination, indeed!

The ones who began to enjoy my company—namely the lesser staff members such as chefs, the janitors, the maids—would stop and converse with me from time to time. They frequently expressed their discontent with how I was treated, but I always dismissed their concerns.

Of course, there were also those who remained indifferent toward me. They were thrilled by the scientific adventure I presented, nothing more.

Most years passed by in blurs, so I only remember that in 1987, they created a working anesthetic. The surgeries and examinations became more intense and harder to recover from. Then, twelve years later, Paul passed away and my rights as a person went with him.

As I was slowly being seen as a monster again, I began to act the part. I would growl or snarl when startled, whimper when in pain. I am uncertain whether I spoke for the years between 1999 and 2004, when I finally became a person in the eyes of those researchers again. I know that sometime around 1995, they built a room for me...a room where I could farm again, with a synthetic sun.

But, oh, there must be something left to tell you...

Ah! Yes. I am vaguely aware of a period of time in which I went mad. It was shortly after Paul passed away, and my treatment altered severely. I received one feeding a day—taken down from three—of some horrid matter I am uncertain was even natural. Due to the terrible food, I felt ill and starved, groaning all the time that I required a day with full meals of meat, vegetables and fruit. My body was deprived, and I was warning them of what might happen if I went too long with such neglect.

They seemed more intrigued than anything, studying my new behaviors. These men and women who dressed so neatly also began to act as though I was an animal. I was never spoken to directly, only spoken of in the third person. The books, record player, and photographs of my family and friends were confiscated. They were replaced with skulls, chains, cauldrons. Things they thought a demon would be satisfied with in an attempt to recreate my "natural habitat," as though I am from some realm of endless cruelty and torture. It was enough to drive an insane man sane, likewise for the reverse.

Tests were done on me more often than I could bear. On some days, I would undergo three separate procedures that left my body feeling bruised, my sheets bloodstained, and my body so heavily covered with stitches and scars that I looked like a new interpretation of old horrors, zombies and other such creations of madmen.

If I recall correctly, they were cutting at the base of one of my horns when my mind snapped. I threw surgical tools, tables, *people*, roaring like a monster. I remember the rage I felt, the fear. It enveloped and controlled me so that I attacked everything in sight.

I ran to what I knew was an exit to the outside world, throwing my fists at it in a fury. In my mind, I know I was screaming for someone outside to come in and help me. One of the people I had called "friend," perhaps, or maybe one of my brothers. It was beyond my comprehension at the time to understand that not one soul who cared would hear my desperate cries or be in any position to rescue me. I was the only person who cared, and I was the only one who had a scrap of hope to save myself.

What halted my rampage was my own foolishness. Blinded by my emotions, I forgot my permanently injured right arm.

So, while banging at that door, my right arm did the impossible—moving straight upward. I was on the ground

writhing before I understood what had happened. From
there, I believe that I was dragged back to what could only
be called my prison. I curled in on myself in the middle of
the floor, shut my eyes against the hideous room and
dreamt of my old home—with the sweet, warm summers
tending to the chickens and hiding behind the corn field—
while I wept myself to sleep.

That was just a decade ago, the year after the turn of
the millennium.

~~ * ~ * ~ * ~~

"Eighteen years after you stopped calling..." mused
Robert distantly.

Cory frowned. "What is the significance of that?"

"Oh, nothing. I'm sorry, please continue."

"I am afraid that there is nothing left to tell," replied
Cory slowly. He sighed heavily. "Although, I did enjoy
this appointment and conversing with you."

Robert shook his head, finding himself defiant. He
wanted to hear that this long, dark tale had a wonderful
ending, but he understood that it did not. It ended where he
was sitting across from Cory in silence.

Robert had to swallow back his tears, forcing a
smile for Cory. "Well, you're here now."

Cory laughed quietly, eyes still distant. "Yes, I
suppose I am."

Robert watched him for a long moment, waiting for
his eyes to return to the present. After what felt like an
eternity, Robert cleared his throat quietly. Cory started,
looking around himself urgently.

"Are you alright?" asked Robert, concerned for his

dear friend. They had gone deep, deeper than the pain of the N.S.I.S.D., to the inaccessible joy of his youth.

Cory took a moment but nodded. "Yes, yes, I will be fine, Robert. I just need time to think. Would it be fine to continue this next time?"

Robert nodded slowly, smiling slightly. "We can continue next visit, of course. I have only one question, however."

"Ask it," was Cory's swift reply, though Robert thought he saw a flicker of fear in his eyes.

"Can you allow the actuality that none of this is your fault—that there is *nothing* that you have done to deserve anything you just told me?" asked Robert, recognizing the self-blame in the demon's expression. Cory sighed heavily, and Robert watched him process.

The atmosphere was heavy while he waited patiently, frowning as he lost track of the slight ticks and pauses in Cory's face. Outside, the world was beginning to change to twilight, while inside Robert wondered if the sun could ever rise again. Finally, the silence was broken.

"Yes, I can," Cory nearly laughed, and Robert could practically see the weight lifting from his shoulders as he relaxed.

Robert laughed as well. "Good, because none if it could have been. Nothing but the best and brightest moments, Cory, remember that."

"I will, Robert, thank you," replied Cory with the brightest smile Robert had ever witnessed. He understood why his family held him so dear, just in finally seeing the smile that Kate had struggled to describe time and time again. The warmth, the joy, the freedom that he expressed was a treasure, and for a moment Robert had to pause and wonder how, when the time came, he could ever let Cory go.

~~ * ~~ * ~~ * ~~

Katelyn returned home from the park with Kyle and Sarah after dark, smiling as they ran off to get ready for bed without prompting. Cory was nowhere on the first floor, and she went upstairs as she began to worry. Where was he? He shouldn't be out right now.

When she entered the bedroom, she found him sitting on the bed, staring at something in his hand.

"Funny, isn't it? All of this time, all of the years in captivity and demands for why, and it was all because of one tiny little ring. A little piece of metal, that's all!" he laughed, the sound ringing with bitterness.

Kate could not move. "...Cory?"

He looked up at her then, tears filling his eyes. He trembled, hand curling protectively around the ring he held. "Kate...I'm sorry. For my theatrics with the proposal, for never fighting hard enough, for forgetting. I never meant any of that, Kate. I never wanted you to endure any of that, and I'm sorry I could not be more for you. I'm sorry, Kate. I love you. I love you."

She stared at him for a moment, struggling to understand just what he was saying. "It wasn't your fault, Cory. None of it was your fault."

"Perhaps not," he sighed heavily, standing to go pull her into a warm embrace. "I'm sorry all the same. I yearn for anything that can give you back everything you had stripped away, and I am so very sorry that there is nothing with that power. I'm sorry that I was too thick to

339

understand that I needed to keep calling, I'm sorry that I never had the chance to meet Charlie. For everything, Kate, I'm sorry."

Kate gasped quietly, eyes watering. "Oh, god...It's you, isn't it?"

He nodded, holding her tighter. "It's me. I'm here, I'm back. I'm home, Kate, I'm finally home."

She wept silently, holding on to the demon for dear life. "It's you! It's you."

"It's me, I'm here. I'm here. I'll never go again, I promise. I'll never let any of you slip away again," he swore, gently pulling Kate away just enough that he could see her face. "Never again."

She stared at him for a long moment before kissing him deeply. She laughed again when they broke apart, tears running down her cheeks. "It is you, you're here."

Cory laughed quietly. "I am."

"Robert kept saying that you might never remember everything, he said—" she stopped herself, taking in the befuddled but happy expression on her demon's face.

"When was he telling you this?" he asked.

Kate considered a fib for a moment before realizing it—Cory was home. The man she remembered, that was who she was speaking to, who was standing in front of her. She could tell him anything.

"Since you were released. I founded the groups that protested for demon rights. After his first visit with you, he made a few guesses, contacted me and we've been communicating ever since," she explained, feeling a hint of guilt for having kept this from him. But he could not recall a thing up until now, he had to be treated more delicately...

Cory just laughed again, louder and more freely as

he uncurled his fingers and held the ring up to see. "That sounds like you, making me earn your time. I don't suppose you would be opposed to wearing this again, until a proper marriage can be arranged?"

Kate grinned in spite of the years they had lost and the years she could feel catching up to her. She shook her head, holding out her hand for him to slip the ring onto.

"I love you."

Demon *Rising*

I can't sleep. I haven't slept in three days. I know I should, but I just...can't. Charlie keeps asking me what's wrong, while Eleanor and Will know. They're the ones who told me that he's dead.

I can't think his name. I don't want to remember his face. It's cruel, but I want to forget I ever knew him. I think it might be easier than being able to remember how good he was. Oh, God, I can't. I can't think that he's—I can't even imagine his face without a smile or his eyes without care. All of it is impossible.

No one wants to hold a service, either. After all, the government won't give us his body to lay to rest. It would only be an empty coffin, but it's better than letting him go unceremoniously. I need that closure. I need to see it all, to be able to have an opportunity to let go. I need to know that I'll never see him again.

If only that were true. I still have the pictures, the books, the albums, his entire room, all of it to remind me of what's wrong. Everything in this town reminds me of everything that is far from right. Nothing could ever be right, not when Cory's dead.

Chapter Nine:
Breaking Point

45th Week Outside

Monday

Where am I?

I knew that I was dreaming. The odd sense of it was disorienting with how vivid the world around me was, but I recalled laying myself to sleep. The sky above me was lit and blue, though. Where was I?

A face came into view above me. It was red, tinged with orange and appearing well aged. Violet, cat-like eyes gazed down at me watchfully. Piercings and tattoos decorated its ears, eyes and nose but they did not take from the strangely powerful grace I saw there. Bright blue lips smiled slowly, as if in response to my confusion.

I frowned, reaching out my hand to touch the face in wonder. I started when I saw that this was not my arm, orange and scarless as it was. The claws of the hand scratched the face above me, making someone nearby cry out in shock. But it was not a human cry. It was deep and guttural, sounding peculiarly like an animal.

"Please, step back from the stranger!" begged the

same voice. The face obeyed and I was able to see the rest of the woman's barely-clothed body. She had wings and a tail with strange, pale bone ridges running along her arms and abdomen. What fascinated me more was that she had no horns.

"He's here," she murmured reverently. Her smile softened. "Great One, we apologize for meeting with you in such an unorthodox fashion. We beseech you, what is your name?"

"My name?" I wondered, starting again. This was not my voice! It was too high! Blinking away my shock, I composed myself. "Cory Lawrence."

"Oh, my!" gasped the woman in surprise. "A human name? Where are you now, Cory Great One? Are you with the humans? Have they captured you? Hurt you?"

"Yes, I live with the humans," I replied, wary to impart the entire truth. This dream felt far too real. I sat slowly and glanced about. "Is there a mirror?"

"Mirror?" murmured the voice that had cried out earlier. An orange-tinted, horned man came into my view. "Whatever for?"

"This is not my body and I wish to see what it looks like." I neglected to mention that I only wanted to know if my face was not scarred.

As if from nowhere, the demon man presented me with a bowl of clear water. I took it and waited for it to still, gasping when I saw the reflection. No scars! But the eyes were so strange, violet set into this orange face. There was a black tattoo at the edge of the left eye, a strange pointed line that traced down the face over the undefined cheekbones. I only had another moment to study the

*narrow face before I gasped and dropped the bowl,
shuddering violently as I collapsed in this imagined body to
wake in my own.*

~~ * ~ * ~ * ~~

"Kate...?" I groaned as I pushed myself from the
floor to my hands and knees. She was at my side in a flash
and helping me to right myself. "What happened? Why
was I on the floor? I—I thought I was dreaming..."

Kate's eyes were concerned and black, capturing me
completely. Even as my own confusion gnawed at me, her
fright and concern pained me. "You don't remember
anything, Cory?"

I shook my head slowly, frowning deeply as fear
slithered down my spine and through my tail. "No...What
happened? Did—Did I hurt you? Or the children?!"

"No, no," she whispered, seeming sad that I made
no mention of myself. "I heard you shout, and when I came
up to see what was wrong, you said that you were sorry
before cutting your arm with the scissors. Don't worry, I
put them away," she added hurriedly, seeing my horror.

I trembled, timid as I glanced at the stinging wound
mentioned. A single, thin black streak of blood was nestled
homily amongst my thick collection of scars. My frown
deepened further. Where was my shirt? I knew I had slept
in it, having relapsed for a night and been too ashamed to
look at my abused body.

"Something is very wrong," I muttered, sighing as I
stood and searched for my shirt. I found it on the floor in
the doorway to the bathroom, stretched and buttons still
done. As though I had torn it from myself in a panic. "Call

Robert. I—We need to know if he thinks it's safe...I will dress."

Kate's hand caught my arm gently, eyes tearing over. "Cory, it'll be okay. We can handle this."

"I hope that you're right." I whispered to keep from choking on my words. As always, she saw. I retreated to the bathroom, needing time alone to process the sharp swiftness of change that cut into our lives.

More of this strangeness, I thought with a deep scowl. *At least my blood is just what it should be...*

I tried to find a way to make this scenario untrue while I washed the blood from my arm. The inky substance ran into the sink, mixing with the water. April had long since passed, so this could be no poorly orchestrated prank. Had I indulged in anything the previous night? Drink or unsuitable food? Not that I could recall...

Drying my arm, I watched myself in the mirror silently for a moment. Was my own image an illusion, as the face in my dream had been? If I asked another individual to describe me, what would they say? Would I hear only what I thought I was?

I sighed, my thoughts heavy as I pulled my shirt over myself, careful not to overstretch my right arm. Checking the buttons to be sure they were well fastened, I left the bathroom for downstairs.

"...be here in twenty minutes? Oh, thank you, Robert, thank you."

"Where are the children?" I asked quietly, concerned by the thought of them having seen me while I was not myself.

"In their room," she replied in a whisper, glancing

at the partially opened door. We listened for a moment before we heard their enthusiastic playing. "They don't know that anything's happened."

I sighed in relief. "Oh, thank goodness. I can only imagine the stress that would have caused them."

Kate shook her head slowly. "No, I think we should keep it quiet from them until we know what's wrong. That way...If it's bad, we can break it to them gently."

I nodded in agreement. "Yes, that sounds preferable."

She stared at me for a long moment. "This will all work out. You'll see..."

I wanted nothing more than to believe her. Could the words still have retained their magic? Could I be saved again, despite appearances? Or was this the end? Already the end...?

I wanted more time! I *needed* more time!

Shaking my head slowly, I took a seat on the couch, unable to answer. I leaned forward onto my knees, the weight of my wings on my back surprisingly heavy. My tail hung off the couch beside me limply, seeming as tired as I felt.

If I were human...

As if Kate could hear the wistful thought, she sat beside me and took my hand in hers. "It doesn't matter what you are. We'll get through this, whatever it is."

I could not help but give her a small smile. "So long as you remain stubborner than fate...I suppose so."

"Damn straight," she muttered, expression resolute. The woman I had known in youth was there, rising again to the surface powerfully.

There was a knock on the door, startling us both.

Kate stood to answer it, Kyle and Sarah sprinting from their room demanding who it was in their adorable little voices. I called them back to me so as to allow Kate space enough to answer the door.

"Robert?!" She stepped aside, blinking in surprise when he entered. Bailey followed him, grinning when she saw the children. "You said twenty minutes. It's been, what, ten?"

He shrugged and replied somewhat breathlessly, "Speed limits changed just a *little*."

"Lead foot!" translated Bailey in a singsong voice, leading Kyle and Sarah off to the Old Thing Room. "Let's go see what's in here, hm?"

"Bailey, can you read to us?" asked Kyle, closing the door and cutting off whatever else was said.

Robert glanced at the door, then stared at me. "She said there was an emergency. What is it?"

"I...I am unaware of exactly what it is," I murmured, staring at nothing.

"He hallucinated, but...he was up and about during it, even recognized me and called me by my name," said Kate quietly. She sounded near tears, but when I looked up at her she was forcing them back.

Robert was pallid. "I...What?"

"Robert, what is wrong with me?" I asked faintly, voice trembling with my panic. Tears moistened my eyes, burning them.

"Cory...I don't know," he admitted tiredly. He sighed heavily, leaning against a wall for support. "It could be any number of things. There are a few mental disorders I know of that generally come up around your age, at least in humans...It could be an entirely different disorder that's

348

only in demons and we don't know how to deal with it! Or there could be emotional trauma that's doing this, but..."

"Could it get worse?" I choked, staring at the floor as my distress ate at me like acid. I wanted to be able to hear some certain reassurance from someone I trusted that all of this would be fine. "Could it happen again?"

His face was pained as a friend's, eyes watering. "At this point, anything's possible. I'm sorry. If...If this happens again, I think we'll need to get you a solitary living arrangement with caretakers, while we figure things out. For now, we'll call the doctors that know at least a bit about your specie."

"And they will tell me they know nothing, but would be glad to study this thing—this defect!" I snapped, stressed by what was happening to me. Solitary living, more damned knives and blood tests and scans that were sure to end at the dead end we began with.

Robert appeared to have already thought on that, nodding sadly. "Yeah, I know. We can only hope we get lucky and find a genius. That's all. It's all," he finished with a realization so strong it brought him sliding down the wall to the floor. I could feel that horror in my own self, too. The knowledge that as my life had begun again it may already be at its end.

"I must start my will. Before I go completely mad, I must write my will," I repeated to myself quietly, brows furrowing as I frowned at the carpet.

That was Kate's final straw to her back. She hurried to my side, biting back her tears until she was in my arms. Her sobs shook her frail frame, so fiercely that I thought she might break while I held her. I understood that she already had, though. Between my own tears I hushed her

349

gently, rubbing her back to soothe her. Anything I did only seemed to worsen her condition.

Robert was still on the floor, just as much a mess as Kate and I. From the Old Thing Room, I could hear Bailey playing one of the records, and was glad for it. It meant that the children were unlikely to hear us in our fit of grief.

It was Robert who pulled himself from the floor and wiped his face first. "I...I'll call some of the doctors, schedule emergency appointments, look up flight times...I'll be back." With that, he left through the front door, cellular device in hand.

Kate and I straightened ourselves in time before the Old Room door opened abruptly. Kyle and Sarah were grinning as Bailey led them out, fairytale book in hand.

"We fixed the story, Grampa!" cried Kyle, rushing over and hopping into my lap.

I laughed, managing to hide my stress from them. "What story? How did you fix it?"

"The one with the demon who steals the princess, and then the prince comes to save her." Sarah climbed into her grandmother's lap with a smile.

"Yeah, yeah!" Kyle nodded enthusiastically. "We say that the prince is the meanie! And the demon really lives, and takes the princess back and lives happy ever after!"

Bailey was grinning. "They wanted to take markers to it to actually *rewrite* the story, but I stopped them when I saw this thing was printed, like, eighty years ago."

"Thank you for protecting it, Bailey," I thanked her, looking to the front door as it opened and Robert entered.

"We need to get to the airport," he said, smiling at the children. "So that we can get to that...ah, demon meeting thing in California."

"There's a demon meet in California?!" cried Bailey, elated. "Can I go? Please? Please, can I go?"

"Ah...I am afraid not, Bailey. Would you be willing to help Kate while I am gone, though?" I asked with a glance at Kate. Her eyes were relieved that he and I had managed to coordinate near our children.

"Aw...Okay. Can I stay the night here, then?" she asked, looking at Kate for her answer. "I'd need to pick up some clothes, but I love these little guys!"

"Oh, that shouldn't be a problem. I can take you by your house, but first I think I should drive the boys to the airport," she replied with a smile. "Could you watch Kyle and Sarah while I'm gone, though?"

"Alright! Come on, guys, back to the room!" She hurried into their bedroom cackling madly, book still tucked beneath her arm. When the door was shut behind all of them securely, I breathed a deep sigh of relief.

"Quick, get packed. The appointment's at four tomorrow," said Robert quietly, watching the door with caution.

I nodded, standing and making my way up the stairs to the room. Kate followed me swiftly. When we were both in the room, she closed the door behind us.

"You're going?" she asked faintly, eyes glistening when I looked over.

"What else is there to do?" I sighed, wandering to the closet, pulling out shirts without a care of what they were. Placing them on the bed, I then went to the wardrobe to find pants.

"Not leave!" she nearly shouted in frustration, but she came to fold the shirts neatly. "Who knows if they'll

351

even know anything? For all I know, you might not come back again!"

"Hush," I murmured, brushing her with my tail as I returned to the bedside. "I will return, my dear. If you need a promise, I will make one. You know that I will keep it."

"I don't need a promise. I just...Why now?" she whispered, face twisted with her turmoil. "Why does this all have to happen now? Why does this always *happen*?"

I wrapped an arm around her. "I don't know. It doesn't matter, though. It will not keep me from you or our little ones."

She nodded with a sniffle. "Alright. Alright..."

I smiled and kissed her, hoping that my face was as convincing as I felt unnerved.

~~ * ~ * ~ * ~~

Tuesday

"Well, you weren't joking," said Dr. Hart in surprise when he saw Robert and I. He smiled falsely. "I read that you live quite a few states away."

"We need..." Robert sighed heavily, shaking his head tiredly.

"I was hallucinating yesterday, and apparently still acting consciously, yet I have no memory of anything but the hallucination," I explained, not wanting to waste precious time with idle chatter. Would I black out again in a moment? Or would it be in an hour? I wished suddenly that those around me had ways to defend themselves from me.

The doctor blinked and laughed nervously.

352

"Straight to the point, I see. Uh, beforehand were you experiencing, um, nausea, dizziness, disorientation, could you remember who and where you were—?"

"He was asleep when he began acting out," interrupted Robert impatiently. "Well, he had been asleep, according to Kate."

"Kate?"

"My fiancée," I replied quietly. Dr. Hart was surprised by this. "She is not here with us because she is caring for her grandchildren."

He was intrigued by that. "Quarter demon—?"

"Can we please focus?" demanded Robert sharply, making me start. He glared at the doctor. "We need to find out what's wrong and treat him as fast as possible, *without* the N.S.I.S.D. finding out. Now, please, what do you think we can do to accomplish that?"

Dr. Hart shook his head slowly. "He somnambulated. That's the best I've got."

"No tests or anything? Just a 'he was sleepwalking'?" asked Robert incredulously. The doctor nodded and Robert sighed heavily again. "Alright. Come on, Cory, let's cross our fingers for the next one."

I stood, startling the short doctor. "It would be greatly appreciated if you told no one about this."

He nodded, eyes wide as he watched me move to the door. "Yeah, won't do that..."

~~ * ~ * ~ * ~~

Aside from the light rain spattering the windshield, the return drive to the motel was long and silent. I was struggling to accept defeat before it came about so that when it did I would not be disappointed. I wanted to hope, though. There was plenty enough to hope for, with too much more to lose. Seeing the dark sky, I wondered briefly if it was weeping. If it was, could it weep for me?

Robert's hands were stiff on the wheel. He was seething, I knew. Why was still a mystery to me, however. He had been quick to anger since we boarded the first plane, snapping at anyone who stared. Even with the evidence before me I could not think that he was angry for my sake. No, he was more likely ireful that he had to follow me across this country and back again for what was going to end with only a confirmation to despair.

When we pulled into a parking space at the motel, he turned the car off with a click. We were both statues in our places. The ominous sky and our silence was beginning to send a chill up and down my tail, making it twitch with the agitation. I remained motionless otherwise, however. I felt like moving would be acknowledging the time I could see racing around me. If I moved, I would be accepting my imminent death of sanity instead of fighting to keep my mind whole.

"Our next flight is tomorrow at noon," said Robert quietly. His words were not startling or loud. They fit the grim scene all too well.

I broke from my defiant trance, nodding slowly. "I recall."

He sighed. When he spoke, he sounded near tears. "There's still some hope. The doctor in New Hampshire might know something."

"Why are we trying?" I asked in a murmur, looking over to see that, yes, he was crying. I paused, disoriented.

He released his hold on the wheel, hands falling into

his lap. "Because we love you, I'd guess."

I turned my attention to the heavier rain on the windshield, guilty rather than embarrassed. "I thought you would have learned from the first time we met: no good comes to those who care for me."

Robert laughed shakily at that. "You make it pretty impossible to avoid."

Now I sighed, looking for some way to brighten the situation. I winced to think that he was sad because of me. That there was reason to be sad was still familiar, even after what was nearing a year.

"Whenever you and Kate want to have that overdue wedding, I'll sign. You'll be officially sane, for a little while," he added, voice breaking. I nodded distantly, smiling.

"Would you be my best man?" I asked, still watching the rain. The topic was both morose and cheerful. A wedding at last, just in time before...

He laughed and nodded. "Yeah. I would be honored."

I laughed to myself, tears coming to my eyes. Bittersweet tears that tormented my thoughts. Finally, I could become a husband. Just like, finally, the years were catching up with me.

"Should we tell Kate the good news?" asked Robert, watching me wipe my tears away.

I nodded, leaving the car without a word. If this was going to be the last of my life that I was aware of, I would enjoy it all as though the ax was not hovering dangerously close to the rope I clung to for dear life. No, I would continue cherishing it as I had in blissful ignorance.

When I was free of the confines of the vehicle, I

stretched my wings to their fullest. The rain was caught by my membranes, tickling the skin like cool fingertips. I smiled, tucking my wings close again. The water was a relieving wash of sensation that I had been needing. I followed Robert to the room, shaking the extra water from myself before entering.

My shirt was wet and dripping, so I took it off and placed it on a hanger in the bathroom. "I hope you do not mind, Robert. It feels very nice to allow my skin time to breathe."

"Just as long as you don't get my bed wet," he replied as I sat on my own, spreading my wings enough to allow them air to dry.

I lifted the corded receiver from the bedside table to my ear, listening for the tone before dialing. I only had to wait halfway through the third ring before Kate answered.

"Hello?" The sound of her voice made me glance about for her reflexively.

"Good evening, Kate."

She gasped. "Did we learn anything?"

"No, Dr. Hart knew nothing," I told her gently, hoping that softening my voice might make the news kinder somehow. I could feel her grief when she replied.

"Maybe the doctor in New Hampshire will know something..."

"Even if he doesn't, we can still continue as we were," I said with a small smile into the phone. The conversation over the telephone was oddly reminiscent of speaking to her while in the facility. Did she feel this as well?

"Whatever happens, I can't wait for you to come home," she sighed tiredly. Glancing at the unattractive room around me, I certainly shared her sentiment.

"I'll be home by Saturday, Kate." *If no one knows what is wrong.* I neglected to add the words. She heard them, regardless.

"In that case, I hope it takes you weeks to come home, if it means that everything will be okay."

I nodded slowly even though she could not see. In spite of my reluctance to be tested again, it would certainly be worth coming home safe and sane. I had tears in my eyes when I recalled just what that could mean.

"I have good news as well, my dear," I informed her, ecstatic by the thought of at last seeing her in a gown.

"Good news?" She sounded incredulous. From her side of the line, I could see how it would be unbelievable.

"Yes. Robert is going to be my best man." I waited a moment, allowing her to grasp my meaning. I knew when she understood by the semi-hysterical laughter that came over the phone.

"What?!" she gasped. "You mean...?"

"Yes, and you will have whatever wedding and honeymoon you desire." I could only imagine the expression she would be wearing. Last time she had begun to plan the wedding, she had been so enthused and invested that it was nothing less than criminal when her dreams were broken. It was only right that she should have whatever she wanted now. "Within the boundaries of destinations where I can legally go, preferably. Whatever you want, whenever..."

She was silent for a long period. I began to worry when she finally replied, "I can't think. I mean, first the issue, now this...I don't know."

"You don't need to right now. You can relax

357

however you need, and I will return home soon to help you." Already, I was dreaming of what that day would feel like.

"That sounds nice..." By the tone of her voice, I knew that she felt the conversation coming to an end as well.

"I love you, Kate," I said quietly, not wanting to chance having no other opportunity to tell her.

There was a rustling on the line. "I love you, too, Cory. Good night?"

"Sweet dreams," I bade her, sighing when I heard the call disconnect. I replaced the receiver, glad that I was dry enough to sleep.

"Good conversation?" asked Robert as I began pulling back the coverings. He was already prepared to switch off the table lamp that kept the room dimly lit.

"It went well." I set myself on the bed carefully, motioning to Robert to darken the light. An instant later the room was nearly black, lit only by a ghostly red glow from the clock. I sighed as I began to settle. "Curse these beds."

"Too uncomfortable?" he asked.

"Too small," I replied, but found a way to sleep with mild comfort, at least.

~~ * ~ * ~ * ~~

Thursday

"Need I say that I told you that Chicago was pointless?" I asked as we climbed into the car again. I rubbed my inner elbow mindlessly. "Besides which, that nurse was rather violent with the needle. They should be more careful with who they hire to interact with demons."

"You never told me that Chicago was pointless, a. And b, that nurse freaked me out, too." Robert sighed as he began to reverse the vehicle before pulling out of the space. He maneuvered through the lot.

"What are you attempting to imply?" I inquired, glad to be back in motion again. The need for action was constant in the back of my mind. It was an odd sensation, not that we should find what was wrong with me, but that I knew what was wrong. I was not in the right place. There was something I needed to do, something I had been planning to do since before I could remember, and I was not doing it...

"That you're being whiny," he teased with a grin. The sun shone through the windows, warming my arm. For once, I was able to sit comfortably in the car.

"You were not the one she stabbed!" I retorted lightly. A truth that I was grateful for. If he had been her victim, it would likely would have meant the loss of his arm!

He nodded, yawning widely from fatigue. "Yeah...Okay, that's three of five doctors in the world down. Two more to go."

I sighed heavily. "This is certainly a long week."

Saturday

We stood at the apartment door of what was supposedly the final possible doctor. Robert looked as exhausted as I felt; both of us were doubtful of this one. The other four had been in large, lavish buildings. What were the odds of a man working from his living room knowing what was wrong?

I knocked gently, startled when the door opened immediately to a wide-eyed, short man. He grinned and motioned us in without a word, laughing to himself when he closed the door.

The home began with the living room, with what appeared to be the kitchen ahead on the left. A modest layout, but for the chair set in the middle of the living room, attached to wires and numerous humming screens. The chair appeared to be sized for either a very large human or rather, a demon. Atop the head of the furnishing, there was a strange device that appeared to be a halo of shining metal and wires.

"So, you're the patient, right?" he asked me with a hint of an accent, still grinning. I noted that he smelled oddly sweet. "Wow, I'm not so much a doctor as mad scientist. This is such a treat! My father told me I was loony for majoring into demon medicine and psychology, but this is just—! Right, right, pardon the rambling and sit in the chair."

"Doctor? We didn't even tell you what was wrong yet," said Robert slowly, frowning in confusion. I glanced at the chair but waited for the man to answer Robert.

"Oh, right, right! What's wrong?" he asked, appearing impatient. "And *don't* call me doctor again. It gets on my nerves. My name is Bernard."

"Okay...Bernard, my client hallucinated on Monday, acting and speaking consciously, but he can't remember what really happened," explained Robert. "He was asleep before it started."

Bernard appraised me with wide eyes. "Get in the chair."

"What is that thing?" demanded Robert, stopping me mid-stride with a gesture. "What are you going to be doing?"

"It's just a brain scan thing, don't worry. It's not dangerous. I'm just going to see what's wrong inside his melon!" he said cheerily, eyes bright. "Now, you. Chair."

With a sigh, I sat in the construction. "Very well. What must I do?"

"Ooh, demon voice! It's so creepy! So, so... Eh," he muttered, shaking his head. He guided my head into the halo, strapping something that I could not see or feel. He placed a cool, sticky device at the base of my jaw on either side. "Right. Now, lean back and don't think."

"Pardon?" I questioned, but faltered mid-thought. My mind went blank as a strange whir filled my ears.

~~ * ~ * ~ * ~~

A whistle caught my attention slowly. I blinked and groaned groggily, coming back to myself. I felt ill as I glanced around. My vision was dominated by the grin of Bernard and Robert's worried expression.

"Hey, guy! Welcome back to la-la land! I've got my scans. All I need's a blood test and then you're clear to go! I'll be sending you the results when I have them."

I groaned again, stomach twisting at the thought of a needle. "No more blood tests, please."

"Not much choice in that, my sub-terrestrial friend. Sorry," added Bernard, lifting my sleeve to clean my elbow. He paused and frowned. "Damn...Those N.S.I.S.D. pricks really did some damage."

"There is no need to be so vulgar," I muttered, turning my head away from his work.

"If you insist." I felt the pinch of the needle passing through my skin. "Almost...There we go. Did you want the red bandage? No, no, kidding. Here."

He placed a beige bandage over the tiny wound and pat my hand as though he were more familiar with me than he was. Robert helped me from the seat. When I stood, the world span out of control and bile rose in my throat.

"Ng...Oh," I sighed, grateful when everything righted itself. "What on earth happened?"

"Well...That's really rather hard to explain. He, uh, was able to not only scan your brains—yes, plural—but he could watch *memories*. It was very...exciting, even before I learned that he was high," he commented offhandedly, guiding me from the apartment.

"He was high?" I asked incredulously. I would not have sat in the chair had I but realized the state of the man whose hands I was trusting!

"Yeah...Apparently, geniuses come in all sorts of ways," he muttered as he helped me into the car. I sat gladly, strapping myself in tiredly. He closed my door for me before materializing on the driver's side. "He also said that you should sleep before we fly back."

"Something I will not argue against," I murmured, laying my head back and fading to sleep again before the engine started.

~~ * ~ * ~ * ~~

Demon *Rising*

July 31ˢᵗ, 2011

The results from Bernard came today. He says that he does not know the direct cause, although I do apparently have a severe vitamin deficiency. He suspects that my horn color—though it was thought to be natural—as well as my abrupt mental illness may be caused by this. However, the problem he explained was that he cannot identify the vitamin or deduce what it is. Again, he has suspicions, though these are that the vitamin may be something that my body produces. He says that he will need time to study, and alert us should he find anything or require further tests.

Robert signed yesterday. Legally, I am sane. Internally, I feel cheated by time. Kate would like to begin planning, but neither of us have been able to find the will to do so yet. I wonder when we will, or if it all truly is too late.

In the meantime, I suppose I shall make the best of everything that I have and not waste any more of my time with this damned paper.

The demon made to close his journal, pausing when he noticed a slip of paper that did not belong. He pulled it out, unable to recognize the handwriting. At first he made to dismiss it, until he noticed his name at the top of the page. As soon as he read it, he tucked it back into the book, hoping to forget it entirely.

Even as he went downstairs, however, the words still burned in his mind:

Cory,

Demon *Rising*

I understand that you're confused about what's happening. All I can tell you for now is don't panic and that I'm sorry for the scare a temporary switch is bound to cause. We're looking for you, and we will find you.

Watch for the skies on my wings.

Demon *Rising*

Demon Sighting In Australia: Hoax?

After nearly twenty years of inactivity in the demon community, there has been a report in Australia of demons appearing. Not just one, but *three* were said to have been seen wandering not on the outskirts of but in downtown Sydney.

The first time any demons have been seen outside of the United Sates of America, they were approached with caution, yet without hostility. The first and only person to speak with them will remain anonymous, but they said that the demons asked, in three separate languages, one thing: "Where is he?"

Then what appeared to be the demon leader of the trio spoke again: "We need to find my master. Do you know where he is?"

When the anonymous speaker replied that they did not know, the demons left without another word and have not been seen since. If you know of any demon whereabouts or have seen any, please contact the Demon Control hotline immediately.

Chapter Ten: Becoming

47th Week Outside

<u>Sunday</u>

I saw Kate at an odd angle, shrinking. Becoming farther away, I realized, leaving me. There was panic...everywhere. So much screaming and shouting in an incoherent language. I was in pain, so much pain. Where was the exit to this nightmare? I looked around for it and found nothing but alien faces.

My heart jolted. I was not home. I was someplace bigger, with more angry people. Why had they brought me here?! What madness was this?! Surely, merely a nightmare. Yes, and when I woke I would be beside Kate in our room on the farm.

"What is that thing?!" someone demanded. "For that matter, what are you doing back here!"

"This is Cory, I'm a doctor. I didn't have enough...supplies, back at my own building. Now, you'll do what I say, when I say."

Paul's voice was commanding people. So sharp and demanding, with words that I did not understand. Words, too many of them...I had my own shallow words. Rasping, because I could not receive air any other way, or speak any louder.

"Paul...? Why are we here? Where—When can I see my family? I need to see them before—before I..."

The word on my tongue was "die" but it felt odd to say it in this dream, this nightmare. I could not die in a dream. Nothing could kill me, not when it was my own mind that conjured the fantastical illusion. Why did I genuinely feel as though Death had his icy scythe pressed delicately to my throat, then?

I saw Paul come to me with a syringe. "No, no, no...Those, they cannot—they never work. No, no, ow! You...You poked me. And my arm...?"

I stared at him in disbelief as I began to lose sensation in my arm, blossoming out from my elbow. The bittersweet freedom spread with a frightening swiftness, coming to my shoulder far too quickly to be real.

"A working anesthetic?" I gasped, frowning. How had he...? Had he known all along? What was the purpose in hiding this? Why?

"Sh, not too loud. No one else can know." He sighed and pat my shoulder, looking away at some other instrument I suspected he needed. "Sleep well, Cory."

Then a man in a black suit came into my view.

I started with a scream.

My heart thundered in my ears, too strong to possibly be contained within my chest. I looked about the dark room in terror, hand fumbling for the switch of the lamp beside the bed. I found it and the room blazed with light, me half expecting to find that suited man there. The man that had taken me. I gaped at the floor in horror as my vision swam before I remembered to breathe.

A hand touched my shoulder and I whirled with a frightened hiss, falling off the bed with a thunderous thud as I did so. I made no move to lift myself from the floor, curling up on myself where I was and fighting sobs. Against my better judgment, I had to know if what I suspected was true.

"Cory?!" cried Kate. On the edge of my vision, I saw Kate leaning over the bed to look at me. Her hand reached out tentatively and recoiled, likely sensing that it would only distress me further. "Honey, it's only a nightmare."

"Why did he take me there?" I gasped, wincing at what she had said. Only a nightmare...My life—only a nightmare. "What reason did Paul give you to take me to that hospital?"

"There was some tool or other that he didn't have and he knew it would be there. Cory, why?" she asked, not grasping the reality I had.

"What did he need? Why did he need it? How did the good pastor lie?" I demanded, staring at the darkness beneath the bed. There looking back at me were those blue eyes, the gentle and thoughtful eyes of Paul.

"*Lie*?!" she cried out, face contorting. "Cory, what are you talking about?"

"How?" I asked again sharply. I kept my glare off of her, making certain that I took none of my anger out on her.

She frowned, straining to remember. "Something about...I don't know, alright! I was too worried about you dying."

I snarled in frustration. Still, I saw no other explanation. Only one more question to answer, though. The one that would determine my sanity or complete lunacy.

"Were you there when they took me in for operation, was I awake?"

"The entire drive there," she replied, seeming to answer both halves of the inquiry. "You wouldn't stop muttering."

"Damn it all!" I swore, uncaring that Kate was present. She flinched in shock. "Damn, it was a memory and not a nightmare."

"What was?" she asked shakily. I saw her trembling slightly as I began to push myself up. I was far from ready to address her yet. I would harm her if I did.

"That whoring devil! What did they give him?" I hissed to myself, staring at the floor as though the answer would materialize before me. "How was the fiend able to hold that kind mask steady before his cruel face for so long?"

Kate was quiet, watching me as though she did not know me. Mild guilt trickled through my system as a part of me registered that she was likely worrying over my mental health. I continued to mutter under my breath, struggling to connect all of the pieces to their proper places. Something, there was something missing.

I stopped short on my ranting when I recalled that, according to the facility, no working anesthetic had been discovered until somewhere in the late 1980's. Paul had known of one since '68, at the latest. Where did he stand, then? Vile monster? Misunderstood man who had made a wrong choice? Or was it that agonizingly annoying middle ground that one could never make heads or tails of?

A tiny knock on the door pulled me from my pondering and I looked up curiously. Kyle was standing there, stuffed bear clutched tight in his little arms. His face was pulled in wrong directions as I recognized that he was trying to keep from crying.

"Are you guys okay?" he asked quietly, sniffling. "I heard yelling and it sounded like someone fell."

Kate hurried up and over to the poor child. "Yes, honey, we're both okay. Are you okay?"

He shook his head, sniffling again. "No, I thought one of you got hit and fell, like Mommy used to. I want to see her!" he bawled, burying his head into Kate's arms.

"I know, hon. We still can't see her for awhile though, remember?" she said quietly, voice pained. I stared at them, anger dissipating quickly.

"But I want to see her now," he keened.

Kate began to shake. "I know. Me, too."

I went to them, pulling them both close. I thought that it may indeed have been a good thing to be unable to mourn a daughter. Not to spare myself any of the grief, no. Just to comfort Kate and her grandchildren. It was reason enough to be composed, knowing that they may be better for it.

Kate leaned into me while Kyle climbed up and into one of my arms, where I cradled him. I held them both to me for awhile. Part of me felt as though we had all just had nightmares; that was the hopeful, wishing part. Realistically, I knew that we were all unsettled by heavy truths and could only calm with time.

I saw Sarah sitting on the top stair, peering at us all shyly, and I gave her a gentle smile. "Come now. Let's go downstairs and I will prepare cups of warm chocolate."

"Chocolate?" sniffled Kyle, looking up at me with red-rimmed eyes.

I smiled and nodded, standing slowly. "Yes, now...Shall I carry you, Kyle?" He nodded vigorously, burying his head into my arm. "Okay."

Sarah raced down the stairs as we came over. Kate followed me down, hand on the railing as always. Sarah was waiting for us on the couch with two movie cases set beside her as well as remotes.

"I already picked some things out for Kyle when he started crying," she said quietly. She looked at Kate, and I was glad to see that this sweet girl was well. "Should I start it?"

"Yes, thank you, Sarah." Kate touched my arm gently before I made my way to the kitchen. The expression she wore said that she had accepted my silence of what I had dreamt. "Would you like me to call Robert?"

I hesitated, thinking of my revelation. Curiously, it did not infuriate me now, my mind unaffected by its previous sharpness. I was also yearning to begin breaking away from my dependency on him, and I felt complete enough to set this matter aside for a few days' time to think it over.

"No, I will wait until I see him next," I told her with a smile. She blinked in surprise but said nothing, going to hug Sarah and begin the movie.

I brought Kyle with me to the kitchen. I grabbed a stool for him to sit on and he watched while I set a pan of milk on the stove to warm. After a few minutes of searching, I was able to find the chocolate. I enjoyed the simplicity of the task, however. It reminded me that my life was my own and I had the *freedom* to get lost inside a kitchen.

Smiling at the comfort, I waited for the milk to warm. Even the past few weeks had seemed relatively peaceful and normal. Maybe I would only require Robert's services for another year or two before we could begin the irregular visits that he had proposed months ago.

I poured the milk into four glasses and asked Kyle to stir while I cleaned the pan. From the living room, I could hear the beginning sounds of an animated film, something about a panda. My smile broadened and I motioned for Kyle to take two cups, one for himself and one for his sister while I carried the remaining two.

"Madam," I murmured, handing a glass to Katelyn with a smirk.

"Madam." Kyle mimicked my movements exactly as he handed the glass off to his sister. She giggled.

"If I could have an inch or so of room to sit, ladies?" I asked politely, chuckling when they both moved to the farthest edges of the couch. I sat in the middle with a sigh, barely having a second's time to settle into a comfortable position before I was swarmed.

As the movie was beginning Katelyn was snuggled into my right side, Kyle into my left, and Sarah had taken possession of my left arm, holding my hand tightly. My little family, putting the nightmare behind them.

~~ * ~ * ~ * ~~

Thursday

I knocked on the fine wooden door as usual,

entering when I heard the muted "Come in, Cory!", ducking into the home. The rich aroma of Anne's cooking greeted me warmly, making me smile. It reminded me of my mother's cooking. When I glanced into the kitchen, of course, I found that it was Bailey and not her mother, although Anne was assisting.

"Good afternoon, ladies," I greeted with a slight nod of my head. Bailey grinned at me. I was glad she had aided Kate while I was gone recently.

"Hey, Cory! Here for Dad?" she asked.

"Every Thursday."

She pointed upstairs, wincing. "He's with Vanessa. Tread softly."

I nodded, climbing the stairs to greet those on the next level. Vanessa shrieked, making me charge up the steps in a flurry, tearing the carpet as I went. Next I heard the scream, it rolled off into laughter accompanied by Robert's own merriment. I rushed over to Vanessa's room.

"Is all well?" I asked hurriedly, blinking in surprise at their predicament. Photographs were splayed out on the floor and Robert was holding one up for her to see more closely.

He looked up at me from the photo, grinning broadly. "Oh, yes. Everything's fine. Sorry, I must have lost track of the time."

"Is it three already?" asked Vanessa with a glance at her wrist. She flinched from it in shock. "Whoa, it's later than that. I'm supposed to be meeting Tina in three minutes. Bye, Daddy, I'll be home around six."

"Drive safe, sweetheart," he called after her as she sprinted down the hall. He sighed and shook his head, pulling himself off the floor. "They grow up fast."

I nodded, thinking more of Kyle and Sarah and how they had grown. Was it truly nearly a year? "Indeed, they do. Should we organize the photographs?"

He waved a hand at it, stepping out into the hall with me. "Nah, don't worry about it. I'll get it later. Where do you want to sit?"

"The living room is fine with me. I admire the openness and broad windows. It is pleasantly light," I decided, smiling as we started downstairs.

Robert nodded. "Can't say that I blame you. Alright, you have patient's rights now, but once we're up I'm taking my recliner."

I chuckled, sitting and settling into the soft leather chair he spoke of. He watched my trimmed claws warily for a moment, taking his own seat. I grinned, placing my hands in my lap to ease his worry, in spite of their being filed.

"How has your week been?" he asked, turning over to my therapist. His face expressed his dedication to the session, watching me.

"Oh, wonderful as always, seeing as I still have my sanity. Although, I did remember something new...From the hospital, after I was shot." That I could speak of the incident so easily made me smile to myself proudly. I was indeed becoming well again.

He kept his surprise careful. "Really? Do you feel comfortable sharing it?"

I nodded slowly, frowning slightly in thought. How did one tell someone what I had to say? "Paul never took me to the hospital in the city because he needed supplies, or because I would be safer there. He had a working anesthetic, the slippery man. Oh, but...He took me to that place to give me to the N.S.I.S.D."

As he realized what I had said his eyes widened, jaw tightening. "He sold you out?"

"I can remember being taken in for operation, and Paul used a syringe. The contents made my arm numb and then the suited man who later came to take me walked over. That is as far as I can recall, but yes. I was sold out. I suspect that the ranger may have even been hired," I admitted with a frown.

Robert took a deep breath to relax. "You seem awfully calm about this whole matter."

"Paul was a good man. I believe that he was merely trapped between a rock and a hard place. Regardless, knowing how everything happened does not change where I am now. I find that it would be a waste of my precious time remaining if I was angry at a dead man."

"You're selfless to your own detriment," he muttered, shaking his head in disbelief.

I laughed, wholly amused by his manner. "Robert, you quite possibly are the most incompetent therapist to be hired, but you are also the best friend I could have asked for. Would you like your chair back?"

He stared at me in surprise. "You...It's been maybe ten minutes."

"And whatever else I have to say I would rather discuss with my friend, not my therapist," I retorted easily, standing with a quiet groan. We exchanged seats. "Ah, the faithful couch. I do love space to stretch."

"I suppose." He was frowning thoughtfully. "But you're certain that you're fine?"

I nodded with a smile. "Yes. To be honest, I feel at ease now that I know how it fully came about. It does not feel so shockingly abrupt. Oh, and it feels even better to have spoken this revelation aloud to another soul. I dread telling Kate..." I added in a murmur, frowning now. She was no longer the strong young girl I had known, and she needed to be shielded from the world so that she could recover. "Maybe I will not tell her, for her sake."

"You didn't talk to her? How did you remember?" he asked with the curiosity of a friend. "Wait, sorry. You normally tell Kate everything."

I chuckled and shook my head. The smell of dinner was becoming intoxicating, making my stomach twist longingly. "No, I had a dream. It was incredibly vivid...I woke screaming, demanding things to know if it was real or imagined. I never told her why. At first because I was unsure, now because I am not able to bear the thought of how heartbroken she would be if I said...Well, you recall when you asked her how she felt that I had stopped phoning."

He was nodding, face sad. "I remember..."

"She has enough to worry about, anyway," I muttered, shaking my head slowly. I remembered the note that was still tucked safely in my journal, promptly placing it out of my mind. "Which reminds me, I have had another week without any hallucinations. A good sign, I hope."

Robert smiled. "Indeed. I'm curious about what color your horns are supposed to be," he admitted.

"Black, perhaps? To match my claws." I glanced at them and shrugged, smiling back at Robert. "I suppose we will know once we are able to deduce what exactly I need."

A call from the kitchen cut off Robert's next words. "Can somebody set the table for dinner?!"

I stood reflexively, grinning at Robert before answering the cry for help. I cleansed my hands and found plates in the cupboards to begin placing at the table. Robert followed suit, utensils and napkins in hand.

"You can take off your jacket when it's the middle of summer. A genius ability, really," teased Robert as he set the table. I set the final plate in place and nodded to myself.

"Oh, I can, can't I?" I asked with a smile, removing the article with a sigh. My skin stung mildly for a moment in the fresh air. It felt wonderful to not be suffocating beneath the jacket, and I was comfortable revealing my scars here.

Robert paused, staring at me incredulously. "What did you just say?"

"It was a confirmation to your jesting, Robert, nothing more," I replied. I stepped out into the front hall to place my coat on a hanger, returning to see him grinning. "I beg your pardon, but what is so amusing?"

"You used a contraction," he said, still grinning widely.

I chuckled. "I suppose I did."

"Wow." He sighed, allowing his grin to fade to a broad smile. "I'll go get the food."

I chuckled again and sat, amused that he could be so elated before I realized exactly why—my relaxation here had become apparent by my speech. Reason enough for celebration, I did suppose.

Bailey came in first with a side dish of vegetables, followed by Robert and Anne. They all sat and began serving their respective dishes onto each plate. Bailey was chattering about her most recent visit with her partner. It took me a moment, but I grasped that she had spoken to her parents about her preferences. I smiled, happy for the acceptance they were receiving her with.

"Your birthday's on Saturday. What did you want to do?" asked Bailey with a grin. "It's your last year as a sixty-some-odder."

I smiled, nodding. "Yes, my birthday...I love the thought of keeping my freedom and want nothing else."

Bailey's grin widened. "See, Dad? Does this mean I can?!"

Robert sighed in defeat to a battle I had not been present for. "Alright, alright. But don't—Oh, well, I guess I can't say 'traumatize', huh?"

"Still, be nice, hm?" chided Anne lovingly.

"Is it a party?" I asked, turning to Bailey.

She paused to think for a moment. "Sort of."

I frowned and Robert sighed, "Go ahead, Bailey."

She cheered gleefully, leaping up from her chair and rushing into the kitchen. We sat in silence, listening to her clatter about in the other room. There was something that sounded like glass being set upon the counter, then a small click followed by Bailey hissing a curse. A few moments later, she reappeared in the doorway, a cake with an endless number of candles on it held delicately between her hands.

"Happy birthday!" they all crowed, laughing raucously at the expression of shock I wore.

"Sixty-nine candles, for ya! I counted," she added somberly.

I grinned, a warm sense of friendship surrounding me. "I suppose I should make a wish on them?"

Anne nodded urgently. "Before they drip onto the

cake!"

"I bet you're really grateful for having eight lungs now, aren't ya?" When I paused, Bailey shrugged. "Read it in an article, now make your wish!"

Chortling, I closed my eyes to think. What could I want that I did not already have? What did I have that I did not want? Ah...

Let none of this joy die.

~~ * ~ * ~ * ~~

July 28th, 2011

My sanity is slipping farther. I can feel it. Something in my mind is...wrong. No, not just my mind, in my entire being. The hallucinations, the acid blood, the vivid dreams. After my most recent dream, I am uncertain of how safe I am near other people anymore. It felt right, though. It felt like the truth, like every other precognitive dream I have ever had. That rightness is what frightens me.

It began with me sitting where I am now at the desk, writing. I heard Kate call out to me from downstairs and I stood to leave, but when I exited the bedroom I found myself staring down a startlingly long corridor with countless doors on either wall. The staircase was at the end, but the living area was not at the bottom. When I reached the final step, I was in the Old Thing Room and the stairs behind me had disappeared.

I went to the door, now wanting to find some way out of this labyrinth that my home had become. When I stepped out of the room, I was in a forest. It was a familiar

place, one I had torn apart in my youth.   There was
something new in this place, however. A tree, or rather two
that had grown not five feet apart, intertwining around one
another ten feet up to create an archway.

When I made to investigate the tree, the world
surrounding me blurred in color, an artist's fresh canvas. I
spun around, attempting to orient myself when I saw the
figure standing directly ahead of me in the archway, now
etched with archaic runes. It waved what I presumed was
an arm and a small dome of clarity engulfed us whilst the
color swirled on around us.

"Who are you?" I asked without thinking, unable to
place their features. For some reason, I could not identify
any of them. Their hair, their face, none of it seemed to be
understandable to my mind.

"I am the nothingness of everything, an ageless
infant. I know who you are, child. Your parents have been
worried many a Mourning Moon," replied the figure
vaguely, voice as indistinguishable as their face.

I frowned, meaning to move toward them but
finding myself frozen. "I am afraid I do not understand."

They laughed, finally taking on a form. My eyes
widened when I recognized Vanessa's smiling face. "Of
course not, with your stubborn attitude of mortality's
importance, young prince. I suppose I can humor you for
just a short while, however."

"Who are you?" I repeated, sensing the strangeness
of this dream. It felt far too solid, this person a whole
personality taking temporary occupancy within my mind to
invade my dreams.

"Oh, I have many names and forms. I am most
commonly depicted as three sisters, the separate forms of

381

my personality." Her smile softened with her eyes as two other forms of Vanessa appeared, one on either side of her. "I am the Fates, ever weaving the maps of time and all that dwell within them. This time, you are my beautiful exception."

I laughed quietly, shaking my head slowly. My, what had I been reading to create such an odd scenario? "I...am still confused."

She sighed, shaking her head as well. "You buried yourself deep, prince, if you cannot understand what it is that I weave."

I sighed to myself. "You...Are you the Creator? Be it whatever myths you go by."

She laughed loudly, truly humored. "Oh, no, no, I am no God, as you understand it. No, far from. I hold more dignity in my art than that."

"Art?" Abruptly, anger pulsed through me from the confusion. "From all that I have seen, I would never call such a tapestry as life art! *The most accurate description would be torture!"*

She raised her brows at me, unfazed. "Oh? In spite of all the pain that you are referring to there is still hope and love, two beautiful things that exist in nearly perfect balance. The secret to any masterpiece."

I made to argue and she held up her hand to silence me. She took a step in my direction before pausing, speaking carefully, "Katelyn. The very name is the most powerful, bittersweet element in your incredibly short mortal life. Can you say that it has only held happiness or pain? Never, because without the one, the other can never be experienced or appreciated for what it is. You know that."

Demon *Rising*

I narrowed my eyes but held back my anger. "Of course."

"The beauty of the day is nothing without the lonely night, hm?" She laughed again, her triplets laughing with her as she stopped in front of me. "Oh, and the weaving hands cannot create without the spirited thread. There must always be one that will not be woven."

She lifted my hand to examine. When she met my eyes again, it was from my own vantage. I stared at the familiar orange face in shock, reaching out a tentative hand to touch the demon's visage while expecting it to evaporate. A dream within a dream...?

"This time, there are two." She spoke with his voice, still smiling at my wonder. "My map is set, and your brother is prepared to help you change it."

"Which brother?" I asked numbly. Both were far too elderly to do much anymore.

"The brother of your spirit. The one who cut you, whose face you wore while he wore yours. But speak of this to no one but him," she warned suddenly, transforming back into Vanessa. Her expression was severe. "All I can do is influence you, guide you to your proper destination. That will never grant you the rights to be reckless. Do you understand?"

Before I could answer she transformed again, this time into Kate. Her eyes saddened, expression still sharp. "Of course, you do. Of all the things you learned...Child, the storm is coming. Do you know what to do?"

I shook my head slowly, confused by this whirlwind dream. "No. Tell me what I need to do, please."

She sighed quietly, shaking her head as well. "No. I can't, you know that. You also know which side of your nature is dominating. Follow it. It can never lead you to wrong."

"No. No, I am not a savage monster!" I denied through my teeth. My anger rose again, turning my blood to fire in my veins. "I have a chance to redeem myself! I will not allow it to go to waste."

She frowned. "Redeem yourself for what crimes? I was led to believe that you lived an honorable life."

"Before or after I fell from heaven?" I demanded sharply, tiring of the dream. I was ready to wake.

The Fates startled me by laughing. "Oh, child, you'll understand that memory in time. And redemption...That road is long, dark and painful. Why would you walk it if you were innocent?" She gave me a moment to allow her question to sink itself into my mind. "Perhaps it is your memory...why you came. Perhaps you were unable to bury yourself as deeply as you had hoped, hm?"

"Bury myself?" I murmured in wonder, anger vanishing as I became enthralled by the power of her presence.

"Yes. Your dreams, your intentions, your purpose, all were born of the skies. You cannot contain the skies, no matter how murky the mortal waters may become!" she exclaimed as if it were obvious.

I stared at the Fates listlessly. "Why would a god care about a lowly demon? Have the humans not caused enough torment? Have you come to torture me yourself?"

Her face became pained, agonized by my words. A small cry escaped her, a tear of glistening perfection falling from her cheek to create ripples across the floor. "Have I not chosen the appropriate form to convey my care for you,

384

Demon *Rising*

child?"

She looked herself over for a moment in sad silence. When she met my gaze again, it was with the eyes of my mother, gentle and concerned. I started, tears stinging my own eyes.

"Mom?" I wanted to reach out but was horrified at the thought of seeing so many scars near her memory.

"No, only your godmother. I had hoped to never see the day when you would know such pains..." She touched my face sadly. "I had also hoped to never be the bearer of such doleful news to your...Well, the sooner you're home, the better, hm?"

"Wait, Mom! I mean--" I sighed heavily. "You can't leave me like this. I...I don't know what to do."

Her smile was gentle. "Follow the crow. Become what you are."

"No!" I cried out desperately, the weight in my chest bringing me to my knees. I shook my head, the weight spreading to my limbs. I stared at my hands in horror. "No..."

"On your knees is no place for a prince," she said gently, reaching out a hand to me.

I refused to look at her. "Why do you keep calling me that?"

"You will understand someday, when you can see my entire tapestry rather than a feeble glimpse," she replied calmly. "Stand now. Your time is coming."

"To do what?" I begged, looking to her desperately.

She smiled. "To be what you are."

"What am I?"

She did not meet my eyes when she replied, "What

will you make yourself to be?"

The Fates disappeared before I could think to reply,
leaving me alone to stare at the swirling color in despair.

~~ * ~ * ~ * ~~

August 9th, One Year After Being Released

<u>Tuesday</u>

"So. No kids, no worries, it's your 69th birthday...What do you want to do?"

I grinned at Katelyn, refusing to be brought down by the thoughts of what-ifs or maybes. I had stepped over the year threshold. I had survived the outside world a full year! What did I want to do?

"Make a reservation for supper. Then, go out for dinner and perhaps follow up with a walk on those park trails you keep telling me about, all the while flaunting quite rudely to those who disapprove of me that I am still alive and doing quite well. Oh, and perhaps frustrate them more by demonstrating an interspecific display of public affection with the most lovely woman to exist. Ah, a good day to be me," I laughed, grin broadening.

"Sounds like a good day to be me." Kate smiled. "You seem to be turning out as quite the little rebel, too."

"I'm late to bloom," I chuckled and stood from the couch, ambling over to the telephone. I paused there, glancing at Kate. "Where would you like to go?"

"Oh, nuh-uh! It's your birthday, mister, it's your choice." She crossed her arms and smirked, then sighed. "You're going to pull some sort of 'It'll make me happy'

386

thing, aren't you? Fine, fine...Um...Well, there's a good Italian place in downtown. Here, I can dial," she added, pulling the phone from my hand and dialing before returning it to me.

I placed the phone to my ear, waiting patiently.

"Vino Mangia, this is Elizabeth speaking. How may I serve you today?" answered a feminine voice.

"I would like to make a reservation," I replied, grinning to myself. Ha! I had that power now! No, not power. *Privilege.* It was a *freedom.*

"Yes, sir. What time?"

"Seven." Kate frowned but I merely continued my childish grinning.

"What name?"

"Lawrence."

"Alright, Mr. Lawrence. We'll see you at seven," she said, sounding chipper. "Is there anything else I can help you with?"

"No, thank you." The line disconnected and I replaced the phone, chuckling. "Oh, that was fun."

Kate was shaking her head slowly. "You are...amazing."

"What are you meaning to say?" I climbed the stairs and she followed, no doubt to also prepare herself for a day out. I found a short sleeved shirt from the closet, confident enough in the day to reveal the fullness of myself to the world. Why had I ever been unnerved by the idea? They were no longer scars to me, things that marred me— they were merely marks that held no significance.

"I'm saying that you're acting twenty and you're the *only* person I know aside from Kyle who could be amused by making a reservation," she laughed, smiling at me as she

387

ducked into the bathroom, clothes in her arms.

"Ah, I see." I made to follow after her, stopping short in surprise when she closed the door in my face with a grin. I frowned at the door for a moment. "I need to comb my hair."

"You can come in if you close your eyes!" she called back. I sighed, imagining that she was grinning now quite playfully. I closed my eyes and smirked, opening the door and stepping inside blindly.

"Why can't I look?" I searched for my comb while stretching my tail out to find where she was in the room. Her hand brushed the flat of my tail aside gently. My smirk turned to a grin. "There you are."

"Oh, no, mister. Just comb your hair," she said, voice coming from the bedroom. I opened my eyes, confused as I combed my hair and pulled it back. What was she hiding?

When I left the bathroom, she was nowhere to be seen. I buttoned my shirt as I left the room, humming merrily to myself. I stopped short when I saw Kate waiting for me at the bottom of the stairs.

"Oh, is *that* what you were hiding?" I asked, taking the steps two at a time. The soft blue dress she wore made me smile happily to see that her own birthday gift was being enjoyed. "You're lovely, as always."

"And you're handsome...In spite of the tourist shirt," she added with a painful glance at what I wore.

"I think it's rather entertaining." We stepped outside and I pulled the door shut, locking it as well. Kate stood beside the car, smiling at me.

"I've got your sandals, by the way. Let's go." She opened the driver's door, waiting impatiently.

Demon *Rising*

"Mm...I think I'll *meet* you at that adorable café in downtown," I told her with a grin. "I'll even race you."

"Um...Go!" she cackled, ducking into the car and slamming the door behind her. I sprinted into the street, taking flight easily before she pulled out of the driveway. I climbed higher, pushing myself faster through the air. With a glance at the street below, I saw her bright yellow vehicle pulling off of our street.

As I thundered through the air in a flash, I could hear birds screeching in terror as they scattered out of my invisible path. Laughter built in my chest, escaping only to be drowned out by the wind and beat of my wings. Below me, the world was a collage of blurred lines, squares and colors. I could not see where Kate was now but I surged forward, seeing the towering buildings of downtown. I aimed to fly between them, feeling sure of my coordination in spite of my wingspan.

I circled one tower to drop lower to the earth and slow my descent. Two blocks away, I saw the sign of the little café. I allowed myself to glide lower and closer, breaking into a run when I landed in a grassy field a block away. As I approached the entrance, Kate appeared there, our hands touching the door simultaneously.

"Tie," I gasped, somewhat out of breath while I grinned at her.

She thought for a moment. "I win."

"No, it was a tie," I contradicted, opening the door to allow her to enter first.

"But I couldn't take all of those shortcuts *over* traffic, and I had to deal with lights. I win," she stated again, making her way toward the counter.

I followed her. "But it *is* my birthday."

"Fine, tie," she submitted, and for a moment it was hard to believe that the year was not 1963. She turned to the woman, smiling patiently behind the counter. "I'd like...Ooh, soup of the day, please."

"Alright, and for you, sir?" she asked, looking to me expectantly. I was glad to be unsurprised that she was handling my presence so easily.

"Ah, just a ham sandwich and the soup sounds like quite enough, thank you." I smiled politely.

"Okay, fifteen forty-two is your total." She waited patiently while Kate retrieved the payment from her purse. "Thank you. Your order will be ready in ten to fifteen minutes, if you could take your seats and we'll bring it out to you."

"Thank you again." I followed Kate to an empty table, set beside a broad window that looked out on the busy street. The café was rather quiet at that time, for which I was grateful. There was a small, nagging recognition that I ignored easily.

Kate was just laughing quietly to herself, opening her napkin to arrange her utensils. "You never changed."

"How have I not changed now?" I inquired, mimicking her actions. I smiled proudly to myself as again I noted to myself that a knife no longer frightened me.

"Sandwich and soup? Your favorite choices of any meal, just short of steaks." She handled the knife, attempting to straighten and then straighten its position again, ever the perfectionist.

"You know me too well, it seems."

"Of course I—Ah!" hissed Kate, dropping the knife in her hand as she might a snake. My heart jumped in panic and I saw the thin streak of blood coming from her fingertip.

"Oh, Kate, are you alright?" I asked as I pressed my napkin to her finger to staunch the bleeding. I held her hand gently in mine. Without looking away from her hand I chided her softly, "You should not be so careless with knives."

"Careful there, he's right. Vampires are everywhere nowadays, and you smell particularly ripe for your age," said a voice behind me, addressing Kate. The owner came into my view, smirking. He was average build and height for a human, black hair falling into his brown eyes. It must have been the lighting, but his eyes seemed to flash red.

I restrained myself politely. "Please leave us be, sir."

He scowled abruptly. "He didn't. Grace, tell me he didn't send us here for a domesticated lapdog?"

Kate narrowed her eyes at him, hand still held in mine. "Look, if you're here to insult someone, you should just find a mirror."

"I like *her*!" he chuckled, grinning. A small, delicate woman appeared beside him. Her eyes were deep blue, contrasting with her vivid hair—red enough to match my skin.

"Vladimir, gentle. He didn't know exactly what we were searching for, so be glad that we managed to find him at all," she scolded him in a soft, musical voice.

"Children, if you would be so kind as to allow us peace?" I asked pointedly, before Kate could begin ranting at them.

The Vladimir character sighed theatrically. "Guess we shouldn't tell them about the demons then, huh, Grace? Oh, well, it's their loss."

They left then, the man leading the woman as she glanced behind at me with a worried frown. I sat for a moment in shock and confusion at the abrupt incident. I warred with myself, arguing that the ignorant children must have been lying.

"Damn it," I swore under my breath, an old dream stirring in my memory distantly. I glanced at Kate, hoping that my expression was not too harsh. "Excuse me a moment, my dear."

I stood and followed after them onto the street, looking about for them urgently. Catching sight of them before they rounded the corner, I raced after them. Around me in my mind's eye, I saw a world turned to wax.

"Wait!" I called, feeling mildly dimwitted for the small spark of hope inside of me. They turned and I wished that I could be certain that they were not playing pranks. "What demons? Where?"

Vladimir bore a satisfied smirk. "Wouldn't you like to know?"

I clenched my fists and swallowed back a growl of irritation while I struggled to remove the image of the crow from my mind. The idea that an aged and erratic dream could hold any meaning at that moment unnerved me, but I knew better than to disregard it completely. "Do you in fact know of the whereabouts or existence of any other demons, boy?"

"We were sent by one to find you," replied the woman, Grace. It startled me to hear how sure she sounded with how quietly she spoke. I expected her words to be lost in the cacophony of the cars blazing by. "He said that you were lost and needed help. We're here to take you home."

Fly, fly, fly!

392

Demon *Rising*

I gaped, breathless. What was this madness?! "I have a home. I *am* home!"

"No, you're not and yes, it's just that obvious," snapped Vladimir, making his behavioral impatience well known. "No demon is at home in a city. I mean seriously, the smell's getting to *me*."

"What?" I could not understand much of what he was saying. I was still too lost to think that he could know so much without ever having spoken to me, and...Other demons? Could they look like me?

He sighed. "Demons are like horses, sort of. Needing lots of space to run around and specific diets otherwise—Well, just look at your horns! How long have they been that color? Twenty years? Thirty?"

"Fifty-seven," I answered quietly, slowly coming from my shock. This was real. "Who are you two? How do you know any of this? Where are the demons?"

"Too many questions," groaned Vladimir, appearing to be pained by them. "Look, we can answer them later. As it is, things are a little risky with us talking to you out here. No, we can't tell you why. Meet us in the park by your *house*, midnight. We'll take you *home* then."

They began to turn away. "Wait! How do you know that there is a park near where I live?"

"First, you wouldn't be so chipper without it. Second, you're not the most discreet flier. Or very observant." He smirked and led Grace away, apparently much more patient with her than he had been with me.

I stood in shock for a long space where I could not tell that any time had passed. Home...? Other demons? When I turned back to return to Kate, I froze. My sense of purpose was screaming at me not to ignore this, regardless of how very like stalkers they sounded. But there was only one chance with this. Could there be others? More importantly, how did I go to them and could I bear to leave Kate behind even for a short period while I explored this?

When I arrived back in the shop, Kate was watching for me.

"Pranksters?" she asked as I sat. Our meal had arrived but it appeared unappetizing to me now.

Follow the crow.

"No. They knew far too much..." I shook my head slowly, numb with my thoughts. "They knew about the vitamin deficiency, of all the things...And they told me to meet with them tonight, so that they could take me back to the other demons."

She stared at me in horror. "Are you going to?"

"I don't know," I admitted in a mutter. I scowled out the window, startling a poor child passing by with his mother. "I think I might, except that I can't leave you or the children alone with a sound mind. Oh, and then there's Robert—"

"I'm coming with you, same as Kyle and Sarah," said Kate firmly. "I don't care about anything those kids might say, you're not going anywhere without your family."

I sighed heavily, closing my eyes to the world. "I...What if they truly are *demons*, not just in appearance but in practice? No, you and your grandchildren should be at home, where I can be certain that you are safe."

"Considering we're demon-lovers? I'd say we're just as safe in that house as we would be in a piranha tank. Either way, it's only a matter of time until they get hungry," she retorted, making me wince. The reminder that things had yet to calm, the glares on the streets and the soldiers that still stood on the corners. It was at least accepted for me to roam without protection, if only begrudgingly.

When I opened my eyes, Kate wore a determined expression that spoke of my defeat in the matter. "Fine. We'll go home, pack...I need to speak with Robert," I realized again, with more force than before. My friend...How would he take to me vanishing for any length of time?

"Alright. We'll get to that, but you need to eat first," she told me sternly.

"I'm not hungry," I muttered, wanting to begin putting all of these plans into action.

She sighed, smiling gently and taking one of my hands to hold across the table. "It's an exciting day. You'll need it."

~~ * ~ * ~ * ~~

"Exciting," I muttered to myself, shaking my head slowly. Katelyn was downstairs, packing for the little ones. "Indeed!"

I was upstairs, double checking that we had completed everything. I had only just finished with the list of individuals to alert that we were going out of town for some time. Glancing around the room, I wondered if I had forgotten anything.

"Packed..." I muttered, glancing out the window and freezing. Standing on the far corner of the street was a tall, lean figure. Bright orange with wings on its back, I could only assume that the mystery demon who had sent the children earlier had also recruited reinforcements.

395

Demon *Rising*

I stared for a moment before the demon met and held my gaze. I flinched away from the window, a memory not my own echoing through my mind, a whirl of ghostly chants and drumbeats. I shook myself free of the strangeness, looking back at an empty corner where the demon had stood.

I shook my head, saying again with wonder, "Exciting."

Rapping urgently on the door of Robert's home, my heart was thunderous in my ears. Those children, had what they said been true? Were there others of my kind? Of course, as I had witnessed one just earlier! Did they all look like me, or just the one? Could I go someplace where no one stared because they all were vividly colored and hideous in appearance? Vivid, yes, but who is to say that the demon I saw was not handsome?

Bailey answered the door, eyes wide. "Cory?! What's wrong? The kids were going to stay the night and come back tomorrow...What's wrong?"

"I need to speak with your father," I told her, finding myself rather breathless. Regardless of the actuality that had occurred, I had to speak with Robert. In one case, it meant that I would be leaving to investigate this demon situation. In the other, I had gone mad.

"Come in then, he's upstairs in the study." She stepped aside to allow Kate and I passage, closing the door behind us. "You didn't answer me though, what's going on?!"

"Bailey, look! Gramma and Grampa are here!"

The children barreled down the entrance hall towards us from the living room. I stepped aside and motioned them to follow their grandmother, all the while rushing up the stairs.

"Robert!" I called, voice as strained and stressed as I felt. "Robert, I need to speak with you!"

He appeared at the end of the hall, face in shadow and scowling. "What's wrong?"

I finished my way down the hall before glancing about to confirm that we were alone. "In private. It's...It's urgent, Robert."

He blanched, eyes widening. In the tinted lighting, he appeared incredibly ill. "This way."

Robert led me to my former room, where the bed and desk were still in place. As soon as the door was shut he whirled on me, straining to keep his face clear so that he could aid me.

"Demons. They began to appear in the seventies, correct?" I asked. Hope was constricting my throat and bringing tears to my eyes.

"Yes, according to reports," he replied in confusion. He frowned deeply. "Cory, what's the meaning of—"

"A young couple approached Kate and I earlier today, claiming to know where demons are." I choked back my tears forcefully to continue speaking. "I need to know if I have finally lost my sanity, or if this is real."

He faltered for a moment, bemused. "I...How could we know? Do you have them here with you? There's no way to tell until it's too late. That's how mental illnesses commonly work. For all either of us know, you murdered Kate before any of this happened!"

"Don't *even* imagine that," I begged, knowing that

he was right. She could have been dead. All of this could be in my mind. It could all be over.

"Okay, okay, I'll talk to Kate and compare encounters," he said, face betraying his hope. The same hope I shared, no doubt. Neither of us could bear to consider the alternative possibility.

"I'll get her, then," I said quickly, leaving the room before he could stop me. I was calling for her as I rushed down the stairs. "Kate, Robert needs to speak to you. He's in the final room on the right, down the hall on your left once you come to the study."

She nodded and began to climb the stairs. Bailey was at my side in a flash, Kyle latching on to my leg even as I made my way to sit in the living room. From there, Kyle clambered up into my lap and settled in as if he might sleep there.

"...Cory? What's going on?" For the first time, I noticed how mortified Bailey was. She was pale and trembling slightly. "I know that you adults have been hiding something from us kids. What is it? Is it...bad?"

"No, Bailey, it is not," I lied flatly. Her condition did nothing to improved. "Everything is fine. Nothing will hurt you."

"It's not me I'm worried about." Her reply made my heart twist painfully. I sighed and covered my face with my hand guiltily.

"No one will be hurt, Bailey. Everyone is fine still," I assured her truthfully. After all, it was truth that I spoke. In my lap, Kyle stirred restlessly.

"Can we watch TV? I'm bored," he chirped. Sarah came to sit beside me, nestling into my side.

"Yeah! Cartoons, please." She patted my hand as

if to command me, making me smile. I pulled my hand from my face. It was a relief to see such a carefree child after the strangeness of the day.

Bailey sat on my other side, switching on the television. She sighed and sat back, seeming to have recovered some, although she still refused to smile. It was some time later that Kate and Robert returned from upstairs, Vanessa following along. Anne had meandered out to sit on the couch beside Bailey. A dark sensation shivered down my spine and through my tail, and I felt as though we had all congregated in response to a cosmic order. What for?

"Okay, kids, let's get you in the car!" said Kate excitedly, making Sarah and Kyle leap up with a laugh. "Come on, we're going to go for a little trip."

"Really? Where?" asked Sarah. I was unable to hear Kate's reply as she ushered them out the door. Robert turned to me tiredly.

"You're alright. Kate told me what's going on. Tell me you've changed your mind, though," he added pleadingly.

Bailey turned to me, eyes accusatory. "What's going on?"

"Just...a vacation, of sorts," I relinquished, uncertain of how to explain this to her. Or anyone, actually. The concept was still somewhat baffling in my own mind.

"A vacation?" she demanded sharply. "Well, what sort of vacation has you coming over at eleven—"

She was cut off by a loud, painful cry from the television. It took us all a moment to orient ourselves. When we were able to hear again, it was the voice of a news reporter. We all turned to the television, unable to even register that Kate had returned.

"...sightings have skyrocketed in the last three days worldwide. Reported so far are 713 sightings. There have been closer encounters, and all persons who have spoken with these creatures have reported that they ask only this: 'Where is he?' Experts worldwide are reluctant to admit what some have come to claim as the demons searching for the antichrist. All that can be said currently is that if you have any information as to who they are searching for, or his whereabouts, report it immediately."

An image of a demon that looked disturbingly familiar flashed onscreen, orange with violet eyes. Had this not been the demon I saw earlier?

We all stared at the screen as the clip began to replay. I was the first to break from my trance, moving and speaking in the same instant.

"I need to leave." The words felt nothing less than right.

Robert started, following after me down the hall to the foyer. "What?! Why?! Where will you go? You can't step outside the house now! The men who used to protect you are going to be hunting for your skin inside the next hour!"

"Those children are the only hope I have now to escape. If the other demons have managed to remain undetectable for the last who knows how many decades, then maybe...Maybe they will protect me as one of them," I suggested hopefully. The concept was certainly appealing.

His expression fell into despair, eyes watering as I watched him submit to the reality I had faced already. "I just...I'm sorry. I guess...I'm going to miss you, Cory."

Bailey and Vanessa appeared beside him, both of

them watching me pleadingly. Anne came up behind them, completing the image of their family. At the door already, Kate sighed quietly.

"It's eleven-thirty," she said quietly, the words sharp in my ears. Shockingly, I had no tears. No, this separation felt right and curiously natural.

It was the Smith daughters that came to hug me first, their parents mimicking so that the family was a small crowd around me. I embraced them all back with my arms, encasing them in my wings as well. It felt warm and safe, here with these humans who had been so accepting.

Why can this not be enough? I wondered, tears touching me now. Why could a human life no longer be enough for me? Had I stayed with my own family, would it have eventually become too little?

"I'll miss all of you," I told them before retreating to the exit, pulling my wings in to duck out the door. When I glanced around at the sleeping street, I wiped tears from my face.

Kate went to the car and climbed in. She met my eyes and gave me a reassuring smile before pulling away and onto the street. I took a deep breath before I made my way to fly. My wings contained a lingering warmth that I wished would dissipate in the night air that was already too hot against my skin.

As I flew, an alien detachment allowed me to understand that I was leaving. Not only leaving one place, but leaving what I had viewed as home for the last year, what I had yearned for my entire life. I did not ache, either. Rather, that I was willingly departing made everything gentler, less traumatic. Vaguely, I wondered if I would find it all so easy tomorrow morning.

Safely landing at the park was simple enough with the lights that surrounded it. Kate was already there, and she came to my side as I glanced about for Vladimir and Grace. I did not realize that I was trembling or in need of comfort until Kate took my hand to steady it.

"Where are the children?" I asked quietly. There was an uncanny sensation that slithered through me, telling me to speak softly lest someone unwanted may hear. I listened carefully for the sure sound of footsteps or guns, things I was far too familiar with. Would it be Thompson who shot me? Could Santos?

"They're in the car, just in case," she replied in a whisper, seeming to have felt the same warning.

I waited an instant longer, the heat of the night stifling. "Where are they? We're not late, are we?"

"No, you're early," rang the clear voice of a woman. I released Kate's hand and whirled, meeting the oceanic eyes of Grace. She smiled serenely, having no fear of speaking at her regular volume. "It's still five minutes until midnight."

My heart was racing as fear managed to break through my comfortable numb. I resisted the burning instinct to bare my fangs as Vladimir slunk from the shadows beside Grace, unable to rid myself of the monster from my nightmare standing in his place. "It is enjoyable to see that you two are not playing jokes. At least so far."

Vladimir's simple smile was curious, and the scent of him that came on a breeze was suffocatingly unnatural. Again, I wanted to bare my fangs and attack.

"Very good of you to join us. The humans are going to be delayed, at least for now. There are others we should worry more about, but if we move quickly they

402

won't catch up with us until we're well into home territory."
His smile broadened and I was able to recognize the tang of
the soldiers' guns in his scent.

"What did you do to the humans by the house?" I
demanded, unnerved. Beside me, Kate seemed to be as
calm as could be expected. Could she not feel the danger
here? Could she not smell what was so apparent to me?

Grace was the one to reply. "Nothing. They're
alive, just unconscious. No more questions for now, we
need to leave."

I nodded tersely. "Where are we going? So that
Kate will know where to meet us."

Vladimir's eyes widened and he seemed to restrain
his anger. The voice that answered slid smoothly from the
darkness behind Vladimir.

"She's too frail to follow." The owner stepped from
the night, as powerful and exotic in appearance as his voice
had been. Violet eyes flicked between Kate and I, a shiver
of recognition terrifying me.

I heard Kate stifle her gasp of shock. "You can't
stop me from coming."

The demon laughed quietly. "You feel strong
enough to keep pace with some angels, of course, but not
considering two demons in their prime?"

I stared at him, then squinted into the shadows,
wondering if he meant that there was another demon with
him. Another person that looked like me.

Kate refused to be fazed. "I will and you won't stop
me."

"Spirited for a human," he noted, then looked to me
with a smile. "And quiet for a demon. My name is Braxen,
and it's best that we be gone before you have the misfortune

of meeting our...adversaries."

The confusing sense that I was in two bodies at once, witnessing through separate minds, had me stumble for a moment, reminding me of the demon I had seen earlier on the corner. "You...I know you."

"The brother of your spirit..."

Braxen appeared startled by my words, as if he may have been offended. I would have apologized had I not seen the terror in his eyes. "You're mistaken. We've only just met, now come. They could be here soon."

"Who?" I asked, barely capable of comprehending his words through the haze of my wonder-struck mind.

He hesitated for a moment while Grace and Vladimir shared a glance. When he spoke, I knew he told only the truth, however. I could feel it, the sense of honesty deeply rooted into our chests. I frowned.

"If you want to survive the coming storm, you'll come with us," he replied gravely.

"Where, then?" I asked quietly, uncertain whether that mattered. If they had told me we were marching into hell, I would have followed. Willingly, I would have led us into the pit.

Vladimir was the one to answer, smiling ironically as he did, "Paradise."

<u>Epilogue</u>

Staring at the sliver of the moon, Bliss knew that his time was soon. He could feel the power and reverence of the old ways dying, and the evidence was there before him. The moon had not blackened on the night it should have. Instead, the sliver of light had gone from one side of the moon to the other. He grinned, wondering if the demons had noticed the change in their precious god.

The Time of Mourning had ended.

Bliss knew why. He had been present when his guardian, master and creator had been forgiven at long last. Oh, his master had been overjoyed and foolhardy. Bliss had seen what would happen if he made the mistake, and now Bliss had a more powerful tool to recreate the world with.

Footsteps echoed across the stone floor, and Bliss tamed his features to only a smile. He prepared himself, not wondering why it was he did not hear the scraping of claws across stone. Perhaps they had made their guest comfortable, as Bliss would have ordered them to.

"My lord," greeted Bravery humbly. Bliss heard him kneel, the sounds of his steel armor distinct.

"Welcome back to paradise, Bravery. I trust that the human world wasn't too...difficult?" he asked, phrasing his question delicately. The master of Bliss's High Guard, Bravery was the least angelic of them all, having had his wings butchered from his back. Of course, Bliss never mentioned that it could merely be Bravery's unyielding and violent tendencies.

"No, my lord, I was not recognized even by the one we sought, though I tended his cradle when he was younger," he replied, standing with the ringing sounds of metal brushing against metal.

"And?" Bliss was ready for this, ready to receive the key to controlling the worlds—human and paradise alike—and more than ready to begin challenging the very heavens that birthed that key.

Bravery's hesitance was palpable. "My lord, they found him first."

Bliss froze, turning slowly. His smile hardened and his hand whipped out to slap Bravery. "You lost him?! The demons have the most powerful being to walk this earth since before our very *creation*?!"

Bravery averted his gaze. "Yes, my lord. The Choir angel and the vampire are with them as well, my lord."

Bliss laughed, startling Bravery by the sound. "Oh, the vampire...So, you mean to tell me that the most powerful being we have ever faced, with his power lying dormant, is going to the place that can unlock that power and turn it against us, *and* our dear Vladimir is there, just waiting around to get a little hungry before KILLING MY KEY!"

Bliss's hands were around Bravery's neck suddenly. He was still smiling serenely, looking into Bravery's eyes. His voice was quiet and threatening as he purred, "I need him, Bravery. I need the boy like a mother, so that I can start giving everyone what *they* need. You know that, don't you? Oh, and he's such a lost little thing. He needs me too, did you see? Did you see all of that pain, all of that uncertainty, all of those scars?"

Bravery nodded carefully, face slowly changing color. "Yes, my lord. I saw, and you have my shame to show the world."

"Oh, you poor child!" gasped Bliss suddenly, removing his hands to cradle Bravery's face. "Oh, I'm sorry. I can't help myself sometimes, when I get upset. But you'll get me what I need, won't you?"

He nodded, rubbing his bruising neck. "Yes, my lord. I will turn him to the angels and against the demons, for your Bliss."

Bliss nodded, smile broadening. He laughed quietly, "Oh, thank you, Bravery. Thank you."

About the Author

Karma Rose is an unschooled teen who has always been a writer at heart. She began with poems and short stories when she was younger, slowly moving toward her first novel, *Demon Rising*. For updates on her current and future projects, visit:

karmiclove.deviantart.com

www.ingramcontent.com/pod-product-compliance
Lightning Source LLC
Chambersburg PA
CBHW030030030726
47500CB00001B/36